MW01659537

In my head I hear my birth mother's angry question, "How could you choose to turn your back on your own people and go out to live among those mind-deaf creatures who are so hard and cruel?" How to answer? In truth it was the wrong question. I never intended to turn my back on the Hadra. And it was not really something I chose. Some hook of curiosity deep in my being had drawn me out of the safety and limits of the Hadra world. Once out there I found it difficult to fit myself back into my old life. For most Hadra, quick encounters with the outer world are enough. Its ways are not our ways; it does not suit our natures. It did not suit mine either, yet whenever I came home I would feel an itch of restlessness to be gone again.

The Smuggler, The Spy and The Spider

Diana Rivers

Bella
BOOKS
2012

Bella Books
P.O. Box 10543
Tallahassee, FL 32302

First Bella Books edition 2012

Printed in the United States of America on acid-free paper

Editor: Medora MacDougall
Cover designer: Sandy Knowles
Cover Illustration by Cedar Kindy

ISBN-13: 978-1-59493-266-3

Other Books in the Hadra Series by Diana Rivers

Daughters of the Great Star—The young women who will become the Hadra find each other, gather together and flee for their lives when their powers become a threat to the Zarn rulers of the land.

The Hadra—In this sequel to *Daughters*, the Hadra journey down the coast through many dangers and adventures, searching for a safe place to build a settlement and create a new life for themselves.

Clouds of War—The Hadra have found refuge in the City of Zelindar they built by the sea but what is to stop the Zarns from invading to re-establish their power on the coast?

The Red Line of Yarmald—The sequel to *Clouds* in which the Hadra, the Koormir and the Wanderers create an alliance to defend the Yarmald Peninsula with a magical line of power.

Her Sister's Keeper—Nhazul, a restless young Hadra from Ossen, travels to the forbidden city of Nhor where she becomes involved in a daring and dangerous raid on the "Gray Place."

Journey to Zelindar—This takes place two hundred years after *Daughters*. Sair is rescued by the Hadra and becomes part of their world after fleeing from the Shokarn city of Eezore.

New Series

City of Strangers—Solene is abducted by strangers and taken to Hernorium as a wife for the future Magistrar. She has to escape and go home with a warning about a planned invasion of her land.

This book is dedicated to all those women who struggle to create a life for themselves in a hostile world.

Diana Rivers lives in the hills of Arkansas on women's land, in a community of women who sustain her life and nurture her existence.

Her house, that she designed herself, was all built by women's hands, including her own. She is an artist as well as a writer, mostly creating cement sculpture with a Goddess theme. Over the years she has originated and helped bring to fruition several venues for women in the arts. She has written poetry, short stories, and performance pieces for Goddess Productions, a traveling theater troupe, as well as six books in the Hadra series, tales of women with powers. *The Smuggler, The Spy and The Spider* is her seventh book in that series.

Part I

Donya

Being a spy in a Shokarn city is strange work for a Hadra. Blessed or cursed as we are with the gift of honesty, lies and deception go against our nature. Also there is much in such places to sicken our spirits, but it is important that we keep a presence there to know what the rulers of those cities may be plotting against us. Most of our spies are only too glad to come home when their pledged time is up. Some, too pained by all they have witnessed, do not even make it that far. Except for Shaleen, who seems to be exceptionally well-suited for the role, no Hadra spy that I know of has ever asked to stay longer—but then none has ever been fool enough to fall in love with a Shokarn.

Is love a curse then? I grew up thinking it a blessing and in my home it was. The open affection between my birth mother and my bondmother was the central core of our lives, the fixed point around which everything else in our house revolved. But for me love has become something else. Love, at least since I met Suinyari, has been a thing that pulled me away from my family and my settlement. It has even made a separation between me and my people, something I could not have imagined before. And it keeps drawing me back against my will to a city I despise. All the time I spend with Suinyari is spent in a web of lies and deceit that must be carefully cultivated and constantly maintained—torture for a Hadra. We are born truthful, just as we are born with powers. But for a love such as ours the truth is dangerous. And for Suinyari it might also be deadly. Only with each other can we share truth; sometimes even that gets distorted by the curious circumstances of our lives.

When I am in Eezore not even my name is entirely my own. I have to go about disguised as a man since men have so much more freedom there, calling myself Donyal, which passes for a man's name but still is one I will remember to answer to. As it is, a Hadra cannot stay too long among the Draiga—the not-Hadra—or she begins to lose her powers. When living in the Shokarn city of Eezore grows too difficult I go back again to my settlement of Ishlair on the Escuro River. It is so beautiful there and life seems so right it makes my heart ache after all the things I have seen in Eezore, yet it no longer seems like home to me or rather I no longer feel as if I have a place in the fabric of that life.

If I return to my childhood home my birth mother, Henori, nags at me angrily, "In all the length and breadth of Yarmald can you not find one Hadra to suit your taste? Why must you go chasing after Shokarn flesh? Live in that foul city? Create a fabric of lies around your life? Here you would be loved and honored and live openly as a Hadra. And it breaks Mauri's heart to think you have left her for that Shokarn woman. If the settlement of Ishlair no longer holds your interest then you could go live in Zelindar or even Bayrhim."

I try to explain to Henori that I have no wish to live in the Shokarn city of Eezore or in the Hadra city of Zelindar either for that matter; it is only that Suinyari and I have some connection that I cannot seem to break and she cannot come to live among the Hadra—cannot or will not. But Henori has no ears to listen to such talk. I think she feels betrayed by me. Also she wonders if she did something wrong in raising me. Then my bondsisters, Tiaga and Laiden, add their voices to her complaints till I am driven out of the house.

Mordica, Councilor for Ishlair, has even called me before her for a more formal scolding, saying, "You have dishonored your training by your unnatural attachment to that Shokarn woman, putting her before your duty to the Hadra."

Shocked at her words, I was so angry that I shouted back, "It was you who sent me to Eezore as a Hadra spy in the first place. I was not eager to go, but you insisted. If not for you none of this would have happened. Suinyari would have stayed in her place and I in mine and we never would have met." Instantly I flushed with embarrassment at having spoken so rudely to our Councilor. I was flooded with shame, but I was also far too angry to try to mend the tear between us at that moment. I turned and left without another word, though she shouted my name several times, wanting to call me back.

It was true that Mordica had pressed me into going by saying, "With your light skin it will be easier for you to pass in that city than for other Hadra." But that was not the whole truth. It was of my own doing as well. After my first reluctance there was something in me that was curious, even eager to go. It seemed that my light skin, which had been an odd sort of curse in my life by making me feel different from my darker kin, might actually be of some use after all. Besides I was curious to see these awful Shokarn whose blood must surely flow in my veins.

All Hadra know who their mothers are, but few know their fathers. Our children are begotten at the Essu, the spring and fall festivals, fathered in darkness at the Gimling. Most of the men are dark-skinned

Kourmairi, but mine must have been a Shokarn. Sometimes I feel marked, set apart, though no one has ever teased me or called me names for my difference. It was with a sense of defiance and some anger that I set out for the city of Eezore, dressed as a man and ready to test my fate. And it was in the course of being a spy there that I met Suinyari—smuggler, trader, Highborn Lady, pretend wife to her cousin, and extraordinary lover to me—the amazing woman who captured my imagination and my heart.

Only my bondmother, Akella, seemed to understand. "Love is love. We do not always ask for it. Sometimes it catches us unawares in its net and flings us into danger. Then, if we follow it, we may lose some part of ourselves. And if we turn our back on it we may lose even more. A hard choice, especially for one so young, but filled with many lessons. My family has long forgiven me and even grown fond of Henori, but at first your birth mother was certainly not their choice. They could not imagine my wanting to live in this little northern settlement when I had all the glories of Bayrhim before me. But Henori's heart and life were woven into this place and the glitter of the city held no allure for me if it meant losing her."

When it grows too oppressive in Ishlair I travel up and down the coast like a Wanderer. Restless and in pain, sometimes I keep to my own company and sometimes visit other Hadra settlements and Kourmairi towns. I have even thought of going all the way to Zelindar. When I cannot bear the separation any longer, I go back to Eezore in my disguise as Donyal, back to Suinyari's arms and to the web of love and lies that awaits me there.

Suinyari

Sometimes I have to wonder about this life that I created for myself after my parents died. On the surface it appears so perfect, but is it really what I want? I must say, I have worked hard for it. And I always try to remember how fortunate I am compared to most women who have to live out their lives in a Zarn-ruled Shokarn city. After all, I am neither slave nor servant to be controlled by another's orders, nor am I an Uppercaste woman so bound up in class rules as to be like a prisoner living in a gilded cage. I have a husband in name only whose existence gives me all the protection of a marriage without its crippling restraints. My father, who knew the truth of my nature, arranged it all before he died.

My husband, my cousin Gordivan, has the same fondness for men that I do for women. He finds the arrangement equally convenient and so is often gone from home on "family business." I am comfortably wealthy and will continue to be so if I can keep my father's lucrative if somewhat shady business afloat—moving goods about, in and out of the city, without payment of the Zarn's exorbitant taxes. In fact Gordivan is my partner in these endeavors and his long times away are not just for lovers' trysts. They are also for trade and contacts as he can move about much more freely than I can. Occasionally I disguise myself as a man to make my own arrangements or to check up on Gordivan's work, but such a ruse is dangerous and punishable by death if discovered.

For a woman in Eezore, loving women is also punishable by death. Even so I cannot picture myself lying under any man no matter how kind or gentle he may be. So I have had to take my chances with a few childhood friends who looked at me in that certain way. Afterward we swore each other to silence and were too frightened to go on with our passionate and forbidden touches. They are all married now and occasionally I see them out in society. We chat in a friendly manner full of nervous politeness, but I never ask if their marriages are also a sham and if they have continued in their old ways. They do not ask me either. After that there were a few times with a maid or two who was willing, but it felt too unequal, as if they only loved me because they had no choice, and so I ended up feeling an even deeper loneliness and more shame than pleasure.

Reading all this you may have grown impatient, wondering what I have to complain about compared to other women. After all, I have a grand house, as much money as I need, friends who are more or less loyal and servants who are more like friends. What could I possibly lack? But it is all artifice, maintained by constant vigilance and watchfulness, stiff and careful and measured, nothing spontaneous or free. I have so much if you count power and material goods, but where is the warmth? The ease? Sometimes I long for the closeness of a young mother to the child at her breast or the intimacy of the little family walking together down the street toward home or the freedom of young girls strolling with their arms around each other, giggling and laughing and whispering together, all innocence.

I had lost my innocence long ago when my father had to warn me that what I thought to be a lovely expression of affection was considered filthy by most of the city and was in fact a crime punishable by death. And so I worked at keeping my desires in check and under control. There is no woman in Eezore that it is safe for me to love. I have tried hard to fill my days with work and my evenings with entertainment to dull the ache of longing. I even tried to resign myself to loneliness as if that was all I could expect from life.

And then, like a shooting star, Donya came into my life, strong as a tree and bright as fire. And different, so different from anything I had ever known, as different as a wild animal that has never known taming, the most forbidden person I could have chosen to love—a Hadra! She met me with a spirit as wild and fierce as my own, and yet tender, so tender and gentle and kind. But it has been hard for me with all my pride and self-reliance, as well as my well-guarded heart, to love someone who can so easily walk through my mind, someone who can read my thoughts and knows me almost better than I know myself.

And there is sometimes as much pain as pleasure in loving her. She is often away. And when she is here with me she is so torn about being separated from her Hadra homeland it hurts me for her. She has asked me often to come and live with her there, but how can I? I am too used to having control of my own life. How can I go live among strangers who all have powers while I have none, like being legless among a tribe of runners or wingless in a flock of birds? They might be kind to me, but how could I stand their kindness and their pity? Besides, what use would I be there among them?

Spider

I hope those of you who read these pages will not judge me too harshly. Remember, if you are able to read at all, you already have some privilege and are likely to have had a far more advantaged childhood than mine. I am different now from the child I write about here and not very proud of some of the things I did then. But that was in another time and I was another person. At least I plan to tell the truth here rather than gloss over it as I could so easily do.

Spider—that is what they called me on the street, those who knew me well enough to call me anything at all. Those in the Thieves Guild spoke of me as "The Spider," wanting to get their hands on me for their own purposes. You might think I was some sort of prize to be snatched up and carried off, but I managed easily enough to stay out of their clutches. I had no desire to be one of their "stable." I did well enough on my own. Always have, ever since my mother abandoned me at the age of five. Or perhaps I should say, abandoned herself.

At some hopeful moment she had named me Aneithia, as if she thought that poor scrawny little baby of hers might really amount to something. That quickly got shortened to Aneith and then Neith before I began to be called Spider for my quick disappearances, my ability to hide in dark corners and my amazing agility for climbing out of trouble. The name fit me and I quickly took it for my own.

And it was not just the Thieves Guild I tried to stay clear of, it was anyone who might want to lay hands on me for any purpose, especially the Procurers. Part of their job was to gather up street-brats for the slave trade. Having already witnessed several of their brutal collection raids I had no wish to add myself to that number. But, in truth, I was even more afraid of the Grayrobes. They were supposed to be holy men, yet I saw nothing holy about them. The very sight of them would set my stomach churning, and there appeared to be more and more of them all the time. Whenever I saw them they seemed to be skulking about to some sinister purpose. Since they always kept their hoods up it was hard to even see their faces. They were like walking ghosts, and the thought of one them touching me made my skin crawl, especially the thought of those bony white fingers coming out of the end of that long gray sleeve. Even the market women seemed cowed by them. Among themselves they spoke of the Grayrobes in frightened whispers and made ugly faces behind the men's backs when they passed.

I had lived all those years by my wits, secretly slipping through the markets like a ball of dirty gray rags on two legs, pocketing a piece of fruit here, a hot potato there, a spiced meat patty from another place, a few coins from still another, and seldom being noticed except occasionally by those in the same business. The boys who made their living that way liked to dash in and snatch what they wanted, hoping they could outrun the keeper of the stall or store. They lived by daring and most of them sooner or later were caught, sometimes with fatal results. I, on the other hand, lived by stealth. Drawing no attention to myself if I could help it, I often followed after such boys and took advantage of the uproar they caused. While the shopkeepers were shouting and chasing the culprits it was a good time to slip in, help myself to whatever I needed, then vanish with my plunder without anyone noticing.

I grew very skilled at what I did, so skilled I was seldom cold or hungry. I made little nests for myself out of my stealings in the corners of abandoned buildings or under the supports of bridges. A few times the boys from the market tried to bother me. I had a knife among my stolen possessions and fiercely defended what was mine. They were stronger, but I was much quicker. A few bloodied hands convinced them to look elsewhere for easy pickings. After that there was even some grudging admiration. Later some of those boys actually became my friends if one can be said to have friends in such a world. I seldom came in contact with other girls; girls did not last long in those streets. I took pride in my skill and cleverness and had no idea at that time how desperately lonely I was.

Mother Melna

I have lived most of my life in Eezore—far more years than I spent in the little Kourmairi village from which I fled—yet I have never really felt myself to be part of this city. I fear I will forever be an outsider in it. The only place where I am really at home now is in this compound of ancient buildings made of weathered stone and red brick, buildings that are just a small remnant of what was once a great Witch Convent, flourishing here before the time of the Witch kills. It is the only refuge for women in this city—also the only place where being a woman and being of dark skin is not a disadvantage.

That the House of the Mother exists at all in this Zarn-ruled city is a miracle of sorts and one I fear may not last much longer. We are not here because of the Zarn's kindness or generosity—nor his tolerance either. It is something more like negligence and ignorance that allows us to remain. We exist hardly noticed at the margins of things, in the cracks between the rocks so to speak, but I fear that will all change soon. The old Zarn is in his dotage, growing ever more foolish and forgetful. When he was younger he was far more concerned with his pleasures than with running Eezore responsibly. Under his rule it has become a bankrupt city, a city of thieves and beggars. Our continued existence is part of that laxness. But Zarn Ozmaryn will die soon and his careless ways will vanish with him. There are already rumors of a wasting illness. His grandson, Lord Gunjorn, the young man who will inherit the Zarndom, is hard, cruel, ambitious and very righteous. He is determined to clear away the mess his grandfather has made and restore Eezore to its former glory, all this under the guidance of Rhaais, the god of war, the one who loves the sight of human blood. I am much afraid we will be part of his ruthless cleansing and our blood may soon be shed to appease this angry god.

Gunjorn is already enlisting eager young men to his cause, mostly the dissatisfied younger sons of Uppercaste Shokarn families, men whose ambitions are thwarted because their older brothers will inherit everything from their fathers—both the power of the house and the wealth. These young men call themselves Purifiers. Already they are making a few quick raids in the markets and on the streets, testing their powers, challenging the Zarn's regular guards to call them to account. They are especially harsh on women. According to their code of behavior women should stay at home, not even show their faces in the public world. Those who sell their pleasures are a favorite target for Purifier attacks. With no protection, several have already died at their hands. And I fear Gunjorn has made an alliance with the Grayrobes, that band of monks also dedicated to cleansing this city from the influence of women.

Knowing all this is happening gives me a great sense of grief and helplessness. I hear most of the news from our young Sisters, our Yellowrobes and Greenrobes who sell our wares at market or beg on the street to get money for the convent. For myself, I seldom go out into the city anymore. There is no pleasure for me there; everything I need is here within these walls. And I wonder how long it will be safe for our young women, how long before they become a target of Purifier wrath.

I suppose it is only a matter of time before the Purifiers turn their fury on those of us who have inherited what remains of the great Witch Convent of Eezore. Then what will happen to the women of this city? They will have nowhere to turn, no refuge or sanctuary. We are the only place left where a young woman can get any learning, also the only shelter for women in desperate circumstances. I am old now and have not much longer to live, but what of the young ones? What will happen to them? Where will they go?

Donya

The way I first met Suinyari is a whole story in itself. It is also part of all the other firsts of coming to this city, a city so different from anything I have ever known, so strange and shocking to Hadra sensibilities that it shook me to my core.

Mordica herself took charge of preparing me to go, trying hard to get me ready for whatever I might meet with there. Among other things she told me that I had to put what is called tack—a saddle and bridle—on my horse Cloud. Unlike the Hadra who speak mind to mind with creatures and ride their horses by consent, the people of Eezore ride by compulsion and need such contraptions for control. Those things are usually made of leather, but we can no more kill an animal for its hide than we can kill a human for its skin. Something else had to be found. Mordica asked Mauri, who was still my lover then, to fashion a bridle for me. It looked like a regular Draiga bridle, but it had no metal bit in the mouth—in fact no bit at all—and rather than leather it was made of braided rope that had been stained and oiled to look like leather. She also made me a saddle of stuffed and stiffened cloth, very tough cloth hardened by being soaked in the juice of batyin bark. When this was done Cloud and I had to practice with these things much to the amusement of the other Hadra.

Being lighter skinned than most Hadra, it took little paste or powder to change my complexion enough to appear Shokarn. In Eezore it would be better for me not to look like a Kourmairi since they are mostly slaves or servants there and so can be stopped and questioned by the guards at any time. The plan was for me to go disguised as a lowercaste Shokarn man by the name of Donyal. Also I worked hard at practicing my Shokarn since Mordica said I still needed to improve my accent.

Before I left I cut paper and sewed the edges together to make a sort of rough pad. This was for writing an account for Mordica of everything that happened in Eezore and also for sketching my impressions. All my life I have made drawings of whatever I saw. This new place would certainly be worth recording. "You will be my eyes and ears there, Donya," Mordica told me. "I have been to Maktesh once, but never to Eezore." For myself I had my own reasons for going that had to do with the mystery of my birth and origins, a mystery that my birth mother refused to explain.

When it was time to leave, Mordica sent me with a caravan of Wanderers who were passing through Ishlair on their way to Eezore. This was a strange new experience for me, being among so many Draiga and especially so many men. Perhaps Mordica intended it as a preparation for my time in Eezore.

How can I possibly convey the first impact of that city on my Hadra senses? As we entered by the West Gate I was instantly bombarded by a rush of strong raw emotions that were certainly not my own. Coming at me from all sides—fear, envy, jealousy, spite, meanness, pain, grief, hopelessness and rage—they were a veritable banquet of troubling and troubled feelings or perhaps more like a festering stew or soup. I had to constantly keep reassuring Cloud that we were safe enough. With my hand on her neck, I tried to settle her down. She kept dancing sideways, tossing her head nervously, flicking her ears back and forth and turning from side to side.

Besides the assault of all those strange feelings, there was the incredible buzz and hum of unshielded thoughts, many of them not very kindly, some actually vicious or dangerous. So little love or joy or pleasure, so much misery all in one place. How could people go about with such cruel thoughts or be so uncaring while their neighbors felt such pain? How could they bear it and do nothing? Much as I was curious to hear their thoughts I had to forcefully shut my mind and shield myself or I would have fallen apart under the onslaught.

From the poor I could almost understand this bitterness. They looked as if their lives were miserable enough. But as I moved through the streets and looked about, I noticed that the well-dressed Uppercaste did not seem much happier than those they oppressed. They were also full of discontent, suspicion and envy, their minds teeming with little petty plots against each other, ways to advance themselves at another's expense. All this I said to Shaleen in a rush of words when I was finally able to locate her small room in a narrow back alley behind the Horse Market. I had been wandering the city for a while, searching for the streets that were marked on the much creased and folded map the Wanderers had left with me. Being so new there I was shy of testing my Shokarn yet by asking for directions. Also I did not mind getting a little sense of the city before I met with her.

Shaleen seemed glad enough to see me—very relieved in fact—but when she answered my flood of questions there was a pitying look on her face. "After a while it gets better or you care less. Believe me, there is nothing you can do, Donya. Do not think to change things here or make them better. It will only break your heart. You must learn to harden yourself, learn to accept and endure what you see and hear and feel or else you are no use to us at all. If you cannot do that then you should go home right now and send another in your place. I certainly hope you will do better than Murial of Ossen whom you are replacing here. She was far too sensitive for this work and had to leave her assignment early."

I was surprised at this; Mordica had not seen fit to tell me why Murial left. Perhaps she had been afraid it would unnerve me. I was about to question Shaleen further, but she went on with hardly a pause, "And do not think to tell these people how much better life is in Ishlair or Zelindar. They hate the Hadra. The things they say about us could turn your hair white. They think us vile and disgusting, worse than animals. They say we mate with our horses. The Grayrobes call us an abomination when they rant and rave against us in their public speeches. Also these people are full of jealousy and envy. They think we have vast hordes of wealth and that incites their greed. Lucky for us they fear us more than they hate us or they would be mounting an invasion force right now to exterminate us. Yes, that is the very word they use. But they still remember their last defeat in Zelindar, and that cools their enthusiasm for destruction.

"And the poor that you pity so are no better than their masters—worse perhaps. They have much anger at their hard lives. Since it is not safe to turn that anger against those who crush them from above, they turn it on us instead. The upper classes of course encourage this, only too glad to fuel that fire as long as it does not turn on them and burn down their fine houses. No, do not waste your pity on any of them. They are not worth it. Pity instead the poor animals they mistreat so cruelly."

Shaleen was breathless and her face flushed by the end of that explosion of words. That was more words than I had ever heard her utter in all the time I knew her in Ishlair. We had been childhood friends there but had drifted apart as we grew older. Now there was little left of the happy, carefree girl I remembered. It was sad to see how much her time in Eezore had hardened her, but I did not argue. She knew better than me the truth of things in this Shokarn city. Still I silently vowed to myself I would never accept the way things were even if I learned to endure.

"I will do my best to serve the Hadra with honor," I said stiffly. Thinking of Murial, I felt determination hardening inside or perhaps it was only pride. I would not be the one to leave early and so disappoint Shaleen again.

When I first came to Eezore I moved about a good deal, always alert and watchful. I did not board with Shaleen. It would not do to be seen too much together. Though I soon developed a network of informants in the markets, still I had no one I could really talk to or trust. The information I gathered was paid for by coins or by the offer of a meal or a drink, not friendship. Finally, just as I was growing weary of my lack of any permanent place, I found for myself a good situation.

I was to meet an informant at The Blue-Eyed Lady. This inn turned out to be a large rambling establishment, painted in blues and greens with gold trim. The whole of it managed to convey an intriguing combination of elegance and shabbiness. While waiting I struck up a conversation with the owner, a widow with a grown daughter. Granthia told me she had inherited the inn from her father. After that she made so much grieving and heartfelt mention of her poor dear dead husband that I began to wonder if the good man had ever really existed. Then I caught from her mind that this was only a needed explanation and protection for her pretty, lively and not very bright daughter.

When I told Granthia I was looking for a very inexpensive room, nothing as fancy as her establishment, she told me she might have just the thing, a room above the barn. She said she would let me have it for almost nothing if I would do some occasional work as stable boy when the inn was crowded or relieve her stableman on his day off. Otherwise I was free to come and go and do as I pleased. That seemed like a wonderful bargain, almost too good to be true. Since my informant had not appeared at the agreed-upon time and seemed not likely to do so, I went with Granthia to look at the room. We climbed steep stairs to a long, narrow space with a low ceiling. Small windows looked out in three directions—the stable yard, the inn and the street. Rough-timbered and crudely built, it was just one end of the barn loft walled off to make a simple room.

Granthia started to apologize for its appearance. "It is nothing much. I had it made for the stableman, but he preferred to have his sleep space down below. He said he needed to be close to his work, that he liked to keep an eye on the horses so he could..."

I grinned at her and interrupted. "Perfect! It is perfect for my needs and quite grand for the price."

She laughed and winked at me, and so we made our bargain.

Granthia appeared to take a liking to me though she said she found my accent strange. Explaining that I was from a farm north of Pellor, I told her it was the accent of my village and as youngest son in a big family I had no prospects at home. The liking was mutual since I found her much more forthright and independent than most of the women I had encountered in the city. Soon I was a fixture there at The Blue-Eyed Lady, eating free meals and helping Granthia with many chores around the inn. This turned out to be an excellent place for gathering information on whatever passed in the city. Being Granthia's man-of-all-jobs gave me a wonderful cloak of invisibility.

Soon Granthia began flirting with me. I wondered how she would feel if she knew the young man upon whom she was lavishing so much attention and free food was really a woman and a Hadra at that. Not pleased, I imagine! I felt badly at using and deceiving her in that way and tried to make up for it with helpfulness. She said she felt safer with me there. I wondered how long it would take before I would have to start refusing her advances and perhaps begin looking for another place to make my bed.

One evening, as I was having my meal, seated close to the door in my favorite place from which I could observe all the comings and goings, a woman came striding in who took my breath away. She was wearing red leather riding boots instead of ladies' shoes and as she entered every head turned. She had amazing presence. Her street clothes were covered with a long red cape, and when she threw back the hood her hair blazed copper against the red. She swept the room with her eyes. For just a moment those eyes touched on my face and I felt a shiver of connection go down my back.

Many greeted her. She nodded or called out salutations in return, but she stopped at no one's table. Instead she went straight to the rear. There she sat down with her back to the wall at a table in a shadowy corner from which she could survey the whole room. As I watched, several different people went over to her table for a few words. When Granthia came by to see if I wanted anything more, I put my hand on her arm to draw her close and whispered, "Who is that woman in the red cape? She is quite a sight, very bold for a woman of Eezore where most women go about with down cast eyes."

"Oh, that is Lady Suinyari of the House of Althor. She has more power in this town than most women. Would you like to meet her?"

"No, no," I said quickly and another little shiver went down my back. "I was only curious; she seems so well known here."

"She is well known everywhere in the city. I think that is part of what keeps her alive and safe in Eezore. I am going back to talk with her right now. Are you sure you do not want…?"

"Very sure," I said quickly, interrupting her question. "Besides, a Highborn lady would not want to meet a stable hand."

Granthia shook her head. "Suinyari is not like that." Then she left me and wove her way through the room, inquiring at this or that table, but heading steadily for the back and the mysterious lady in the red cape. I told myself I should leave right now. Instead I sat staring at that shadowed table where Granthia and Suinyari were soon deep in conversation, heads bent together. Suddenly Suinyari looked up and I felt her eyes staring back at me. I quickly dropped my gaze to my plate and my unfinished dinner.

I was still slowly working my way through my now cold food with my mind elsewhere when I sensed someone advancing on me. Looking up I saw Granthia coming my way with Suinyari close behind her. Granthia stopped right in front of me and said, "This is the lad that inquired about you. Donyal, this is Lady Suinyari of the House of Althor."

"Just Suinyari will do well enough without all the rest of that decoration. Good evening, Donyal. To what do I owe this interest?" A pair of bright green eyes were gazing down at me with lively curiosity and her tone was full of light mockery. I blushed deeply. When I opened my mouth to speak no words came out. While I struggled with my silence she looked me up and down as if examining a horse at a Kourmairi horse fair.

Finally her eyes met mine. It felt as if she was staring right into my head. Smiling with amusement, she said, "What a shame, you seem to have lost your voice. If you gain it back and want to ask me some questions, come to my house later this evening. It is the big one made of red stone with white marble trim, standing at the corner of Althor Street and Morlan Way. You can hardly miss it. I am sorry to have struck you speechless." Then, light as a bird's wing, she ran the fingers of one hand up my cheek. In the next instant she swept past me and was out the door.

Shaking my head in surprise I beckoned Granthia to sit down by me. "Granthia, tell me, what was that all about? What does that woman want with me? Is she always like that? And how does a woman alone come to have so much freedom in Eezore?"

Granthia laughed and winked at me. "So many questions. I see you have regained your voice. Well, in the first place Suinyari is not alone. She is a married woman, but her husband is often away, and so she goes about the city on his business—or at least that is what she says. And no, I have never seen her like that with anyone else. If you are so curious, you could go and ask her. She certainly has given you a clear invitation. If I did not know better I could imagine she had taken a fancy to you, but I think she does not much fancy men in that way."

Those words rang in my head and made me blush again as I remembered the brush of her fingers against my cheek. "She seems dangerous to me. I think I will stay as far away as possible."

"Oh, there is no harm in her; she has a good heart. I think she is only dangerous to her enemies."

Granthia took away my cold food and brought me some hot cider which I sat nursing for a while, musing over what had just happened. I vowed to myself that I would never go near that woman, that I would do everything possible to avoid her in the future, but Granthia's words, *Does not much fancy men in that way*, kept replaying themselves over and over in my head. I finally finished my cider and stood up to leave, intending to go back to my room. Instead I suddenly found myself on Cloud's back headed for Althor Street as if I had no will of my own and no brains at all. *No harm can come of this*, I told myself, *I am just curious. I will only take a quick look at her house and then ride on by.*

Suinyari

I left the inn that night in a fever of curiosity. Granthia might have been fooled into thinking Donyal was a young man; I knew better. My business, my safety, my very life depends on an accurate observation of people. Though her square jaw, her heavy dark brows and her strong nose might look "mannish" enough to fool the eyes of others, I could see through to the woman underneath. And then the softness of her cheek under my fingers confirmed my suspicions. Yet her gaze at the moment that our eyes met had been direct and piercing, unlike the women of Eezore who avert their eyes. Few Shokarn women would look directly into another's eyes that way and certainly no Kourmairi. Then she had quickly glanced away, acting as if struck dumb. I think she did not trust herself to speak for fear of giving herself away. But in that instant that our eyes touched, something sparked between us, something attractive and very dangerous.

Who was she? Where was she from? What was she doing here? And why this disguise that could cost her life if discovered? I was determined to find out and had decided to draw her to me, using whatever means I could. I had already set about devising a plan, but in the end it proved unnecessary. She came to me all on her own, no doubt also drawn by curiosity and attraction.

Donya

Suinyari was right that I could not miss the house. Though not as big as some of the Great Houses of the city, it was still quite imposing. Tall and with many spires, it had a certain arrogance, standing there on the corner with its striking contrast of red stone and white marble trim, too tasteful to be gaudy, but still demanding attention, much like its owner.

In spite of my wariness, the same impulse that had put me on Cloud's back now got me off again. With no rational thought on my part I found myself propelled under the white stone arch, through black metal gates that were open with seeming welcome and on up the flower-lined walk. There all sense of welcome ended. I was met by a stern-faced woman who opened the huge red door partway and glared at me suspiciously. She blocked access and asked sharply, "Are you expected? Who shall I say is calling?" Behind her a dog was barking wildly.

"Yes, I am expected. Tell Suinyari that Donyal is here."

"Well, Donyal, I see you can speak again. Thank you, Bethron, I can deal with him. And take Dondo with you. That is enough barking for one evening." Suinyari's voice had that same mocking quality I remembered from the inn. She had appeared behind the woman she called Bethron. That one gave a grunt of disgust and slowly backed away, watching me the whole time as if I might suddenly grow fangs or a tail. As soon as she was out of the way, Suinyari swung the door wide and gave me a smile that went right to my heart. "Be welcome in my house, Donyal."

Gone was the red cape, but she was still just as striking. She wore a long gown of sapphire blue and had let down her red hair. Easy to see why the men had turned to look at her. She was enough to turn any man's head and perhaps any woman's, certainly mine. There I was standing in her house after vowing to myself I would stay well clear of her.

"Bring us some tea in my bookroom," she called to Bethron's departing back. Then she guided me into a charming room full of low comfortable furniture, very different from the stiff formal appearance of the other rooms I had glimpsed as we passed. As well as being a sitting space, this "bookroom" as she called it seemed also to be an office; one corner was occupied by a wide desk full of papers and accounts. Somehow it reminded me of Mordica's office in the Zildorn back home. With a wide gesture of her hand, Suinyari motioned me to sit on one of the brightly cushioned couches arranged at the front of the room.

Bethron brought the tea immediately, almost as if it had already been prepared. She was closely followed by a younger woman carrying a tray of delicate little pastries. That one stood staring at me wide-eyed. I sensed that she was there out of curiosity, not because Bethron needed help. Suinyari gave them a nod and said quickly, "Bethron, Alliya, thank you. Please close the door when you leave and let no one disturb us here, not even Gammo." They left, though reluctantly. As she poured our tea, Suinyari gave me a searching look and asked, "So, now, why are you here, Donyal? I had hoped to see you again, but I did not really expect you to come, certainly not so soon."

"I am not sure. Curiosity I suppose. You seem so…so different from other women in Eezore. And besides you…" I shrugged. What I wanted to say was, *You cast some sort of spell over me*, but that sounded much too bold to say to an almost-stranger.

"You feel you know me in some secret way, is that it? Well, I feel as if I know you too—from a heart place—and it disturbs me greatly. I do not like anyone to have power over me, especially over my heart. I also know you are not what you seem. And I too am curious, very curious as to who and what you are and why you are playing this dangerous game. Not the young man you appear to be, that much is clear. Not a man at all, I could tell that from the touch of your cheek. Who knows, perhaps there is some business we could do together if you will only tell me your secret."

At her words a ripple of fear went up my back. "Secrets are to keep silence on or they are not secrets for long. They may even become very dangerous. Why should I tell you anything?"

"Because you are here to find something that is missing in your life or you would not have come. Now you must give something in order to find it, make me some sort of trade."

I stared hard into her eyes, trying to understand the woman who lived behind them. For an outsider, a Draiga, she had a good shield. It was hard to get a clear reading of her thoughts, yet I could sense no harm in her, no trap waiting there for me. Finally I said, "I think you also have a secret, Suinyari, and something you need as well. If you want my secret so much, you will have to give me yours first. Then I will know if it is safe to speak."

"You drive a hard bargain, stranger." In her turn she stared hard at me, trying to see into my heart or my head. Then she sighed deeply and finally spoke. "Well, my curiosity is overcoming my caution and so I will talk first. You must promise that you will speak next." I nodded and she went on, "The truth of my life is that I followed in my father's steps and took up his business when he died. I am a trader of sorts, someone who facilitates the movement of goods in and out of the city without the payment of the Zarn's unfair tax, not such a dreadful secret after all, but it could cost my life." Though she avoided the word "smuggler," I could hear it loud and clear in her head. "And now tell me what it is you are hiding and why you go about dressed as a man."

"That last part is easy enough to answer; I dress as a man because that way I have far more freedom to move about in this city. As to the rest of it, if I tell you, you may not believe me. If you do believe me, you may well betray me."

She shook her head emphatically. "Not likely. I hold many secrets safe. That is part of my work. I think this is just an excuse for your silence. You made me a promise. I believed you. Now I have made myself vulnerable to you with nothing in exchange. I am a merchant, a trader. I expect a fair return. I can tell you right now, this does not please me."

I held up my hand. "Wait, Suinyari, please give me a moment." I could sense her mounting anger. Behind my silence, my mind was frantically darting back and forth, weighing alternatives. As a Hadra spy I was pledged to secrecy, but it was very lonely in this city with no friend or ally save Shaleen whom I seldom saw. It would be a blessing to have someone here I could trust, someone with whom I could speak openly and be myself. This woman certainly appealed to me for many reasons.

"Well?" she said impatiently. "Are you going to wait all night to uphold your end of the bargain? Are you going to tell me the truth of who you are and what you do here or do I have to call my stableman to come and shake it out of you?"

That made me laugh. "And that would do you no good at all, no matter how big and brawny he might be." She raised her eyebrows in surprise, and in that moment I decided. "Open your mind to me, Suinyari."

"What do you mean, open my mind? What are you talking about?"

"Just that, shut your eyes, take a deep breath and open your mind to me. Then I will know if I can trust you."

With a sigh of annoyance, she did as I asked. It took a few moments for her to release, but finally I felt her energy shift and the barriers go down. Probing her mind, I could sense no harm there, just impatience and a lively curiosity. Besides, she was not likely to turn me over to the guards. She herself was an outlaw of sorts and probably did her best to avoid their attention. Holding her secret in trust made it less likely that she would betray mine.

"Thank you. You may open your eyes now."

She shook her head and rubbed her fingers vigorously through her hair. "What in the name of Rha-ais was that? It felt like some nasty spider crawling through my brain. What are you, Donyal?"

"Forgive the intrusion; I had to know if I could believe your words.

Now I will tell you, but you must promise to tell no one else, not even the people of your house."

She nodded, watching me strangely. "I promise," she said almost in a whisper.

I nodded in turn. "The truth of it is that I am a Hadra from the north coast of Yarmald, here as our eyes and ears in the city of Eezore to make sure there is no harm to us brewing in this place. We have been the target of hostile invasions from Zarn cities before, and we need to be forewarned and prepared."

"A Hadra!" she exclaimed, her eyes going wide. "A Hadra spy!"

"Shh, be quiet, no one else must know. You have promised me your silence on this."

Suinyari nodded. Then, eyes sparkling with mischief, she began to laugh. When she spoke again, she leaned forward and said almost in a whisper, "So I cast out my net and fished up a Hadra spy. No, I do not doubt your word. I felt you there in my brain, a most startling experience. Who but a Hadra could do such a thing? And no, I will not betray you to anyone, most especially not to the guards or to the Zarn. I myself have no love for the man though I hear he has a soft spot for me. That would change quick enough if he ever caught me at my games. Then he would probably crush me to pieces with no mercy."

I had avoided using the word "spy," but she seemed to relish it. "The smuggler and the spy, what an interesting combination," she went on with sly amusement in her voice. Then, in a more serious tone, she added, "So now we have entrusted each other with our most deadly secret and are equally endangered. Our lives are in each other's hands. We need to form a bond of mutual trust, something I do not do easily in this peculiar life of mine. In fact, I never talk this way to anyone, least of all a stranger. How did you manage that?"

Watching her, seeing the quickly changing expressions that flashed across her lovely face, catching the sparkle in her eyes and the shimmer of her red hair, noticing how her hands echoed her words so expressively—I began to feel a strong tug at my heart. It had been a while since I had felt such feelings for anyone. My love for Mauri had long since turned into sisterly affection. Even that was threatened now by our conflict over my going to Eezore. Much to my surprise, I was finding myself attracted to this woman. Challenging and intriguing, she was certainly very different from any other woman I knew. Warnings of danger throbbed loudly in my head. In spite of that I reached out and impulsively took her hand in mine. "Suinyari, you must tell me the story of your life and I will tell you mine. That will make our bond even stronger."

"So be it then. It is probably not at all wise, but what is done is done. This may be a new beginning. I have certainly been feeling there was something lacking in my life."

Afterward we sat up almost till dawn, sharing our lives. I slipped back into my room just as it was turning light. Before I went on my rounds in the city that day I took out my pad of paper. In it I wrote down this account of everything that had happened so far in Eezore. I also struggled with drawing Suinyari's likeness. No matter how hard I tried I was not satisfied with the result. Suinyari's beauty was not easy to capture. Flat paper could hardly do justice to the liveliness of her face in motion, but I could not afford to crumple up paper and throw it away so I set it aside to work on later. Once more I decided that it was too dangerous to see her again, and once more, come evening, I found myself back at Suinyari's door. This time she answered the door herself. I could tell by the look of welcome on her face that she had been expecting me.

Suinyari

Of all the people I could have chosen to love, a Hadra was probably the most dangerous. And yet how could I resist? Here was someone who loved women as her birthright, not as a criminal trying to conceal her crime. What freedom! To be able to share love with an equal, not someone who would betray me out of fear or carelessness or under torture or for some personal gain and advantage. Imagine that, here I am thinking of love when I hardly know this person, have only spent one evening in her company. We have not even touched in the manner of lovers. And yet, in some way, I feel we already know each other deeply. But then, perhaps she will not even come back. Or perhaps she only sees me as a good source of information, someone to cultivate for her work. Well, this evening will tell the tale. If she does not come back, then that is an end to it. And if she does, I will know instantly the truth of the matter. She may have a reading of minds, but I have a reading of hearts. I will know by her face, by the look in her eyes.

Donya

I had been subjected to endless warnings about not trying to change the evils of Eezore; no one had thought to warn me about the dangers of falling in love there. Perhaps no one had been able to imagine such a thing. It was as if someone had cast a spell or thrown a net over me. Not Suinyari, I think. She seemed just as surprised.

After that first night when I found myself sharing with her the secret of my identity I had a very clear sense that any connection with this woman was dangerous. I should stop this before it went any further. At least that is what I told myself by the clear light of morning. But the pull was still there, a string fastened to my heart, tugging me in the direction of Althor House in spite of my resolve.

I managed to resist all day, finding plenty in the city to keep me occupied. Then evening came and I turned in that direction as surely as a flower turns toward the sun. This time I went on foot. My intention was only to tell Suinyari that I could not come back again, that an association between us would distract me from my work and was in fact very dangerous. These were my thoughts as I strode purposefully through the evening streets, carefully preparing the words in my mind. What I planned to say was strong and clear and altogether right. There could be no arguing with it. I was quite sure of that until Suinyari herself opened the front door of her house and smiled at me. Then all my words dropped away like pebbles. For a moment I was struck silent again by her very presence.

Suinyari

I was very glad to see Donyal at my door again or rather Donya, for she had told me the night before that was her real name. I had been watching from behind the curtains and when I heard her knock I told Bethron and Alliya to stay away and let me answer the door. "But that man is a stranger," Bethron fussed at me. "How do you know you can trust him? Would it not be better for me to hide somewhere in the hall?"

"No, it would not!" I said in a tone of finality that allowed for no further argument. "Now leave me some privacy. And take Dondo with you; I do not need a dog barking. And keep everyone else away."

She grinned and winked at me. "Ah, so is that how it goes now?"

I stamped my foot. "Away! Now!" Bethron retreated with Dondo at her heels. Alliya followed, and I went to the door.

When I swung it open, Donya was standing there, looking nervous and expectant. She stepped in, her eyes searching mine. I pushed the door shut. Then, with no idea I was going to do that, I suddenly held out my arms to her and Donya walked into them without a word being spoken between us. We held each other for a long time in that way, pressed tight, body to body, everything said in silence, each heart pounding against the other's. No other woman had ever held me that way, so fearlessly and so completely. With other women in Eezore there was always too much fear and hesitation, a moving forward and at the same time a moving away, a guarding against. Besides, women in Eezore are trained to be timid; they never use the full strength of their arms or bodies that way. Actually no one in my life had ever held me like that, man or woman. She was holding all of my self with all of her self. I felt as if I had finally come home. Just as that thought went through my head she said aloud with her lips warm against my cheek, "I feel as if I have finally come home." No need to tell her that I had thought the same thing at the same moment; she already knew.

At last we both stepped back to catch our breath. For a long while we stared at each other in silence until I finally said, "Well?"

Donya made a slight bow and said with total seriousness, "I am yours tonight, My Lady, for whatever you desire."

"And afterward?"

"Afterward as the Goddess wills it, for surely at this moment we are in Her hands. No one else could have brought us together in this way."

"The Goddess eh? Well she is certainly a better guardian of love than this Rha-ais men seem so eager to worship." Before she could change her mind I took her hand, drew her down the hall, and led her up the stairs to my room. I did not want to be robbed of this adventure even at the risk of my life. Never had I felt myself more present to my life, more open to a lover or more careless of the consequences. My body throbbed with desire that bloomed with a delicious ache between my legs and ran up my body in waves.

Donya

It was not my usual way to be so forward and reckless in matters of the heart. In fact my Hadra sisters were more likely to tease me for my caution and reticence. In spite of that, and with hardly a word spoken between us, I found myself following Suinyari up the stairs and down the hall to her room. It did not take Hadra powers to know that this time we were not going to chat all evening.

When she threw open the door to her room I stopped in my tracks with a little gasp of amazement. The dizzying riot of color before me was a startling contrast to my glimpses of the rest of the house which—except for Suinyari's bookroom—seemed furnished in an almost austere manner with heavy dark wood furniture that looked very well made, was probably expensive and appeared to be more for show than for real comfort. This could hardly have been more different. Tugging impatiently at my hand, Suinyari drew me in. Then she quickly shut and latched the door behind us.

Looking around I felt as if I had just stepped into a dream. The only furniture in the room was a bed raised on carved legs, a large ornate clothes cupboard and a dressing table and chair. The rest of the space was filled with cushions and rugs and drapes in brightly clashing colors and endless swirls of patterns, reflected back over and over by the round mirror over the dressing table and the long one on the clothes cupboard door.

I turned round and round, trying to absorb what I was seeing. Suinyari laughed with pleasure at my surprise.

"The other rooms are just for show. My father furnished them that way to establish our position in this city that cares so much about position and I have kept the house much as he left it. This is where I really live. This was my parents' room. Now it is mine—my nest, my refuge, the heart of the house for me. All this is Muinyairin work that my father collected. It reminded him of his life on the road as a Wanderer. Most Wanderer wagons are furnished with Muinyairin rugs and cushions, items of trade. But he kept it all out of public view. It was his own private passion. The other Great Houses in Eezore have far more Muinyairin work on display.

"My father began this collection and I continued it. When things go wrong in my life or in my business I come in here for warmth and comfort and to remember who I really am rather than who I pretend to be. My father once told me that my mother hated it at first, said he had made their bedroom look like a brothel. After a while she acquired a taste for Muinyairin handwork and became almost as knowledgeable about it as he was."

This work was all far more elaborate than any Hadra weaving I had ever seen. Sensing my interest, Suinyari started naming the different styles to me, saying what region of the Drylands they were from, but my mind started wandering. After a while I could hardly follow her words since I found myself wondering who she had shared this space with before and what she had done with them here…these cushions… that bed… Abruptly I shook my head to clear it. "Surely you did not bring me up here just to show me your knowledge of weaving styles," I said a little tartly.

At that she laughed again and this time her face flushed. "No, surely not. I was suddenly struck shy and it seemed easier to talk about weaving than…"

With sudden courage I took her hand in mine and raised it to my lips. "We should put all these lovely rugs and cushions to use." Perhaps the boldness of the patterns was making me bold as well. I started by kissing her hand. When she did not withdraw it, I began to run some little kisses up her arm. She shivered slightly and then turned her face toward me expectantly. The kisses ran to her shoulder, up her neck, along the line of her jaw and came to rest on her lips. She opened her mouth and drew me in, soft at first, then hard and demanding.

I sank into that kiss, surrendering my caution. The sudden shivers that ran up and down my body were as much from desire as from fear. And with the thrill of fear came a rush of excitement. I had never made love with a stranger before. Every woman I had ever shared loving with was someone I had known since childhood. With some I had even played those first girlish games of exploration before we grew more serious. Suinyari was more than a stranger. This woman I was about to give myself to was not even a Hadra. She was a Draiga, an outsider, something forbidden, tantalizing, dangerous. The unknown was drawing me in—frightening and seductive.

As my hands ran up her body and slipped under her clothes to touch warm flesh I could feel Suinyari opening to me, letting down the barriers of her mind. I was certainly as strange to her as she was to me, more so perhaps, but she seemed not to care. Now that we had started down this road she did not hesitate. Her joy at being really free to make love to another woman seemed to override all caution.

Soon we had shed our clothes and were rolling about among those cushions, sucking and nibbling, thrusting our hands between each other's legs, groaning and crying out with pleasure, all shyness and fear forgotten. Suinyari was alternately laughing and crying. That cool mocking woman had disappeared and left a wild creature in her place. I followed her into pleasure and with a last wild cry we peaked together. Afterward, as we clung to each other, Suinyari began to cry in earnest. It was a while before she could talk again, and then her words came out in an anguished whisper. "All those lost years, so much feeling and passion that I have had to hide, burying it under work and social pretensions. Why does it have to be so hard? I envy you growing up where you were free to be yourself."

After that I gave up all pretense that I was ending this connection. I did not have the strength. Even thinking of it made me go weak. In fact it was clear to me that this was just the beginning. Certainly I knew it was not wise, but I rationalized this unlikely affection by telling myself that Suinyari's house would be a good source of information about what was going on in the city. Soon I found myself dividing my time between my little room at The Blue-Eyed Lady and Suinyari's bed at Althor House. Granthia would give me knowing looks in which salacious amusement was mixed with a little tinge of jealousy. Perhaps she regretted introducing us. I know she had fancied me herself, at least in my guise as Donyal.

Actually it was more than Suinyari's bed I was sharing. I quickly became part of the household. Bethron, who saw herself as Suinyari's guardian, became less hostile and suspicious. In fact she was the one who insisted we needed some proper explanation for my presence in the house. "You cannot have a young man visiting here over and over unless he is a relative. It will make talk and talk will make trouble, something this house does not need." That was how I became Suinyari's distant cousin on her father's side, trying to make my way in the city. Alliya, the other maid, became positively friendly. As for Dondo, he stopped barking each time at my arrival. Instead he became an adoring nuisance and took to following me around or lying on my feet.

I also met the other permanent members of the household, Gammo the cook and Torvil who was the stableman, the yardman and whatever else was needed at the moment. The person I did not meet at that time was Suinyari's husband, the mysterious Gordivan. He was off on some sort of business. The thought of his return made me a little nervous in spite of Suinyari's reassurances that this was only a sham marriage and he was not really her husband in that way.

After the first few times I was there, Suinyari told me to come into the back courtyard and enter by the green door. "The red door is for formal guests, the green door is for intimates," she said with a wicked grin. As we spent more time together I came to understand that this lovely woman—rich, powerful, capable, with many friends and connections—was actually very lonely. She had no peers, no equals with whom to share her life and her thoughts, certainly no one with whom to safely share her passions, not until this Hadra spy came into her life.

Mother Melna

When Nafrini, the newest of our Yellowrobes, asked where Olya and I had come from and how the House of the Mother had begun, I was surprised. Most of the new ones are not so curious when they first come to us. Many have just escaped some horror in their own lives and are too desperate to think much about others. They are just grateful for shelter. If they think of us at all, they think we are old as the hills and have been here forever. Often they are quite shy with us and would not dream of asking such personal things. But Nafrini is bold and outspoken. She reminds me of Olya when we were young. Her outspokenness is no doubt the cause of that pattern of painful-looking bruises on her face and arms and body. I was glad to see that beatings had not broken her spirit.

Answering Nafrini's questions took me back to that early time. There is so much to do here, so much that keeps me occupied, I hardly ever think of it anymore, how we had first come to this city and begun raising these old rocks. When Nafrini asked her questions she and I were working together, planting spring greens in the early beds sheltered against the stone wall of the barn. It took me a while to pull back the recollection of those times. She probably thought I was not going to reply. Finally I cleared my throat and began in a voice rusty with memories, "We were very young women then, scarcely more than girls really, your age perhaps. Looking back it seems so far away it might have happened in another life or perhaps to another person.

"Olya and I had always known each other. We had grown up together, our families being neighbors in the little Kourmairi village of Naklis. And we had always been good friends though we were as different then as we are now. I was the kind, caring, soft-hearted one who hated to hurt anyone's feelings, the one whose heart bled at the sight of injury. I was also the peacemaker who soothed troubles and restored harmony. Olya was as bold and blunt and outspoken then as she is now. She spoke the truth as she saw it regardless of who might be hurt or offended, and she often wore her own set of bruises for it. She was not kind, at least not to others, but she could always be counted on for honesty. She could also be counted on for loyalty—at least to me.

"You might well ask, how could we be friends and be so different? Perhaps we valued in the other the very thing we did not have in ourselves. Mostly it worked quite smoothly for us though sometimes I had to go about and patch up troubles that Olya had made, explaining that she had really meant this and not that, mollifying without outright apologizing for her which would have made her even angrier. All this was made up for by her sense of daring that took me into many little adventures I would never have experienced on my own. And it was her sense of daring that eventually took me out of the village of Naklis and all the way to the city of Eezore, which I could never have imagined before it actually happened. But I am getting well ahead of myself here.

"The way it happened was this—we were about to be married off to two brothers from a neighboring town in a double wedding. Our parents thought this a wonderful idea, especially since those men had paid a very high bride price for us, surprising since our families were quite humble compared to theirs. But, in truth, I think we were very beautiful when we were young or at least that was the talk at the time, not that it mattered much to either of us in that way. We were both in despair at this prospect. We had no wish to be married. We did not like or trust these two brothers and what they planned for us. I had overheard some talk between them of how they might trade us back and forth or even lend us to their friends for a price. We tried to tell our parents; they would not listen.

"Most of all we did not and could not love these two men or any others because we loved each other in that way. All our protests were to no avail, though of course we said nothing about that last part. Our parents were delighted with the prospect of such a good match. And this time they were adamant, especially since we had resisted several other offers. They were probably afraid they would be stuck with us forever. They were particularly pleased that the bride price had been paid in coins instead of cattle and crops.

"I was in tears all the time. Not Olya. For her part she stormed and stamped about. Either way it was hopeless. Our families and neighbors told us it was the way of young girls to be shy, that we would soon get over it and be very glad for our good fortune. I knew I would never be glad and saw before me only years of misery.

"The night before the wedding I could not sleep. My pillow was wet with tears. I tossed about in a sweaty tangle of sheets. Then there was a tap on the window, and Olya slid in over the windowsill as she had done so often before for a night of loving—and never would again.

"I sat up quickly. 'I had hoped you would come to me one last time, but it is so late I had almost given up.'

"'I was making preparations. This wedding is not taking place tomorrow because the brides will not be there. We are leaving tonight. The horses are saddled and ready.'

"I was shocked. 'Not possible. We cannot do such a thing. It would be too…' And then I ran through all the objections I could think of, but under my words there was a little tremor of hope. Olya answered the first few questions as if she had been ready for them. Then she said impatiently, 'Enough talk! Time to go.' She spoke so forcefully that I found myself on my feet, stuffing some clothes into a sack with her help. 'But what about money? How will we live?'

"'I took the bride price for both of us. It will do for a while.'

"'You stole the bride price!?' I was so shocked I almost choked on the words. 'What about our parents? How will they…?'

"'Think of it as their contribution to our future.'

"I opened my mouth to object and then shut it again. There was nothing left to say. The alternative was just too terrible.

"Soon we were sliding out the window together, trying not to giggle or knock against anything. We slipped out of the village, walking our horses. Olya had tied rags to their feet for silence. Once we were far enough away we unbound their hooves and mounted. Then we rode faster than I had ever ridden before, heading toward the Zarn's highroad. There was just enough moon to see by. I concentrated everything I had on keeping Olya in sight and not falling from my horse at that speed.

"Dawn found us in a place I had never been before, a long straight road that stretched before us into the far distance. It was very different from home. Instead of a patchwork of woods and hills and little farm fields with barns and sheds there were huge flat fields planted as far as you could see in a single crop. Everything looked gray and desolate in that early light. The mountains were way off to the side, blue with distance. Looking about me I was full of fear in this unfamiliar place. Some part of me understood that I could never go back, would never see my family or my village again. What I had done that night was irreversible and unforgivable. I would have to find the courage to live with the consequences. At the same time I was thrilled not to be getting married that day and even more thrilled to be traveling with the person I loved most in the world, riding into a new life. When we had slowed enough to be able to talk again I asked timidly, 'Where are we going?'

"'To the Shokarn city of Eezore. I have thought long and hard about it. We cannot go to any Kourmairi village or town. If they found out who we were, the Kourmairi would think nothing of capturing us like escaped horses or pigs and returning us to our families, especially now that we have taken the money. And you may be sure the word will be spread from market to market by those who go from one to the other. Dangerous though they may be, the only safe place for us to hide is among the Shokarn.' The answer was far from reassuring, but I did not think to argue. It was much too late for that.

"And so we got to Eezore with our horses, a small sack of clothes, our stolen money and no idea in the world what we were going to do there."

I groaned suddenly and stood up with much difficulty. My back hurt and all those little green plants were swimming before my eyes. "I am going to lie down for a while. I have shown you what to do and now you can finish here."

"But what about the rest of the story? What happened once you got here?"

This one is not at all shy, I thought to myself. "Come tomorrow to the clothroom. I will show you how to work the spinning wheel and tell you the rest."

As it was, many other things intervened, many little emergencies that demanded my immediate attention. But Nafrini was persistent, so one evening after dinner I took up my tale again.

Donya

To me it felt as if the connection between us deepened every time Suinyari and I came together. I had given up the struggle, surrendered to it, let go of any idea that I was going to break free of her, and so I was hurt and surprised when she met me at the door one evening with what appeared to be anger on her face rather than affection. She grabbed my hand and rushed me down the hall to her bookroom. Once we were inside she shut and locked the door, then leaned her back against it. "We have to talk, Donya. I need to have some questions answered. I want to understand what I have gotten myself into here. What does it mean to be a Hadra? What are these powers I hear spoken of by others with such fear? Are they for doing harm?"

I shook my head. "No, not for doing harm, just the opposite." With a sigh I sank into a chair and sat staring at her in silence, wondering if I would be betraying the Hadra even more by my answers.

Finally Suinyari grew impatient. "Well?" she asked sharply.

I had never spoken to a Draiga about such things but I felt as if I had no choice. I took a deep breath before I started. "Those powers you speak of are what we call our Kersh. It is a gift. It keeps us safe in a dangerous and hostile world. But it is also a mixed blessing for it makes the Hadra feared and hated by those who find differences frightening and like to invent falsehoods. First off we have the power of self-defense. Whatever harm is sent to us goes back to the sender. This is nothing that we can do or will or even prevent, it simply happens. It also means we can do no physical harm to another. If I were to try to stab someone the knife would turn back on me.

"Besides that we have the reading of minds. We can speak mind to mind with each other as well as with animals. That is why we cannot eat animals or harm them. We can feel their pain. Luckily we also have the power to shield so we can keep our thoughts private or shut out another's thoughts from our minds. Otherwise we would be bombarded, especially in a city like this with so many disturbing thoughts. Beyond that we have some physical powers of strength, speed and endurance. Of course these are all things we take for granted in our ordinary lives and within our own cities and settlements. They only become a strangeness when we are out here in this world where others do not have such powers. And there you have it, Suinyari. I have explained as best I can. If you have more questions you need only ask."

As I was speaking I watched many expressions pass across her lovely face, surprise, fear, envy, even admiration. After I finished she stared at me in silence for a long moment. I thought perhaps this was the end of the road for us, that her Shokarn pride would not be able to deal with such unequal power. Finally she nodded and then her face broke into a big grin. "Amazing! Look what I have fished up here. Human and yet not human, maybe something more than human. Well, so long as you stay out of my head and do not try to bend my will I think we can continue to be lovers."

"I can put up a shield between us if that is what you want," I answered tartly. "As for bending your will, Suinyari, I cannot do it, not even if I wished to. My powers prevent it."

"Well then, let us get on with our lives." She reached down to pull me up into her arms.

I ducked away from her kiss and said into her ear, "You must say nothing of this to anyone." I did not return her kiss and shook my head when she tried again. Then, as soon as she opened the door, I found myself walking down the hall and back out into the street with no word of explanation or goodbye.

For a while after that I felt hurt and distant, especially when I thought of Suinyari saying, "And yet not human." What did that mean? Did she see me as some strange sort of creature? Actually I stayed away for several days until she finally sent me a note at The Blue-Eyed Lady begging me to come back. I was very glad she was the one to reach out. I was already missing her but could find no way to make the move myself. Afterward, as if by mutual consent, we never talked about that conversation. Later I came to understand that Suinyari had cleared the air with her questions and now there could be more closeness and honesty between us.

Suinyari

Sometimes, after loving, we just lay beside each other, talking and talking. We had lived such very different lives. I found the Hadra world fascinating and never tired of hearing about it. One of our many differences was that Donya had two mothers whereas I had been raised mostly by my father. One night she showed me a drawing she had made of her mothers, a clever little portrait drawn by her own skilled hand. She said she always carried it with her. I held it tenderly, looking into their faces. "I envy you having two mothers. Mine died when I was quite young and I still miss her."

Donya shook her head. "Not always so easy," she said ruefully. "Especially with my birth mother. We seldom see eye to eye. In turn I envy you your father since I had none."

"But you must surely have had a father. Even with all their powers the Hadra are not able to…"

"No, it takes a male to make a baby. I have already told you about the Gimling, but we do not know our fathers. I wish I knew mine. I think he holds some secret to my life. My skin is light enough that he was likely a Shokarn—was or is. Perhaps he is in this city right now, walking these streets."

"Your mother could probably…"

"No doubt, but she tells me nothing. And I cannot read it from her mind. She keeps a tight shield on the matter. I am not even sure my bondmother knows. Now tell me about your father. It seems you were very fond of him."

I nodded. "My father was not like other men in this city and he certainly was not like other fathers." Feeling again the old grief and loss, I fell silent, wishing Donya and my father could have met, thinking how much they would have liked each other. With my father I could have been honest about what this woman meant in my life.

"Tell me," she repeated. "Different in what way?"

Carefully I set aside the portrait of her two mothers. Then, with a sigh, I drew her down into my arms. "My father…How I wish I could call him back for just a day, just an hour. Even now, after all this time, I could still cry for him. Yes, I will tell you something about my father—also about my wedding and my marriage. If we are to continue being close, you need to understand these things.

"My father was an amazing exception in this city where class, power and privilege count for everything. He had been born into a Wanderer family and so learned early the skills of trading and buying and selling for advantage. But he did not like the roving life. At a young age, probably in his fourteenth year, he decided to stay in this city and try his luck here. He set himself up in a market stall. Because of his Wanderer connections and his natural skill at trading he did very well here. Soon he moved from the market to a little shop and then to a larger one. Not long after that he was approached by someone from the Thieves Guild about smuggling in some goods without the payment of the Zarn's tax. My father was a shrewd man, but also an honest one, with a basic Wanderer code of conduct, so he told the man he had to think about it.

"He said he stayed awake all night pondering the matter. As he explained to me, 'I had to think long and hard about who it would harm and who it would benefit. On the one hand the tax was exorbitant and harmful to trade. It benefited only the Zarn to the great detriment of the people of Eezore. On the other hand I would be allying myself with the Thieves Guild, doing something illegal with potentially deadly consequences for me and the possibility of violence. Also it was something that would require constant watchfulness and deception and I was basically an honest man, not used to lying. Finally I decided I could not pass up the opportunity and so I became a smuggler as well as a merchant. I have never wished it undone, but I have had my moments of doubt and regret.'

"He did very well at his business, both the legal and the illegal side of it. In a few years he had amassed enough money to build Althor House and in a few more years he was ready to marry. There were many among the market women who would have been glad to be his wife, but there was no one there he loved in that way. Then he went to a party given by an Uppercaste Shokarn gentleman who had fallen on hard times and had several marriageable daughters. Though my father was becoming a wealthy merchant, he was surprised to have been invited to such a fancy party—until he discovered the real purpose of the evening. It was to find husbands for girls who otherwise would be stranded at home, fast eating up the host's much diminished resources.

"By the time my father understood how the land lay he had already met the young woman who was to be my mother and had fallen instantly in love with her. For her part, my mother had reciprocated his feelings. After that night they met a few times in secret and consummated their love. She was the youngest daughter and when my father came to ask for her hand the old man tried to convince him to marry his oldest daughter. My father told him it was too late, she was already his. Besides, if he could not have her he would never marry anyone. The old man might have had him killed right on the spot for his audacity. He might have had my mother killed too for that matter. In Eezore he would have been well within his rights to do so. Instead he decided to make the best of a bad bargain and gave his youngest daughter in marriage without a dowry. I think it was quite a scandal at the time."

"And your mother, how did she feel about this?"

"Oh, she had no regrets. She told me she much preferred the easy affluence and casual atmosphere of camaraderie in our home to the pinched pride and poverty of her father's house. And she did not at all mind helping my father in his business. It made her feel useful, gave her a sense of purpose and freedom. She even knew about the other side of my father's business though he kept her away from it.

"We had a good life for a while and I remember being a happy child. Then unexpectedly, in my tenth year, my mother caught winter fever and died almost before we understood how sick she was. My father was struck down with grief, turning in that instant from a laughing man into a somber one. It was understood that my mother had been the one great love of his life and he would never marry again. Though he had the raising of a child on his hands he did not look for a stepmother for me as some men might have done.

"My mother had been teaching me sums and letters at home, not much, but more than most girls in this city are taught. After she died my father sent me to the House of the Mother for my learning. She would not have approved of my being sent out of the house that way, but he said, 'I will not raise an ignorant daughter. I expect you to know as much as I do. After all, you will have the running of this business when I am gone.' I understood nothing of what he meant by 'this business,' but the words 'when I am gone' sent chills of fear through me. After all, I had already lost one parent.

"That is how I first came to know the women at the House of the Mother, and it has been a useful connection ever since. At the time I was certainly no great gift to them—an angry, rebellious, grieving child who had no use for discipline. The Mothers and Sisters may have been strict and stern, but they were also kindly, especially Mother Melna. She gave me love in spite of my careless thoughtless ways and my wild escapades that certainly must have tested her patience to the utmost. At home my father turned to Bethron and Gammo for help and for a while they became my mothers."

"How is it that the servants in this house are treated more like friends, whereas, from what I hear, in other houses they are more like slaves?"

"True, in other houses in the city there is a deep divide between the masters and their slaves or servants, almost as though those who did the work of the house were not human and had no human feelings. But my father was different in that way as well. He had been raised as a Wanderer where all were respected and had value. Though he ended up living in the style of an uppercaste Shokarn, he never forgot his origins, never turned his back on them, no matter how wealthy he got. In my father's house the servants were part of the business and were treated like equals. Though he still had the final say, it was not till he had heard everyone's opinion that he made his decisions. And they got a part of the profits as well as their pay—still do. They loved him and had a fierce loyalty to him that they have passed on to me, especially Torvil. My father had bought him out of prison, probably saving the man's life or at least saving him from the mines."

"And your marriage? How did you come to be married to this Gordivan when you have no such interest in men?"

"That was my father's doing. Before he died he had arranged this match for me. My father knew about my ways and thought this would be a good cover for me, for both of us in fact since my cousin is as fond of men as I am of women. 'If you are to survive in this city you will have to marry. It is the only way you will have any protection. Otherwise, when I am gone, you will be besieged by suitors, men who will think they can manage the business much better than you can. They will want to get their hands on that money as well as on you. And in this city everything a wife has belongs to her husband the moment they are married. With Gordivan you will be safe. I have made a legal arrangement with him that pleases him very much. I have settled a sum on him that will come to him each month. All at once might have been too much of a temptation and he might have quickly squandered it. The house and the rest of what I have is yours, as well as whatever you can make out of this business. I know you have a good head for it.

But Gordivan cannot have a totally free ride. You must teach him the business. You will need him.'

"I was shocked to hear his words. 'But why are you talking this way, Father? You are young still. You will be here a long time, running things as you always have. Besides, Gordivan is a lazy wastrel. I love him well enough; he has always been like a brother, but I know his ways. If you think it so important I am willing to be his wife, but in name only—and certainly not his business partner.'

"He looked very stern and spoke in a tone he had never used with me before. 'Suinyari, I have let you have your head in most everything, but in this you will do as I say. It is important; you will need him.'"

"I did as he told me, teaching Gordivan the business in the coming weeks. My father had wanted me to be the teacher so Gordivan would look to me for guidance. To my surprise he learned quickly and was quite good at it. I think secrecy and subterfuge were natural to him. Then, in less than six months my father was dead, and Gordivan did indeed become my business partner, better at it than I could ever have imagined. It entertained him, seemed to give him a sense of purpose though clearly I was the one in charge, just as my father had been, just as he had planned for me to be.

"When my father died I was disconsolate. I wanted to die too. I even thought I would. He had been the constant in my life and I was sure he would go on forever. I could not imagine the world without him."

"And what of Gordivan?"

"Ah yes, Gordivan. I will say this for him, though he was my husband in name only, at that time he acted like the best of husbands, staying home, taking charge of things, giving whatever comfort and support he could, letting me cry in his arms for as long as I needed to. It made a deep bond between us. But I am getting ahead of myself here. Back to the wedding.

"That wedding was everything one could have imagined or wished for and more—an abundance of food all beautifully displayed, masses of bright flowers, every sort of drink flowing freely, the chandeliers aflame with candles, music for every mood and several hundred elegantly dressed guests. For my father it was not just a family social occasion. It was also a chance to advance his business and make connections and he lost no chance of doing that. I, the lovely bride—dressed in a long embroidered peach-colored gown that clashed daringly with my red hair which was piled high on my head—went about smiling and flirting and making myself visible while in reality I felt as fake and invisible as it is possible to be. Not that it made me unhappy. I got a sort of perverse pleasure from the fine show we were putting on, my father and myself and Gordivan and our whole household, as if it were all a grand theater piece and I was the daring actress at the center of the stage, having to be very careful not to fall into the pit.

"When the dancing began I spent the first while in Gordivan's arms, whirling round and round with my handsome, charming husband while being watched with envious eyes by a crowd that no doubt thought us a loving and devoted couple, the luckiest people on earth. We laughed and chatted, heads bent together fondly. Altogether we gave a very good performance. After a while my father claimed a dance with me. 'So how is it going with you, my girl?'

"'As well as can be expected when it is such a fraud. I am having a grand time and everything is very beautiful, but under all the gaiety some part of me is a little sad that it cannot be real, that I can never marry someone I really love in that way.' I did not want to hurt my father's feelings since he had gone to much trouble with this, but we had always been totally honest with one another.

"He gave my hand a little squeeze. 'How well I understand. But it is the way of it in this part of the world. I would change it if I could, but not at the risk of your life.'

"Right in the middle of the floor I stopped him with a big hug. 'Thank you for everything,' I whispered in his ear. 'I know this was the best thing you could have done for me and I am very grateful.'

"After that I danced with other men and then even some women. Though we are not allowed to love each other, still we are allowed to dance together at such occasions. Then I danced with Gordivan again, though by now he had so much drink on his breath that he did not seem quite so charming anymore.

"It seemed the party was going to go on forever. People were having too much fun to think of leaving. But Gordivan and I had other plans. Finally he gave me a long, very public kiss, then took my hand and led me up the stairs. At that there was much loud clanking of mugs and a roar of toasts, good wishes and waving hands, some of it quite bawdy and suggestive, all of it very far from the mark. I am sure there were many fantasies that night about what was happening upstairs in our bed. Actually nothing happened, not between us at least. Very soon Gordivan slipped down the back stairs and out, heading for his favorite tavern. I hoped he would be discreet and not call too much attention to himself.

"So there I was, abandoned on my wedding night. Did I cry myself to sleep, wetting my pillow with tears and hugging it to me for comfort? Not hardly! In fact I got very little sleep that night." Suddenly I stopped talking, finding myself in an agony of embarrassment, blushing furiously at the thought that I had been sharing all this with my lover and now she could probably get the rest of the story right from my head.

"And then what happened?" Donya urged, her eyes sparkling with interest. I shook my head, promising to finish on another night. Hoping she would forget later, I jumped up quickly, saying, "I need to go check the doors. I think Bethron went to bed before us and may have forgotten." As if Bethron would ever forget such a thing!

Donya

All that talk the night before about Suinyari's father had rekindled my longing and curiosity about my own. The next morning I left Suinyari sleeping and went out early. Walking through the streets of Eezore I found myself searching every Shokarn face I saw—at least every male face—for something familiar, some sign, some hint of connection. *He* could be in the next shop or around the next corner. *He* could be the next man I passed on the street. Clearly this was craziness. There were thousands of men in this city and three other Shokarn cities just as large or larger and many other Shokarn who did not even live in the cities. He could even have become a Wanderer. He could even be dead. My chances of finding him were almost nonexistent. It was like finding one particular pebble in the length of a riverbed. Yet sense had no meaning to me at that moment. I even convinced myself that if I encountered him, I would know. My Hadra powers would tell me. Foolishness of course, but at that moment I was obsessed. I had searched before, in fact I had searched ever since I had first come to Eezore, but never so intently or with such a sense of purpose as that morning.

Most Hadra do not think one way or the other about the identity of their fathers. They certainly do not go in search of them. Hadra grow up knowing that the man who fathered them was an anonymous Kourmairi their mother coupled with at the Gimling during the spring or fall Essu. We do not even really have a concept of fatherhood except as we see it among the Kourmairi, certainly nothing that we envy or long for. A birth mother and a bondmother and endless aunts by blood or friendship with our mothers—aunts to give advice or scold or keep watch over us or act as our mothers' eyes—are quite enough love and guidance for our young lives. But then most Hadra have the dark skin of their mothers. They do not look like some pale washed-out copy, nor do they find themselves plagued by strange insistent questions every time they glimpse their reflection in a darkened glass or the still water of a pool.

Though I was not teased for my difference, still I could see those same questions in the eyes of others. No doubt some of the older Hadra knew the answer. When I asked they just said, "Ask your mother." All I could catch from their shielded minds was some sort of dark violence. Henori, of course, would tell me nothing. I only knew there was much pain there, an old history of pain that, in some way I could not understand, kept us apart. Shielding hard, Henori would say, "That is all in the past. Let it be. No need to think about it, Donya." No need! Easy enough for her to say when the demon of curiosity had me by the throat. Besides, it was not in the past. It stood between us in the present, a hard invisible barrier like thick glass.

The dreaded Shokarn! I was so fascinated by them and at the same time repelled. I watched what they did and how they did it, sometimes even mimicking their movement or gestures, trying to understand, trying to see if there was anything of myself in them. In truth they were not a very pleasant lot, at least not the Uppercaste, the Highborn as they called themselves. They, of course, lorded it over everyone else and seldom walked in the streets. Instead they rode their fine horses or went about in fancy carriages and expected all others, even little children and bent old women, to clear the way for them. I have seen people hit with whips for not moving quickly enough, and once a little girl run over and killed by a speeding carriage whose occupants did not slow down or even look back.

The merchant caste was not much better, almost as merciless to those below them, though of course they had to bow and scrape before the Highborn. In spite of all that, I looked hungrily at Shokarn faces whenever I could do so without being obvious. Naturally lower castes are forbidden to stare at their superiors. And even as they repelled me, I thought, *Your blood runs in my veins. In some way I do not yet understand, I am related you.*

That day I took with me the little pad of paper on which I kept a record of everything. Sitting on a park bench or standing on a street corner, I drew what I saw around me, trying through marks on paper to understand this strange city and its people. At some moment I was seated under a tree, totally absorbed in a careful rendering of the arched, scrollwork gate in an old stone wall, when a Highborn suddenly jumped from his horse right in front of me. With barely restrained fury he began berating a Shokarn commoner. The scolded man bowed and bobbed in a totally servile manner. He kept apologizing for whatever sins he had committed—all to no avail. The Highborn even went so far as to grab the man by the shirt and shake him. Then he began to hit him. To all this the other man made no resistance, not even putting up his hands to ward off the blows. A little warning voice in my head said, *Danger! Danger! Leave quickly! Go now!* But there was something in the cast of the Highborn's face and in his gestures that seemed slightly familiar and so held me rooted to the spot.

I do not now remember anything that was said—not a single word—but the sight of that incident is still blazoned on my memory. Quite a crowd had gathered though they kept their distance. No one made a move to interfere or come to the man's defense. I was so horrified by what was happening right in front of me that I stared at the Highborn, open-mouthed, completely forgetting that the lower castes are forbidden to stare at their betters that way. Suddenly he became aware of my gaze. Letting go of his victim, he turned on me. "What are you staring at, you fool? Are you feebleminded? It is not allowed for such as you to stare at the Uppercaste." Then his glance fell on my drawing. "Were you drawing me? Doubly forbidden! Give me that pad this instant!"

I leapt to my feet and whirled to run. There was no way I would let him have my precious pad. Not only did it have my drawings in it, which I valued personally, but every word written there was danger to me in another's hands. And if he tried to grab me I was afraid my Hadra powers, my Kersh, would be instantly revealed.

"Guards!" he shouted. "Guards, stop that man! Bring him here!"

Clutching my pad tight against me and using all my Hadra powers for speed, I fled down the street, dodging grasping hands. The streets were instantly full of shouts and cries. I was afraid I would meet the guards head-on as I ran. Actually no one seemed to put great effort into capturing me. I doubt that particular Highborn was very popular with the people on the street. Gradually the sounds faded behind me. I ran on until I had no more breath. Suddenly I was gasping, doubled over with pain, unable to move.

As soon as I could breathe again, I backed into an alley and watched the street. I was much relieved to see no signs of pursuit. When I finally looked at my pad I saw that my drawing was all smeared from being pressed so hard against my sweaty shirt. Well, the repairs would have to be done from memory. No way was I going back there again!

That night I did not go to Suinyari's. I went instead to my room over the stable. I wanted to be alone to brood and ponder. I nailed up all my sketches on the crude wood walls. Then I stared at them for a long time. What if that man really had been my father? Would I have wanted to claim him? Not hardly! After that day I still looked for my father as I went about the city, but never again with the same intensity or hopefulness.

Suinyari

In spite of Donya's love there was still a large empty place in my life, a longing, a hunger which if I was really honest with myself I had to admit, much to my surprise, was the longing for a child. Of course that was not to be. I would never have a child for Eezore, never give birth to a daughter who must be trained in submission. Nor could I imagine carrying in my belly a son who might grow up to lord it over his mother as if it were his natural right. Never! And yet the hunger and the discontent persisted.

As I went about the city on my various errands that were in truth business deals, accompanied by Bethron and Alliya, I often saw abandoned children in the streets and markets, surviving as best they could, stealing or begging or hiding in doorways. The guards drove them away from the Uppercaste sections of town, but they were everywhere else, thick as vermin. I have to confess that for a long time I thought of them that way, as if they were simply an unpleasant part of the scene, of no more account than stray cats or dogs but more of a nuisance and far more dangerous. I never gave money to beggars and

I made sure that thieves got not one cent from my pockets.

I thought my heart was well hardened against every sight in the city streets. I even carried a knife visible in my belt and liked the feel of it against my thigh. It pleased me to think that no one dared to mess with Suinyari and that included those bands of ragged children that floated homeless through the city. So when did I start to notice her in her bundle of rags? When did I start to see her as separate from the others, a child, a person, an entity who reached through to me even when I thought nothing on those streets could touch me? A child whose eyes met mine and somehow shifted my world?

I rode or walked quite freely around Eezore in a way that was probably considered somewhat scandalous, but I always said I was on my husband's business and that I went about that way at his bidding. People may have disapproved, even disbelieved, but on those rare occasions when Gordivan was home we gave grand lavish parties, inviting everyone of importance. People—even those who disapproved of us—hated to be left out. Because of that they made themselves pleasant to us the rest of the time. On those evenings we always made a great display of our boundless affection for each other. Ah, but I am losing the trail of my story here.

Back to the child. She quickly became an obsession for me. I only caught occasional glimpses of her. Dirty and ragged, there was nothing very attractive about her. It was her eyes that caught me, some combination of spirit and sorrow, defiance and vulnerability. Perhaps I recognized something of myself in her. I know she felt something for me too, curiosity or kinship or the beginnings of trust for I began to see her more often. I even thought she might have taken to following me. But the moment I turned my attention on her or tried to beckon her over she would scuttle away, vanishing instantly, almost miraculously. I knew she was called Spider, a name that suited her all too well.

When I questioned the market women they told me that she had been abandoned by her mother in her fifth year and was an expert little thief. Wilder than a feral dog, no one could lay hands on her. Now I was more intrigued than ever. I took Bethron and Alliya into my confidence. Alliya, who has a warm heart, said instantly, "Why not bring her to Althor House? We could tame her and take care of her and make a home for her here." Her own little boy had died of winter fever and left a hollow, empty place in her life.

Bethron was much more wary and probably more realistic. "Why would we want to do any such thing? Likely she is infected with bugs and diseases. She would probably turn the house upside down, steal everything you have and run off with it. That child has a terrible reputation. She is one of the worst of the wild children."

"But hardly the worst. I have never heard of her torturing dogs or knocking down old women in the street or stabbing someone and leaving them for dead—all things that are done by some of the wild ones. Stealing to stay alive—that does not seem to me like such a terrible crime. The child is quick and clever. She does her stealing well and so she has survived and never been caught. I say good for her."

"Do what you please," Bethron answered grudgingly. "I know you will no matter what we say. Why not? After all, you are mistress here. But you asked me what I think and I will tell you. What I say is that you would only be bringing trouble home, more trouble perhaps than even you can manage. Why not bring home an Oolanth cub? It would probably be just as cuddly and charming."

Only once in my life had ever I seen an Oolanth Cat, those huge tawny creatures that live in ledges in high wild places and are the most powerful and feared creature known to man. I was with a group of riders going to Maktesh. Unwisely I had gotten off my horse to look at some flowers and so fallen behind. I was standing next to a rock outcrop when this huge animal dropped from above onto the road right in front of me. My horse gave a scream of terror. It jerked the reins from my hands and fled. I was sure I was as good as dead, facing an animal that could rip into a horse's flank or tear off my face with one swipe of its giant claws. And yet I was not afraid. Perhaps I was too stunned with surprise. I knew enough not to run, that such action would only set off its hunting lust. And so, while I tried to steady my breath, we just stood regarding each other for a very long moment, cat and woman face-to-face in the road. Then it gave a low growl of acknowledgment. With another bound it crossed the road, streaked through the field and disappeared, leaving me sobbing with awe and fright. I never forgot those lovely deadly golden eyes that had regarded me so calmly, measuring the worth of my life.

I knew Bethron was right about the dangers of bringing home this child, but my heart leaned elsewhere. Shaking my head, I said, "Not an Oolanth cub surely, but at least a street cat. I can hardly bring her home; she lets no one near her. But if I succeeded in catching her would you help me with her?"

Alliya said joyously, "You know I would," while Bethron answered more thoughtfully, "If that is really your heart's wish, Suinyari, how could I deny you? Your father entrusted your happiness to me. I have been a sort of mother to you ever since your own mother died. If this is what you must do then I even have some thoughts on how to capture the child."

"Besides," I said with a sudden grin, "she might be useful to us. A child who is so quick and clever and can disappear that fast from sight might be good for carrying messages."

At that Bethron laughed. "Well then, let us set a trap and capture our wild little messenger."

I had not yet told Donya of my plans. Sooner or later she could have them easily enough from my head, though at the moment she was often away and seemed too occupied with her own affairs to pay much attention to mine. And I was dreading telling Gordivan when he came back. Basically my beloved husband-cousin was a very self-indulgent man who did not like his comforts disturbed in any way. But I was determined and would not allow anyone to change my mind. After all, it was my house and my life.

Donya

I was very curious to meet the man who was my lover's husband, also a little apprehensive. Suinyari kept assuring me there was no need for that. "You already know Gordivan is not my husband in any ordinary sense of the word. We grew up together, like brother and sister, but better, closer perhaps because there was none of the jealousy that sometimes plagues children in the same family. Our mothers had been first cousins and best friends. When my mother died, Gordivan's mother, Naidiri, made sure we remained close. She thought it was good for him to play with a girl, that it might tame his wild nature. Little did she realize that in all our pranks and adventures I was more often the leader than the follower. I was a year older and he looked up to me. I am still the leader and he still looks up to me, takes my guidance in all things. And you know from my stories that he has as little use for women in his bed as I do for men in mine, so you see there is really nothing to worry about."

Still a little anxious, I listened to her words and reserved judgment.

The first few times I was at Suinyari's house Gordivan was still away, but one night he was the one who answered the door. He gave me a charming smile, saying, "Please come in. You must be the Donyal that Suinyari has told me so much about. I am her husband, Gordivan. So glad to finally meet you." Of course, even without those words, I would have known instantly that this was Gordivan. As he spoke he looked me up and down. I suppose I did the same with him. After all, he shared this house with the woman I loved.

With his dark hair, dark eyes, pale skin and even features the man was as handsome as Suinyari was beautiful. I had a momentary flash of jealousy, thinking what a fine-looking couple they must make and how people probably spoke of them that way. He was elegantly attired in dark blue velvet with silver trim. His long hair was pulled back and fastened with a leather thong. He had a small, trim mustache and a neatly clipped beard. Altogether a very impressive appearance and his words to me were impeccably polite, but under them I heard his confusion. He thought I might be a young man of his kind and a very attractive one at that, but he could sense none of that energy coming from me toward him. Besides, if that was what I was, then what did Suinyari want with me?

I made a slight bow and said in my deepest voice, "And I am also very glad to meet you, Gordivan. Suinyari has told me much about you as well." Good that he did not have the Hadra skill of reading minds. My words sounded false even to my own ears, not lies really, but certainly not the whole truth either. After that stiff exchange there was nothing much to say. We stared awkwardly at each other for a long moment until Suinyari rescued us both. She dashed into the hall and put an arm around each of us. "My two favorite people, my husband and my good friend, meeting at last." After that we went in to eat.

Poor Gordivan, he did not know how to treat me. Was I a potential rival? Or a potential lover? Or something he did not understand at all? One moment he was painfully flirtatious and the next competitive, almost combative, challenging everything I said. That night he sat next to Suinyari and opposite me. He engaged in lively conversation with Suinyari about things of which I had no knowledge as if to purposely exclude me. He also ate huge quantities of food as if he had not had a good meal since he left. And he kept glancing at me with a curiosity that bordered on rudeness or perhaps outright hostility. Several times he asked us questions about my relationship to Suinyari. Finally he said to her, "I still cannot understand how I can have a cousin, a whole family in fact, that I knew nothing about."

With some impatience Suinyari answered, "But I have already explained to you, Gordivan, he is *my* cousin, not *yours*. You and I are related through our mothers. He is related to me through my father's people. Why should you know of him?"

"But your father's people were Wanderers."

"Not all of them," she answered sharply. "Now leave it be and stop pestering us with questions. You are making Donyal uncomfortable." I did not say aloud what I was thinking, that making me uncomfortable was the very purpose of his questions.

He gave me a speculative look. "Did they teach you swordplay in that far-off place? A handsome young man like you needs to know how to protect himself in this turbulent city." There was a challenge in his words.

"I know much about crops and cattle and almost nothing of swordplay. It was not needed where I lived."

"Then perhaps I could teach you, Cousin." He said that last word with spite. Under his seeming helpfulness I could sense the desire to test me, to find out who and what I really was.

"Thank you for you kind offer, but it would just be a waste of your time and skill. I am very clumsy at things that require agility and would likely only injure myself." It would not do of course to have him come up against me and discover my powers of self-defense.

"I think that is not the real reason, but if you are afraid to try…"

"Enough, Gordivan!" Suinyari said sharply. "Now you are being rude to our guest."

He grinned and shrugged, looking like a bad boy who does not much care that he has been caught at his mischief. After that he ignored me and turned all his attention to Suinyari, but I could feel his mind turning the puzzle over and over, trying to find answers, clearly not satisfied with Suinyari's explanation. He was a threat to my secret. I saw I would have to watch myself around him.

After we ate Gordivan was only too glad to escape as soon as politeness allowed, going back to his "city lairs," as Suinyari called them. It was clear he would never be comfortable with me until he knew the truth. Suinyari was all for telling him, but I held back, shaking my head. "Words, once spoken cannot be retracted. I need to know him better before I can trust him with my life."

"But I know him and trust him. Is that not enough?" She looked slightly hurt.

I shook my head again. "I am sorry, Suinyari. I need to observe him a little longer before I can find my own place of trust." Personally I could see nothing about Gordivan that inspired trust. Hoping to distract her from that subject, I said, "Now that he has gone out and is likely to be away a while, it is time to tell me the rest of the story of your wedding night."

She blushed hotly. Even her ears turned pink. "Not possible," she said shaking her head vigorously. "It is much too embarrassing. I should never have told you any of it. I should never even have started."

"Yes, but you did and now you must finish. You have promised. And not here where we could be interrupted. Up in your bedroom where I can put my hands on you while you talk." I could feel heat rising in my body and I was probably blushing too. With no more words I reached over, took her hand and drew her to her feet. She stumbled slightly, but she came with me willingly enough.

Suinyari

At Donya's insistence I took off my clothes and lay down on the bed. She began running her hands over my body in a way that sent little shivers of pleasure up and down. "Now the story, Suinyari. You cannot delay any longer. The story of your wedding night in all its glorious details."

"Are you sure, Donya? Are you sure it will not hurt your feelings or make you jealous?"

"A little jealousy can be a good thing," she said, winking at me. Then she slipped her hand between my legs and began to move it with slow arousing motions that made me shiver with pleasure.

And so, floating between the sensuousness of the present and the past, I began the part of the story I had never told anyone else. "Soon after Gordivan left I heard a little tap on my door. I had been expecting it. When I opened the door, there was Yania, grinning expectantly. I quickly drew her into the room, shut the door behind her and bolted it.

"'Are you sure, Suinyari? On your wedding night?'

"'Why not? What better time? Gordivan is already off to his pleasures. No one will disturb us.'

"'We are alone? It is safe?'

"'Quite safe. Stop worrying. If there is noise from my room people will be expecting it. What better way to celebrate my wedding, a lovely present for the bride. Besides we so seldom have the opportunity. Why waste it?'

"'Why indeed?' She took my face in both of her large hands and gave me a big wet kiss the effects of which reached right down between my legs with a sharp tug of pleasure. Ordinarily Yania was a dignified, respectably married market woman ten years my senior, but she still enjoyed an occasional romp on the other side of the sheets. We had been at this game since I was fifteen. There was no question of love between us, just lust and a sort of rough mutual respect. If her husband knew he politely looked the other way, probably thinking it had nothing to do with him. And that was true. She loved that solid kindly man, but she also had a taste for what he could not supply. Still she had to have some cover or excuse. She and Orun had supplied the fruit for the wedding table. Then he had gone on his way while Yania had stayed to help with the cooking and serving.

"When she stepped back from the kiss her eyes were sparkling with mischief and desire. 'I told Orun I might have to stay the night as the party would probably go very late and it would not be safe for a woman alone on the streets at that hour. And he said, 'Well, I know you will be safe enough at Althor House.' She was laughing as she said it.

"'You will indeed,' I said, grabbing her arm and tugging her toward the bed.

"'But will you be safe, that is the question?' She said as she scooped me up in her broad strong arms and dumped me laughing on the bed. We scrambled to get out of our clothes, tugging at our own and helping each other. Luckily I was already in my nightdress or my lovely wedding gown might have gotten ripped in our careless hurry. It had been much too long since my last encounter of this kind. I was burning with desire. It ached in my throat and down between my legs. There were too few opportunities in this city where this kind of love could mean your death.

"Before she was fully undressed I made a grab for her large full breast, pinched her nipple and twisted hard enough to make her moan.

'Ah yes, trust me to keep you safe,' I murmured as I covered her other breast with my mouth and sucked hard while thrusting my hand down between her legs. For just a moment I could feel her melting in surrender under me. Then she heaved me over and sank on top of me, her large softness enveloping my body. 'Not so fast, girl.'

"She pinned my arms to the bed and began kissing me all over my face and down my neck. Usually we struggled a little with who would be on top first, amusing ourselves by pitting my young strength against her weight, but at that moment I surrendered with a groan of pleasure, only too glad to let her have her way with me. When I crested I let out my cries with abandon, knowing that if they were heard they would be accepted as proper and fitting for a wedding night.

"After that I lay very still for a while, stunned with pleasure, hardly breathing while the echoes of my cries reverberated in my head. Then energy flowed back into my limbs and with it a different kind of hunger. I slithered out from under Yania's weight and turned her over. She struggled with me. We mock-tussled until we were half out of the bed. Then, with all my strength, I pinned one of her arms and whispered fiercely in her ear, 'Stop moving. Lie still and let me love you.' She quieted and I slid to the floor. Her legs were hanging over the edge. I spread them, knelt between them and put my arms around her thighs. Then I put my mouth on her and sucked and licked as if I were starving while she moaned and wriggled under me and rose to meet my mouth. I was lost in a trance of desire when her long shuddering cry went through me right from the top of my head down to my very toes. Afterward I stayed where I was with my face against her thigh until she pulled me up on top of her. Then we lay there, breathing in time with each other. After a while of stillness we began again, but more slowly this time and with more thought. Finally, thoroughly satiated, we fell asleep together, a luxury we were usually denied.

"That next morning, after a little more loving, lazy and casual this time instead of frenzied, Yania gave me a parting kiss. Then she slipped away down the back stairs while I sank back on my bed, replete with pleasure, my hand between my legs, enjoying the last echoing tremors of our time together.

"When I finally went down there were many still asleep in the great room, on the tables and on the floor, as well as on chairs pushed together—tradefolk mixed together with higher classes as was the way in my father's home. Our usually orderly house was in appalling chaos—spilled drinks, dropped food ground into the floor, dirty crockery and scattered clothing. I quickly set about helping Bethron and Alliya, who were hard at work, trying to clear away the mess. Alliya wanted to shoo me away. 'It is your wedding morning, Suinyari. You should still be sleeping.'

"I laughed and said with a careless shrug, 'Well, the groom is not there in my bed to keep me company so I would rather be with both of you than spending this morning alone.'

"As our guests woke, yawning, rubbing their eyes and their probably aching heads, they gave me knowing, salacious looks and seemed surprised to see me. They had no doubt heard our cries of pleasure. I gave them little smiles and ducked my head shyly. Perhaps I even managed to blush a little, the timid new bride found out in her passion and embarrassed by it. Well, let them think what they wanted; it had been a wonderful wedding night. The only thing better would have been if I could have married a woman.

"Not long afterward my father appeared, shaking his head in disgust and looking about ruefully at the temporary ruin of his house. 'You are certainly up early.' He was regarding me with surprise.

"'And so are you.' I answered, grinning at him. 'You look distressed. Have no fear, this will all be set to rights soon enough, just as if it had never happened. I had hoped you would sleep a little longer so it would have been done already.'

"'Never mind. It does not matter. Tell me, did I not find you a good husband?'

"'The best,' I said loudly enough for anyone to hear. Then I whispered in his ear, 'I only hope he did not get so drunk as to be indiscreet or lose too much money at the tables. And I trust that whoever he shared a bed with last night will keep his silence.'

"Later I went up and found Gordivan asleep in his own bed, looking like an innocent child. Gazing down at him, I remembered that I really did love him. Yet, all in all, though I may have loved Gordivan, I certainly had no illusions about him. Handsome and charming, he was also reckless and careless, not much able to keep his mind on anything. His mother had spoiled him and doted on him, never correcting his faults. Though his father's death had left the family in poor circumstances, still Gordivan somehow expected the best of life to be his due without much effort on his part. I, on the other hand, having been raised mostly by my father, expected to work hard for everything I got, to pay attention and keep a sharp eye about me. I thought my new husband might sometimes be a handful and a trial.

"The next time I saw Yania at the market she looked me up and down with a questioning, critical eye and asked, 'Well, girl, now that you are married are you going to start popping out one baby after the other like most of the other married women that I know?'

"'No, of course not.' I told her indignantly. 'Why would I do that? I am a muirlla, a lover of women. I have no intention of making a child with a man. Besides this is a sham marriage, a pretense. You better than anyone should know that.'

"'And Gordivan, what of him? Now that he is a married man, will he not want to be a father?'

"'Gordivan? What would he want with a baby? How would he care for a baby when he can hardly care for himself? I would certainly not stay home and take care of it for him. And anyhow, we are never together in that way and never will be. Also he is seldom home for long. What makes you ask such a thing?'

"She shrugged. 'Ah well, time changes all things. The heart takes many turns. You may someday find yourself longing for a child.'

"'Not me! Never!' I exclaimed. I walked off, shocked and annoyed that Yania would even think such a thing. I had been very sure in my answers. Even so she had forced me to consider questions I had never thought to ask myself before."

I did not say aloud to Donya how much those very questions were haunting me at that moment. If she heard it in my head she made no comment. She was much too busy re-enacting the story of my wedding night on my body. With a groan of pleasure I sank down to join her, glad to be done with words for that moment.

Donya

When Suinyari told me that she and Gordivan were going to give one of their lavish, twice-yearly parties to which half the city was invited, I thought to make myself absent by going to The Blue-Eyed Lady for the evening. I imagined regaling Granthia with tales of my little adventures and misadventures in the House of Althor, but Suinyari would not hear of it. "If you are going to be at my house so often you must meet the people I know and we must tell them all our story that explains your presence here. I want to show you off a little. Besides, what better place to get the information you seek?"

The idea of being shown off made my skin crawl. I was about to protest until she said that last part and then I acquiesced. I knew she was right. Better to meet these people and tell them an agreed-upon story than to let them wonder and speculate and make up their own, maybe hitting on the truth by accident.

"But what will I wear? I have nothing that would be suitable for such an occasion."

"I will ask Gordivan to loan you something." Before I could object she had gone off to find him. And that is how I found myself on the night of the party in Gordivan's room, being dressed for this event that I dreaded. He offered me a green velvet suit that had gold embroidery down the front and with it a white silk shirt, ruffled at the sleeve and collar. I said it was much too fine; he insisted. I was about to take it all into Suinyari's room and dress in front of her mirror when Gordivan said, "Come, lad, you need not be so shy with me. After all we are made the same. I want the pleasure of seeing you in those clothes before the others do."

I hesitated. Then I thought, *What is to lose? There will never be peace between us until he understands that part of the puzzle.* By now I knew him well enough to feel a little trust so I dropped the clothes on the bed and said, "So be it then," as I stripped off my tunic leaving my broad breastband in view. Watching the puzzled look on his face, I unwrapped the breastband, letting it fall to the floor and revealing my bare breasts. Gordivan blushed deep crimson and began to stammer, "Oh, I see…Yes of course…So very sorry…I did not mean to…Please forgive me…I only thought…"

"Come, Gordivan, surely you have seen a woman's bare breasts before. It is not so shocking as all that. Now that you know I must trust you to keep your silence on our dangerous secret." As I picked up the breastband and rebound my breasts, I said, "Will you please help me with these unfamiliar clothes so I do not do something wrong and make a total fool of myself down there?"

He nodded and seemed to collect his wits. After that he became my able dresser. He even seemed to enjoy the fraud. He pulled my hair back and tied it at the nape of my neck, gave me cloth boots after I objected to the leather ones, powdered my face, turned me this way and that, and finally declared me "a very handsome young man and fit for any company." Then we laughed together like two conspirators, and he reached for my arm. "We should go down together and make a grand entrance," he said with a wink and a grin. I shook my head, saying I needed a moment to gather my thoughts. After he left I stood staring in the mirror, wondering who that was staring back at me in that fine green suit. I saw almost nothing of my true self in that reflection.

Feeling strange, awkward and oddly distant from myself in my elegant borrowed clothes, I hovered at the entrance to the great room, watching the swirl of activity. Most of the rooms in Suinyari's house were very large compared to Hadra rooms in Ishlair. This one was big enough to have contained a whole Hadra house with space left over. I hardly ever set foot in it, as it seemed to me cold and cavernous. It was seldom used. The furniture was usually draped with dust covers and the heavy red drapes were kept closed, giving the room a strange sort of dismal crimson gloom.

Now it had suddenly and miraculously been transformed into an island of light and gaiety. The curtains had been thrown open onto the terrace and the dust covers removed to reveal brightly embroidered upholstery. The patterned marble floor had been polished to a high gloss and the room thronged with hired servants as well as guests. The huge chandeliers were lit, throwing brilliant sparkles of light into every corner. There were masses of flowers everywhere and long tables of food against one wall. The center of the floor was left open for dancing and musicians were already warming up. I remembered Suinyari's description of her wedding and thought I would soon have the dubious pleasure of seeing her dancing in Gordivan's arms. I might have slipped away again if Bethron had not spotted me at that moment and asked me to help her bring in more chairs from the hall. She was not very impressed by my fancy clothes.

People were beginning to flow in, more and more of them. I saw Suinyari and Gordivan moving about the room, talking, laughing, greeting people and making introductions. They seemed easy and charming and openly affectionate with each other, two beautiful people with not a care in the world but the comfort of their guests and their obvious love for each other. Seeing them together that way I felt a twist of jealousy, that most un-Hadra-like and uncomfortable of emotions.

Then Suinyari saw me and beckoned me over. While Gordivan wandered off on his own, she introduced me as the son of a distant cousin of her father's from the countryside north of Nhor as this was the story we had both agreed on. I nodded and chatted and smiled, trying all the while to remember the details of my invented life and making sure I did not let one word of truth slip through. And meanwhile a silent and very different conversation—the thoughts from those around me—was whirling through my head. This conversation was not nearly so pleasant and charming. In fact it was often full of spite, envy and anxiety.

After a while Suinyari left me on my own. I drifted about the room, shamelessly listening to both levels of conversation, the spoken and the silent. I was somewhat shocked at what I was hearing from people's thoughts. There were many in that room who loved Suinyari, but also some who did not, some in fact who wished her ill and were actively plotting it, though their spoken words betrayed nothing of their thoughts. I knew I needed to warn Suinyari and tried hard to remember which face went with which ugly thoughts.

Finally I saw Suinyari on the other side of the room, talking intently to some man who kept glancing at me. She noticed, beckoned me over and introduced me to Lord Arnzil, a thin, ferret-faced older man who was surveying the room with bright clever eyes and a cynical expression. "So this is the Donyal that I have heard so much about," he said as he turned his sharp glance on me. Though he continued talking to Suinyari for a few minutes he kept looking at me as if I was an interesting specimen that might be useful to him in the future.

I was instantly uncomfortable with this man and was trying to think of how to leave his presence as quickly as possible without open rudeness when I suddenly began hearing his appalling thoughts as loud as spoken words. *Old Althor should never have left everything to this chit. I helped him make the business—my connections, my cleverness. If he had left his worth to me I could easily have paid off my debts without having to come here and borrow money. How I hate to ask her for anything. She thinks herself so clever. No woman should be so full of pride. This young Donyal is very handsome. I wonder if she fancies him? Perhaps I can use him against her in some way to bring her down. Maybe there is something here to interest the Grayrobes. How I hate those slimy creatures, but they have their uses. With Suinyari out of the way I could...* At the same time he began asking me probing questions about who I was and where I had come from.

I was trying my best to dodge Arnzil's questions with charming smiles and evasive answers when out of the corner of my eye I saw Alliya carrying a huge tray. I made a quick bow and said with my best fake smile, "I hope you will both excuse me. I promised Alliya I would help her with the trays. I was so caught up in conversation that I have totally neglected my promise. Lord Arnzil, very glad to have met you and I do apologize for leaving so suddenly, but I am sure we will talk again."

"Yes, I am sure we will. And you are certainly forgiven," he said with a polite nod, giving me back his own fake smile. As I hurried away I heard him thinking, *That one has something to hide, wish I knew what it was, could be very useful.*

I went up to Alliya and said in her ear, "Let me help you with those. I am trying to escape that man over there."

"I should be glad of your help and you were smart to make an escape. That Arnzil is not to be trusted no matter how witty or charming his conversation."

I helped Alliya for a while, glad of some useful work to ease my awkwardness. Then, needing to withdraw a little while from the noisy chatter and the swirl of activity and most of all from the necessity of telling constant lies, I went to sit on a bench that ran under the window. The end of it was somewhat hidden by the drapes. As I was in shadow it was a good place to observe the room without being seen. I had no sooner settled myself there with a sigh of relief when two men who I knew to be friends of Gordivan's came to stand by the window. They were so close I could have reached out and touched them. A chill went up my spine as they started to speak and I heard my own name, or at least my fake one.

"So who is this new fellow, this Donyal? He is a little on the pretty side for my taste, but not too bad."

"Some find of Suinyari's. You know how she picks people up on the street. This one is supposed to be a distant cousin, but I hear he was a stableboy at The Blue-Eyed Lady for a while, all covered with yard muck when she first saw him."

"Well, he cleaned up rather nicely. He even has a certain elegance about him, more than some of this tiresome company. It might be worth getting to know him better. He is certainly ornamental at a party."

"Do you think Gordivan has taken notice of him yet?"

"How could he not? The real question is—has he gotten his hands on him yet? I rather think Suinyari fancies the lad herself."

"It is not Gordivan's hands I would wonder about, but some other part of his anatomy." At that they burst out laughing, braying like two donkeys. Then they walked off together, arm in arm. Face flushed with shame, I felt sick with anger at being talked about in that manner. I even wondered if they had known I was there. Perhaps it had all been for my benefit. I was about to stand up and leave, not wanting to be trapped that way again, when three more people, two women and a man, stopped right in front of my hiding place.

"Now tell us, Loryni, what is this secret you have?" one of the women asked.

Loryni peered about to see if they could be overheard. Seeing no one nearby at that moment she leaned close to the other two and said in a low voice, "I have it from a friend who works at the palace. In a few days word will probably be all over the city, but we will be among the first to know."

"Get on with it then," the first woman said impatiently. "Stop gloating. Tell us and be done with it."

"Well, this is what I heard," Loryni continued with relish. "But you must not tell anyone until it is official. I heard the Zarn is planning to get a new paramour and rid himself of the other. I think he is trying to prove to his grandson and the rest of Eezore that he is still a strong and vigorous man, capable of ruling a while longer. Zarn-to-be, Lord Gunjorn, is pressing very hard on his grandfather, perhaps even urging him to step down. He has many young men on his side."

"Many young hoodlums you mean," the man said. "I hear they are training south of here to come and challenge the City Guard."

"Best not to talk that way, Jorgan, if he is really going to come to power any time soon. I suppose this is a last little show of strength on the old Zarn's part."

"How old is this new girl? The other is only eighteen and has just been with him two years."

"Sixteen or there about. He probably has worn out all the possibilities with the other one and wants to try someone new. What happens to Rashindra? Will she go back to her village?"

"I think not. I have heard that the Zarn cannot bear the idea of having another man touch what he has once possessed. They are never allowed to live. Some guards will probably take her out of the city in the direction of her home and dispatch her when they are far enough away."

The first woman shook her head. "A hard fate for one so young."

"Come now, Nishal, you are too softhearted. She should have thought of that when she was parading around with her nose in the air wearing all those strings of pearls and those yards of green velvet." Loryni sounded hard and angry.

Nishal said quietly, "And what choice did she have? The Zarn no doubt had someone buy her from her family. They were probably glad enough to get rid of a daughter for a goodly sum of money, but if they had resisted she would have been taken anyway and they would have been killed. She does not dress of her own free will. She would wear pearls or cow dung at the Zarn's command. And I doubt she found much pleasure in sharing her body with that skinny old man. I am glad it is not my job."

Loryni laughed. "Never fear. There is not much likelihood you would be chosen."

Nishal ignored her remark and turned to Jorgan. "So you think the power is shifting between grandfather and grandson."

Jorgan nodded. "I have no doubt. I think it is likely to shift for good and very soon, no matter how many young girls the old Zarn deflowers and has put to death. And I would not be at all surprised if the Zarn-to-be has some hand in his grandfather's demise. But truth be told, it would amaze me if Gunjorn manages to hold onto power once he has it. Lord Tarkin is giving him support at the moment, but I think he has his eyes on the throne for himself when the time comes, and he is a ruthless and powerful man. Gunjorn would have to move very quickly and cleverly to hold out against him." Then he gave them a bow. "The night grows long and I have a thirst growing in me again. Perhaps you ladies would like to sit here while I fetch us something to drink."

I held my breath and stayed totally still. He was gesturing toward the very bench I was sitting on. To my great relief Nishal said, "Thank you for the offer, but I see an old friend I need to speak with. I want Loryni to meet her too."

"But not me?"

"No, not you, Jorgan. You are too much of a rascal and would only break her heart. Get yourself something to drink and we will talk later."

They went off in different directions while I quickly got to my feet, crept out of my hiding place and slipped outside into the courtyard, very glad for some fresh air that was not overladen with smoke and perfume and food and drink and the stench of too many bodies in the same space. I was sucking in great gulps of fresh air when I sensed someone close by. He had kept himself in shadow just as I had done moments before and he whispered his words right in back of my ear. "I am Zathrun the Wanderer. Ask your Lady to come out and speak with me. Tell her to come to this exact spot and I will stay in the shadows. This is not a party where it would be wise for me to be visible."

Reluctantly I went inside, found Suinyari and gave her the message. Later, after she had spoken with Zathrun I asked her what had transpired. She looked at me coolly and shook her head. "Some things are better for you not to know. I fixed things with Zathrun, that is all I need to tell you."

I felt a quick flash of anger and had to resist the temptation to have the truth from her head, something I had promised not to do. Instead, when the party had quieted somewhat, I drew her into a quiet corner of the garden. There I told her in a whisper what I had learned from people's minds, especially what I had learned of Arnzil's treacherous thoughts. Suinyari shook her head. "I am hurt and saddened, especially about Lord Arnzil whom I had counted as my father's friend—but not altogether surprised. Later you must point out the others to me. This Kersh certainly has its uses."

"Oh, Suinyari, how can you live with such deception and cruelty all around you?"

At that she whirled on me in anger and said loudly, "What! Do you think yourself so superior to the rest of us because you had the good fortune to be born a..."

I quickly put my hand over her mouth and finished her sentence for her, "...born in the country. Well, it does affect one's view of things, to be country rather than city bred." In her ear I whispered, "Do not say that word aloud this night. There are too many listening ears bent on mischief. Do not say it ever!"

She nodded, leaned against me with a sigh and said softly in my ear. "So sorry, Donya. It was the hurt and anger speaking. I will be sure to watch my tongue in the future, you may trust me on that."

Then I told her what I had overheard about the Zarn and asked if there was anything she could do for Rashindra. She shook her head, looking troubled and puzzled. "Usually I am the first to hear news of the palace. This does not bode well for the future of my enterprises. This young Zarn-to-be is going to be hard to deal with. He will not be nearly so lax as the old one. I think he will let nothing pass by him."

When I asked again about Rashindra, she said sharply, "No, I can do nothing for her. After all, I am only one woman. I cannot save everyone. And besides it would endanger us all. Now I must go back to my guests or they will wonder where I am and may even come looking for me." She sounded angry as if I had accused her of something, though in fact I had said nothing more, only nodded at her words. Then her face softened. Suddenly, she gave me a quick kiss and left me standing alone in the garden, shaken to the core, wondering how I had become so deeply entangled in her very complicated and unsavory life.

Suinyari

That next morning I lay very still, watching Donya sleep. Curled on her side, she looked soft and young, almost like a child. I was flooded with love for her. At the same time I felt a great wariness. This was no ordinary person. She was dangerous, someone to be afraid of. She could read minds, she had powers. How had I let her slip into my life and into my heart so quickly and easily? This had never happened to me before. I had always kept my heart well guarded. Had she cast a spell on me with her Hadra powers?

The evening before, she had gone among my guests, hearing their thoughts. I was grateful for the information. Some of it was vital. Some might even save my life. But nonetheless it felt strange, like a betrayal of all those people. With no warning I had set a spy among them.

And between us? She had told me she would not spy on my mind, would leave that door shut, but could I really trust that? What of those moments when she felt threatened or found something to justify her curiosity? She told me I had a good shield, almost as good as a Hadra, but could I even trust that or was that just another way to disarm me? What she told me about Arnzil was deeply distressing and also hard to believe. He had been my father's friend for years and then mine—or so I thought. Was that really the truth or had Donya said it for her own purposes as a Hadra spy?

I slipped out of bed and tried to quiet my mind. I did not want to risk waking her by the force of my thoughts. Sooner or later we would have to talk about all this, but now was not the moment. I could not face such a discussion with my head throbbing painfully and my eyes out of focus. Clearly I had downed more drink than was wise the night before. And on top of that I had to think what to do about Rashindra, an unwelcome burden Donya had just added to my life. At that moment all I wanted was to sit in my office with a very strong cup of tea, going over my accounts. Compared to human interactions, numbers were clear, simple, precise and uncomplicated.

Donya

I woke late that next morning feeling thick-headed and nauseous, an altogether unpleasant sensation. It was as if I had been drinking hard, though of course I had only taken a few sips for the sake of appearances. Hadra do not take strong drink, it muddles our powers. The one time I had tried had been quite enough to convince me it was not something I wanted to repeat, but it felt as if I had somehow absorbed some of it from the drinkers all around me the night before.

As I lay there scenes of the party began floating through my head, most of them not very pleasant. With few exceptions I did not much like Suinyari's friends, acquaintances and associates. Their thoughts, so different from their words, had left me feeling slimy and dirty. In fact, truth be told, when Suinyari was with them I did not much like her either or at least not that side of her. With them she was all cleverness and artifice, never natural, never her real self, her charm all calculated for effect.

I wondered again what I was doing here and how I had allowed myself to become so entangled with Suinyari when in truth I knew so little about her and what she actually did. It was as if she had let me into her house and into her bed, but not into her life. I knew almost nothing of this business of hers except what little I had observed.

Sometimes people came and went from Suinyari's house at all hours. If it was dark, the excuse was a little evening gathering with music and food. I would join them for a while, but then she would give me a slight nod and I would excuse myself. During the day there was often building work being done on the west side of the house so there was sometimes a flow of workmen as well as carts and wagonloads of materials, all quite legitimate since she had discovered some rot there and much needed to be torn out and repaired. Somehow the work never seemed to advance very fast no matter how many set their hands to it. Some of those who were rough workmen during the day would appear a few evenings later dressed in evening clothes or with instruments under their arms.

Suinyari had also started work on the garden on the east side of the house. She said all the hedges there had grown spindly and needed to be replaced, also some garden beds had to be replanted and the paths laid again, all of which meant much more coming and going of carts, wagons and men. Meanwhile the front of the house that was the formal entrance remained serene and ontouched. So did the back of the house with its high dense hedges guarding it from the street. That was our private place to gather with each other and lounge about at our ease, equals away from prying eyes.

I knew there were chambers under the house, perhaps as big as the house itself, but I had never been down there though I had occasionally heard noises from those depths. About all this Suinyari herself said nothing. If I tried to ask, she just shrugged and deflected my questions. Or she turned her lovely smile on me, flirting and kissing me until I lost interest in such things.

Needing to talk to Suinyari about all this, I forced myself to get up. I dressed with some difficulty, fumbling with fastenings, glad I did not have elaborate clothing to struggle with. If this muddle-headedness was the result of a few sips of hard drink it was a wonder that people ever grew accustomed to it and even had a craving for the stuff. *No accounting for the ways of the Draiga,* I thought sourly to myself as I stumbled down the hall.

I found Suinyari in her office, bent over a pile of papers, accounts by the look of them. When she heard me she looked up, startled and not particularly welcoming. She even dropped her arm protectively across the papers. Though she did not invite me to, I sat down in the chair opposite her and blurted out. "I am troubled by some things between us. That party opened my eyes. But perhaps this is not the best time to talk of such things."

"You are here and we are talking so this must be the right time," she said curtly. "I also have been thinking, but you sought me out so you should go first." Her tone was not at all encouraging. In fact she seemed like a rather hostile stranger, not the Suinyari I loved so much.

I went on, trying to find words that would make sense of what I was feeling. "I am almost living in your house. I share your bed and the intimacy of your body and yet you share nothing with me of your work. I feel like a plaything in your life, a toy. It is as if your real life is lived somewhere else, never to be talked about—at least not with me. I woke this morning wondering what I was doing here."

"And I share my heart and my body with you, that will have to be enough. It is more than anyone else has ever had. Since you are not about to become a partner in this business, the rest is better for you not to know. Do I ask you what you do as a spy? What you report or who you report to? That is your business and none of mine. Safer not to know. I only have to trust that you will do no harm intentionally or by mistake to me or to those I love or even to this city. Beyond that it is not my affair.

"As to what I do in my work, I can promise that you are not in bed with a monster. I have caused no death and no hardship. On the contrary, I have aided the flow of commerce that the Zarn's exorbitant taxes tend to block. I have moved a lot of goods and seen to it that the benefits, after I take my share, flow down instead of up to those who already have an excess. In fact I do a service to the city, though those in power would hardly see it that way. But the less you know about that part of my life the better. It is no use to question me."

Her tone made me angry and I thought, *I could have it from your head if I wanted to.*

"You had better not," she said sharply as if she had been reading my mind instead of the other way around. "And do not cross me in that. I would know and I would never forgive you the intrusion."

Whether or not that was true, I had no intention of trespassing there. In spite of my Hadra powers Suinyari was not someone I wanted to cross. She had her own kind of power and so far it had kept her safe in that very dangerous city. It was part of her fascination for me, but at that moment it was not fascination that I felt—it was distance and strangeness and sadness.

Her words stung. I stood up suddenly. "I am going away for a while, riding south to look into some matters." I spoke coldly. I had not known I was going to say that or that I intended to go until the words were coming out of my mouth.

I felt her hurt like a stab in my heart and saw her trying to hide it under a cool exterior. "When will you be back?" Her voice was cold.

"When you see me." I was angry at being shut out that way. I was hurt and wanted to hurt back. As I said those words I was sucked into her mind against my will by the force of her feelings. I saw Suinyari as a child, standing in the hall, waiting for her father to come out of her mother's room. A tall man, he stepped through the doorway, shaking his head. "She is gone, Flame, it is over." The child did not cry or throw herself into his arms. She just went very still, staring at him in silence, all her grief held deep inside. Suinyari was staring at me with that same expression now. I felt dizzy from having been drawn into her mind so suddenly and was disarmed by her pain. I might have relented, said something loving, been kind, but she instantly covered her pain by saying sharply, "Good journey then," and glancing back down at her papers. I had been dismissed. Without another word I turned and left, went to gather my few things and saddle my horse.

Torvil offered to do it for me, but I shook my head. Actually I wished I could leave all those hateful trappings behind and just ride away on Cloud in Hadra style, our own free selves together. Torvil was watching me with speculative curiosity. "How is it you ride with no bit on the bridle?"

"Cloud has always been my horse. I trained her that way from the time she was young. She has never had metal in her mouth." Not a lie exactly, but not quite the truth either—like almost every word I spoke in this city.

"Do you guide her with your mind then?"

"I guide her with the reins," I told him sharply. There was something in his questioning look I did not like. He was too close to the truth.

Before I left the city I went to see Shaleen. I told her everything I had heard at the party and said I wanted to look into the rumors of men training in the south. She was my superior there and could have sent me on such a mission or forbidden me to go. She just nodded encouragement. "I was opposed at first to your association with that woman and to you living in that house, but I see now it is being very useful."

"I am not going back there when I return to the city. My time with Suinyari is over." For the second time that day I found myself saying something before I had even thought it.

"Why, since that is such a good source of information for us?"

"I cannot be someone's lover just for the sake of information."

"But I thought..."

"Hadra and Draiga, we are too different. It is not natural." I wanted to say, *And it is really none of your business.* I resisted, but I could tell that she had caught it from my mind. I just wanted to leave, to be gone from Eezore, to be alone on the road with only Cloud and my pain for company. My throat felt thick with unshed tears.

Later, as I took the road south, I wondered if I would ever see Suinyari again. Perhaps she had not really intended for me to leave, but she had certainly not offered any words that would have induced me to stay. I would move back to my room over the stable, that much was clear. Though my heart ached with the thought, I knew we would never be lovers again. I had made up my mind and this time the decision was final.

Mother Melna

When I took up my story again several days later, it was only because of Nafrini's persistence. Now I had several more in my audience, a whole circle of young Yellowrobes who stayed to listen after the table was cleared from the evening meal.

I began slowly, feeling my way back into the past. "You must understand that I was just a country girl at the time, only accustomed to my little village. I had never traveled beyond the Kourmairi market town of Maldron. As you can imagine, my first sight of the city was so overwhelming I almost wanted to turn around and leave—too many people, too much noise, troops of guards riding through the streets ordering people about in a frightening way, everything too big and scary, buildings that loomed over me and blocked out the sun, towers so high I had to bend my head back and look up to see to the top of them. Olya kept having to remind me to shut my mouth and not to stare so much.

"So there we were in Eezore without the slightest idea of what to do with ourselves. We had a stash of money with us, but we knew enough not to be in any rush to spend it. We wanted a place to stay that cost very little, at least at the beginning. The first thing we did was go to the market, always the best place to gather information. We asked a few of the women there if they knew of any lodgings that were cheap or free—an old barn perhaps or an abandoned building. One of the women gave a quick glance at the others, then said with a funny little smile on her face, 'The abandoned ruin of the old Witch Convent is nearby. Parts of the roof are still intact and will give shelter.'

"Another woman said quickly, 'But it is haunted, Jani. How could you think to send them there?'

"She shrugged. 'They asked for free shelter and that is what they will find there. They look to be young, maybe they are brave as well. Surely some old ghost will not scare them away.' Then she laughed and her laugh was more mocking than friendly. Clearly we were green girls to her, right from the country, and she was enjoying teasing us.

"In spite of my fears I said quickly, 'Please tell us the way.' I thought they might change their minds to protect us from this ghost.

"As soon as we had our directions we bought ourselves some food and supplies from those women. Then, not having eaten since the night before, we stopped in a small park, tied our horses to some trees, sat on a bench and quickly gobbled down some vegetable tarts before we went on to look at our new home. And that is how we found ourselves here on Varmorl Street, staring at a huge structure of gray rock and red brick, mostly in ruins, visible through an archway covered with a wild tangle of vines and berries.

"It was easy enough to see where the roof was still sound and would offer some shelter. By now it was getting toward evening. We quickly inspected a few spots, found one that seemed suitable to set up our camp and laid out our few things. Enough weeds and grass were growing up through the cobbles so there was plenty for our horses to graze. We made ourselves a fire from the litter of branches that filled the cobbled courtyard. That gave us a little cheer and warmth in those strange surroundings. Since we had only been able to stuff two thin covers into our sacks our plan was to stay as near the fire as possible. One of us would sleep while the other sat up and fed the fire, turn and turn about. First we thought to both lie down together for just a minute or two and rest. Of course we fell sound asleep the moment we snuggled in together.

"We were both awakened in the middle of the night by strange frightening sounds—laughs, shouts, eerie singing, dreadful moans and then more cackling laughter. We sat up, clutching each other. 'The ghost!' I said through chattering teeth.

"'I think not,' Olya answered quickly. 'To me it sounds more like a madwoman, some street trash who has taken up residence here. I am going to see.'

"I grabbed at her sleeve, but before I could stop her she was on her feet. She made a little torch out of a twist of grass she dipped in our dying fire. 'Come with me or not, Melna, but I am going. There is no way I can sleep again unless I know what it is. You can stay here by the fire if you want.'

"I was not sure I would be able to sleep again when we *had* found out what it was. But I was more afraid to be left alone there so I followed where she led. It was easy enough to track the source of the sound. When we found her she was sitting under another of the roof shelters by her own small fire. Beyond her I could see that the shelter had been made into a little home of sorts with makeshift shelves. There was a small altar space with a clay image of the Goddess, some flowers in a bottle and several ritual objects carefully laid out and arranged.

"Olya coughed several times, but the woman—at least I took it to be a woman, though at the time it was hard to tell with all those rags and in that poor light—did not look up. She continued singing her strange song with occasional bursts of sound and sudden incomprehensible words.

"We waited and waited. At last Olya said, 'I know you know we are here. Why are you ignoring us that way?'

"'Because I am in the middle of a ritual and you are interrupting it. But then the young have no manners, so I suppose I will have to forgive you.'

"'Are you the ghost?' Olya asked boldly.

"'I do my best. It keeps people away, the ones that are not supposed to be here.' When she looked up, a dense tangle of dark gray hair framed a face that was immeasurably old and wrinkled, a face filled with grief and pain and also a glimmer of spiteful mockery. She gave us a questioning look out of dark, deep-set eyes. 'So you have finally come. It is about time. I have been calling you for a long while.'

"'Calling us?' I asked, my voice shaking. A shiver went up my back. 'You do not even know us. How could you have been calling us?'

"'You or someone like you—no matter. I need to pass this on, this place and everything I know. Then I can rest. I am very weary. I am the last of the witches who once ran this convent and I cannot just let it all die.'

"She must have been as old as she looked. If she had been part of the last Witch Convent, even if only a student there, by quick calculation that would make her almost a hundred and fifty years old.

I had heard that witches lived to be that old, but had thought that was only stories for children. Had she been waiting here all this time? I was about to inquire when Olya asked suspiciously, 'What do you want from us?'

"'Not much, nothing you would not be glad to do, but I will tell you in the morning.'

"'You can find us at…'

"'I know well enough where to find you. I am not a total fool. We will speak by morning light.' Then, pulling her hood over her head, she seemed to disappear into her black shawl as if she were a darker hole in the darkness instead of a person sitting there. Glancing back at her I thought perhaps she was a ghost after all or that this had just been a trick of alternating candlelight and darkness.

"True to her word she was there in the morning. I opened my eyes to find her sitting on an old stump, staring down at us. The intensity in her eyes made me shiver. We both sat up and Olya turned to face her. 'Now what is it that you want from us?' Olya's tone was confident, almost belligerent. Under it I could feel her fear.

"'I want you to rebuild this place and make it into a shelter for women in this dreadful city.' This time grief quavered in her voice and it cut to my heart.

"'And just how are we to do that?' Olya demanded. 'We have no money and no tools, only our own hands.'

"'You have money enough to start. A good bride price will go a long way on this project.'

"'How do you know that?' I asked sharply, another shiver rippling up my back.

"'What makes you think we want to do it?' Olya asked at the same time.

"The old woman turned to me first. 'I have my ways. I look in the bowl of water and I know what is happening. Rather I see it. I have been watching you all the way here.' Then she turned to Olya. 'Do you have anything else to do with your life? Anything better? Perhaps be married to a handsome pig who plans to rent you out to his rich friends for a plaything? Believe me, you are better off here. I will teach you everything I know before I leave, everything I know of these buildings and everything of what was taught here. You should feel flattered that I would chose you two ignorant country girls to spend my time on—very flattered in fact. And I promise it will not be easy. I am a hard teacher and there is much to learn. My name is Lurghan the Witch.'

"When Olya started to speak Lurghan shook her head. 'No need for that. I already know your names. And if they ask in the market about the ghost just say it has not bothered you yet. Do not tell them of my existence. The less those nasty gossips know about me the better.'

"And so started our new life. It was as if we had agreed to it all without a word of agreement being spoken. She was right that she was a hard teacher and a relentless one besides. There was so much to learn it made my head spin. Sometimes I felt as if I were drowning in new things that often served to show me my own ignorance. And meanwhile we were also clearing away rubble and trying to make some livable space.

"One evening, as the three of us sat together by a fire, she said in a very serious voice, 'When the others come, when this has become a House of the Mother, you, Melna, will be the Mother Superior. You have the gift of love and kindness. You will be the one to hold it together at the center no matter what conflicts or difficulties arise. And there will be many, I can promise you that. Olya, you will be the truth sayer, the one who sees things clearly as they really are and is not afraid to say it. You will be the one who makes sure everything stays on course and keeps moving forward. But you have no gift with people, they will not follow you. Leave it to Melna to weave everyone together.'

"'What do you mean when others come?' Olya asked in her usual testy way. 'Why would anyone else come to a haunted ruin with no place to sleep and nothing to eat? So far there are only rats and roaches here to follow us.'

"'You will see,' the witch said abruptly, clearly finished with her talk.

"Before the week was over two young women had come to join us and soon after that another three. When six months had gone by there were ten of us there, learning and clearing and building, falling into bed exhausted at night. Lurghan taught us how to read and write and do simple figures. She also taught us whatever skills she had for building. And she taught us whatever our heads could hold of geography and history and astronomy and geology—much I had never heard of before, never even considered. I am sure we were a trial to her. We were so ignorant of everything and she wanted to leave the whole body of knowledge that had been contained in the Witch Convent in our poor sieve-like heads, not possible of course. She only had a few books out of what must have been a great library and not much paper to spare.

"What with feeding everyone and buying blankets and sleeping mats and materials for building, Olya and I were going through our money so fast it frightened us. We could not stop now and we knew we could not go on in this manner. Then, after a while, some money began to come in. The first young women who came were poorer than we were, but soon an Uppercaste family sent us their daughter who was terrified of getting married and wanted some book learning. Though she was difficult at first, they sweetened the pot with a large sum of money for her board and so we were able to keep going. After that, even though we were living in something that was not much more than a ruin, more wealthy families sent us their daughters since this was the only place girl-children could learn anything and they sent us money as well. Then the building began to go faster. Lurghan drew plans and we were even able to hire some stonemasons to help. We were not attempting to rebuild the whole Witch Convent, only that portion that it seemed practical to occupy. Later we could enlarge if we needed to do so.

"The gifts continued, though not all in coins. Poor families who could not afford money gave us other things—some food that could be stored such as potatoes and onions and a bag of tarmar grain, some chickens, two pigs, a milk goat, chairs and a table, some outworn clothes. Women in the market were friendly to us now, especially Jani, smiling and winking as if we had a little conspiracy between us. 'Good to see you girls are not afraid of ghosts,' she would say as she handed us something to eat and shook her head at payment.

"At moments it seemed to me as if there were two cities. The visible one belonged to men and—except for the market—it was run by them. The other, hidden just under the surface, was a secret city that belonged to women. There the differences of class and color were much less important than in that outer city and there seemed to be surprising connections across those barriers between market women and servants in the Great Houses on the one hand and the wives and daughters of the men who ruled on the other. I think the Zarn tolerated all this as women's charity, something foolish and frivolous to keep women occupied. In truth he should have been afraid, especially of the convent. There women were learning many things men might not have wanted them to know.

"Along with everything else she was driving into our heads, Lurghan began teaching us about herbs and healings. She even went on to show us a few simple spells, at least to those of us who seemed to have some talent for it. And with everything she taught there was a sense of urgency as if each day might be her very last chance to impart all this valuable information.

"Besides that sort of teaching she had us growing a garden under her watchful eye. 'You cannot expect to continue living off the charity of market women. You have to grow your own food. Surely as farm girls you know how to do that.' There had once been a large garden at the convent and we set about rediscovering it, weeding the old beds, mending the stone walls, unearthing the herbs where they had been almost choked by weeds. Lurghan had maintained a small herb and vegetable garden for her own needs, tucked away in a secret little places, but it was not nearly large enough for all of us.

"In those first few months of frantic activity, I began to notice a woman in a dark cape passing the archway and glancing in. She seemed very interested in what was happening here, yet if I tried to speak to her she hurried away down the street. If I even looked at her she rushed off. Once I saw her getting into a large fancy carriage at the far end of the block. Though she seemed in a hurry to leave she always came back. When I asked Lurghan about her she just shrugged and turned away, though I sensed she knew something. I was very curious and tempted to go after this strange woman, but I was far too busy to indulge that impulse. Besides, she would probably have just hurried off faster. When I asked Lurghan again, she said impatiently, 'Leave her be and she will come to you.'

"Finally, one morning, when I went out to take table scraps to our new chickens, I was startled to see a figure in a dark cape sitting very still on a stone bench in the courtyard. For just a moment I thought it was Lurghan though she seldom sat still that way. Then I realized that the cape was not ragged and tattered as hers was, but of good heavy cloth with a raised design around the edges in dark purple cording. I could hardly believe it. It was our mystery woman, here in the yard and sitting still for a change, not rushing off down the street. She beckoned me over and very timidly I went to sit beside her. She had thrown back her hood. I saw she was quite beautiful and surprisingly young, a woman of about my age.

"'Who are you? I whispered. And what do you want of us?'

"'I am the Zarn's daughter. I came to see what is happening here.'

"'The Zarn's daughter?' I drew back as if stung. 'Are you here to spy on us and report to him?' I was trembling. I pictured all our hard work being destroyed and ourselves being thrown out of the city or imprisoned.

"'No! No!' she said quickly, two red spots suddenly appearing on her very white cheeks. She laid a reassuring hand on my arm and I could feel her trembling also. 'He has no idea I am here. It would be very dangerous for me if he did. Please tell no one but your friend Olya who I really am. Lurghan says I can trust you both. I am here for myself. I needed to see a place where women are free to make their own lives. Will you show me?'

"I nodded. 'Who shall I say you are?'

"'Say that I am a friend of Lurghan's and that my name is Valdain, nothing more. Can you do that?' I nodded again and stood up, slightly flustered and amazed that I should be the guide for such a guest. She rose and followed me.

"Valdain, as I shall call her, soon set me at ease with her keen interest in everything and her gentle but observant questions. All the while, as we walked about looking at the most ordinary things which she seemed to find of great interest, I could feel her barely controlled fear. Here was the most pampered and privileged young woman in the city, yet from her comments I gathered that she envied us our lives and saw value in everything we did. I think she would willingly have traded beds with any of us. When we reached the bench again she motioned me to sit and passed me a sack of coins. 'For your work here, so that you can soon shelter more women. I will send some each month and I think I can find others to do the same. But I will not come back again. It is too dangerous for me. Thank you for all your kindness.'

"Stumbling over my words, I thanked her for her generous gift. Then she was gone, slipping out the archway and going speedily down the street to that same waiting carriage.

"Valdain had said she would not be back, but she came back many times. It was as if she could not bear to stay away and soon she began bringing her maid with her. She seemed more relaxed after a while, eating a humble meal with us or helping with simple chores as if that was the most exciting thing in the world, but the fear never altogether left. I thought she must live her whole life in fear, that it was an act of great courage to come to us at all. I grew to like her very much and looked forward eagerly to our talks, but I worried that if she were discovered among us it might call us to the Zarn's notice in a dangerous way and bring his wrath down on our heads.

"Before anything like that happened she stopped coming. I both missed her and was much relieved. Then I heard she was betrothed to be married. For a while sums of money kept coming at regular intervals, then that also stopped, but by then we were getting enough from other sources. Next I heard she had started having children. They were all girls, one after the other for several years, much to the disgust of the old Zarn who desperately wanted an heir and had not been able to produce a son of his own. Gunjorn, the young Zarn-to-be who is such a menace to us now, was her only son, her lastborn, the too-large baby whose birth ended her life. A mystery how such a nasty man came from such a gentle, generous woman, but of course he never knew her, never had the advantage of her kindness in his childhood. I grieve for her life and think of her often as we go about the routine of our days. How I wish we could have stayed friends. More than that, I wish she could have been free to live her life as she chose. Perhaps then she would have stayed with us and still be living.

"By the end of that first year we had enough of the old building rebuilt so that we could live in it with a degree of comfort. We no longer walked through holes in the walls; we had an actual front door. And we had roofed over other parts for our growing family of animals—pigs, sheep, cows, goats and chickens that we had been given. We had mended some other places to make a pottery shed and a weaving shed. We had even begun making things for sale in the market as well as for our own use.

"When more women came, we were able to take them in without too much hardship. Many of those who came to us changed their names, taking names of their own choosing if their birthnames carried ugly memories or might endanger their lives. 'A new name for a new life!' became the saying among us. How amazing to think that some of those same women are still with us today: Mother Nazeem who is in charge of healing and herbal remedies; Mother Cindral who supervises all our cloth production from seed to loom; Mother Ulwin who manages the kitchen and the food; Mother Golvini who is responsible for the animals and the barns; and of course Mother Olya who is our housemother and manages all our finances, as well as teaching the skills of combat for protection and self-defense. After Lurghan left I myself supervised the learning of everything else. We were not and never could be a real learning institute like the great Witch Convent on whose ruins we were building our new lives, but we made sure all girls and women who came through our doors and stayed for any length of time learned the rudiments of reading and writing and sums and whatever else Lurghan had tried to teach us in her short time among us. Just as she had predicted, I also became the peacekeeper, the final authority, the highest equal in a community of equals, though I always tried to rule by consent.

"How young we were then! Young and inexperienced and hopeful and foolish—so many mistakes! Now those of us who survived are all purple-robed Mothers, a little wiser perhaps, slightly bent with age, complaining to each other about our aching backs and our failing eyesight. But I am getting way ahead of my story here.

"Back to the tale. Exactly a year from the day we had first come to this place Lurghan left—vanished actually. She said nothing to any of us, left no note and took none of her things, not even her horse. She had never moved into the house with us, preferring her little shelter, though we had rocked in the sides to make it more comfortable in the cold. Everything was just as it had been. She even left the figure of the Goddess on her altar. We kept it that way, as a shrine to the woman who had made our lives here possible, lighting a candle for her every night and leaving flowers on her altar. I thought of her often that next year though I knew we would not see her again. I missed her deeply, but I did not miss the lash of her tongue when we were too slow or too stupid to learn something she wanted to impart."

I was just telling this last part when I heard Suinyari's voice saying, "I am so sorry to interrupt, Mother Melna, but I have some urgent news."

I looked up to see Suinyari sitting in the circle. I had been so absorbed in the story, so lost in that far past, I had not even noticed when she came in. "How long have you been here?"

"Almost from the beginning. A fascinating story. I knew some of it, of course, but I have never heard it all strung together that way."

"And you thought I would go on forever so you had to stop me."

"Forgive my rudeness, Mother. I am here because a friend overheard someone say at my party last night that the old Zarn has gotten himself a new sweet-girl."

At that I jumped to my feet so quickly my chair fell back on the floor with a clatter. "I was afraid this might happen. Come to my accounting room so we can talk." Then, as we were rushing out, I told Nafrini, "Find Mother Olya and send her to me as quickly as you can."

As soon as we were all three in the room Suinyari said urgently, "This time we must do something. Last time we were already too late. He intends to have Rashindra done away with in the next day or so, probably assassinated on the ride home. If we can find a way to free her, will you take her in?"

"Of course," I said instantly.

I turned to Mother Olya and raised a questioning eyebrow. She hesitated a moment and then nodded. "As long as we are careful and secretive so we do not bring the Zarn's wrath down on our heads and risk everything we have built here."

"Then we must make a plan," I said urgently.

Spider

Of course I knew who Suinyari was. All the market brats had noticed her. It was impossible not to, what with her showy style and her fine clothes and that bright red hair flashing all about. Most had thought of trying to snatch her purse, though none had succeeded. She wore a long knife on her sash, right out in plain sight in a fancy sheath, and kept a sharp eye out all around her. *What is a grand lady like that doing in such a place?* we had all wondered to each other at some time or other. A few times I had followed her, watching what she did and who she met with, all the while trying to keep myself well out of sight. She would come with those two maids of hers, the pretty one and the ugly one, and appear to be shopping at this or that stall. She never came away loaded with bundles, but each time she met with many different people, some of them Wanderers, even some from the Thieves Guild. Altogether she seemed to do far more talking than shopping. There were always stories about her, even some talk of her being a smuggler. I was never sure what to believe.

I remembered seeing Suinyari for the first time not long after my mother vanished into the pits and hellholes of Sarvo Street. I was only five at the time and very sad. The sight of her took my breath away. Of course I had seen other grand ladies but always in carriages, always at a distance, none so near to me. There were moments when she came so close to my place of hiding I could have reached out and touched her, could have counted every button and bow and ribbon on her dress. For some reason the sight of her always set up a strange ache of longing in my heart. But that was back when I still pined for my mother and cried myself to sleep each night. After a while I grew accustomed to seeing Suinyari going about her business as I went about mine. Soon I gave little thought to her. I was too busy learning how to stay alive in the harsh world of the streets to pay much attention to some misplaced Lady.

Those last few months, just before it happened, had been different. Whenever I saw her I felt a sort of hope or lightness as if maybe my life did not always have to be so hard. One day I even shared my thoughts about her with Argan. He was one of my few friends on the streets. After I had stabbed his hand when he tried to steal my things and then beat him in a card game where he was plainly cheating, he had begun to respect me. He had even tried to protect me from the older boys, not that I ever needed anyone's protection or asked for it, but I suppose he was lonely too. As I talked to him about her I found myself enjoying saying her name aloud—Lady Suinyari this and Lady Suinyari that. "Whenever Lady Suinyari sees me she gives me a look that seems to be full of meaning. Maybe she wants to take me home to be her daughter. Maybe I could have a mother again."

At that Argan burst out with a harsh ugly laugh that sounded more like a croak. There might even have been some pity in his eyes, though we did not have much of that to waste on each other. "Daughter!? Is that what you think? What a fool you are! How could you have lived so long on the streets and be so dumb?" He spit with contempt. I was not sure if it was for me or Suinyari or both. "Besides, that woman is no Lady," he went on with his lip curling. "She may put on grand airs, but she is a smuggler, not much better than a thief herself. Daughter indeed! If she wants to take you home it will more likely be to sell you to others or to use as her love slave until she tires of you or wears you out and throws you back on the street. I hear she has an unnatural appetite for women. Watch yourself, Spider, that woman is dangerous. She can swallow you whole or chew you up and spit out the pieces. Besides, for people like us it does no good to become too attached to anyone. They can be gone tomorrow." That was just a week before Argan himself was caught by a stallkeeper and taken away by the guards; I thought it likely I would never see him again.

After that I watched Suinyari even more closely, but in a very different way. Maybe Argan was right, maybe I was a fool—and a baby too—pining for something I could never have, still looking for a mother when I had done well enough for myself those past four years without one. I had been watching Suinyari with one thought in mind. Quite likely she had been watching me with an altogether different one.

When I saw her questioning the market women, especially Kelameer and Turian, I thought it must be about me. Turian even nodded and gestured in my direction. From where I was hiding in back of a pile of potato baskets I felt betrayed, even endangered, but at the same time somehow warmed at the thought that someone actually noticed me and cared about my existence. Turian was my favorite among the market women. She never tried to hit me with her long stickhook. Sometimes she even offered me food or some shelter under the far corner of her booth when rain came suddenly. Of course I never let her come close enough to set hands on me, but I also never stole from her or from any of the women near her.

From my hiding place I saw Suinyari buy a new pouch from Turian's booth, a beautiful thing of soft red leather embroidered with gold and blue and green. I had coveted it myself. Now I watched her fingering it, caressing the leather, holding it up to the light while her maid, the pretty one, clapped with delight. After a while Suinyari nodded and slipped another pouch from the concealment of her sash. I saw the flash of coins, then she emptied the contents of her old pouch into the new one and fastened that pretty thing around her waist, right there on display for anyone to see. After that she went off arm in arm with her maid to join the other one, the one with the harsh face and stern look. Then she continued about the market with her new pouch in plain sight, bright red and tempting against her dark skirt. At that moment I vowed to myself that I would have it from her no matter how long it took. She thought to get me and I would get her instead. Some of the market boys even dared me to do it.

After that day, whenever Suinyari came to the market, she always wore her new pouch, but her maids stayed close to her and she seemed watchful and alert. Then there came a morning when she stopped at a bookseller's stall and became so engrossed in one particular book that after a while, the pretty maid called the other one away to look at something—a bolt of fabric, I think. I saw my chance. Slipping around the corner of the booth I knocked over a stack of books. The bookseller began dashing about, cursing like a madman, trying to gather up his wares. When I saw that Suinyari was bending over to pick up one of the books I knew this was the moment.

In the confusion I slipped up behind her and was about to cut the strap on her beautiful new pouch when my arms were suddenly pinned behind me and a strong hand slipped over my mouth. I fought like a wild thing to get away until this voice in my ear said, "If the guards come you will be marked as a thief, maybe end up in the dungeons or worse. Better to come quietly with us." That stilled me. I had heard enough ugly stories of the dungeons that ran under the city, cold rooms carved out of living stone. I had also heard that sometimes children were sold from there into child brothels where children of any age and sex were kept for use until they died. Whatever Suinyari wanted of me could not be quite as bad as that.

Now it was plain that she had set a trap for me. And thinking myself so clever, I had walked right into it. Argan was right that I was a fool. I heard Suinyari say to the bookseller, "We will deal with the child. She will make no more mischief in this market. Here is something for your troubles." Then I heard the sound of coins clinking on the counter. I could see nothing because of that large hand over my face.

Taking my hand in a firm grip, Suinyari said in my other ear, "Will you come with us willingly or must we bind you? No one here will help you, of that you may be sure. You are well known as a clever little thief. They will be only too glad to be rid of you."

No one had touched me since my mother vanished out of my life and Suinyari's grip on my hand was not altogether unpleasant. For quite some time now I had been feeling weary of my life, especially after Argan was taken away. In spite of what he had told me, I thought this might be a chance of something better. I nodded and the ugly one took her hand off my face. With Suinyari holding one hand, the pretty one the other and the ugly one following right behind with a hand on my shoulder, we walked out of the market and up to a waiting carriage. As we went along I stared down at my feet, embarrassed to have been so easily caught after so many years of cleverness. I looked at no one until we passed Turian's booth. Then I nodded at her in a sort of goodbye. To my surprise she grinned and winked at me as if I had been the one to catch the fish instead of the other way around.

I had never been in a carriage before that day and it frightened me. It looked like a large cage, like the one that was used to bring the dancing bear to the market on feast days. I had just a moment of wondering again about their intentions and whether perhaps they were planning to put me on display. When I hesitated in front of that dark interior, Bethron, the ugly one, gave me a good shove from in back so that I suddenly sprawled across the seat. Suinyari laughed and slipped in beside me. Alliya got in on the other side and Bethron climbed into the place right in back of me.

"Well done! Well done!" Suinyari shouted gleefully. "Easier than I expected! Drive home, Torvil, so we can see how well she cleans up, what kind of jewel lies hidden under all that grime."

Now I was sure that Argan had been right. The woman meant me for some ugly purpose. Like a fool I had let myself get caught much too easily. When the coachman said, "Some prize, Suinyari! Is this what we came here for? It looks like a cockroach and smells like a week-old basket of dead fish," I blushed furiously, wanting to kick the man where it would hurt the most. And that was how my new life began.

Suinyari

There is an old saying in the markets, "Be careful what you wish for, you might get it." All too true! I had captured this wild child almost too easily. Now I had even less idea what to do with her than the newest stable hand knew of training a green horse. Just being a woman did not automatically make me a mother. What had I wanted? A child who was docile and loving? One who would sit in my lap while I read to her and fed her sweets?

And in truth, what had I expected? I had not been a docile child myself. My mother had been sickly and then died when I was young. After that I had been a wild child, angry and unmothered, wandering restlessly around the house and even exploring out on the streets whenever I could slip past my guardians. I spent my time being a trouble to the servants who were supposed to watch over me and a worry to my father who loved me, but was seldom home, then a plague to everyone at the House of the Mother. Yes, indeed, what had I wanted with this child? The younger sister I never had to fill the empty, lonely spaces in my life? A younger version of my own self who would get good mothering this time because I would be the one to provide it? Maybe a way to feel more like a woman and less like a freak in this city that had such a deadly hatred for my kind? Whatever my reasons, the child certainly did not cooperate. I could as well have brought home a skinny, half-starved, feral cat and expected to turn it overnight into a well-mannered lap pet or, as Bethron had warned me, brought home an Oolanth cub to tame. In truth the girl was even worse than Bethron had expected, ruining my peace of mind, almost destroying my home and turning my well-ordered household upside down.

The first afternoon should have warned me what to expect. We locked all the doors so she could not go running out. She had tried that the moment we set her down in the house and would have succeeded if not for Torvil's quick action. In his hands she kicked and spit and cursed. Torvil got a long bloody scratch down the side of his face for his troubles and ended up cursing too, yelling things I had never heard from him before. Bethron and I began arguing loudly and Alliya rushed about wailing in distress.

All the commotion drew Gammo from the kitchen. "Stop that!" she shouted at everyone. It had the silencing effect of a thunderclap. We all stood still, even Spider. "Take care of that scratch and get it clean," she told Torvil with a toss of her head. "Who knows what that child has under her nails." Then to Spider she said sternly but not unkindly, "You need a good wash. You are smelling up the house. And those clothes have to be burned; likely they are full of bugs. Now we can do this hard or we can do it easy, your choice, but we are going to do it. Let go of her, Torvil."

"But she will…"

"She will not!" Gammo stepped over and took the child from Torvil's grasp. Then she hissed in Spider's ear, "Try any of that with me and I will crush you in my big arms. Do not think to test me or you will regret it."

Spider's curses subsided and she stopped struggling in Gammo's grip. Gammo went on, "Torvil, when you are finished, go out and lock the door behind you. Keep watch outside in case she tries to make another escape. The rest of you come in the kitchen and help me. Bethron and Alliya, fill that big tub with warm water. Suinyari, get the scissors and start cutting off those rags while I hold her still. Then throw them out the kitchen door for Torvil to burn and make sure to lock it again. We do not want her running about the city naked."

I did as I was told. When Gammo gives orders in that manner there is no choice but to obey. As I started cutting off the rags the child had been wearing, she began wailing in real distress and struggling again. "No! Please! Do not hurt me! Just let me go. I will never try to steal from you again. Please do not hurt me. I am too young for that, too little. Find someone older."

At first I could make no sense of her words. Then the horror of them hit me and I flushed with shame. So that is what she thought of us. "We are not going to hurt you," I told her in a soothing voice as if speaking to a frightened animal. "You are safe with us. We have no bad intentions. We are only going to bathe you and dress you in warm clothes and give you some food."

After that she seemed to calm a little. She did not really fight when we put her in the tub and began to wash her. She even seemed to enjoy it and to relax a little in our hands. I was shocked to see how thin she was with every rib protruding. Her arms and legs were so stick-like that her knees and elbows looked like big knobs. I wanted to cry at the sight of her poor little body all blotched with scabs and bruises. The rags she had been wearing had made her look larger and bulkier than she really was.

For a while she dozed in the warmth of the water and even allowed me to cut the tangles out of her hair. Afterward she let us dry and dress her without too much difficulty. I was foolish enough to be hopeful, to think things might go more easily, might even be well—an idle hope as it turned out.

Everything changed the moment we tried to eat together. Alliya and Bethron and Gammo set food on the table and called Torvil in. I brought Spider in and showed her the place at the table that had been set for her. Instead of sitting down to eat she gave a cry, almost of pain, and grabbed up the whole platter of meat. Then she dashed out of the room with it and crawled under the hall table, pushing herself back into a corner where she crouched, growling and gobbling. Torvil was all for trying to pry her out of there. "Leave her be," I said quickly. "When she has eaten her fill maybe she will calm down. She has been slowly starving all this time on the street." Afterward, of course, she was terribly sick, but she would let no one get near her.

I hoped things would get better after that, but it was not to be. Whatever I may have wished for in bringing this child home it was not what I got. I heard nothing but complaints about her—from the seamstress, the stable hands, the maids, even Gammo. Platters broken, food stolen, tables and chairs overturned, covers and pillows taken to make nests in corners and under furniture because she could not get accustomed to sleeping in a bed. No one praised me. No one told me how clever I was to bring home this little street-rat.

And anyone who tried to discipline her risked a bite or a kick or worse followed by a spew of vile language and spit. That child had heard more nastiness on the street in her short life than I had in all my years on this earth. It was amazing to see even Bethron blush scarlet at some of her talk. It might have made me smile if I had not been so desperate myself.

Alliya tried to stay loving through it all. Even for her it was a strain. As for me, I was beside myself. I could not imagine turning the child out in the streets again, though Bethron and Torvil both urged me to do so. Nor could I live with her this way much longer. I have to confess, I had hoped for a little gratitude—not much, but a little. After all, I was supplying food, clothes, a warm shelter, even some love if only she could have accepted it. Instead I had let loose a monster of chaos in my house. I was very glad Gordivan was off on one of his trips and fervently wished that Donya had been there with her reading of minds and some good advice. Maybe I would send the child to live with the Hadra; maybe they could tame her.

She called herself Spider and I tried to call her Aneithia since I knew from the market women that was her real name. That was only one of our many struggles; I refused to call her Spider as it seemed too much of a street name. It was unsuited for the house and would only serve to remind her of her other life. For her part she refused to answer to Aneithia. Instead she would curl her lip, turn away and ignore me. Finally I compromised by calling her Neith and that seemed to do—not that she responded politely, only with a little less rudeness.

Bethron said she was an ungrateful brat and thought she should be smacked for her insolence, but I saw no good that could come of it and told her to leave the child be. "After all she did not ask to come here." Besides I could not imagine who could do such a thing without getting themselves kicked or bitten or worse, not a very useful outcome to attempts at discipline. Alliya thought she could love the girl into tameness. In her nasty way Spider thought Alliya a fool. She told her so quite plainly, sometimes reducing Alliya to tears.

Spider

Everything there was strange to me and had to be learned: how to dress, how to eat, how to sleep, how to relieve oneself. And perhaps I was the strangest thing of all, a street-rat in that fine fancy Shokarn house. My first bath and my first meal were almost as frightening as my capture. It was not a good beginning and I think I behaved quite badly. I know Suinyari expected something from me. She no doubt deserved better than I could give. I was so full of rage at the way I had been forced to live while others lived in such comfort that all I could give back was anger, certainly not gratitude. Underneath it all I was terrified that they would throw me back out on the streets. In fact I thought that was what I deserved.

When things in the house were too confusing I sometimes went to hide out in the kitchen since that place seemed to me the safest. Gammo the cook was the one who finally helped me to sort things out, the first one I could really talk to. That came later. At first there was no one. Certainly not Alliya. I did not trust her. She seemed too sweet and kind to be real. I might have liked Bethron. She was rough and honest—more like the women I knew from the market—but at first she had no use for me. Several times I heard her say, "Bring home a wild animal, expect to get shit on." I thought she was right.

Torvil I stayed away from altogether. He said I should be hung by the feet from the garden wall. "Just say the word, Suinyari, and I will tie her up, throw her in the carriage and dump her out by the West Gate." *First you have to catch me, you pig!* I would think spitefully. Suinyari would just shake her head and look sad.

I loved Suinyari with a passion, but she seemed so far away, so unattainable, so high above me that I could not imagine getting close to her. So instead I was rude and hostile, expecting at any moment that she would get rid of me, though she never said any such thing.

She puzzled me; in fact the whole household puzzled me. I had heard that the Shokarn were harsh cruel masters and that being a servant in a Shokarn house was not much different from being a slave. In that house they all sat down to eat together. Though Suinyari seemed to have the final word on most things, they discussed and argued over most matters. No one seemed to be afraid of anyone else, certainly not of Suinyari. Also I knew she was supposed to be married and that married women are under the rule of their husbands, but there was a great deal of business being done by everyone there and no husband around to give the orders.

Altogether it was easier to be with Gammo than with anyone else in the house. She did not scold me for my bad ways like Bethron or try to talk to me in a sweet high false-sounding voice like Alliya, as if I were some wild animal to be tamed and gentled. Gammo had no great hopes for me, no plans or expectations like Suinyari. And I had no need to impress her. She was just Gammo the cook, big and solid and very sure of herself.

At first she would just set some sweets on the counter for me, some little cake or candy, and talk aloud as though to herself about the day or what she was doing, but I knew the words were really meant for me. When I dashed out to snatch the sweets and dashed back into hiding again to eat in safety she would not turn to look at me, but she might talk about how good the raisin cookies were or how sweet the apple tarts tasted while she ate some herself.

After a while I grew more daring and might even come and sit by her on the bench. Wordlessly she would give me a knife to help cut up the vegetables or a spoon to stir the pot she pointed to, saying, "Keep stirring, do not let the bottom burn." Those were the first useful things I did in that house. Then she would tell me stories or sing songs. Sometimes, if I felt safe enough, I would lean against her. She might even stroke my hair or put a hand on my shoulder and I would let her, at least for a few moments. In four years no one had touched me. No one had ever laid a hand on me, neither with kindness nor with anger. Even in this safe house it was hard to allow it. It was really Suinyari's touch I longed for, but I could hardly admit that even to myself, much less to her. Indeed I did everything to make that impossible.

It all changed one afternoon. I said something rude and insulting to Suinyari. When she tried to speak to me, I ran into the kitchen to Gammo, as if for protection. When Suinyari followed me there I hid behind the cook's broad back. Instead of giving me shelter, Gammo stood up and slammed her hands down on the table, her face all in a dark scowl. "This has gone on long enough, Neith. Let that be an end to it. This rudeness stops now. Suinyari has been nothing but kindness to you and this is how you repay her?"

"I thought…"

"You thought I would go on protecting you forever? I saw you trusted me a little and I did not want to shatter that trust with scoldings. I am not Bethron. I was trying to be patient, waiting to see if you would come to your senses on your own. But now I am done with waiting. Enough is enough! You are too hurtful. And stop trying to hide behind my skirts now. Stand here in front of me, look at Suinyari and tell her you are sorry for your meanness. Then we will have no more of it."

Ashamed, I glanced at Suinyari. She mumbled quickly, "Not necessary, Gammo. After all, she is just a child."

"Child or no child it is necessary or this will never end. We need some peace in this house. *I* need some peace in this house!" She pulled me in front of her, held me there and shook my shoulders with her large strong hands. "Say it! Say you are sorry."

It was no lie. I really was sorry, sorry that Gammo was angry and very sorry for what I had said to Suinyari, especially when I saw the look of pained bewilderment on her face. Why did I say those things? It was as if I had some demon inside that would not be satisfied until I had done something hurtful. "I am sorry, Suinyari," I whispered.

"Louder," Gammo said and shook me again. "You were loud enough with the ugly words."

This time I looked right at Suinyari. "I truly am very sorry. It is as if some evil thing gets hold of my tongue. I do not really mean to say such things."

"It is all right, Neith, I understand." She turned away quickly and left the kitchen, but not before I saw the tears in her eyes.

When she left Gammo pressed me against her in a big hug that almost crushed the breath out of me. Suddenly I was crying—wailing really, howling with grief, all the grief of four years on the street, grief I had never given voice to before. Gammo sat down on the bench, pulled me into her lap and rocked me like a baby, crooning one of those songs with words I did not understand, while I spluttered and sobbed and hiccuped my way to calmness. I must have fallen asleep that way. When I woke I was in my own bed and it was morning.

Gammo never had to scold me that way again. I had finally made my peace with Suinyari. My tongue no longer ran off with itself that way or at least not so often, and I actually learned how to say I was sorry when it did. Also I took more care with my own appearance since that seemed to matter to her, keeping myself clean and my clothes in better order. After that first disastrous haircut where my hair had been chopped off to rid it of filth and snarls, Alliya had trimmed it off evenly. It turned out to be a pretty reddish brown, several shades lighter because of being clean, and it began to curl rather nicely around my face, something I learned from looking in a mirror. Suinyari wanted me to grow it long again but I refused. "I never want to be tangled in hair again. This feels so much freer. Besides I do not want to fuss with it or have anyone else needing to fuss with it."

Aside from the issue of my hair I became a compliant child, at least as much as my nature would allow. I would follow Suinyari around, trying to help with chores, or sit by her while she read to me, amazed that a whole fabulous story could fit into those little squiggles. Seeing my fascination with the mystery of books, she began to teach me my letters and also how to do simple sums. All the members of her household were very skilled at sums. They could also read and write, something rare for women in that city, rarer still for servants. Suinyari was very determined that I learn as well. I was a clever child and I think my progress pleased her. As for my fear that she wanted evil things from me, that was totally unfounded. She seemed in fact to want nothing from me, and I began to yearn for some useful task to prove my affection and my loyalty.

The first task I set for myself was to learn some skill with the glue pot. I felt a need to mend some of what I had broken in my rage at the world as well as my clumsy unfamiliarity with household objects. Gammo had saved everything that had any chance of being made whole again. She watched me, nodding with satisfaction. "Much easier to break than to mend," she told me several times as I struggled to hold all the pieces together. With that in mind I learned to watch my temper and to move around the house with more care.

As time went on I also tried to make myself useful to Bethron and Alliya and Gammo. I even helped Torvil out in the stables. He said I had a natural hand for it and he no longer threatened to hang me up by my heels. In fact, when he saw how well I did working with horses, he offered to teach me to ride. I shook my head. "Maybe later," I told him. The thought of it frightened me. I was not yet ready for that. Horses' backs seemed much too high and I still felt too small. Working among them was challenge enough for me.

I kept asking Suinyari what she wanted from me, what I could do for her. Finally she told me that she might train me as a messenger, but not till I was ready and then only if I was willing since it might be dangerous. Thrilled by the idea, my heart filled with pride at the thought that I might do something useful or vital for the house, but whenever I asked if she had some message for me to take she told me it was not yet time, that I would have to wait. By then, of course, I knew that Argan had been right and that the business of that house was nothing Suinyari would want the Zarn's guards looking at too closely.

Then, just as I had begun to be comfortable at Althor House, to feel I had a place there and that Suinyari really loved me, this Donyal creature appeared to claim all of her attention.

Donya

After the party I went south, partly to observe the men training because I needed to do this for my work and partly to be away from Suinyari. The sudden close connection with her had shaken me to my core; her party had been the final twist. Finding myself abruptly plunged into her strange life had left me in a state of deep confusion. The Hadra part of myself seemed lost in her household. I was fast becoming a stranger to myself. As a spy I should have been overjoyed. What better situation could I have found for gathering information? Instead I felt deeply disturbed. Riding alone with just Cloud for company gave me the time I needed to think.

Detailed observations from my trip are all in my report to Shaleen, so I will only say a few things about it here. Going south I wore shabby ordinary clothes and did nothing to disguise my skin color. I could be taken for a dark-skinned Shokarn or a light-skinned Kourmairi, in other words an ordinary poor man, not worthy of any notice. Though the Shokarn try to keep sharp divisions between themselves and others, in reality there is much crossing of the sheets and most of the common people look much as I do.

From asking questions in the markets of the towns I passed through, I discovered easily enough where Gunjorn's followers, these so-called Purifiers, were training and where their camp was. Each time I asked I was warned not to go near them. Several times I was told, "They are quick to kill anyone who spies on them." Then, with both relish and a shiver of fear, someone might go on to tell me a story about a cousin or uncle or friend who had been done in by their curiosity, someone who had gone to look and never come back or whose body had been found days later, crushed and mangled. By the time I neared their practice field I considered myself well warned.

Even before I heard the shouts of men, I felt the presence of their sentries, ringing the field. I dismounted quickly, sending Cloud off to graze and wait for me. I told her to stay out of harm's way and not let anyone get near her, not in words exactly—horses do not understand words the way we do—but in pictures. Then I went forward on foot, keeping myself out of sight behind trees. The practice field seemed to be in a bowl. Not too far away I could see a little rise with a rock outcrop at the top, an excellent place for observing what was happening below. Of course there was a sentry posted there.

I was just wondering how I was going to get past him when a loud gong rang down below. He left quickly and I could neither see nor sense anyone coming to replace him. I made a quick dash through the trees and up the slope, then slipped forward on my belly to look down. It was indeed a perfect lookout spot, giving me a clear view of the whole field. Knowing it would not be mine for long, I looked around for a place to hide. The rock face was not solid. It had many crevices, ledges and overhangs. I quickly found a spot where I could tuck myself away in the shadows, see everything and not be seen. None too soon. Moments later I heard the crunch of boots on the rocks. Then the smell of food made my stomach clench with hunger. The sentry settled himself above me to eat with no idea anyone was nearby.

Looking down, my first surprise was how many men there were, far more than I had expected. In numbers they might almost rival the City Guards. Soon after I was safely hidden in my crevice, several supply wagons came into the clearing, foodstuff probably from the eager way the men rushed forward to help unload. After the wagons left and the supplies were stashed, I watched while the men drilled and practiced. I made note for Shaleen of comings and goings, numbers of men, ratio of captains to soldiers, ways of fighting, types of uniforms, levels of skill, styles of command, the nature of the encampment itself and anything else I thought might be useful.

Just as I was beginning to feel restless and itchy, wishing I could leave soon or at least move about more freely, I saw a large contingent of men riding in with an ornate, gilded carriage in their midst. Horns blew and then the drums began. In an instant the whole camp was in a flurry of activity with everyone sheathing their weapons and quickly dashing about to form two orderly lines down the field. The man who rode at the head of this troop was clearly the leader. He looked quite young, only a little older than most of the men on the field. As he rode between the newly formed lines all the men bowed deeply. I heard the name Lord Gunjorn said several times. So this arrogant young twit was the Zarn's grandson, the one who hoped to be Zarn himself one day. He looked hard and cruel. Under that I could sense his fear, a dangerous man who was planning to stand the city of Eezore on its head to prove himself. Not very soon though, at least not until these fighters were better trained. Their numbers might be frightening, but they still had far more enthusiasm than fighting skill.

Riding with Gunjorn were some Grayrobes and a whole contingent of important-looking Highborn, quite a bit older than the men on the field. A throne-like chair was quickly taken from one of the carriages and set up with a commanding view of the action. I expected Lord Gunjorn to be seated in it and was surprised when he ordered his men back to their practice, then rode up and down himself, shouting commands and pointing out faults. He was very visibly in charge of the scene. With the flood of biting criticism that poured from his mouth I was glad not to be one of his men. His voice and sometimes his words easily carried to where I was hiding. Nothing pleasant, but at least a distraction. It was hard to stay still for so long. My whole body ached from contact with the hard rocks and the strain of trying not to move.

The throne-chair was soon occupied instead by a very white, very broad man who climbed down from the gilded carriage with much help and some difficulty. He needed assistance to seat himself on that grand chair. By the deference paid him I assumed him to be quite important. He looked about with a mocking smile on his face and seemed contemptuous of all this rushing about playing at war, almost as if it was beneath his notice. Nonetheless he watched intently and appeared to be making suggestions to the young captains who came up to confer with him. I heard them call him Lord Tarkin and looked at the man with renewed interest. This must be the same man Jorgan had spoken of at the party, a man to watch out for, a man hungry for power, a man who might be even more dangerous than Gunjorn himself.

Some of the Grayrobes stayed near Lord Tarkin, seeming to be an important part of whatever consultations were going on. Others spread out in the field. There they gathered groups of men around them and appeared to be exhorting them to more passion and dedication in the Purifier cause. Mostly I could just see their gestures, but occasionally I caught a few shouted words about the old Zarn's corrupt ways or the evils of women being allowed in public places.

When Gunjorn and his party finally left, taking Lord Tarkin and the throne-chair with them, as well as all the Grayrobes, a collective sigh went up from the field. Soon the men gave up all pretense of working. They milled around eating, then settled down to smoke or play cards or even sleep. I thought I would have to stay in my hiding place until dark, but the man who was supposed to be standing watch must have been sitting or perhaps even lying down. Soon he was snoring gently. I was able to uncoil from my hiding place, stiff and sore, and slip away to go find Cloud while it was still daylight. I had seen enough and was only too glad to be riding away.

Afterward, in no great hurry to return to Eezore, I wandered about for a while, observing how people lived and what they did. I did not think my news so urgent that I had to rush back to Shaleen. Also I did not expect to return to Suinyari's household. I was determined never to set foot there again, but the longer I stayed away the more I missed her. I began to remember all the good things we had shared, to hear her voice, see in my mind a certain turn of her head or gesture of her hand, catch a flash of her red hair. Then my heart would ache with longing. Finally the rest of it seemed less and less important. What did I really care about her work and whether or not she shared any of it with me? She was right that I shared little enough of mine with her. Maybe it was better not to know, better just to be each other's plaything and leave the rest of it in the hands of the Goddess. Was there any real harm in that? The thread that connected us started to tug at my heart more and more strongly. As I turned north again I began to think that at least I should go see her.

First I had to report to Shaleen. She shook her head and seemed very worried about what I told her. "That many men? Even if they are all fools they can cause a great deal of trouble. I fear this city is going to explode in violence soon. It is just a matter of time. The old Zarn can only hang on a little longer. And I wonder what it will mean for the Hadra. Drunk with new power, perhaps these young madmen will think to extend that power westward. Each new generation of Shokarn seems to forget the lessons learned by the last one about the powers of the Hadra or not to believe in them or to consider us a challenge to their manhood. We will need to keep a close eye on all this." Afterward Shaleen actually praised me for my careful observations, something she had never done before.

When I left I was filled with both apprehension and eagerness, turning Cloud in the direction of Suinyari's house. *These two women in my life,* I thought with amusement, *they could hardly have been more different.* It was certainly not Shaleen who worried me at the moment, it was Suinyari.

As I rode toward her house I wondered if she would give me a warm welcome or shut the door in my face. Actually she did neither. She met me at the door, her face closed and wary. Without a word she beckoned me to follow as she walked down the hall. When we were in her bookroom she turned to me and asked, "Are you coming back? Or are you just here to tell me you are leaving me for good?"

"Coming back to live if you will have me." There, I had said the words. Now I knew what it was I was going to do.

"Are you sure?" Her eyes were still guarded and there was as yet no welcome there. I knew what it had cost her pride to even ask that question.

I nodded. "Very sure. The longer I was away the more I missed you."

She nodded in response and was silent for a moment. Then very thoughtfully she said, "And I missed you too, Donya, more than I care to admit. No one has ever had such a hold on my heart. I have never allowed it. At first I tried to tell myself it was good you were gone, that we were too different at the core. I decided you were right, there was no place for you in my life. But I have to say it was the same for me, the longer you were away the more I missed you."

And still she did not reach out to me. It was as if she was waiting for something, maybe we both were, both frozen behind a shield of pride and fear. Forcing myself to speak, I went on, throwing words into the gap between us, "I decided it did not matter to me whether or not I knew anything of your business. And that the differences between us did not really matter so much either."

She gave a shrug. "Ah yes, the differences, that I cannot make you into a Shokarn and in any case would not want to. And you cannot make me into a Hadra no matter how you might wish to do so."

I was about to reach out to her when a sudden thought flashed through my head, no doubt from Suinyari's. "The child? What of the child? Did you…?"

"Yes, the child. We caught her in the market. She is taming nicely although there are still some rough edges. We had a little trouble at first, but now she is even learning sums and letters. You will meet her later. She is out at the market with Alliya."

I caught from Suinyari's mind that a little trouble had been a whirlwind of chaos and destruction and thought I was probably lucky to have been gone for the worst of it. "And Rashindra?"

"She is safe. What made you ask that?"

"You were almost shouting her name."

"Stay out of my head." She stamped her foot and her green eyes flashed anger at me.

I took a step back but could not resist asking, "Did you help to…?"

She interrupted me with a sudden laugh, "Mine to know and yours to guess. I do not have to tell you everything." With that her head slammed shut to me and she gave me a sharp warning look. I thought how beautiful she looked at that moment, staring at me defiantly, challenging my Hadra powers.

I knew then that I would have to be the first one to make the move and it frightened me. I took a deep breath and said very softly, "Show me how much you missed me, Suinyari." With that I leaned forward to kiss her, feeling as if I were leaning across a very deep chasm into which I might fall at any moment and keep falling forever. If she stepped back, I was lost. Instead she stepped forward into the kiss. I brought my arms up around her. With a deep sigh of relief she pressed her whole body into mine. The kiss deepened and deepened. All the longing, all the missing of those past weeks flowed into it. Suddenly my resistance melted away and I remembered what we really were to each other. Soon our hands were moving all over each other's bodies. I felt my knees growing weak and her weight getting heavy in my arms. I think we might well have sunk to the floor and taken each other right there as if we were in her bedchamber with the door shut instead of in a semi-public place, had I not felt a sudden pain in my back. It was as if I had just been stabbed by a sharp thorn or the point of a knife.

With a cry, I turned to see a child standing in the doorway. Had I not been so lost in Suinyari's kiss I would have sensed her presence much sooner. She was glaring at me with such feral ferocity that it sent chills up my back. If not for my Hadra powers I might really have been afraid of her.

Suinyari actually smiled at this little monster. "Come here, Neith.

I want you to meet my dear friend Donyal."

"I know well enough who that is," the girl spit out with a sneer of sullen contempt. Dragging her feet, she shuffled to Suinyari's side, never taking her eyes off me as if I were a snake that had suddenly appeared in her bed. I could see I was going to be subjected to some of those rough edges Suinyari had spoken of. Not a very good beginning surely. Suinyari pretended to ignore all of this and said in a quite serious tone, "Donyal, this is Neith, who is now the daughter in this house."

The girl muttered, "What she means is, here is the street-rat I dragged home."

I did not say, *Glad to meet you, Neith*, could not have forced out the words. Nor did I reach out my hand; she might have tried to bite it. Instead I made myself meet her angry stare with a steady gaze.

"Anyhow my name is not Neith, it is Spider," she said in a furious voice that cracked with an edge of grief.

At that instant I saw her as the child might have looked to Suinyari when she was living on the streets—lonely, hungry, ragged and in despair. Pity slashed open my heart like a knife. I nodded. "Well, Spider, I hope we shall be friends. If that is not possible, then at least not enemies."

Not wanting to shame the girl with a spoken reproach in front of this stranger, Suinyari put a hand on her shoulder and gave it a warning squeeze as if to say, *That is enough now.* We continued staring at each other for a long moment. I thought this awkward silence might go on forever. Fortunately Bethron saved us by appearing to announce that the noon meal was ready. Just as Neith turned to follow Suinyari, she muttered to me out of the side of her mouth, "Not friends."

Life is full of surprises. I had ridden back ready to break off with Suinyari, had even rehearsed the hurtful words I would have to say. Instead I returned to discover a wild child living in the house and was amazed to find myself instantly eaten up with jealousy, a most un-Hadra-like emotion. Suinyari had talked about her interest in this Spider or Neith or whatever she was called, this street-child, but in truth I had thought it was just a whim, a fantasy. I had not really expected her to act on it. I wondered if she had waited for a moment when both Gordivan and I were conveniently away.

I must say, the jealousy was mutual. Whenever Neith was nearby, I could feel the little darts of hatred from her eyes. It was not hard to read her blazing thoughts, especially when I went off to Suinyari's room at night.

Our first meal together was no pleasure. Neith helped Bethron to bring platters from the kitchen. She set everything as close to Suinyari and as far from me as possible until Suinyari looked as if she had a little fortress of food built up around her. Each time Neith set something down with a little thump, she would give me a spiteful look. Suddenly she sniffed the air and looked me up and down insolently. "And what sort of thing are you anyhow? You dress like a man, but you smell like a woman."

"Neith, that is enough! Sit down here with us and mind your mouth." Suinyari tried to sound stern, but a little smile crept into the corners of her mouth and then she burst out laughing. "Well, the child is certainly perceptive even if she has no manners."

Neith scrunched up her face in anger. "I will go sit in the kitchen with Gammo. She cares more about me and never tells me to be silent."

With that she turned to go. Before she could reach her goal she was met in the doorway by Gammo who had obviously heard everything. She gave Neith a look that could have scorched wood. "Find your manners, girl. You shame Suinyari in front of her guest with your rudeness, and you shame the rest of us. Sit there and eat your meal without any more nastiness." Neith sat down abruptly. Gammo served her a plate of food, served herself another and sat by the child. "Now we will have no more of this. Donyal is a member of this house just as you are and must be treated with the same respect." I smiled inwardly. I could see who really had the final word here at Althor House.

Later everyone else left, even Neith after a pointed command from Gammo to come help her in the kitchen. Finally Suinyari and I were alone. She stretched out a hand to me. "If you are willing to tell me I should like to hear of your trip south."

She was asking, giving me a choice. I nodded and then told her everything I had observed about the men training in the great meadows. At the end I added, "They are young and inexperienced, not very skilled at combat, but frighteningly earnest, passionate even, and very full of anger. There are many Grayrobes among them, giving spiritual support, validating their hate, making them feel they have a sacred mission. The surprise to me was the older men, Highborn by the look of them, who were there too. The most visible of them was Lord Tarkin. He seemed almost as much in control as Gunjorn himself. I think they mean to use these young men to their own ends. They themselves hardly appear to be Purifiers. I cannot imagine that they share those beliefs."

Suinyari nodded, looking thoughtful, even worried. "Thinking they can control the outcome, they probably hope to use these Purifiers to get themselves into a position of power over the old Zarn's loyal followers. I doubt they have any idea what forces they are toying with. I very much fear they will find themselves plowed under in the chaos that follows after letting loose these creatures on the rest of us."

"Maybe it is time to leave here, Suinyari."

"Leave and go where? This is the only life I know and the only place I know. All my connections are here, my livelihood is here. I will just have to hope I can ride out this storm as I have ridden out so many others."

I shook my head. "Not likely this time. Why not come back to Ishlair with me if things get much worse here?"

"And be a Shokarn among the Hadra, powerless among women with powers. Would you go back if you had lost all your powers?"

Losing my powers was not something I even wished to contemplate though I knew it was a risk I took by living among the Draiga. "Of course. I would still be a Hadra," I answered sharply. "A bird that cannot fly is still a bird."

"Is it? I doubt that very much. Let us hope you never have to test that theory. I am telling you quite clearly, I will not go live among the Hadra. Do not ask me again. Now tell me, how did you observe so much without getting seen or caught?"

I grinned at her. "Mine to know, yours to guess. We Hadra also have our secrets."

She grinned back at me, then took my hand and drew me to my feet. "I think we need to go share another kind of secret and finish what was so rudely interrupted." I had no argument with that and followed willingly where she led. My body was already humming and burning. I had been away much too long.

Later, when I asked the others about Neith, they all had a different opinion. Bethron told me with a sniff of disapproval, "Suinyari brought her home in spite of our advice. You are lucky you stayed away so long, you missed the worst of it. She was like a wild animal let loose in this house. It is a surprise there is a single dish or glass left in one piece. I thought she was going to bring the walls down around us before she was done." Alliya with her eternal kindness said, "There is a warm heart under all that roughness. She only needs a little more patience." Torvil nodded, "Yes, she raised the roof, I can tell you that. She is not much for manners that one, but except for you, she is the best hand with horses I have ever seen. Besides Dondo likes her." And Gammo laughed, saying, "She is not so bad. She reminds me of my own wild, angry self when I was young. And she has tamed down nicely. She even makes herself useful here."

After that first hard beginning, Neith and I settled into a sort of surly truce. When Gordivan came home it was a different matter. He set out to charm her. Much to my surprise he succeeded. He flattered her and teased her and gave her little trinkets from his trip. He told her stories. He made her feel special and important. Soon she was following him about, asking his opinion on this or that and demanding more tales about his travels. Suinyari and I watched all this with amazement, along with a mix of resentment and relief. Soon all her talk was peppered with Gordivan's name till we grew quite sick of it.

A few weeks after I came back, I was in Suinyari's study examining a map of the city with a magnifying glass when Neith suddenly appeared. I had not heard her coming or sensed her presence. Dondo, who had been sleeping at my feet, only raised his head at the last moment. Just as I was bracing myself for another attack of rudeness, Neith surprised me by saying, "Donyal, you are more like me than any of the others in this house. I have given it much thought; I know who you are. You are one of the wild ones they tell tales about in the market. You are a Hadra."

Shocked by her words I asked sharply, "What makes you think that?"

"I watch and I listen when no one knows I am there."

I could easily picture her slipping unseen into rooms or hiding in dark corners. There were probably few secrets in the house she was not aware of.

I felt a little tremor of fear. This child could hurt me. "It is not safe for others in the city to know this. It might endanger my life; surely it would endanger Suinyari's."

"Your secret is safe with me. I know how to keep my silence on things; I have done it all my life. Donyal, I need to ask you something. They all call me Neith in this house, thinking to better tame me. I want you to keep calling me Spider so I can still remember who I was."

I nodded. "I can do that easily enough. Is that the price of your silence?"

"No, I would keep my silence no matter what you called me, for Suinyari's sake if nothing else." She took another step closer, put a hand on my arm and looked me in the eye. I could see tears at the edge of her eyes. "But there is something else. I want you to help me find my birth mother. No one here will tell me anything. You go about the city and have many contacts. Ask some questions for me." Before I could answer she slipped away and was gone as quietly as she had come.

Later, when I asked Suinyari about Spider's mother, she shook her head. "I know where she is, but she is not ready yet to see the child. Best to let it be."

I felt like a traitor to Spider, but after all I had only been asked, I had not given my Hadra word on it. I did however remember to call her Spider in spite of Suinyari's frown. I knew how important it was to have one's real self acknowledged. That was the least I could do for the child.

Mother Melna

It was a long time before I heard the story of Rashindra's escape in her own words. By then we had already renamed her Rhosharn and totally changed her appearance. Of course I had already heard Suinyari's version, told with much laughter, some of it probably a cover for her fear. In spite of the risky way she lived her life I doubt that Suinyari had ever done such a daring and dangerous thing before. Each time I had asked Rhosharn what had happened she just shook her head and kept her silence.

Rhosharn mostly went about her work among us with quiet efficiency, but there was a stiffness in all her motions, a deadness in her eyes that hurt me to see. I almost never heard the sound of her voice. Then, almost a month after she first came to us, as we were gathering eggs together, she began to speak, very softly at first, almost in a whisper, "Hard to believe, he would have had me killed—almost did too. I had heard stories about the last one, but he promised me he would send me home safely and with enough money to do some good for my family and for the farm. I believed him. I thought he loved me or at least was fond of me. That was what he told me over and over. He kept saying I made him feel so good. Goddess knows I did my best. Not that I knew much about such things when I first came there, but there was a woman at the palace who taught me; it was her job. I learned fast and I was eager to please. And really he was not such a bad man, not like everyone says. I saw another side of him. He could laugh and make little jokes. He could even be tender and very sweet sometimes."

I had to bite my tongue. *Ah yes, so tender and sweet he would have had your throat cut for the sake of his vanity. Tender and sweet? Tell that to the people rotting in his dungeons or the ones hanging at this very moment on his death-posts.* But I kept my silence. We each have our own reality. I nodded to encourage her to go on.

"I tried my best. It was not my fault if he could not always…you know. After all he was an old man and those parts get tired just like the rest of the body. At those times he would get very angry with me and shout and sometimes even hit me, though he was always sorry later. Then we would try again and usually it would happen. When he was well satisfied he would give me little gifts and whisper things to me that made me blush.

"Then, one day, with no warning, he told me I was about to be replaced. I cried and begged, but he said it was too late, it was done. He already had a new woman. With seeming regret he told me, 'I promised your family I would send you home at the end of the second year. I hate to have you leave me, but I need to keep my word to your people.' All lies of course, every bit of it, terrible heartless lies when I think of what happened later."

Hearing her talk I suddenly understood why he needed her dead. It would not do to let the Zarn's lover live and tell tales of him that showed his weaknesses and made him not so different from ordinary men, ordinary feeble old men. Better to silence her forever. And easy enough to do, or so he thought. "And then what happened?" I asked softly. She had stopped and was staring off into the distance.

She gave a little tremor and seemed to come back to herself. "Then he had me pack everything, even the dresses he had given me, even the jewels. I never thought I would get to keep all that. I thought it was only for my time at the palace. 'But I will have nowhere to wear such things, not on the farm.' I protested.

"'Take it all with you. You never know what may happen in your life. I gave you those things. They are my gifts to you. I want you to have them.' Little did I know that his only gift to me was going to be death and he planned to gain back all his gifts, maybe for the next one."

I shivered. The horror of all this chilled me beyond belief. When I nodded again, Rhosharn said, "After that he sent me riding off with two nice young guards, a horse for me and an extra horse to carry my things. Sad as I was to have been replaced I was excited to think that I would soon see my family again and very pleased to be bringing them some money, more than they had ever seen in their lives.

"As we rode the guards joked with me and sang songs and shared out the food one of the cooks had sent with us. I learned that the dark-haired one was named Arn. He was the leader and slightly older. The younger one with the crooked nose and straw-colored hair was Danuth.

"Under all that pleasantry there was something strange in their manner, something evasive and secretive, but I really suspected nothing bad as we rode through the day, not until that afternoon when they left the road we had been following west, the one that went home to my village. Suddenly we took the fork north instead. When I questioned them they grew very nervous. Then Arn turned to Danuth and said, 'This is probably far enough. We could just take her into the woods here.'

"Suddenly I understood. It had all been lies to keep me docile and cooperative. They were not taking me home after all. This was about to be the end of my life. With a cry I kicked my horse and tried to make it run, but there was a rope tied to Danuth's saddle, for safety they had explained to me though I told them that as a farm girl I knew very well how to ride. Now I understood the reason for that too. Though there seemed to be no one around at that moment I screamed as loudly as I could.

"Before they could get their hands on me a woman in a long dark cape and high yellow hair stepped out into the road. She had appeared suddenly from behind a large tree that blocked the curve of the road from sight and she began calling out plaintively, 'Help us, please help us,' as she came hobbling toward us. 'We are in terrible trouble. The horses got stung by bees and ran off with our carriage. The coachman fell out and died of a broken neck. Now the carriage is mired and we are stranded here. My husband is also badly injured. Without help we may die in this place. I have no idea what to do. I have never handled such things before. My husband always takes care of everything and now I am all alone. You have to help us! Please!' With every sentence her voice got a little shriller and more hysterical. She seemed to totally ignore my screams and my plight. Instead she focused her large dark eyes on my captors, first one and then the other.

"Danuth seemed tempted. Arn said sharply, 'We are on a mission for the Zarn. We cannot dally here.'

"'I am Lady Aldernith, a great friend of the Zarn's, may his reign go on forever. It will not go well for you if it is discovered that you abandoned me here. And you look to be strong young men. It will only take you a moment or two to free the carriage. Then possibly I could drive it back to safety and get help for my husband. Please, I beg of you."

"Arn finally said with a shrug, 'It can do no harm to look. Come with me, Danuth, and keep tight hold of her horse.'

"If I had not been about to die I might have been tempted to laugh at such craziness. Here they were about to kill me and instead they were stopping to rescue this ridiculous woman. I hoped there might be some way to escape in the confusion, but Danuth pulled my horse close to his and kept me right next to him.

"As the lady in front of us hobbled along, groaning with pain and holding her side, I suddenly noticed that her boots were men's boots and very large for a woman. At that moment she turned and took hold of the reins of Arn's horse, saying, 'Hurry! Please hurry! My husband may be dying right now.' Her voice was full of a terrible urgency, yet she seemed to be holding him back, slowing him down instead of pulling him forward.

"The next moment we went under a limb of the tree that supposedly hid the carriage from view. There was a rustling in the leaves. Then a body dropped straight down from the branch onto Danuth's horse, landing in back of him and wrapping a choking arm around his neck. At the same time the helpless, hysterical woman who had been leading us, shed her cape with one jerk of her arm and became in that instant a man with a raised sword and a yellow wig. "Off your horse if you want to live," he told Arn. Two more men leapt out of the ditch and pulled Danuth from his horse. In no time at all my two captors found themselves standing in the middle of the road, disarmed and with their hands tied behind them.

"'Brigands,' Arn said with disgust. 'We have been captured by brigands before we could carry out our mission for the Zarn.'

"'Good, that is what you will tell the Zarn when next you meet with him, tell him you were captured by brigands and your captive was stolen right out of your hands. Tell him that you were lured to your downfall by a lovely lady in distress. Too bad it will take you a while to walk back as we will have to take your horses with us. We cannot risk having you follow us or causing any problems.'

"This person who had dropped from the tree branch was dressed like a man, but she had a woman's voice. She was sporting a little black mustache and a frightful black wig of the kind people wear on turnabout day. I saw that her face might have been pretty if she had not added some ugly, thick, dark eyebrows. The man who had started out as a woman still wore the high blond wig which gave him a very droll appearance, though I was not ready yet to laugh at anything. I was not sure if these people were my salvation or only another kind of trouble.

"Arn shook his head. 'We cannot go back, not now. We were told to kill her and to bring back her little finger with his ring for proof. He said she was young and pretty, that she would likely plead for her life and we might be tempted. Without that proof we cannot afford to go back.'

"The woman gave a harsh laugh. 'Well, now that is a pretty story. That Zarn is always full of charming surprises.' The man in the yellow wig, the 'lovely lady,' aimed his sword at Arn as if he meant to finish him off. So did one of the men from the ditch, but the woman shook her head. 'No use to add two bodies to this mess. People ask questions about bodies and it takes too much time to bury them. Besides they are finished as guards. They cannot go back to Eezore, not if the Zarn is expecting a little finger with a ring to be presented to him.'

"With a shudder I pulled the ring from my finger and tried to throw it away. The woman caught it out of the air. 'No use to leave that here for someone to find and be curious about.' With a quick turn of her wrist she put it in the red pouch she wore at her waist. Then she swung onto one of the horses that had been tied beyond the tree. There was no carriage there, of course. To the two men from the ditch she said, 'Hold them until we have been gone for a while, then send them on their way and bring the extra horses. We will have to doctor their appearance a little before they are salable.' To me she said, 'Will you ride with us now?'

"I felt a little shiver of fear. What if they wanted me for some terrible purpose? I tried to look into her eyes and see what was there, but the combination of the wig, the mustache and those outrageous eyebrows just made me want to laugh. 'Are you really brigands? And what do you want with me?'

"'To save your life, that is all.' Then she shook her head. 'No, not brigands, not in the way you mean it, though we may have to take this baggage of yours and deal with it to our profit. But rest assured, you will come to no harm at our hands. We will take you to a safe place. We cannot take you home to your village. When the Zarn realizes that you are not dead he may send someone to look for you there.'"

With those words Rhosharn set down her egg basket and turned to look at me. For the first time I saw a little life in her face, some spark in her eyes and a touch of color in her cheeks. "And that is how I came here. Before we reached the city gate they stopped. The man put the yellow wig on my head and pulled the dark cape around me so I would not be known. I never got to see what he looked like since he turned away and put on a large dark hat that almost covered his face."

"Do you know who they are?"

"No, I have no idea, only that the woman had a little red hair showing under her black wig."

"Say nothing of that part to anyone. It could be dangerous."

Then I told Rhosharn the story of the mysterious finger since I thought she had a right to know. "Shortly after you came to us I had heard through a friend who works at the palace that a package had been delivered at the palace door. The one leaving it said it was for the Zarn and no one else. His face was well concealed and he disappeared before the guards could grab him. Then the package was brought to the Minister in case there was something dangerous in it. The Minister and several of the council members and some guards were all assembled in the Council Chamber along with the Zarn when the Minister opened the package. He took out a bundle of cloth and when he unwound it a human finger dropped out on the table. It was of a size to be the little finger of a young woman. On it was a wide band of gold dotted with bright red rubies that looked like tiny drops of blood.

So you see you are officially dead as far as the Zarn is concerned."

"But who…"

I shrugged. "Someone already dead who sacrificed a very small part of themselves for the living."

"Who would do such a thing?" She sounded shocked.

I shrugged again. "Better not to ask. Just accept the gift." Then I gave her a big grin. "Rashindra is dead. Welcome to life, Rhosharn."

She gave me an uncertain little smile. Then, suddenly, her face lit up, she threw back her head and laughed. It was a young woman's wild, boisterous laugh. I had not heard her laugh since she had come among us and it warmed my heart. "Life after death is not so bad after all," she said grinning back at me. Then she gave me a crafty look. "And whatever happened to all those valuable belongings that were traveling with me?"

"We had the Thieves Guild convert everything to coins and take their cut for the service. After that, part went for your upkeep here, part was given to your parents, a large share went to 'the brigands' for their daring work that day and some has been set aside for you in case you decide to leave this place."

Rosharn shook her head and looked thoughtful. "Strange brigands, they could have kept it all. They certainly earned it. I would not grudge them one cent of it. If not for them, I was as good as dead."

"They are fair; they got their share of it."

"How is it that you know thieves and brigands and all that sort of folk? You seem so…" She appeared to be struggling for the right word.

"So what? So pure? So innocent? Is that what you are trying to say? Perhaps I am the biggest thief of all. I steal women from their homes and off the streets and out of brothels and I make a place for them here. For that I need a lot of help and a lot of money. I am not too particular where it comes from. But enough of all this. Best not to talk of it. There are too many ears about, too many things hidden in crevices that it might be dangerous to have revealed in the light."

Rhosharn picked up the egg basket again. She looked me right in the eye and nodded. "I like it here. Not as fancy as the palace, but more to my taste. I think I will stay for a while."

Spider

After I finally made my peace with Suinyari, I came to depend on her, not as a mother exactly, but as the center of my little world, the most important person in my life, and in my own way I tried hard to please her. One could even have imagined that I had begun to settle down. I am sure that is what Suinyari thought, so this next part fills me with such shame I find it hard to write. I can feel the flush rising to my face at this very moment. But it is part of my story so I will try my best to tell it honestly.

There was a period when Suinyari was away much of the time or so it seemed to me, gone on errands for the business to other parts of the city or even beyond, sometimes even to Pellor or Maktesh. Then I was left in the care of the rest of the household. I felt they did not have much love for me and I resented Suinyari's absence. Had she not said she would try to be a mother to me though she had little skill at hugging and holding? And now she was abandoning me just like my own mother. Never mind that Suinyari was nothing like my mother and had provided for me in every way she could, I still resented her absence. I also resented her presence since this street-rat, this market-trash, felt so unworthy of it. Under my surface compliance the old hurts still festered, spreading their poison. This child, who had owned nothing and now had so much, wanted everything. Ingratitude could have been my name at that time. I was a glutton of insatiable needs with an ugly monster of resentment sitting in the middle of my heart. In truth, even her loving made me angry. It made my heart ache and since I never had a heart before, somehow I blamed Suinyari for my pain.

In one of Suinyari's many times away—when Donyal and Gordivan were also out of the house—I evaded Bethron's watchful eye to slip into Suinyari's room. There I was, trying on some of her embroidered vests in front of the mirror, parading my image back and forth in the reflection. Afterward I found myself idly poking around at the things on her bureau. I was taking lids off jars in search of some face paint when I made a sudden unexpected find, a pot full of money, gold coins to be exact. I gave a gasp of surprise. Shivers of greed went up and down my spine. Thrusting my hands in among the coins, I lifted them up and let them run through my fingers. I loved the cool weight of them and the soft clinking music they made.

Now, before you judge too harshly, you must remember that I was a child of the streets. I had trained myself, or been trained by circumstance, to take advantage of every possibility that came my way in order to stay alive. In my whole life I had only seen a few gold coins and here was a whole pot of them right under my hands, there for the taking. I felt a rush of rage at Suinyari for carelessly leaving them out that way, conveniently forgetting for the moment that they had been in a closed pot and I had unscrewed the lid, forgetting too that I had been snooping uninvited in her room. I wondered angrily if she was testing me or if she had so much gold she could afford to be careless of such things.

Surely, I thought, she would not miss a few coins out of so many. I pocketed a few coins and then a few more. Then I replaced the lid and slipped out of her room, feeling both very clever and very guilty. The next day, when she still had not come back, I took a few more coins as if to punish her for her absence. And the next day, after a big argument with Bethron about all the books and cushions I had left out on the floor, I snuck in and took the whole lot, stuffing my little pack with gold. My quarrel with Bethron had ended with my yelling at her, "You are not my mother! You have no right to tell me anything!" and her slapping me across the face. At that moment, with my face still stinging from that slap, I decided that everyone in the house hated me, Suinyari most of all. I convinced myself that she was staying away until I left and justified taking the gold so I could live on the streets again. I was able to slip down the back stairs and out the kitchen door without anyone seeing me. Then Torvil spotted me from the stable and waved. I did not wave back. I was done with those people. If they did not care for me then I did not care for them either.

The instant I was on the street I knew it was all a big mistake. Pride and stubbornness kept me going. Several times in the next few days I saw Gordivan out looking for me and thought of surrendering, but each time I slipped away and hid from him. I will not say much about that time on the streets except that it was dreadful—punishment enough for my bad deeds. I felt keenly all the discomforts I had been numb to before, the filth in the streets, the danger, the hunger and thirst, the hard dirty ground, the lack of any way to keep clean or relieve myself. It was not so easy to steal food now. The pack with the weight of all that gold was an encumbrance and I no longer had my gray rags for concealment. It was like a cruel joke to be carrying a fortune in gold on my back and not even be able to buy food. Once I tried to buy bread with a gold coin. When the baker asked where I had gotten it, I blushed and stammered. He shouted, "Thief!" and chased me down the street. I even thought of going to the Thieves Guild to trade my gold for spendable copper, but I knew too little of numbers to make such a deal. On the third day I finally decided I had had enough.

It was dusk, not a time when I would usually be out. The decision was made for me by the thought of trying—one more time—to find a safe place for the night. I would rather go home and face a beating if that was what it came to. I hoped that Suinyari had not yet discovered my theft. Maybe I could just replace the coins secretly and be done with them. They had certainly become a burden on my back. With my mind so preoccupied by worries I was not using my street alertness.

They came very suddenly, four of them, boys a little older than me who were skilled in ambush. I never heard them, never even saw them until they were on me. "Give us the pack easy and we let you go. Hold on to it, I slice you up and we get it anyhow." He had a grip on my arm and a knife in his hand, but I still had some of my old street skills. I was very desperate to hold on to what I had. It was my ticket home.

With a scream I jerked out of his hold. Then I clawed, bit, kicked and punched anyone who came near me, shouting the whole time, "Help! Assassins!" Finally I tried to run, but there were just too many of them. They soon had me down on the ground with one kicking me in the ribs while another cut the pack straps. They might have finished me off if someone had not opened their door just then and shouted, "Stop that noise!" At that they ran off in one direction while I scrambled to my feet and dragged myself off in the other.

That night, not much caring about safety, I found an alley to crawl into and cried myself to sleep. Suinyari's house was closed to me; now I could never go back. It was so close, only a few streets away, but so far it might as well have been in another city. I was not sure how I was going to get up to face another day of this miserable existence and then another.

This time Gordivan saw me at almost the same time that I saw him. Suddenly he was running toward me with his long, easy strides, shouting, "Neith, wait!" In that instant I slipped into a crevice between two buildings thinking I could slip out the other side and disappear before he could run around the building. Unfortunately I had eaten too much of Suinyari's good food. I was no longer the skinny little Spider of the streets. Hard as I tried there was no way I could get through. Gordivan instantly came and placed himself in front of the opening making a dark shadow there. "I know you are in there, Neith. I am not leaving until we talk."

"Go away, leave me alone. Even if I die here I am not coming out until you leave."

"Well, that may be a long and boring way to die."

"When I get thin enough I will slip out the other side and you will never know. You will be left standing there like a fool. Now leave me be. This is no affair of yours."

"It certainly is. Suinyari has sent me out every day to look for you while she waits at home in case you return on your own. I am getting tired of playing tag with you all over this city. You are coming back with me today."

"I can never go back," I said with a sudden sob. "I was on my way to bring back the money I took from her and then it got stolen from me by some older boys. They beat me and cut the pack from my back. Now it is too late to go home. Now I can never make amends so Suinyari had best forget about her gold."

"It is not gold she weeps for every night when she tries to sleep. She is afraid she did you some unkindness that made you run away. Her heart is breaking. Come back with me so she can be happy again and there can be some peace in the house."

"It is not worth breaking her heart over me. I am a thief and a liar and probably always will be so her love is wasted here."

"Well, then come out for my sake so I can get a decent meal. She told me that if I come home again without you I will be sent to bed with only bread and water for my dinner."

This made me laugh and when I laughed it made my ribs hurt where I had been kicked. Gordivan could always make me laugh; it was one of his gifts. Suddenly it all seemed very silly. Why was I standing out in the street, crammed into a dark crevice, arguing with Gordivan, when I could go home to a hot meal and sleep in my own clean bed that night? Most of all I wanted to see Suinyari's face again and beg her forgiveness.

"All right, but only for the sake of your dinner," I said with seeming reluctance. When I tried to get out, I found I could not move. I was wedged fast between the rough stones. At the price of my pride I had to ask Gordivan for help. He laughed uproariously at the thought of my being stuck there. When I saw his hand reach in and grope around, I was suddenly tempted to sink my teeth into it. He must have heard my thoughts for he said loudly, "Take my hand. If you bite me, I leave you here to die." I took his hand and he pulled while I sucked in my breath, trying very hard to be thin enough. Still it took a lot of grunting and tugging to get me out. By then my clothes were shredded and tears were running down my face from the pain in my ribs.

Dondo met us at the door wagging his tail furiously. With a bark of welcome he bounded at me. When he put his big paws up on my chest to lick my face, I gave a cry from the pain in my chest and ribs. Gordivan pulled him down for me. I bent to hug and pet the dog, but it was Suinyari I needed to see. Gordivan brought me straightway to her bedroom. She had been lying down. At the sight of me she leapt up instantly, rushed over, grabbed me up in her arms and whirled me around. I was in pain again, but I did not care. I had never seen Suinyari so demonstrative. "Oh, Neith, you frightened me so. What happened to you? Who did that to your face? You must never, never run off that way again. Whatever possessed you, child? Did I do something so bad you could not stay here anymore?"

The moment she set me down I started talking, words pouring out of me as if they would never stop. "Not you, Suinyari, it was me, I was bad. I was angry that you were away so much and I found the gold and ran off with it and then I was trying to bring it back to you when some bigger boys caught me and beat me and stole it from me and then I knew for sure I could never come back, but Gordivan found me and told me that I must and that you were very sad and so I came with him and now I am so sorry for all the pain I caused you and maybe I can work somewhere and earn some money so I can pay it all back."

"Slow down, Neith, I cannot follow your story. What gold are you talking about?"

"The gold in the pot. I was trying on vests and then I wanted to put on some face paint and I found it."

Gordivan gasped, "That gold!" It seemed to me for a moment that Suinyari went very white and her hands shook. Quickly she turned her back to me, went to the pot and opened the lid. She stayed that way, staring into the empty pot, for a long while. I was afraid to breathe, afraid of what she would say, but when she turned back there was color in her face again, and she was smiling. "So you found my little stash of counterfeit coins. That was play money for the next banquet we were planning, tin covered with gold paint. Now we will not be able to shower it on our guests from the balcony. What a shame. But of course they will never know what they missed. Now I suppose my false coins will be floating around the market instead, causing all sorts of trouble. I hope you did not try to pass any."

Too confused to find the right words, I merely shook my head. I saw a quick look pass between Suinyari and Gordivan that I could not fathom. "Are you going to punish me for what I did?" I asked anxiously and was embarrassed to hear the quaver in my voice.

"No, I think someone else has done too good a job of that already. Let me put some healing salve on those cuts."

As she daubed my cuts she spoke very softly to me as if her words were for my ears alone. "I am sorry you were angry at my long absence, Neith, but sometimes I have no choice; I need to be gone on the business that keeps food on our table. Find some other way besides stealing to speak your anger. When your mother abandoned you on the streets, you had to teach yourself to steal in order to survive. It kept you alive from day to day. Here we are honest with each other in order to survive and it keeps us alive from day to day. We may be a house full of smugglers, some would say not much better than thieves, but we must be able to trust each other. If we stole from one another the house would fall apart in mistrust and quarreling and we could not manage. You are a member of this house now. Remember that if you are ever tempted to put your hand in the jar again."

Thinking I deserved far worse, I stood very still against the sting of the salve and the sting of her words. Everything she said was true. When she finished she asked almost casually, "These boys who beat you and took the coins, do you remember anything about them?"

"There were four of them. It was dusk and they had their faces covered so I hardly saw them. I just remember that one had a limp and another was very big, man-sized really, though he acted like a boy. One was called Toad and another Ghost. Those were the only two names I heard and I have no idea which was which. That is all I know."

It seemed very little, but Suinyari nodded and said with satisfaction, "Good, now we shall see what we can do with that information."

Gordivan coughed as if to remind us he was still there and indeed I had almost forgotten. At that Suinyari grabbed my hand and said gaily. "Come, let us go eat. You must be starving from your little adventure. I am too. I have scarcely eaten since I knew you were missing. And Gordivan should have quite an appetite from chasing you all around Eezore for days."

We went down together to eat a grand meal. Food had never tasted so good. Everyone from the house was there, even Torvil who had also been out looking for me. Only Donyal was late. When she came in she seemed much relieved to see me. She gave Gordivan a wink and a meaningful look as she took her place. I wondered if she had been out looking for me as well. I was very glad she did not choose to comment on my absence. She only gave me a little nod of acknowledgment before she started eating. I understood that she was leaving me my pride.

There was silence for a while, at least no words, only the sound of silver against china and the munching of food. Glancing around at all their caring faces, I knew I would never be so foolish again. I really had come home at last.

Mother Melna

Sometimes I see the child on the street. I watch her with curiosity, wondering what she thinks of this new life of hers. But I try to keep myself out of sight and of course I do not speak to her. That would be meddling; it is not yet time. She looks so different now with a clean face, new clothes and her red-brown hair curling softly around her face instead of standing up in a wild matted tangle. She wears real boots rather than rags wrapped around her feet and she walks with confidence, no longer skulking around.

I wish we could bring Neith to the House of the Mother for teaching, but it is not yet time for that either; soon enough I hope. When I ask Suinyari how she is doing she smiles and tells me proudly, "She is filling out so fast it is hard to keep clothes on her back. She is even learning to read and do sums and has become a real help in the house." Anyone with eyes can see how the child is growing and how well she looks, but I know from talking to Bethron that

Neith caused Suinyari and indeed everyone in that house a rash of trouble and heartbreak. That seems to be over now. I think Suinyari was too proud to say anything about it. I had warned her that Neith might be more than she could handle. She was so set on it there was no dissuading her. Now I am very glad she did it. Poor Suinyari, I hope this child does not break her heart. With my far-knowing I see Neith already set on a course that will take her out of that house and far away from here but I keep my silence on it.

Suinyari

That pot of gold coins was our cache, our stash, our escape money, our "in case money," such as in case we got a warning from the Thieves Guild that the Zarn's guards were on their way, about to raid the house and take us all away to the dungeon. It had to be kept somewhere close and accessible, someplace where any of us could lay our hands on it in an instant. We all knew where it was kept. I trusted the others in my household as much as I trusted myself. That Neith would come on it by accident had never occurred to me, though it should have if I had just stopped to think about it, but I was still not used to having a child about the house.

That gold was our security in a not very secure existence. I was in the habit of checking on it every few days. Interestingly enough, with Neith's disappearance, I had not once thought of it. I had been too frantic with worry about the child, confused and mystified too as to why she would run off that way. I had sent everyone out looking for her. Some folk in the Thieves Guild had spotted her quickly enough. She was not so good at hiding anymore, but I wanted Gordivan to be the one to bring her back. And I wanted her to be willing, not returned to me by force.

It was only when Neith started talking so frantically about the gold that I thought to look in the cache pot. I almost fainted when I saw it was empty. In that instant I understood everything she had been saying, more in fact than I wanted to know.

How would we ever replace it? And what if we needed it soon? It had taken us quite a while to accumulate such a sum. Much of our wealth was tied up in goods that could not be quickly turned to cash. I had to keep my face turned away so Neith did not see my expression of distress. It would not do to let her know the truth. I was afraid that guilt and shame would drive her into running off again. This time I might not find her so easily, might not find her at all. By the time I had myself enough under control to turn back I had thought of a charming lie. I flashed Gordivan a warning look not to contradict me. Meanwhile my mind was already at work on getting the gold back.

Luckily Neith had given me enough of a description so those boys could be traced. I sent Bethron out to find Makelmac of the Thieves Guild. We had traded favors over the years and been friends of a sort. The last favor had been a plus on my side. I had saved his life when he had gotten himself into a bad scrape, bribing his jailer so that he made his escape before he could be taken off to the dungeon. Makelmac was a strange-looking man with only one eye, one leg shorter than the other and a badly twisted back. He had been a randy young Highborn by the name of Makian before some girl's father had decided to teach him a permanent lesson. Somehow he had managed to survive. Afterward he joined the Thieves Guild. With his clever mind he became a threat to every honest household in the city, starting of course with the man who had crippled him.

That night he came to my back door wrapped in a dark cloak. When I told him my problem he shrugged and said lightly, "No problem at all, Lady. Rest your mind easy on it. I know just the boys we are looking for. Old Makelmac even knows where to find them. They have been doing a little foolish bragging." Two days later we got back most of the gold, minus of course the Thieves Guild commission. I never asked Makelmac what methods he used and likely I was happier not knowing. As soon as it was in my hands I replaced the gold in its hiding place. Except for Gordivan, no one else in the house knew it had been gone or that Neith had taken it. Next I called Neith into my room, lifted the lid on the pot and showed her the stash of coins. Her eyes went wide at the sight. "It is all safely back where it belongs now. This is only for emergencies, Neith. It should not be touched otherwise."

She nodded and gave me a long thoughtful look. "It was never pretend money, was it?" It was more of a statement than a question.

"No, but I was afraid if you knew the truth you would…"

She interrupted me. "I never believed it was. I saw the look on your face just before you turned away. But thank you for the lie; I understand that it was kindly meant. Suinyari, I promise you I will never touch that money or anything else of value in the house. And I will not run off that way again, you have my word." I heard the truth in her voice. At that moment she looked so serious and unchildlike it nearly broke my heart.

Two good things came of that incident. One was that Makelmac and I renewed our old connection and did several mutually profitable dealings. The other was that Neith became good, at least for a while—considerate, thoughtful, helpful, even polite as much as she was able. I have to say it was a great relief. It also worried me a little.

For this moment at least I have a family of sorts—a husband, a lover and a child. Though it was a little rough at first, now it all seems to be coming together quite smoothly. When I visit Mother Melna at the House of the Mother she says she is happy for me. I have my own doubts about whether such luck can last. And of course we both have our fears about the future of Eezore and what such changes could mean for all of us.

Part II

Spider

I had lived in Suinyari's house for more than a year and was well content. I had everything I needed there: food, clothes, a dry roof, love. Occasionally I even had some little bit of work to do; Suinyari had begun using me as an occasional messenger. Though still not riding, I was learning my way around the city, trusting my feet to keep me safe. Gordivan and Donyal and even Suinyari were often away, but I had finally learned to trust they would come back—though the last time Donyal was gone so long I thought she had left for good. I was surprised at how much I missed her. Without my even noticing it, she had actually become part of my life.

Poor Suinyari, she wanted so much to be my mother, but she had no skill for it. It was not her trade. In terms of affection Gammo was more my mother than Suinyari could ever be. As for my birth mother, I had finally stopped looking for her, though occasionally I would still dream of her. On those mornings I would wake strangely troubled and confused. Sometimes I would go to Alliya for comfort, sometimes even Suinyari.

Perhaps I was not exactly the daughter Suinyari had longed for, but at least I was becoming "less hostile, more trusting and compliant" or something like that. Those were the words I overheard her saying to Gammo. With a secure place in Suinyari's home, my years as a market waif were beginning to fade. And yet, though I had learned new ways of walking and talking and dressing and moving about in the world, I had not altogether lost my animal wariness. I still carried a little knife hidden on me when I went out into the streets.

That memorable morning I was shopping on Strathorn Street, looking for a shawl for Suinyari to give to her friend Drusia on her nameday. I liked to run errands for Suinyari; it made me feel important or at least useful. I spent a lot of time looking at every shawl in the shop. Finally I settled on a very soft one in a sort of rose color with purple flowers. It had caught my fancy and I hoped Suinyari would like it.

The moment I stepped out of the shop I was aware of one of those yellow-robed nuns from the House of the Mother, lurking in a doorway. She was watching me strangely. I sensed her as much as saw her. Then I remembered that I had passed a Yellowrobe on my way into the shop. At the time I had thought nothing of it. Now a shiver went up my back as I recalled stories I had heard of the nuns snatching women off the street. I had already been snatched once and had landed right where I wanted to be. I had no wish to be snatched again.

Totally alert, giving no sign that I saw her, not even glancing in her direction, I walked to the corner. Turning down the next street I quickly ducked into an alley from which I could watch the street without being seen. I had vanished nearly as fast and neatly as Spider herself might have done. I slipped my knife out of my sleeve and held it ready. Soon I heard rapid footsteps. Almost immediately that nun appeared at the corner. She turned all about in bewilderment, looking up and down the streets. Then she threw back her hood to see better. For the first time I saw her face clearly. With a cry I jumped out of hiding, shouting, "Imalia! Mother!" The last thing in the world I would have expected to see was my mother in a nun's robe.

She opened her arms; I rushed to her and threw myself into them. For just that instant I was a child again, safe in my mother's arms. She crushed me against her robe and held me tight. After a moment or two of such closeness my nose began to itch against that rough fabric. Also I remembered who I had become, how good my life was—and with no help from her. Pushing myself away, I stood looking at her, the first time I had really seen her in six years. She looked much stronger and healthier than I remembered. Her eyes were clear, her skin fresh and clean. Though she seemed about to cry, her face no longer had that familiar pinched and haunted look.

"When I never saw you anymore I thought you had died, but now I see you looking very well indeed," I said sharply. Much as I had missed her, I suppose I had never forgiven her for deserting me that way. My words, innocent enough in content, were full of angry accusation.

"I also thought you dead. I grieved for you until Mother Melna told me you were living at Suinyari's house."

"But you did not come there looking for me."

"Well…no…I…" Her words faltered. Her face flushed and she looked away ashamed, seeming about to cry. Then, taking a deep breath, she gathered herself together and slipped her arm through mine. "Come sit with me and tell me everything that has happened in your life."

I tried to pull away. "I am on an errand for Suinyari," I said holding up my bundle. "And I must go back." Out of some perverse cruelty I almost said "my real mother." At the last moment I bit back the words.

"Come now," Imalia said with a nervous little laugh. "The Lady will not grudge you a short talk with your mother."

With my heart so full of a mix of rage and love I thought it would burst, I let myself be led along Strathorn Street until we found a stone bench and sat down under some trees. It took a while of urging for me to get past my resentment. Then, in a sudden rush of words, I told her everything: my hard years on the streets, being snatched from the market, the strangeness at first of Suinyari's house and all my adventures since then. Well, not all, I knew well enough that some things that went on in that house were not to be spoken of to anyone outside, not even my own mother. And I left out the part about taking the gold.

While I talked she kept staring at my face as if she could not quite believe it was me. When I finished she ran her hands over my head and gently down my cheeks. "She is good to you then? She does not harm you?" There was a quaver of anxiety in her voice.

"Suinyari treats me like a daughter. Those ugly stories about her are quite untrue. Not that you cared anyhow. You never came to fetch me away from there." My words were like a lash. I saw pain crumple her face. To stop myself from going on in that vein I said quickly, "Tell me how you came to be a nun. I would never have expected such a thing."

"Nor I, not in my wildest dreams. Listen, Aneithia," with those words she took my hands in hers and I allowed her to hold them. "They saved my life, those women, and they gave me a new one, though I must say at first I did not make it easy for them. At that time I was barely eating, food being hard to come by and not much in my thoughts. If they had not found me that day I might not have lived much longer considering the path I was following. Full of the pain of living and the guilt of leaving my child, I was wandering the streets, looking for the next man who would pay me enough for the use of my body so that I could buy oblivion again in any form: drink or drugs, liquid or powder or smoke; anything that would soften the anguish of being human.

"I had just come around the corner onto Sarvo Street and was heading for The Green Skull and a glass of forgetfulness when I was startled to see three nuns blocking my way. The one in the middle was old as a crone and dark as narl-wood, an ancient creature in a robe of deep purple with a young nun on either side of her dressed in bright green.

“I was amazed at seeing them on such a foul street and was about to slip around them when the old one said, ‘There she is! That one!’ and pointed her bony finger straight at me. Her eyes burned like fire in her dark face and I was struck with terror. It felt as if those eyes stared right into me, into my rotten life, into the very depths of my corrupted soul. The two young ones stepped forward quickly and grabbed me by the arms. Even with my scant strength I struggled wildly out of fear, not just fear for my life but some deeper kind of fear, fear for my very soul. I had heard stories of these nuns snatching women off the street and imprisoning them in their convent. What did they want with me?

“I needed to be away from those women and quickly, but that was not to be. There were two of them to my one. They were young, strong, very determined, and I was in a feeble condition. The shorter of the two—I later learned her name was Anishen—hissed in my ear, ‘Stop struggling or you will draw unwanted attention to yourself.’ The other, a tall, skinny thing called Lozell, was beginning to bend my arm up behind my back, saying, ‘Do you want the guard to come? A woman like you needs to stay clear of the guard. Just come quietly with us. I promise we will not harm you. You should feel pleased that Mother Melna has chosen you this day.’ Then, by sheer force, they started moving me along with them against my will.

“‘Let me go!’ I shouted. ‘Let me go! Let me go!’ At that moment, such was my fear, I would have welcomed the guard if it would have freed me from those women, but when a guardsman did finally appear, probably drawn by the commotion I was making, Mother Melna said loudly, ‘Clear the way! This woman is delirious with the fever. We must get her home before she dies here in the streets.’ Her powerful voice rang out clearly. The guardsman instantly and without question set to doing her bidding, but probably her own words did much of the work. At the word ‘fever’ the street cleared as if an invisible tide had moved through. People disappeared into doorways or down other streets as I heard ‘fever’ echoing before us. The only faces to be seen were at the upper windows. I looked up, wanting to appeal to them, wanting to shout, ‘Lies, all lies, I am being forced against my will,’ but what good would that do? Who would be fool enough to come to my rescue? Instead, feeling hopeless, I dropped my head and stumbled along between them, half dragged and half carried through the city.”

I shivered, hearing my mother’s story that was so much like my own. She gave me a look of concern and I nodded for her to go on.

"Soon we came to quieter, cleaner streets. No one moved to block our progress. In fact, even here they quickly stepped out of our way. Resigned, I no longer struggled or cried out. I let myself be borne along unresisting to my fate. If it was death it hardly mattered. I had been courting death for a long time. If it was slavery it might be better than the slavery of the streets.

"Finally we came to a little, winding, tree-lined street, more like an alley, with wide yards and gardens and red brick buildings on either side. We stopped at a set of huge wrought iron gates, built into a brick archway. Mother Melna gave me a curt nod and said, 'This is the House of the Mother and you are very lucky to be here. Remember that.'

Then she rang the bell and two green-robed women came to open the gates which had been chained shut. Beyond them I could see a sunny cobbled courtyard with flower-filled pots set about and climbing vines along the walls. Several women wearing different colored robes crowded in behind the young gatekeepers to stare at me. Among them was another old woman who looked almost as ancient as Mother Melna herself. This one looked me up and down with contempt, a look that had not one shred of kindness or mercy in it. 'Well, Mother Melna, what sort of trash have you brought us from the streets this time?' she asked in disgust, pointing in my direction. 'This one looks to be a right foul specimen, smells too. What is her story? Drugs? Drink? Jitters? Some leprous disease? All of it? What?'

"Stung by her words I tried to pull free of my captors and stand up a little straighter. 'I never asked to come here and would be only too glad to leave right now,' I shouted back at her with sudden courage.

"At that she laughed harshly, a sound even more disconcerting than her voice. 'Woman, you have no idea how fortunate you are to be here. Take her to the baths. Her smell is fouling my hall.'

"Mother Melna gave us a nod of dismissal. With that Lozell and Anishen rushed me through the entryway and across the courtyard. This time I went willingly. Anything to get away from that harsh, grating, accusing voice. Behind me I heard Mother Melna say calmly, 'Come now, Mother Olya, she is no worse than others who have come here. Given the chance she might even make a fine nun. Even battered as she is there is still some spark of life there. Besides, look at her. How could I leave her out there on the street searching so hopelessly for her spirit when she could easily find it here among us?'

"'Who was that?' I blurted out as we dashed off.

"Lozell laughed, saying, 'That is Mother Olya, our house mother, not known for her kindness. She is not so bad as she sounds, but she is responsible for keeping everything here running smoothly and hates disruption. She always makes nasty comments about Mother Melna's little 'shopping trips' as she calls them because it means more work and always some changes, but Mother Melna is Mother Superior here and her word is final. If she says you stay, then you stay.'

"At the baths the tubs were all lined with tiles and hot water bubbled up continuously from some deep invisible source. I was handed over to a big-shouldered woman in a red robe who also looked me up and down but with amusement instead of contempt. 'Another of Mother Melna's finds? She must have dug deep this time. This one looks pretty sorry, but she might clean up all right. My name is Haldrun and the baths are my domain. When you are here, you do what I say.' With that she made me take off all my clothes, leaving me not a scrap of modesty. Then she scrubbed me down with rough kindness. After that she gave me a robe of bright yellow to wear and sent me off to the dining hall. That was the first real meal I had eaten in months. I was very hungry, but I kept looking around suspiciously, thinking someone might suddenly take away my food or try to force me into something terrible."

I had no wish to hear my mother's whole entire story at that moment. I had my own questions that I needed answered. "How long have you been with the nuns?" I asked abruptly.

"Almost two years now."

"And in all that time you never thought to come and look for me?" My anger was quickly overcoming whatever love I might feel for her.

"The first year I was too sick and too crazy. All I could do was try to heal. They were not sure I would survive. My body was poisoned with everything I had ingested and my spirit was even worse. Besides I was virtually in prison there. They told me if I left I could not come back. Mother Melna said, 'It is up to you; if you leave, the street will swallow you up again. This time I will not go chasing into every cesspool on Sarvo Street to save you. One chance is enough. It is all you get. If you want life you will stay here with us. If you want death it is easy enough to find out there.'

"She talked as if I was really free to choose, but in truth they kept a close eye on me. Though I was almost a prisoner I had very kindly jailers. More than once Mother Olya or one of the younger ones actually blocked my way when I wanted to leave. Even with all their teas and healing brews, the longing for drugs and drink nearly ate me alive. There were times when I pulled out my hair and clawed my face bloody. Other times I thrashed about with fits and two or three of them actually had to hold me down to stop me from hurting myself or others. That is past now. I cannot imagine being carried away by that craving again, but at that time I was of no use to myself or anyone else."

"And what of this last year? Did you even remember that you had a daughter or was I just some trash from the past, a thing to be swept up into a pile with the rest of the garbage on the street?"

"Oh, Aneithia, I loved you so much, more than you can possibly imagine. I was just not a very good mother. I could hardly take care of myself. I knew you were at Suinyari's and I hoped you were safe there. Mother Melna told me. Then Suinyari herself talked to me. She wanted me to come see you, but I was much too ashamed and embarrassed. What could I offer compared to all her bounty? Besides, I thought you might hate me for leaving you. Now I can see that you do."

"Also you thought Suinyari might have snatched me up for some ugly purpose of her own and you were afraid to find out, so you stayed away and left me there to rot." I never for one moment had any cause to regret living at Suinyari's. In fact I had often blessed the day when she caught me in the market, but now I was suddenly feeling very sorry for myself as if I really had been terribly misused. Imalia looked at me with tears in her eyes and I felt a nasty satisfaction at seeing her pain.

"How could Suinyari know where you were and not tell me? She knew I was looking for you. She knew how much it mattered to me." Now I had another target for my anger.

Imalia shook her head. "Do not blame Suinyari. I begged her not to; I was afraid. She kept trying to persuade me to see you. In fact she was the one who arranged for us to meet. She sent me word where you would be today."

So they had conspired together. "And what about your nuns. Did they even care that you had a child?"

"The nuns have often urged me to come and see you. Today when I hesitated, full of my own fears, they almost pushed me out the door.

Come back with me and meet them. You will see for yourself how wonderful they are and they would be delighted to meet you."

"Why would I want to meet them? They have stolen away my mother," I said, full of puffed-up bitterness. Suddenly I heard Suinyari's voice in my head saying, *Take what is given with love, never turn it away. Life is full of uncertainty and who knows what tomorrow will bring.* I had cried for my mother, longed for her, dreamt of finding her again, yet here she was before me in the flesh and all I could think of was making her pay for the past. I stood up suddenly. "Well, what are we waiting for? Show me the way." The tremulous smile on my mother's face melted the last of my anger, at least for that moment. It would be worth going to meet these nuns if it made her so happy.

I had expected them all to be silent and serious, almost solemn. The few nuns I had met with on the street seemed stern and unfriendly. Instead the place was a noisy bustle of activity. I heard laughter, raised voices and even an occasional shout. There was a whole little world inside those gates: gardens, orchards, a pond, animals, even sheds for making and repairing things. My mother showed me around proudly. The nuns themselves were friendly and curious. They came to greet me and look me over and ask me questions. They seemed fond of my mother and eager to meet her daughter, but they soon drifted off, back to their work. When I had seen enough and was ready to go, Imalia said, "Before you leave, come and meet Mother Melna. She is the one who saved me from the streets. She is the real heart of this place."

Mother Melna was the oldest woman I had ever seen, her face brown and deeply wrinkled. She had on a robe of dark purple, different from what most of the other nuns wore. She was working in some flower beds, but she stopped the moment she saw us, gave me a big smile of welcome and beckoned us over to sit on a bench. I felt as if she wanted to give me a hug and barely restrained herself. "So this is Aneithia. Well, child, you are almost as beautiful as your mother. You look to be strong and healthy and growing well. What do you think of our place here?" She went on talking to me in this way, as if she knew me, as if we had some shared secret, as if she owned some part of me. It made me quite uncomfortable. Kind as she was I wanted to be away from there and on my way home, back to Suinyari's house where I was safe. I felt this place reaching out to lay some kind of claim on me and it frightened me.

Soon another old woman in purple came by and she was anything but friendly. "This must be Aneithia. I had heard she was here." She did not sit down with us, but stood there looking me up and down, shaking her head as if I was a horse she was thinking of buying and then had decided not to. I thought her very disagreeable and was about to say so. My mother said quickly, "Aneithia, this is Mother Olya who keeps everything running smoothly here. Mother Olya, this is my daughter." Then, slightly flustered, she added, "You must both be very busy. We will not keep you any longer." After that she stood up quickly, took my arm and walked away with me.

As soon as we were out of hearing I shook her hand from my arm and hissed, "That old woman, that Olya, is certainly a nasty piece of work."

"Hush, Aneithia, someone will hear you. She is not so bad when you get used to her."

"Well, I do not plan to get used to her. I have to go now. Suinyari will be worried. And anyhow my name is Neith now, not Aneithia." I knew I would never get her to call me Spider. She gave me a puzzled, wounded look as I rushed away.

I went back several times to the House of the Mother to visit with Imalia, looking for something, something I did not seem able to find, some part of myself that was still missing. I would always go hoping I had forgiven my mother for abandoning me, sure in fact that I had. Then I would suddenly find myself saying some angry, hurtful words and storming off, probably leaving her in tears. After that I would feel a terrible guilty pleasure at having hurt her. *But not nearly as much as she hurt me,* I would tell myself to justify my meanness. Each time I promised myself that I would not go back again and that if I did go back I would be kind instead of cruel. For a while I would resist until the pull grew too strong and it would all start again.

Mother Melna

Poor Imalia, she suffers so. When she first came to us she seemed to be sleepwalking, only half awake. Now that Neith has come back into her life she is fully alive, but she goes back and forth so quickly between joy and grief it makes me dizzy. Whenever the girl comes to visit Imalia is so hopeful, so eager to please, so full of fragile happiness that it is painful to watch. Of course, sooner or later, Neith says something mean and hurtful, all that happiness is dashed and Imalia is in tears again. When Neith leaves Imalia is always sure she will never come back.

Yes, I could weep for her. Even with all the terrible things that have happened to her, all the dreadful things Imalia herself has seen and done, she still has a sort of innocence, a hopeful tenderness that breaks my heart. Mother Olya, of course, says I am much too softhearted, an old argument between us. "She has made her choices and now she has to live with them, just like the rest of us. No need for you to bleed for her. You have too much heart and too little backbone." She herself is just the opposite, always has been, too much backbone and too little heart. I think I am the only person she has ever really loved. And the child is much like her, too much backbone and too little heart, though I think her heart is growing a tiny bit now, just enough to let in a few people. On the street she could not afford a heart; it would have killed her.

I know Neith loves her mother, but she also hates her, old anger at all she herself has suffered from being abandoned in that way. And when the chance arises she cannot resist a few cruel words, the demon of meanness in her. She needed that demon before. It was her friend, probably the only thing that kept her alive on the streets when other girls would have died. But it is time to put it to rest now. Time for it to sleep unless it is really needed.

I felt that I had to talk to Neith, but I did not want to do it at the House of the Mother where we could easily be interrupted or overheard. Also I did not want to wait for her next visit. I talked it over with Suinyari and she let me know when she would send Neith to the dressmakers. Suinyari's new dress needed some alterations or at least that was the excuse. When Neith stepped out of the store, I was already there on the street, seeming surprised and delighted with our "accidental" meeting. "How nice to see you Neith. Come walk with me a little and let me tell you a story."

Instantly suspicious, she took a step back and asked quite rudely, "Were you waiting here for me? Why should I want to listen to your story? What does it have to do with me?"

Having rather expected this, I was more amused than ruffled by her tone. Apparently she still saw me as the woman who took her mother away from her rather than the woman who had saved Imalia's life. "Listen to the story for just a little while. Then you be the judge of whether or not it matters to you."

"There is no time. I need to go home. Suinyari sent me to fetch her dress."

That made me laugh. "Nonsense, she is not about to wear that fancy dress at midday. You can tell Suinyari you stopped for a few minutes to talk to me. She will not care two figs how quickly you get home with her dress, but I can tell you she would not be very pleased with your manners."

The child blushed a little at the truth of my words and gave me a grudging nod. "Well, then, tell me your story if it is not too long."

I returned her nod, began walking slowly, and started my story almost as if telling a magic tale for children, "Once, in the city of Eezore, there was the Great House of Modrun. The young man who was the son of the Modrun and would someday himself become the Modrun had just reached the age of marriage. With the help of his father he became betrothed to a very beautiful young woman named Hermione, whom he found quite charming. He thought himself the luckiest man in the world for not only was this young woman beautiful, she was also docile and attentive and from a very rich family. Of course he was a fool for he really knew nothing at all about her, only what showed on the surface. He certainly did not know that she was weak and sickly and that her father was very eager to make a good marriage for her quickly before these flaws were discovered.

"The young couple married with great ceremony and soon they had a child. That child had the great misfortune of being born a girl. After that first baby Hermione was not strong enough for any more children. The young man felt cheated, as indeed he had been since he had expected a batch of fine strong sons, after which a daughter might have been acceptable. Instead he had a rather puny daughter who took after her mother. The young man had been cheated by life and by his wife's father, but of course he turned his anger on his wife and daughter. When he was not upbraiding and terrorizing them, he ignored them and found his pleasures elsewhere. As Hermione was heartbroken and ill, she also had little time for the child. Imalia grew up raised by servants and starved for her parents' love."

At the sound of her mother's name, Neith sucked in her breath and her eyes grew wide, but she said nothing and I went on as if I had not noticed. "When Imalia was fifteen a new manservant was hired for the house, a very handsome Kourmairi youth. He paid all the attention to Imalia that she could possibly have wanted. He thought her dazzlingly lovely, open and innocent, like a flower just coming to bloom and with all the allure of the forbidden. As is the way sometimes with young people, these two were fatally drawn to each other in spite of all the obstacles of caste and color. For a little while, Imalia had all the love she could possibly have wanted in her young life and everything was magical. When the fruit of their love began to show in Imalia's swelling waist her father beat the truth from her. Then he had the young man killed in front of her eyes for disgracing the family. First he had the youth's hands cut off and then his member.

"Imalia fled the house in horror. She ran screaming into the street, wanting to kill herself, but something stopped her. She was carrying the child of the man she loved, all that was left of him. Later her mother sent the servants in secret to find her and take her some food and money. She even arranged for a little room where her daughter could stay until the baby was born.

"Two years after the baby's birth Hermione died. For a year or so after that Imalia stayed on in that little room, doing some work for the landlady, but she was so shattered by everything that had happened that she was really not much use. After a while the landlady lost patience with her and put her out. Then Imalia began to drift, going from place to place with the child.

"Her father meanwhile had become the new Modrun when his father died. He had wasted little grief on the death of his sickly wife. Now that he was free, he quickly married again, choosing a strong, buxom, much younger woman who bore him two fine sons in quick succession before she too died, of the fever this time. The older son, Gairloff, is much like his father and will be Modrun in his turn. The younger one, Lairdun, is a gentle quiet boy, more like the half sister he never met."

"What happened to the child?" she interrupted impatiently.

"Ah, so you have been listening after all."

"Of course I have been listening."

"Oh, yes, the child. I suppose she is important in the story. She was not weak and frail like her mother. She was tough and hard and strong like her father or maybe her grandfather. She must have been born that way or she would probably not have survived since it was a hard life she was born into."

"Not her grandfather!" Neith shouted angrily. "That man was a monster!"

"Well, she was certainly not softhearted. That much I can tell you. The mother tried to take care of her child, but she could hardly take care of herself. Her spirit had been shattered and was not very strong to start with. As a daughter of the Uppercaste she had no training in doing anything useful and no experience in living hard. The shock of her lover's death had destroyed her soul and all she wanted was forgetfulness, oblivion, perhaps even death though she had not the courage to seek it directly. She began selling her body to survive and drifting more and more into drink and drugs. She thought sometimes of going back to her father, but she was afraid he would take away her child and sell her as a slave or perhaps kill her or perhaps kill them both.

"After a few years of this life, Imalia let go of her daughter altogether, lost her in the streets while she went on a month-long journey into the black pit. When she came back to herself the child had disappeared. Assuming the child was dead, she was full of terrible guilt and remorse so she began drinking more than ever. This went on for a year or more until finally the nuns of the House of the Mother found her wandering the streets near death and brought her back to live with them. The rest you know." At that point I stopped my story, stopped walking and stood staring off into space, thinking of all the misery we humans cause each other with our strange ways.

"But what about the child?" Neith shouted impatiently, tugging on my sleeve and abruptly bringing me back to the present.

"The child? Ah yes, the child. I keep losing my story. Her mother had named her daughter Aneithia, after her mother's mother who had been kind to her when she was little, but the girl took the street name of Spider and it suited her better, perhaps too well. She was a mix of her two parents. She had her father's dark hair and dark eyes and her mother's lovely features, though her skin was somewhat darker. But she had none of her mother's delicate temperament. The girl was tough and resourceful, I will say that for her. When her mother abandoned her, she learned to live on the street by her wits, becoming a skilled and clever little thief. She was what we call a survivor, the kind we like to recruit for the House of the Mother."

"Never! I am not about to become a nun!" she shouted furiously, whirling around to face me.

"No, of course not. I was not speaking of you. I myself would be opposed to it. You would be far too troublesome, much more of a nuisance than you are worth. I was speaking of the child in the story. Now, to continue. It took the mother, Imalia, almost a year to recover and come back to her senses. Many times during that year we thought we were going to lose her. When her wits returned she was flooded with guilt about the child she had left and was sure she was dead. But when we located the child—no easy thing I must tell you—she was also afraid to see her, afraid the child would hate her, with good reason. It took a while, but when we discovered Suinyari was longing for a child we found ways to point this one out to her. Those two formed a sort of bond on sight. Finally Suinyari captured the child and brought her home, but she was like a wild thing, not easy to live with, certainly not easy to love. Full of anger at everyone, she turned the house upside down. She had survived, but her heart had turned to stone inside. Now that is the end of my story."

Neith stamped her foot and her face flushed an angry red. "I have every right to be angry. That was no way to treat a child."

"So true. Yes, you have a right to be angry. Life treated you very badly. And you have a right to grieve for what you did not have. But these streets are full of terrible stories. If these stones could cry they would weep for years, weep tears of blood. If these stones could cry we would all be carried away in that flood of tears. And what of Imalia? She also has a right to be angry for what was done to her. Instead she is full of sorrow and guilt."

Neith stared at me, seething with resentment and hostility, not giving an inch. Under all that fierceness, all that anger, I could feel her terrible grief. "It is not a crime to cry," I told her softly.

"I am not crying," she said angrily as she rubbed her sleeve hard across her eyes. Then she burst into tears.

Spider

I had not asked for my mother's story. Now I had heard it twice over. I suppose they thought to soften my heart that way, make me kinder. Not likely. I am who I am. It felt as if Mother Melna had forced her part of the tale on me. I am sure it was no accident that she met me on the street that way. That was twice now that I had been ambushed with Suinyari's help, first by my mother and now by Mother Melna. I had no doubt that Melna had it all planned. She wanted me to change, wanted me to be good and kind like she was, but it was not in my nature.

So my mother had a hard life. Well, so did I! But she had been born with advantages. If I had been given those advantages I would have found a way to keep my baby and make a life for us both. I would not have given up everything and ended in a ditch like trash. I would not have left my child on those streets like thrown away garbage. Why should I feel sorry for her? She could have done something different. She was not a fool.

At the end of her story Mother Melna said I should cry. What for? What good would that do? I stared at her angrily, meaning to stare her down. No way was I going to cry—not for my mother, not for myself, not ever!

Suddenly, with no warning, against my will, I found myself howling with grief. Great, terrible, gulping sobs were shaking my body as I cried for all those years of fear and hunger and loneliness on the streets. I thought I would break in half with the pain of it. I gasped for breath. My knees began to buckle and I could hardly stand. I might have fallen if Mother Melna had not caught me. "Oh, it was so hard, so hard," I wailed to her. "No one knows how hard it was."

"I know, child, I know." Old as she was she sank down on the street and held me in her arms while I cried out my grief in her lap much as I had done earlier with Gammo. This was even deeper and longer. Perhaps I cried for my mother as well as myself. I suppose people stared at us in passing. If they did I had no knowledge of it and did not really care. Finally the grieving lessened, the sobs quieted and I sat up, feeling clearheaded and clean as if a great storm had passed through and the rain had washed me inside and out. When I thought of my mother I had no anger left, only love and pity. When I thought of Suinyari I was filled with love and gratitude. A little embarrassed to be sitting in someone's lap at my age, I struggled to my feet. Mother Melna reached up her hand to me. "I am too old to get up off the street with no help."

I helped her to her feet and tried to thank her, but she shushed me. "Go home now before Suinyari worries over you. You will have to hang that dress out over some steam. I fear we have crumpled it badly."

Suinyari

Gordivan has been gone for almost a month now, far too long for the simple errand I had sent him on. Sometimes he stays away on his own pursuits, but this is such a stretch of time I have grown worried. I even thought of contacting some of the Wanderers who might be heading north to Pellor, asking if they would look for him, or talking to those who had just come back to see if there was any word from there. That very morning I was just getting ready to go to the Fish Street Market to put out the word when Gordivan himself rode into the courtyard with a companion, bringing the winds of sudden change into all our lives.

As Gordivan came in I rushed to hug him, scolding fondly. "Where have you been? What happened to you? You have been so long away that I began to worry. That was not kind of you." Then Dondo came bounding up to Gordivan, barking and wagging his tail, but he stopped at the sight of the stranger and growled deep in his throat, sounding so menacing I had to ask Bethron to take him away.

"Do not begrudge me my time away, Suinyari. We have been having a wonderful adventure and now we are here." Gordivan nodded toward his companion. It was startling. The young man who had followed him into the house looked enough like Gordivan that he could have been his brother or even his twin except that the expression on his face was so very different—arrogant, surly, devious. Looking quite pleased with himself, Gordivan proudly introduced him to me as Nosharn of Pellor from the House of Anshwar. "I met Nosharn on the way and he took me to his father's Great House in Pellor. We have become fast friends and I said he must come back with me to meet my wife and see our house."

"Be welcome in our home, Nosharn. Any friend of Gordivan's always has a place at my hearth."

Handsome, graceful, looking quite at ease with himself, Nosharn bowed to me, then gave me a charming smile as he glanced around. "Lady Suinyari, your house is as lovely as Gordivan told me, a fine setting, but not nearly so lovely as the Lady that is its most treasured jewel."

I gave a slight bow in return. "I am sure this is only a humble place compared to your family's Great House. And I am not a grand lady who is used to flattery, only a very ordinary woman who works for her living." I was both charmed and amused by his little speech, but at the same time chilled by something in his eyes, something calculating and predatory as he looked about. Clearly Dondo disliked him and that added to my suspicions. Hiding my feelings, I laughed and went on lightly, "Do you always talk to the ladies that way? If so you must have quite a flock of them following you about. Since you like my entranceway so much you must come and see the rest of the house." Then I blushed, realizing the flirtatious double meaning of these words I had just exchanged with a total stranger.

"It would be my great pleasure," he said with a quick little smile that hardly touched his eyes.

As Alliya was fluttering about and Bethron was watching all this with a grim frown, I sent them both off to ask Gammo to make us a light lunch. Then the three of us walked through the house with Gordivan doing most of the talking. He seemed different with Nosharn there, more self-assured and confident, his voice sounding louder, deeper, more authoritative. Even his carriage was different. He was holding himself upright instead of moving along with his usual slouch. This was the first time he had brought home a companion. I could see this Nosharn was good for him. As we went along he kept giving the man adoring glances that seemed to be reciprocated. I should have been happy for him. Instead I felt this warning shiver that went up and down my back. I was wishing that Donya, with her reading of minds, had been there to advise me, but I had no idea how soon she would return.

When we came back from our stroll around the house and gardens, I took them into my bookroom to sit and talk until the meal was ready. I wanted to find out more about this Nosharn that Gordivan seemed so smitten with. The man made me uneasy. I planned to question him under the guise of polite conversation. Before I could begin Neith came dashing in and threw her arms around Gordivan's neck. "You are back. Where have you been? We thought you dead on the road somewhere."

"No, no, I am not so easily lost as all that." He gave her a rough, jesting hug, then instantly fell to chatting and teasing. Neith asked him endless questions about his trip and hardly listened to his answers while he pulled little trinkets out of different pockets for her. I was amused to see the look of distaste on Nosharn's face.

"Nosharn, this is my daughter, Neith. Neith, this is Gordivan's friend, Nosharn of Pellor, who has come back with him to visit us."

Neith only gave Nosharn a quick sidelong glance and no greeting at all. Her jealousy was easy enough to see. In a half whisper she asked Gordivan, "Is he your brother?"

Gordivan shook his head emphatically. At the same time, Nosharn exclaimed, "Your daughter?" as he looked in surprise from me to Neith. Of course we look nothing alike.

"My adopted daughter," I said quickly. "She had been abandoned by her mother."

"Ah yes, so this is the girl Gordivan told me about. I have to say, Suinyari, you must be the heart of kindness." He continued to look at Neith as if she were an obstacle or an object to be puzzled over rather than a living child. "Adopted legally or unofficially?"

"Oh, not legally. We are not very formal here."

"Ah, I see. Well, Neith, I hope you realize how very fortunate you are to have been rescued by this lovely and generous lady."

"Oh yes, very fortunate, I think of it every day," Neith said with a little bobbing curtsy.

Though the words were polite enough, underneath them I could feel the girl's smoldering anger. I thought it might be best to get her out of the room before that anger turned dangerous and ignited something. "Neith, would you be kind enough to fetch us the tea tray from Gammo? Bethron and Alliya are busy with setting out lunch." She gave a nod and was gone in an instant but not before giving Nosharn a spiteful look.

We talked of their journey for a few minutes, then Nosharn went back to the subject of Neith. "Very good of you to take her in, but do you trust her with your things? I have heard that feral children can never really be tamed."

"I would trust her with my life, sir, and that matters more than objects."

"Even so, you would do well to keep an eye on her. Such children can be dangerous. I fear you are far too softhearted and kind for this sort of thing and will only get taken advantage of. The best policy is discipline and more discipline. A good thrashing for impertinence can do no harm. And even that may not suffice. It is said that they usually revert as they get older. I have heard stories…"

I felt a little shiver and looked up to see Neith standing in the doorway with an odd expression on her face. She was watching Nosharn intently. I had no doubt that she had heard his words. She set the tray down on the table with great care. Then, as she handed Nosharn his cup of tea, she tripped over something on the rug and dropped the cup, splashing him with hot tea. He leapt up with a shout of mingled pain and outrage. Neith instantly went down on her knees. "Oh, forgive me. So sorry, so sorry. I am terribly clumsy. Here, at least let me help you wipe that up." She grabbed up some napkins from the tray and began dabbing ineffectively at his trousers.

"Enough, Neith, leave us be. Nosharn can do that better himself." Neith scuttled out of the room and I apologized several times for the child's clumsiness though I did not believe for one moment that it had been an accident.

After that we got on reasonably well. Gordivan took Nosharn up to his room for a change of pants. When they returned Alliya came to say the meal was ready and the three of us went into the sunroom for a light lunch. The rest of my household stayed away and Nosharn soon went back to charming me with flirting and flattery. I accepted being charmed as the best way to learn more about him and managed to slip in some questions of my own. He was, as I suspected, the frustrated younger son of an Uppercaste Great House, a man with no great prospects and much ambition. Meanwhile he himself had many questions, also veiled in politeness, some of which I did not want to answer and some that would have been dangerous to us all. It felt like trying to walk on the edge of sharp blades without getting cut and showing blood. I found myself resorting to uncomfortable evasions and half-truths, trying to maintain a surface of casual charm while fighting an invisible duel with a very clever enemy. Gordivan was wonderfully oblivious to it all, just happy to be basking in Nosharn's light.

Later that day Gordivan and Nosharn went out into the city, no doubt for Gordivan to introduce his new friend all about. They stayed away at dinner so Neith and I dined together with Neith sitting as close to me as possible. Then Alliya and Bethron came in to join us. It felt like family except that I was missing Donya. For the next day or so Nosharn and Gordivan came and went but did not dine with me. I cannot say that I missed them, at least I did not miss Nosharn. Gordivan I did miss, but he seemed almost like a stranger to me now, someone I did not really know anymore.

The fourth night Nosharn was with us we all sat down to eat together. The atmosphere at that table quickly became thick and heavy. It was enough to give one indigestion before even taking a single bite. Except for Gammo who steadfastly refused, Gordivan had talked the rest of my household into joining us. Donya had even returned from wherever she had been gathering information—spying as I would call it—but of course she could say nothing of that in front of a stranger.

Neith insisted on eating with us though I had suggested she take her evening meal with Gammo. I knew how much she disliked Gordivan's new friend. Since Gammo had already said she would not sit down to eat with him it seemed a good idea. My mistake! The girl was instantly insulted and turned obstinate. "I am not letting that dog's breath take my place and drive me away from the table," she hissed in my ear. I hissed back that she had best behave if she was going to eat with us or I would carry her out to the kitchen myself. Better I should have insisted she eat with us. Then she could have defied me and stormed off to eat in the kitchen.

This mystery of a child, she loves me and would likely defend me to the death. She is also painfully jealous of anyone who comes near me. Yet she defies me at every turn. No, not always, only when she feels threatened. At other times she is loving and compliant, like a kitten. And just like a kitten she is soft one moment and all claws and teeth the next. Ah well, she reminds me of myself when I was younger. Perhaps that is why I love her so. My father had much the same complaints of me.

I was sure Nosharn did not approve of "servants" being treated as equals. He was proper and polite but mostly silent at the beginning of the meal, probably observing and gathering his thoughts. I think he wanted to establish his place in the house or perhaps Gordivan had told him it would be wise to eat at home a few times. It amused me to watch the many different faces the man wore. With Gordivan he was attentive but masterful. With me he used his charm and flattery though under it I could sense cold contempt. He ignored Neith as if she was not there, looking down his nose, sometimes interrupting her in mid-sentence. Donya he was wary of as if she might be male competition of some sort and he had to show himself to be superior. Alliya and Bethron he tried to treat like servants though they did not allow it.

Altogether the meal proceeded with painful slowness since there was not one honest word being said at that table. We talked of the weather and the gardens. Then Nosharn launched into a glowing description of his father's house and grounds, clearly intended to impress or perhaps intimidate. Several times I saw Donya and Neith—usually not very friendly with each other—exchange conspiratorial glances across the table. It took no Hadra mind reading to know what they were saying with their silent looks. Nosharn missed it because he was too busy holding forth, trying to impress the rest of us or to prove himself in front of Donya who sat next to me and occasionally said a few words in my ear.

Bethron, who had no patience for cant, caught my eye and gave a little impatient shake of her head. Nosharn saw her and abruptly stopped the flow of his story. "Is it usual in Shokarn households for servants to be so familiar with their masters and even eat with them at the table?"

"Probably no more than in Pellor," I said quickly, feeling myself flush with anger. "But in this house the people you think of as servants are more like companions who are paid for their work."

"That is a most unusual arrangement and speaks for your great kindness, but perhaps not for your…" He seemed to be searching for a word that would show superiority and disapproval without being rude.

I was about to suggest the word "wisdom" when I saw that Torvil was about to rise. His face was almost purple with anger. I said quickly, "Torvil, would you please look to the horses? I think I heard some commotion from the direction of the stable."

"With pleasure," he answered with a slight bob of his head. I breathed a sigh of relief as I saw him leave. I knew his reputation for temper and the rampage of anger that had left two men dead and put him in the dungeon before my father bought his freedom.

Seeming unaware of the danger, Nosharn went on recklessly, "Personally I have to say that I agree with my father. He says he much prefers slaves to servants. Slaves have no choice and so no opportunity for inconvenient self-will." Then he launched into some tale of how his father had enforced absolute obedience from his slaves. It was an ugly story full of cruelty and malice, a story that turned my stomach. I let him talk unopposed, hoping Gordivan would hear the meanness in his words, but I fear Gordivan was too busy looking admiringly at his lover's profile to judge his meaning.

Then I noticed the look on Bethron's face and how her hands

were clenching. I thought she might be tempted to do some damage with a platter. Before she could do anything, Donya, who had kept her silence for most of the meal, spoke out in a loud clear voice, "Personally I prefer to live among free people who are neither owned nor owners. Of course most Shokarn find that hard to understand."

"You are not Shokarn then?" Nosharn looked at her with surprise as if he had not really seen her or rather "him" before.

"Of course I am a Shokarn. It does not mean I agree with everything the Shokarn do. Perhaps there are some things we could learn from others."

"You do not believe that the Highborn should have a right to rule over other castes?" He sounded incredulous.

"No, sir, I do not. I think everyone should use what skills and abilities they have for the common good."

"Such views could lead to chaos and the total breakdown of the social order. In Pellor that would be considered treason."

Donya pushed back her chair and stood up suddenly. "Then I am glad I do not live in Pellor." Without a backward look she strode out of the room. I could hear her loud footsteps going down the hall and then the sound of the back door slamming. Bethron and Alliya rushed after her. The rest of us sat for a moment in stunned silence. Then Neith said angrily, "Now look what you did! You drove Donyal out of the house!"

Nosharn looked at her as if he were seeing dog dirt on the bottom of his shoe. He did not answer, instead he turned to me. "Suinyari, my dear, I hope you are not raising this child to think of herself as your equal. That would be doing Neith a grave disservice later when she has to go out into the world. Shokarn cities are not as casual or kindly as your household. The moment this girl opens her mouth to speak there is no disguising that she comes from the street no matter what fine clothes you may dress her in."

I was staring at the man, trying to think of an apt response that would make my feelings known, but not be irreparably rude. Suddenly Neith took care of it for me. She jumped to her feet so forcefully that she knocked over her chair with a loud crash. It shook everything on the table so that glasses tipped over spilling wine and water together across the white cloth in a great bleeding stain of red.

"My name is Spider, you fool, not Neith!" she shouted at Nosharn. "And you are no better than a rat's backside all dressed up in fancy clothes! I hope you go home soon to your father's big fat fancy house." Then she whirled around and dashed into the kitchen. Actually what she had said was a street expression that was much more crude and vulgar than rat's backside, but also much more difficult to write down. Nosharn's face turned red and his eyes bulged while he struggled for breath. Meanwhile, I struggled not to laugh. She had said it so much better than I could have.

When he was able to speak, he whirled on me and said with very little of his usual charm, "That is just what I mean, Suinyari. That girl will grow up insolent with her betters and only make trouble for herself. She is a wild thing with no respect for others. I hope you will reprimand her sternly and beat some sense into her."

I nodded. "I will speak with her later. Right now she is not likely to hear anything I say, not till she calms down. But I will not beat her. No one is beaten in this house, it is not our way." Then I righted the glasses and stood up abruptly. "Please forgive the child. When she feels threatened or insulted sometimes she reverts to street talk. I believe you may have unintentionally offended her, Nosharn, by ignoring and interrupting her. She is very sensitive. I hope you will both excuse me. I am weary now and need to be alone for a while."

As quickly as I could I took myself out of the house and into the back garden before I exploded with laughter. When I looked up, I saw Neith and Donya huddled together on a bench as if they had been conspiring or commiserating with each other, a most unusual sight. They were both staring at me with a look of shocked surprise on their faces and that set off another gale of laughter that almost doubled me over. With that Donya jumped to her feet and came striding over. She shook me by the shoulders. "It is not funny, Suinyari. That man is dangerous."

"Oh, but it is," I burst out. "You should have seen the look on his face when Neith called him a rat's backside. He is such an arrogant fool that he deserved it."

I was laughing again and now Neith was laughing with me. Donya was not amused. She shook me again and said in her sternest voice, "You are the fool here and this is no laughing matter. I am telling you the man is very dangerous. Under all that flattery he means you ill. He has plans for using Gordivan to bring you down."

"Oh, Donya, I can manage him well enough. I have dealt with fools before, even dangerous ones. It is Gordivan I worry about when the shades fall from his eyes and he sees Nosharn for what he really is."

"Gordivan is an even bigger fool than you are. Do not count on his ever seeing the truth. Anyhow, let him look out for himself. It is you I am worried about."

"Not tonight, Donya. Please not tonight. I have had enough of Nosharn for one evening. Not another word about the man. We can talk seriously tomorrow. For tonight, I think I saw a cake as I passed through the kitchen. Let us take it up to my lair, just the three of us. There we can drink tea and eat cake and tell stories."

"Yes! Yes!" Neith was jumping up and down, probably very relieved that she was not about to be scolded or perhaps punished, maybe even beaten for her insolence as Nosharn had suggested. When we went back into the kitchen we found a cake with rich dark icing and a pattern of red petals in the shape of flowers. With it was a note. The first of it was in Gammo's large scrawling hand.

> *Dearest Lady, your slaves have run off for the evening to carouse around the streets of Eezore so you will have to look out for yourself tonight. Please do not beat us too badly when we come home. There is dessert here for those who deserve it, Gammo.*

Under that Bethron had written in her hard angular print.

> *Dear One, please rid us of this creature. It is hard to be in the same house with him. I think he is a danger to us all. I am not sure I can stay if he does not leave soon, Bethron.*

I stared at the note, wondering if Donya and Bethron were right, if something was happening that I would not be able to manage as skillfully as I had managed everything else in my life. Then I shook myself as if shaking off a chill. "Neith, would you heat us some water? And Donya, will you set out cups and plates on the tray? I am going to cut half this cake onto a platter for us and leave the other half for our runaways."

Giggling as if we were conspirators in some childish mischief, we took our laden tray up to my room. There we set it on the floor and put cushions around it for seats. Then we ate till we were stuffed and slightly nauseous while we told stories about our lives with even Neith joining in, turn and turn about. Though we never once said Nosharn's name, still his presence hung heavy in that room.

Donya

It was time to go home, back to Ishlair, back to give my report on conditions in the city of Eezore. I had to leave. I knew I had to leave. And yet I did nothing. Every day I made plans to go the next day, but when the time came I could not do it and so would plan to leave the day after and then the day after that. I hated Eezore more each day. I was actually afraid my powers might be waning from being so long away from the Hadra, living among outsiders, among the Draiga. Even Suinyari's house, where I had known so much pleasure, became hateful to me when Nosharn was there. Whenever I heard his loud, arrogant voice in the hall I would make myself scarce or go elsewhere. Even so I did not go home to Ishlair. Some powerful spell seemed to be holding me in Eezore day after day, despairing and confused, eaten up with homesickness, filled with longing for the clean, beautiful streets of Ishlair and the sounds of the Escuro River.

The morning after the cake feast, Suinyari and I had our second fight, shouting at each other in furious hissing whispers for fear of Gordivan and Nosharn hearing us. They, of course, were not even there. I had awakened early. With a terrible sense of foredoom I looked in puzzlement around the pretty pillowed room. Then I spotted the messy remains of our tea party. With that I remembered the ugly dinner the night before and the reason for my uneasiness. I had a hard time waking Suinyari. Even when she did wake she did not want to talk.

Ever since Gordivan had met this Nosharn in Pellor and brought him home things had changed; Gordivan himself had become a different man. Before he was totally loyal to Suinyari; I would have trusted him with her life. Now there was something ugly and murky in his thoughts, some tangled threads of greed and lust that made him untrustworthy, even dangerous. And this Nosharn clearly was a plotter and a planner, a greedy discontented man who meant Suinyari no good behind that charming smile he turned on her. How could I leave her with these two men no matter how much I might want to be gone? I sensed danger all around her, but she was much too confident to be afraid, too used to running her own life and having her own way. It was when I tried to talk to her about Nosharn that we had our fight.

"He is a guest here, Gordivan's guest, let me remind you. What do you expect me to do? Throw him out in the street?"

"Oh, Suinyari, open your eyes! He is not just a guest, he is a menace! The sooner he is gone the safer you will be, all of you. How can you be so blind?" When she kept arguing I went stomping off in a huff.

Later, when I came back, we had some cooler words. Actually, Suinyari agreed with me about Nosharn, but she felt trapped because of Gordivan. I even got her promise that she would ask the man to leave—soon. But could I trust her to go against Gordivan's wishes and so cause her beloved cousin pain? As time went by I kept pressing her on the matter and she kept telling me "soon."

In the meantime, since Nosharn was often at the house, seeming intent on claiming a place there, I was often away. In fact I moved back into my room at The Blue-Eyed Lady. Granthia teased and questioned, trying to pry some information from me. "I hear there is a handsome young man living at Suinyari's. Has he taken your place with her? Or is it Gordivan he favors?" Then she would wink suggestively, waiting for some good gossip. I would only shrug and shake my head. No matter what way she asked I kept my silence on what was happening at Althor House. It seemed safer that way.

Spider

Things had changed at Suinyari's—and not for the better. Nosharn seemed to have moved into our lives. Donya was mostly away just as I was beginning to like her. Really she was not so bad, especially compared to him. And she certainly had more interesting stories to tell. I knew, of course, to keep my silence on her secret and to remember to call her Donyal. She even shared my feelings about Nosharn and so I could talk to her freely. Out of loyalty to Suinyari the rest of the household kept their silence with me on that subject.

With Nosharn it was just the opposite, the longer he stayed the more I disliked him and his loud, boastful, insulting ways—and the feeling was certainly reciprocated. I also felt as if I had lost Gordivan;

he no longer paid much attention to me. I even felt as if I had lost Suinyari since she was so troubled and preoccupied. She hardly ever read with me anymore or helped me with my sums. As for Bethron and Alliya and Torvil, they went about the house silent and angry. Only Gammo was not much changed, but I think that was an act of will on her part. Besides she mostly kept to herself in the kitchen.

I hardly ever ate with Suinyari anymore, at least not when *he* was there, but one night she asked me to, saying she thought he had changed and I should give him another chance. Not believing that was possible, I did it for her sake. Nosharn, of course, was his usual insulting self, at least with me—not changed at all. I think Suinyari was even embarrassed by his behavior. After dinner I slipped away as quickly as I could. She might have wanted me to help serve beverages and sweets in the sitting room, but I could not bear to hear the sound of Nosharn's voice any longer. It was making me ill. I needed to make my escape. I even heard Suinyari calling me and I ignored her, something I never did anymore. I was mostly only too glad to be needed by her for something useful.

Instead of going up to my room where I could be found easily enough, I scurried down the hall and slipped into Suinyari's bookroom at the back of the house, a room where I had spent many wonderful hours learning to read, as well as exploring books and charts and maps. There was already one dim lamp burning. For fear of being discovered I lit no more. Thinking to read a while, I took out a book and lay down on the couch, but after a page or two of struggling to see in that dim light I dozed off.

I was awakened later by the sound of angry voices from close by. It was Nosharn and Gordivan arguing. My first irrational thought was that Nosharn had followed me there to inflict himself on me one more time. Then I heard what they were saying and froze, lying still as the dead, terrified they would find me there though the back of the couch was toward the door, probably making me invisible, especially in that dim light.

Nosharn was saying angrily, "And you are a spineless fool! If you do nothing you will always live in her shadow. She has everything. You are only here at her goodwill. She could ask you to leave tomorrow. What kind of future will we ever be able to build? And if she dies will she leave it to you or to that street-brat she treats like a daughter? By rights, it should all have been yours. How did she ever manage to seduce her father into leaving it to her? In Pellor such a thing would not have been possible. The nephew would have inherited before the daughter. And how did he die? Was he helped on the way, a little poison perhaps? You have been cheated out of what should rightfully have been yours. Only by getting Suinyari out of the way can you ever really stand up and be a man."

"Nosharn, I could never hurt her. She is more than a cousin; she has been like a sister to me. We grew up together. Besides, I owe her my livelihood. She is the brains of this business. I could never run it alone."

"But I could, or rather I could run it with you. I know as much as Suinyari of such things. We could be partners in this and you would reap far more of the profits than you do now."

"She has always been more than fair with me. I have no complaints."

"You are a worm! How can I stay with such a worm? I tell you if nothing changes here I am gone and you will never see me again. I cannot bear another meal with servants at the table and my lover being treated just like one of them. She has kept you on your knees. Yes, unless you are willing to stand up like a man and take what is yours I am out of your life. You will never see me again, Gordivan. Now is the time. You must choose between me and Suinyari."

"I cannot bear to lose you, Nosharn. You have become my life. I have nothing without you. But no harm must come to Suinyari, you must promise me that."

"No harm, I promise you. We will only take her away for a little while and persuade her to turn over to you what was rightfully yours to begin with. Then she and her maids and the child can go live at the House of the Mother where I hear she spends much of her time already. After that you and I can make a real life for ourselves here. Of course I may have to make a fake marriage to cover our 'friendship,' but that can all be arranged in due time."

"How could we ever get Suinyari to go with us? She is no fool and I fear you are not her favorite company."

"*We* will go with *her*. We must watch for the right moment, wait for a time when Suinyari is going off on some business alone as she often does. Then we follow, her invisible escort. After that just let me manage the rest. It will all fall into place very nicely, I promise. Then we can have a real life together."

"But no harm to Suinyari, that has to be a pledge between us."

"No harm, you have my word."

It was all I could do to keep my silence. I wanted to shout to Gordivan, "What a fool you are! How can you believe him? That man is a lying snake. He plans to kill her and put the blame on you." I bit my lip to hold back the words. Nosharn was still speaking, saying in his most persuasive voice, "Besides it is only a matter of time for women like Suinyari. As soon as the old Zarn dies and the young Zarn comes to the throne all women like her—the ones with any power—will be swept out of the way, out of public life altogether and kept behind closed doors. We want to be in a good position when that happens. Otherwise the Zarn himself may lay claim to her property and then it will be too late for you; it will all be confiscated anyhow. You must make her understand that. You have to get her to agree."

After that Gordivan mumbled a few words I could not understand, then Nosharn mumbled a few and it sounded as if they embraced, making a pledge between them. I felt sick with horror at the thoughts of what that kiss promised. Soon after that I heard them walking away.

The moment they left the room I slipped out of my hiding place and crept to the door. I had to warn Suinyari as quickly as I could, make her see what great danger she was in. As soon as the sound of footsteps was gone and the house seemed silent I scurried down the hall, listening for any movement. No one seemed to be about downstairs, but when I got to the top of the stairs I heard voices from Suinyari's room. I was too late; Gordivan had gotten there before me and they were arguing. I heard Nosharn's name being said in anger. Ordinarily I would have slipped away again and left Suinyari her privacy, but this was much too urgent. Trembling, I knocked on the door, then walked boldly into the room without being asked. Gordivan whirled at me, red in the face with anger. "Out!" he shouted. "Have you no respect for closed doors? What kind of manners has my wife taught you?" He had never spoken to me this way before.

Ignoring him, I said frantically to Suinyari, "Sorry for the intrusion, but I have to speak with you alone for a moment. It is very important."

She looked surprised at my rudeness and said coolly, "Whatever it is, surely it can wait until tomorrow."

"Please, Suinyari, you have no idea…"

"That is quite enough, Neith," she said sternly, interrupting my words. "You can see that Gordivan and I are having a private talk. You are interrupting. Please close the door as you leave." Now I had no choice but to go. There was no way I would have said a word of what I knew with Gordivan there. He would have lied and contradicted me or perhaps called for Nosharn and taken her right then. I made a little bow and backed out of the room, not wanting to turn my back on Gordivan for one moment. As I was leaving Suinyari softened and gave me a brief smile. "Good night, Little One. We will talk in the morning and sort it all out then. You will see, whatever it is may not look so bad by morning light."

I shuddered when she said those words, but I had no choice. As I left I closed the door behind me. After a quick glance up and down the hall, I pressed my ear to the door. Suinyari was saying, "What I told you before that interruption is that Nosharn has to leave. He cannot spend another night in my house; I forbid it. He makes everyone here miserable; he frightens the child; he has driven Donyal away; he insults the people of my household; and in turn they all complain to me. None of my friends will come to visit while he is here. He is even rude to me under that cover of courtly manners. When he is here it does not feel like my home."

"You are driving away the man I love. When he is gone from here I will feel like a stranger in this house and the house will be a stranger to me. When Nosharn is absent, then it is not my home."

"Gordivan, I never thought to say these words to you and it breaks my heart to do so, but the house is mine from my father's will, and my husband is a resident here, not an owner. The choice is yours. You will have to decide how to live your life though personally I cannot understand why a man with such a warm, open heart would want to spend it with such a cold, cruel man. I love you. You are more than a cousin to me, you really are a sort of husband. Know that you are always welcome here, but Nosharn is not. And it is not for want of trying on my part."

Gordivan gave a shout of anger, then I heard him sobbing. After that there were more words from Suinyari and more from Gordivan, though not so loud now, not loud enough for me to understand. It seemed as if this might go on all night. I was afraid I would fall asleep with my ear to the door and be found there in the hall. Clearly I would not have a chance to talk to Suinyari that night, but perhaps all would be well after all. I could tell that she was very determined to have Nosharn out of the house by the next day and that might put a stop to their mischief. Perhaps I would not have to tell Suinyari these terrible things after all. Hoping for the best, I stumbled off to bed. Once there I went to sleep instantly as if I had no worries or problems.

Suinyari

After Gordivan left, I had a hard time falling asleep. Restless and troubled, I kept tossing about, hearing our conversation repeating itself over and over in my head, questioning if I was really doing the right thing. One moment I would think it was the only thing to do and wonder why I had not done it much sooner as Donya, and indeed everyone in my house, had urged me to. Then the next moment I would wonder if there was not some other solution, something less painful to Gordivan and less likely to make a permanent rift between us. I also puzzled over what Neith had wanted to tell me that was so urgent, and now I regretted sending her away. Sleep, when it finally came, was fitful and dream-ridden.

Feeling as if I had only just dozed off, I was suddenly wakened by the sound of footsteps in my room. Opening my eyes in the dim predawn light I was amazed to see Nosharn cautiously approaching my bed. I sat up instantly and hissed in an angry whisper, "What is the meaning of this intrusion into my private space?" I was much too outraged to be properly frightened.

"We need to talk you and I."

"Indeed we do, but this is neither the time nor the place," I snapped.

Faster than I could have imagined he was at my bedside and had grabbed my arm in a painful grip. "Keep silent and listen to me if you value Neith's life."

"Neith! Where is she? What have you done?" My indignation shifted instantly to cold fear. In my head I gave a silent scream of terror.

"She is with Gordivan and he has a knife at her throat. If you make any noise to rouse the household she is as good as dead."

"Gordivan! Gordivan would never hurt her. He loves the child."

"Perhaps you have not noticed, Suinyari, but Gordivan is my man now, not yours. If you want Neith to live, you will do exactly as I say. You are going to come with us voluntarily and make no sign to anyone. We are riding out of here as soon as the horses are ready. You will come with me riding on your own horse and Neith will be riding up in front of Gordivan. Now get up this instant and dress quickly. Wear your riding boots. Put a cloak over your clothes and the hood of it over your red hair."

As soon as I dressed, we went down by the back stairs and out into the courtyard. As we left my room Nosharn resumed his grip on my arm and kept a firm hold the whole way, not releasing me until I stood next to my horse. Gordivan was there before us, already mounted. He had Neith up in front of him, partly concealed by his riding cloak and he held the reins for the other two horses. No one else was about.

I held my breath, caught between wanting someone to come running out to stop them and being terrified that any commotion would be the cause of Neith's death. When I mounted it was with a terrible dread in my heart. I turned, trying to catch Gordivan's eye. He kept his face averted and started off in the lead the moment we were all mounted. Nosharn pulled my hood forward so it almost covered my face. He rode right next to me and kept one hand on my reins, bending close as if we were good friends carrying on an intimate conversation. In this way we rode out unquestioned through the South Gate and took the road toward Pellor. It had all been accomplished as if it had been well rehearsed. Even I had played my part flawlessly out of my fear for Neith.

As soon as we were away from other people I threw my hood back and said sharply, "Let me see Neith. I have to know that she is unharmed." Gordivan opened his cloak. He was carrying a bedroll stuffed under it. "What have you done with her?" I shouted. "Where is she?"

Nosharn laughed harshly. "Home in bed, asleep as she should be. Do you think we would be fool enough to bring that brat with us? She is nothing but trouble. Besides, you are the one we need and now we have you. Neith is no use to us."

My eyes stung with tears of rage and frustration. I had been a fine fool. No doubt this was what Neith had tried to warn me of the night before. I remembered the suspicious way she had looked at Gordivan and how she had backed out of the room. I vowed that if I got out of this alive I would never ignore her again. "What is your game, you two? They will be looking for me by now and then you will have to answer for this."

Nosharn laughed again, a very nasty sound that made the hair rise on the back of my neck. "No one will look for you, Suinyari. I told your stableman that the three of us were off on some business and not to expect us back before the month was out. It has all been taken care of very neatly."

I wanted to shout in his smug face that Neith probably knew the truth, but that would hardly have been wise. Instead I turned to Gordivan. "What is all this? I thought you were my friend as well as my husband and my cousin. Are you planning to kill me?"

"No! No! Certainly not! No harm will come to you. Nosharn has promised me that."

"And you believe him? What kind of a fool are you? Open your eyes, Gordivan! The man is lying to you."

"He would never lie to me. We are too close for that."

Now I looked at Gordivan with more pity than anger. My poor cousin, so besotted, so hungry for love that he mistook Nosharn's carefully crafted mix of flattery and attention for the real thing. Wondering what end this strange play was leading to, I shook my head and said flatly, "Cousin, he is more likely to lie to you than to anyone else in the world. His every word to you is a lie, his every calculated look."

Nosharn said sharply, "Woman, if you cannot be quiet I will have to gag you. And put that hood back over your hair." Then he tied my reins to the pommel of his saddle in case I had any idea of kicking my horse and trying to dash away. The thought had crossed my mind. Now I watched that door between me and my freedom being closed.

A look of pain and confusion crossed Gordivan's face and he pleaded urgently, "Please, Nosharn, do not gag her. I will vouch for her. Suinyari, as soon as we stop everything will be explained and you will see that it is all for the best. Now, will you give me your word to be silent, Cousin? It is really better to ride quietly with us."

"If you say so," I answered curtly, giving my assent without giving my word. In my head I pledged to myself that I would shout for help the moment I had the chance, but I saw it was no use trying to talk sense to Gordivan. He would go on believing Nosharn's lies because he needed to.

As it was I had no chance to shout. We soon turned off the cobbled road onto a little rutted dirt lane that led into a deserted barn. Part of the roof had fallen in but one end was still sound. There were piles of hay for sitting and supplies had been stacked in the sheltered end.

Now I understood that this little escapade had been organized and planned for well ahead of time.

Nosharn pulled me roughly from my horse and crossed my hands in front of me. Though I struggled he was much stronger. "Tie her wrists," he shouted at Gordivan.

"Is that necessary? Surely we can just sit here and talk and in the end she will see the sense of what we are saying."

"Do as I say. Even now she is fighting us. It will be much easier to be persuasive if her mind is not on escaping. Also she is probably a neat hand with a sword or a knife. Better not to give her the chance."

I knew nothing of the skill of swords. I had always relied on my wits, but I promised myself that if I survived I would learn. Reluctantly Gordivan tied my wrists and Nosharn pushed me down on the hay, saying, "For your own good, listen very carefully to what your cousin has to say. We need to settle all this and quickly." There was a long tense moment of silence, then Nosharn growled, "Talk to her. You know what needs to be said."

Gordivan began hesitantly, scuffing his boots in the dirt, not able to look me in the eye, but he grew more confident as he went on. "We needed to get you away from that household of yours so we could talk without interference. Nosharn has showed me how it was not proper for you to have inherited the house and the business from your father. You must have tricked him into it somehow. A grave injustice has been done. You stole what was rightfully mine. As the closest male heir it should have come to me instead of you and now all we want to do is set things right again. We mean you no harm.

"When you have signed everything over to me I will settle a sum on you and you can go live at the House of the Mother where you will be much safer and better cared for. You can take the child with you and your maids and the cook. It is much too dangerous for a woman to be out on the streets, doing the work you do. And besides it is not proper. You see how well we have thought it all out. We have the papers here for you to sign."

So that was the way the wind blew, betrayal of the worst sort all bound up in a pretty story and the worst of it was that Gordivan had made himself believe it. He could never have been my father's heir. He was not even his nephew, except by marriage. I wanted to scream, to curse, to laugh like a maniac, to shout at him for being such a fool, to spit in his face. Instead of indulging myself in such foolishness, no matter how tempting, I thought I had better consider my options. Clearly whether or not I signed their papers Nosharn meant for me to die, likely soon after I had signed. There was no way he would let me return to Eezore. And after me probably Neith and maybe the rest of my household would have to go and possibly even Gordivan himself after he also signed a few papers, but I knew there was no way my cousin would believe me. Any more said in that direction was a waste of breath and dangerous besides. He had talked himself into being the injured party and words from me would fall on deaf ears. After he finished I sat in silence for a while as if pondering all this. I wanted to make them think I was actually considering their proposal. What I needed was time. I was sure Neith knew the truth and would send help. I had to stretch this out as far as I could. Let them make the next move.

"Well," Nosharn finally said, "what do you have to say to this? It would certainly be wise to sign these papers of your own free will before we have to bring anyone else into the matter."

I smiled slightly, thinking this threat gave the words "free will" a whole new meaning. I let my silence go on a while longer. Then, when Nosharn looked as if he was about to explode, I nodded and said thoughtfully, "This is certainly something new to consider. I had never thought of it quite that way before. In truth, of late I have grown weary of this life of danger and had some thoughts of changing my ways, becoming more settled and respectable, but surely we could have talked of all this back at the house like civilized people without this wild morning ride. What sort of sum were you thinking of settling on me, Gordivan? It would have to be enough to start a whole new life. Perhaps I am not suited for the House of the Mother or they would not have me. We have to seriously consider that possibility. And I doubt that Neith would want to go there, so we have to think of settling a sum on her also. This is not something to be jumped into lightly. There is much involved that needs careful thought and consideration."

Gordivan named a sum, Nosharn told him he was a fool and for a few precious moments they argued with each other. Time, a little more time, that was all I needed. Then Nosharn said impatiently, "We could just have you sign these papers now and the rest of the details could be worked out later. Besides it is only a matter of time before it will all be resolved one way or the other. The old Zarn is dying, and believe me, when the young one takes his place, many things in Eezore will be very different. You will see, he has no patience for women in power. Soon all that will change. Women like you will lose everything. But he might confiscate your property himself and then it would all be lost. This way at least it will stay in the family."

"Ah yes, and that of course is very important to me. But what if Gordivan should turn it over to you? I need some guarantee that this would never happen." All this was just a performance on both our parts for Gordivan's sake. The two of them could easily kill me, then Gordivan could sign my name to any agreement they decided on. He had often signed for me in the past and knew my writing well enough. Who would question it but the "servants." But Nosharn still needed Gordivan's cooperation for his plans and so he needed to keep fooling him. Killing me was clearly not part of their agreement.

I saw the look of barely contained fury on Nosharn's face. He was probably gnashing his teeth, wanting to hurry me along, but not wanting to upset me if I was really going to be fool enough to take part in his little plan. I shook my head. "No, no, I think it very important to work it all out at the same time and to me the sum is not just a detail. It matters a great deal. It is my future and the sum Gordivan named is much too low. You must understand, Gordivan, if I agree to this we are making some very big changes here so perhaps you would also sign some papers for me, especially about keeping it in the family. After all this is an important life decision. Whatever I give my word to I honorably intend to carry out." I looked right at Gordivan, and for the first time he met my eye, hopeful perhaps that this was all going to be peacefully settled. Poor Gordivan, I was also using him. He was in for some rude shocks whichever way this all fell out.

"Fine talk for a smuggler!" Nosharn suddenly burst out, losing patience.

"Even smugglers have honor," I said lifting my head high. "My father taught me that." In the distance I heard a dog barking. The others seemed not to notice. To cover the sound I began talking quickly about many different possibilities—sums of money, business prospects, whatever nonsense came to mind. Through my words I heard the sound I had been listening for, the sound of horses, riding fast.

Donya

That night, filled with unhappiness, I had gone as I sometimes did to a tavern on the far western edge of Eezore, a place called The Brass Bird. There Thieves Guild, Wanderers, Shokarn and Kourmairi all mixed together, many of them in the city on various shady errands of their own, folk who sometimes managed to slip in and out without coming through the well-guarded gates.

Shaleen, the other Hadra spy in Eezore, was there too. Except for her, we were all playing an endless game of darts. Filled with a burning, itching anger at my life that seemed to be turning in on itself and going nowhere, I was bragging and being generally insulting to everyone around me. I had even taken a few drinks, something Hadra seldom do as it weakens our powers and clouds our minds. I was indulging my anger in the game, using my Hadra powers recklessly to win each turn. In the process I was gathering up a fair-sized pile of money and antagonizing all my opponents. Shaleen kept trying to signal me to end this madness. In my head I could hear her shouting, *Donya, stop being a fool! This is a dangerous game you are playing!*

I paid her no heed. I even half hoped that some drunken fool would challenge me to a fight and find himself flat on the floor. That might have satisfied my itch of anger. Finally, as the night was turning toward morning, a man who had lost all his money to me smashed his mug on the table in a rage, shouting, "Now I will take care of this rotten filthy cheat." Yelling some further obscenities, he was about to attack me with the broken shards when I heard Suinyari's cry of distress in my head. I had a moment of such blinding pain it rocked me on my feet. With a shout I threw all the money down on the table and dashed out the door. Shaleen was close at my heels. I could hear the man's angry voice rising behind us as we ran for our horses.

Spider

Exhausted by my fears I slept like the dead until I was awakened in the gray dawn by Dondo's terrible howls. Leaping up, I dashed down the hall to Suinyari's room. Too late! She was already gone. The room was in disorder as if she had left suddenly and unwillingly. I rushed to Gordivan's room and it was empty too. Everyone in the house was up now and stumbling around stupidly. Gammo released the dog who had been locked in the pantry and he began running around and barking frantically. A rag had been tied around his muzzle to silence him. He had apparently managed to chew it or paw it off. It hung in shreds from his collar.

When Bethron asked me tersely if I knew what was happening I told her to gather everyone in the kitchen. Though I was the child of the house for that moment I was the leader. Quickly I told them all what I had overheard. Torvil groaned. He was twisting his hands, almost in tears. "I thought there was something wrong. I never saw her this morning. It was Gordivan who came to tell me to ready her horse along with his and Nosharn's and that with no warning at all the night before. I set to work in the dark. It was just gray light when Gordivan took the horses away saying, 'We will all be gone for some time on business. Do not look for us before the month is out.' She did not come to give me any instruction of what to do in her absence or even to say goodbye, something she has never done before. I should have known then something was very wrong."

At that moment Donya burst into the house, shouting, "Where is she? What has happened? Where is Suinyari?"

Donya

We had to ride hard across the whole city to reach Suinyari's house. When Shaleen and I came bursting in, the others were all assembled in the kitchen. They whirled to look at us. Distress was plain on every face and Dondo was howling mournfully. In a few quick words Spider told me what had happened. "We must hurry. I think Nosharn plans to kill her. Dondo can lead us to her."

"You cannot go, it is much too dangerous. Besides you cannot even ride. Shaleen will come with me. We will take Torvil and the dog with us. When we get closer, I can use mind touch."

"I must go! I must!" Spider shouted, grabbing for my arm. "I could not warn her in time. Now I have to save her life. I can ride in front of you on Cloud."

I evaded her hands. "Gammo, Bethron, hold her back. She cannot go with us, it would endanger her and slow us down." I dashed out of the house, hearing Spider's cries of protest turn into screams in back of me, but there was no time at that moment to deal with her gently. Suinyari's life hung in the balance. The moment we had Torvil's horse saddled we were gone into the early dawn with Dondo running in the lead.

The ride seemed endless and I was terrified to think what we would find at the end of it. Finally Dondo turned off the main road onto a little dirt track that led to an old barn. With the sound of Dondo's baying we had no advantage of surprise so we made the most of our advantage of speed by galloping straight into the barn.

After that it all seemed to happen in an instant. I saw Nosharn leap to his feet, saw the flash of the knife in one of his hands, saw him grab Suinyari's wrist with the other. With no hesitation I leapt from my horse to throw myself between them. Nosharn swung the arm with the knife. The blade missed me altogether, but to my utter amazement his arm struck my chest and he was able to knock me away with such force that I fell flat, sprawled on the ground with the breath knocked out of me. Before I could get to my feet again he had Suinyari clamped against his chest and the knife at her throat. "Stay back all of you or she dies."

Gasping for breath, I was struggling to get up when he growled at me, "Stay down Hadra, do not move if you want her to live." At the look of shock on my face he laughed that ugly laugh of his. "Oh yes, I know who you are. I know all the little secrets of Suinyari's house and I plan to use them well. Gordivan has told me everything. And I see you are losing your powers from living among the Shokarn. What a shame."

I had never felt such a sense of utter helplessness as I did at that moment, seeing Suinyari in that man's grasp while I lay sprawled on the ground, unable to move. Gordivan meanwhile was shouting, "No harm! No harm must come to her, Nosharn! You promised! That was the only reason I came with you. You promised she would not be harmed."

"Shut up, you fool! This raid changes everything. This was not what we planned for."

At the same time Torvil was shouting, "Let go of her, you horse turd. If Suinyari dies your life is worth nothing, less than nothing."

Meanwhile Shaleen was taking slow steps in Nosharn's direction, holding out her hand and saying calmly, "Give me the knife right now before anything happens. You do not want to kill Suinyari with all of us watching. Think on it carefully. After that what happens to you?" As she took another slow step, Nosharn whirled toward her like a cornered animal, snarling, "I warn you, not one more step."

I wanted to shout at Shaleen to stop and stand still, that she was endangering Suinyari's life. Before I could open my mouth Dondo launched himself at Nosharn with a fierce growl and grabbed the man's leg in his strong jaws. When Nosharn's knife hand jerked away, Suinyari saw her chance. She drove her bound hands straight up into his chin and then ducked away.

With a cry of pain and surprise, Nosharn staggered back a step or two to keep his balance, blood pouring from his nose and mouth. Instantly Suinyari threw herself sideways out of his reach. At the same moment Torvil flung himself at the man and took him down while Dondo leapt out of the way. Nosharn was strong, I knew that from my own recent experience, but Torvil was a tower of a man with muscles bulging from years of working horses. Besides, his fury gave him extra strength. Nosharn did not stand a chance against all that. He crashed to the ground like a felled tree, and his knife slipped from his hand. Before any of us could say a word Torvil had grabbed up the knife and stabbed Nosharn several times with his own blade. He was about to slit the man's throat when Suinyari shouted, "No, Torvil! Stop!" At that moment Gordivan began to scream, a terrible, heart-ripping, blood-chilling sound.

When Torvil stood up he was covered with blood, but all the fury had gone from his face. With icy calm he wiped his hands and the knife on his pants, then bent to cut the rope on Suinyari's wrists and give her a hand in rising. "Why did you stay my hand, Lady?"

"Stab wounds can be explained. A slit throat is a whole different story. Besides, he is already dead."

Nosharn had been thrashing about. Now he lay still, blood pouring from his wounds and his eyes starting to close. Still screaming, Gordivan threw himself on his lover's bloody body. With that Torvil turned and raised his knife, shouting, "The second rat to kill." He seemed fully intent on dispatching Gordivan as well, but Suinyari grabbed his arm.

"No, Torvil, for my sake not Gordivan. One death is enough for today. Besides he is a fool, not a villain."

Thinking he was likely both, I slowly and painfully got to my feet, wondering if anything was broken in the fall. Then I saw that

Suinyari's arm was streaming blood and she was swaying on her feet. Leaping forward, I caught her in my arms and gently laid her down. Instantly Torvil had his shirt off and was tearing the unbloodied back of it into strips. Shaleen took them from him and set to binding up the cut while Suinyari lay shaking her head, saying over and over in a strange, dazed way, "He meant to kill me, he really meant to kill me and Gordivan had a part in it all."

Though she was very pale, she recovered her wits quickly enough. As soon as Shaleen finished, Suinyari asked me to prop her up against a hay pile. Then she called Dondo to her side. The dog was trembling all over, not sure if he had done the right thing or not. She stroked him and praised him. Finally he lay down next to her and put his head in her lap. Taking command, Suinyari called the rest of us to come over to her. "You too, Gordivan, you can finish grieving later."

To my surprise he obeyed her, though he kept his distance from Torvil. He was covered with blood, his face twisted in pain. "You did not have to kill him!" he yelled accusingly. "You could just have knocked him down. We could have talked some sense to him. I know he did not mean to harm Suinyari. He had promised me that."

Furious, Torvil whirled on him. "Fool! Fool if you believed anything that man told you! What do you mean not harm her! He meant to see her dead and out of his way. Likely you would have been next. Once Suinyari was dead he could have killed you and come back to Eezore in your place. He looks enough like you. Then it would all have been his. We would have known who he was, but who would listen to the word of 'servants' over the word of an Uppercaste Lord? You are an idiot if you think Nosharn would have listened to anything from us. I did what I had to do. As long as that man was alive Suinyari would never have been safe. Never!"

"You always hated him. You saw your chance to do him harm. You wanted to kill him."

"Enough!" Suinyari said sharply. "You can quarrel later. At this moment it matters little who was right or wrong in the matter. Right now we have a body to account for and we must have a story to go with it, a story we can all agree on. This is a time when the truth, no matter how satisfying, will not serve. The truth, in fact, is dangerous to us all and will put us in the dungeon or worse."

"We could just bury him out here somewhere and say he had gone home," Torvil said curtly, glaring with anger at the dead man.

Suinyari shook her head. "And when his family comes to ask questions? Everyone in Eezore knows he was a guest at our house. Gordivan saw to that by parading him around everywhere in the city. And no doubt there are some who saw us ride out together this morning. One way or the other we have to have a story."

"Nosharn is dead, that is all that matters to me. What do I care about some story?" Gordivan said stubbornly.

"Because you know the punishment in this city for men who are too fond of other men. The truth would be your doom, Gordivan, worse than death, so you had best listen well and remember every word." With that he sank down and began to weep with his face in his hands, but he did not argue anymore.

And so Suinyari sat there, her bright red hair tangled with hay, her face streaked with blood, her arm bandaged with lumpy rags, while she boldly wove out, with all the details, the story of how two bandits disguised as tradesmen had come for her in the early morning saying they were holding her daughter and the child's life was at forfeit if she did not ride off with them. She went on with how that same daughter, watching out the window, had become suspicious when she saw one of the men take Suinyari's reins and so had alerted the house. After that had come a wild ride with the dog as guide and poor Nosharn's brave defense of her life that had cost him his own—a grand bold tale of heroic rescue and tragic death that even bore a twisted resemblance to the truth and could have brought tears to a listener's eyes. She spoke so convincingly I could see it all as if it had really happened that way. She told how the bandits had been wounded but had escaped. She continued with how poor Nosharn had breathed his last on the floor of a barn, his head in her lap. She even had a description of the men, taken from her father's account of bandits that had attacked a Wanderer caravan in his childhood. Watching her at that moment I think I had never loved and admired her more or found her more foreign to my own Hadra ways.

After that the camp was quickly gathered up and Nosharn's body bound to his horse. Shaleen and I were to have no place in this small mournful procession, carrying the hero home. There would be neither praise nor blame for our part in the events—we had not been there. We needed to disappear, take a different road home and stay far away from the others.

We rode off first. I was silent for a while, very shaken by what had happened. I had never witnessed a killing before and the backlash of all that pain and rage was crashing around in my head. Also I was shocked at the loss of my powers and what that meant for me—very frightened really. I just followed Shaleen, not really knowing where we were going.

Finally Shaleen broke the silence, saying forcefully, "You must go back to Ishlair with me this day before any more of your powers slip away. This is very dangerous for you."

"But I cannot leave Suinyari at this moment. After everything that has happened, how can you even ask that of me? I must meet her back in the city, be some help and comfort to her there."

"A week then, promise you will go with me in a week. This is for your own sake, Donya, your life may depend on it. Promise and I will say no more on the matter."

"I promise," I mumbled, regretting the words as soon as they were out of my mouth. But I was a Hadra, not a Shokarn story-weaver like Suinyari. I knew I would have to honor my word, though I had given it mostly to satisfy Shaleen.

As it was, a week was more time than I needed. After the funeral was over Suinyari seemed to forget my existence. As for the funeral itself it was something I had hoped to avoid, but both Suinyari and Torvil said that it would look strange and might raise some unwanted questions if Suinyari's cousin, who also happened to be a member of the household, were to be absent. Gordivan did not seem to care one way or the other. Truth to tell, at that moment, Gordivan did not care much about anything. The question about Gordivan was whether we could get him sober and keep him that way long enough to get through the funeral without his doing something disastrous. Torvil assigned himself to be Gordivan's guardian and keep watch over him.

It seemed as if half the city came to the funeral. The graveside was buzzing with malice and gossip. Suinyari had spent what seemed to me a foolishly large sum on a grand namestone. Looking grief-stricken, she told the story we had all agreed upon with even a few embellishments, heaping praise on Nosharn and making a hero of the man. It quite turned my stomach to hear it. Then Gordivan said some heartfelt words about his friend before Nosharn was finally put in the ground where he could do us no more mischief. Neith stayed close to me the whole time. I could feel her vibrating with eagerness and anxiety. I think she wanted to get her hands on the shovel herself and move that pile of dirt into the hole.

Anxious for this all to be over with no incident, I tried to stay at the edge of things and talk as little as possible. I especially did not want to be asked any questions. The grave had just been filled and some last words spoken when a friend of Suinyari's, a man I had met at the first big party I attended, slipped up next to me and said in my ear, "I cannot say I grieve for him. Alive I thought the man a braggart and a scoundrel no matter how much Gordivan blew the horn for him. Interesting that in death he should have become a hero. Somehow I would not have pictured Nosharn as someone who would risk his life riding to Suinyari's rescue." A chill ran up my back. He knew! I could read it from his mind. He knew the truth of it all or at least enough to be very dangerous. I could not think of what to say to keep us safe. The Hadra are not very good at this kind of game. Then our eyes met, he gave me a slight nod and I knew he would keep his silence. He stepped back, winked at me and was gone before I could say a word.

Once home Suinyari seemed to sink into a numb, bottomless grief. "How could he have planned such a thing? We were children together; we grew up sharing our lives; he was like a brother to me; I would have done anything for his sake. How could he betray me in this way?" She asked the same questions over and over, hardly aware of my presence. Bethron, Alliya and Gammo hovered over her, changing the dressing on her wound and fussing at her to eat while Dondo lay by the bed, head on his paws, watching everyone warily and growling low warnings at the rest of us.

I felt superfluous, in the way. The whole house seemed sunk in gloom. Gordivan took to the bottle in earnest and started to drink as soon as he woke, seeking to escape the shame and grief that waited to ambush him if he should ever have a sober moment. Torvil stomped about in a sullen rage and the sight of Gordivan would set off a string of curses.

I myself was no source of love and light either. My head was teeming with questions, none of them very pleasant. I wandered the streets gutted and empty, feeling as if I had lost my center, not really sure who I was anymore. I was like a bird with a broken wing or a horse with a broken leg. "A bird that cannot fly is still a bird." I remembered saying that to Suinyari. "It does not suddenly become a dog or a fish." But will it ever really be a bird again? Was I still a Hadra even without my powers of self-defense? And what did I have to learn now to keep myself safe in the world? Would my powers come back if I went home? And what would it cost me? Was Ishlair really my home anymore?

Meanwhile Spider begged me every day to take her away from there. "It is like living among the dead. Suinyari barely speaks to me. I am not even sure she knows me. The others treat me as if I am not there at all. I will die if I stay much longer in this boneyard. No one will even notice. Please, Donya, take me with you to Ishlair. I want to meet other Hadra and see how all of you live. Please, please do not leave me here among these walking corpses."

I did not want the burden of a child at that moment and so I said curtly, "You could go to the House of the Mother and stay with your mother there." I tried to harden my heart to her pleas, but when she burst into tears and clung to my arm I felt my resolve weakening. It was Shaleen who settled it. When I suggested taking Spider with us she said gruffly, "I do not want to be saddled with a child. I already have the responsibility of getting you safely back to Ishlair with your diminished powers. That is enough."

Finally there was nothing left but to tell Suinyari. She hardly seemed to notice or to care that I was leaving.

Spider

I felt abandoned by everyone: Suinyari, Donya, Gordivan, even Gammo, even Alliya and Bethron who went about with long faces and short tempers. Shortly after Nosharn's death, Donya left to go back to Ishlair. A few days later I ended up at the House of the Mother. It was not because I really wanted to be there, but it was better than Suinyari's dreary house of doom. Torvil took me there mounted on the front of his horse. "I do not feel the streets are safe for you at the moment. With Suinyari and Gordivan indisposed it is up to me to make such decisions." Indisposed indeed! Is that what he called it? One of them had fallen into the black pit of despair and the other into the bottle.

I think Torvil expected some resistance. For once I did not argue or insist I could perfectly well take care of myself. Actually I agreed with him. I did not feel safe, not after what had happened. It had shaken me to the core to know that Suinyari herself was not safe in that city. I was actually grateful for Torvil's protection, though he was probably doing this as much for Suinyari as for me. And I have to say I was glad Nosharn was dead. I certainly shed no tears for the "hero," but when anyone outside our house spoke to me about him I remembered the story and knew to keep up the pretense.

When we were on our way, Torvil said matter-of-factly, "As soon as you come back I will teach how to ride. It is time you learned. You are certainly old enough." I nodded and bit back the tears. His words warmed me, gave me something to hold on to at that bleak moment. It meant he thought I was coming back; it even meant he cared.

When I had gone to say goodbye to Suinyari she had hugged me and said, "Do not stay away too long, Neith; I shall miss you." The words sounded kindly, but the dead flat tone of her voice robbed them of any meaning.

Donya

Caught up in my troubled thoughts, I was not very good company on the ride back. Shaleen did not seem to mind. She herself appeared to be quite preoccupied arranging her own thoughts. There would be much to tell when we got home. Also she was going to have to find a replacement for me. When we were a day's ride away from Eezore, we found a stream and cleaned the last of the paste and powder from our faces. Then, much to my relief, we dressed again in our own Hadra clothes: long embroidered tunics, loose pants of a contrasting color and boots of tough woven fiber. After that we rode another two days before we came to the edge of the Drylands.

That night, when we camped, I wondered about the Muinyairin. Going back and forth between Ishlair and Eezore I had always managed to find a Wanderer caravan going at least part of the way and so had avoided them. I hoped to be as lucky this time. "Do not count on it," Shaleen said dryly, reading my thoughts. "The Muinyairin are very active at this time of year. When the weather is mild they hold big gatherings. For myself, I always enjoy meeting with them on the road, though of course not now, not with your powers at such a low ebb."

Personally I was hoping for no more challenges to my failing powers.

The next morning we left when it was still dark, hoping to reach the oasis of Silver Springs well before the noon sun came beating down on us. As soon as it grew light we began entering the Drylands with its great stretches of sandy soil and sparse scrub growth. I knew we would soon come to a place where there was nothing but sand as far as the eye could see. Before we had gone far, Shaleen stopped and unrolled a Hadra flag, the flag of North Yarmald with three horses running—one black, one red, one white—against a background of bright green. "That should keep us safe enough. The Muinyairin know better than to meddle with the Hadra," she said as she slipped the end of the pole into a long narrow sleeve in her horsepack, made for that purpose. There it boldly waved its warning in the breeze.

I shuddered. Reading my mind she gave me a sharp look. "Do not think so much about them. You will draw them to us." Sure enough, not an hour had passed before five Muinyairin men rode over the top of a nearby dune and came charging down at us at full speed. They must have been watching the road from up there. If my powers had not been so diminished I might easily have sensed their presence. I tensed with fear, that strange new feeling in my life. Shouting some kind of challange they galloped right at us with their swords pointing straight out in front of them. Shaleen wheeled her horse around.

"Hold your ground and face them," she told me coolly. "They are only trying to frighten us, their idea of a game or a good joke. And let me be the one to talk." She sounded as calm as if we were being approached by a group of merchants with a wagonload of goods for sale instead of being charged by five armed Muinyairin. I was only too glad to let her do the talking. I would have been glad to hide behind her. Though it would probably cost me my life, what I really wanted to do was turn and run. My little experience with Nosharn had made a coward of me.

Going out to meet them, Shaleen rode forward several steps, sitting very straight on her horse. In a shower of sand the leader reared his horse to a stop just a few feet away from her. The others quickly gathered right behind him. Shaleen made a slight bow. Speaking Muinyairin, she said in a loud clear voice, "Greetings, Lords of the Desert. The Hadra of North Yarmald salute you. I am Shaleen of Ishlair and this is my companion, Donya of Ishlair and Eezore. She tells me she is sorry to have missed you on her way to Eezore."

The leader drew back his lips in a wolfish grin. "Well, she may be the only young woman in the world ever to say she was eager to meet the Muinyairin. We do not have a very kindly reputation." The men in back of him laughed and it was a chilling chorus of echoes. "Good morning to you, Hadra of the North," he went on. "Take our greetings back to Ishlair. I am Shamir of the tribe of Ozzan and these are all my brothers. That is a very fine horse you are riding, Shaleen. Would you like to trade me something for it? I could make you a very good offer." Although the words seemed innocent enough there was a tone of threat humming just below the surface.

"Lord Shamir, I must assume you are jesting. You know full well that the Hadra cannot trade in horses; it goes against our natures. Timpani is like my sister. We are bonded. I could no more trade her away than you could trade one of your brothers, no matter how tempting the price." She made her slight bow again as if saying, *Your turn now.*

Shamir's grin grew truly menacing. "And what if we simply took your horse and left your body to rot in the desert."

Shaleen shook her head. "I hate to think you would try to force me to go against my nature. Besides she would not stay with you, but you are welcome to try. I am at your mercy." With that she held out her hands in a gesture of total surrender.

At that Shamir roared with laughter. "You are no more at my mercy than an Oolanth Cat. I have seen what you Hadra can do against the strongest and best armed men so I suppose you must keep your horse then no matter how much I may fancy it."

"I am deeply flattered that you think my horse worthy of your attention for I know the Muinyairin are experts in the matter of horses."

Shamir gave her a nod, "Well done, bold words, Shaleen of Ishlair; you are a brave woman. Only the Hadra could sit erect and proud, staring back even though they are outnumbered and unarmed. Since you will not trade me your horse perhaps you would care to race with us. That horse must be very fast if you value it so much."

Shaleen laughed in turn. "We would like nothing better than to stay and race with you and no doubt win, but not today. We have been long away from home and must get back with urgent news. They are awaiting us and it does not do to make our Councilor angry. She is not known for her kindly patience. Some other time, Shamir, and you had best keep that horse of yours in good shape against the day."

Shamir nodded, seeming quite pleased with this whole exchange. "Well, since you must be on your way, I want to give you something to remember us by." With those words he untied the sash from around his waist. It was a beautiful thing, richly beaded and embroidered in bright colors. He tied several knots in it till it almost formed a ball, then called out to Shaleen, "If you can catch this it is yours," as he tossed it at her. Shaleen sat very still as if trying to figure which way the wind was going to blow. She came into motion at the very last instant, catching the scarf though she almost fell from her horse to do so.

"That is a gift from Shamir of the tribe of Ozzan to the Hadra of Ishlair. Give it to your Councilor if she scolds you too much for tardiness. Otherwise wear it yourself in good health."

"Thank you, Lord Shamir. It is mine now. I will wear it in memory of this day." I was amazed that she could speak at all. My tongue was frozen in my mouth, and I had been keeping my jaw clenched so my teeth would not rattle.

Shamir bowed to us both. "I will pass the word to others that you are not to be stopped or bothered in your journey through the Drylands. May your path be easy and your days be cool. May you never thirst along the way."

With that he wheeled his horse around and galloped off amid flying clods of sand. He was closely followed by his four brothers. In that whole exchange these brothers had not said one word and neither had I. At the sight of their departing backs I finally let out the breath I had not even known I was holding.

So was this fear? Was this what ordinary people felt much of the time? If so I had much admiration for them as well as great pity. How on earth did they endure it? My whole body ached from the tension of hiding my fear and trying not to flee. Shaleen rode over to me and handed me the sash. "This is for you, Donya, earned this day."

"I could not possibly…"

"No arguing. Put it on and wear it for courage. You will need it until your powers return."

Suinyari

Sitting here at my writing desk, I find myself staring out into the courtyard, feeling hopeless and weary. Things need doing, business must be taken care of, but nothing gets accomplished here. Tears drip down and stain the pages. Ah, Donya. Now that she is gone my heart aches with missing her. And I fear she may not ever come back. Why should she, with the way I treated her? After that daring rescue I scarcely spoke a word to her. I acted as if she did not even exist though I knew she had plenty of troubles of her own and needed care and kindness. When she told me she was leaving I paid it no mind, hardly said one word of missing her, of hoping for her safe return. I never even thanked her for coming to my aid, for in fact saving my life. If not for her who knows where I would be now. Most likely dead or a prisoner, helpless in some small dank place.

I had so much pride of power that I never saw it coming, could not imagine anyone daring to treat me that way, though Donya tried hard to warn me and so did Neith. Poor Neith, I have deserted her too. My heart has closed in on itself and I live only in a tiny corner of it. No wonder she wanted to be away from here. I heard her tell Donya that this house was "full of walking corpses." Who knows if she will come back to me either.

Oh, Gordivan! How could you do that to me? For as long as I can remember you were part of my life. We were raised together. You were the cousin who was more like a brother, no, better than a brother for there was never the curse of jealousy between us, never any rivalry or meanness. We shared all our dreams and secrets with each other. When we grew old enough for lovers we shared those secrets too. Lovers came and went in our lives, but we always had each other, at least until now. I would have trusted you with my life. I did and look what happened. How could you have betrayed me this way? I suppose I should hate you for what you did. Instead I pity you.

Enough of all this rubbish! I have to stop grieving, pull myself together and get back out into the world. Bethron and Alliya are holding together the business, but it will soon begin to flounder if I do not take hold of it again. People want to see me; friends to give comfort and express support; rivals to see if my hand is really slipping and it is time to carve up my interests between them. I need to show myself in public.

How I wish I had Donya here at my side at this moment. Most of all I wish I could tell her how sorry I am for the way I treated her. But letters do not run easily between Shokarn cities and the Hadra settlements of the coast. Perhaps I will go look for Zathrun the Wanderer. He will know who is going west and might have a way to send a message. And maybe we could even do a little business at the same time, he and I.

Right now I need to put in a grand appearance, wipe away these tears, deck myself out in my finest gown and have a little gathering here, fifty or so close friends and rivals. That would make Gammo happy. She complains that it is a waste to cook for us since Gordivan is seldom home and I have taken to eating like a bird. I wonder if I can keep Gordivan sober long enough to attend and put a good face on things. Yes, if I am going to live then I have to hold up my head and reclaim my life. And this is the day to begin.

Donya

As we rode into Ishlair I was overcome with waves of feelings. Familiarity rushed up at me all mixed in with a painful ache of longing that tugged at my heart and choked my breath. This was my settlement where every person had been part of my childhood and everything was known to me, every tree, every bridge, every turn of the street. Was there still a place for me here?

We were quickly surrounded by women eager to greet us, my mothers and sisters among them. I was glad to see them all, but there were too many questions flung at me, too many eager expectations, and I was very weary. I disentangled myself from everyone and said I needed to be alone with the river for a while. I think my mothers were hurt, but I had to catch my breath and center myself.

The Escuro River had always been a comforting friend and asked nothing of me in return. I sat on the bank, leaning against a tree. After a while I shut my eyes and just listened to the flow of the water. There was music in it, the sound of wordless voices singing. I let myself float away on the pleasure of it. When I finally stood up to leave, I felt calmer, but still uncertain of what the future held. I had come back with crippled powers, not sure what that meant, not even sure I belonged here anymore.

When I got home my mothers were both beading at the kitchen table and my bondsisters were there helping. They all welcomed me so warmly I almost let myself feel comfortable. As they settled back to their work, they asked me to tell them about Eezore. They seemed to be listening with interest, but as soon as I told the story of Suinyari's capture and rescue, Henori interrupted angrily, "When you told me about her last time you were here I said that woman would cause you nothing but trouble. Of course you were too proud or too stubborn to listen to me."

Then Tiaga, the older of my two bondsisters, added spitefully, "Why do you always have to be so different? So special? Every time you come home you cause some sort of upheaval." At that my younger bondsister, Laiden, tugged on my sleeve. "I hope you never go back to Eezore again, such a nasty place. It is time for you to be home here with us." By that time any sense of comfort I had felt was gone.

After I first returned it seemed very strange to be back in my childhood home, staying in my old room and sleeping in my own bed. After the big spaces in Suinyari's house everything appeared so small, cramped even, familiar and yet foreign—a skin already shed or clothes I had outgrown and could not fit back into. It was not that I missed the large rooms in Suinyari's house. Most of them seemed to me wasteful and cold. It was only that for a few days I kept bumping into walls and doorways until I regained my Hadra sense of space. We Hadra build for use and comfort, not to impress others with our wealth or power. Since we build everything ourselves we make spaces no larger than we need. And indeed who would we impress? The neighbors who have helped us build and to whom we now owe an exchange of labor? A waste of time and effort. Truth be told, in some ways we live almost like the poor in Eezore, those folk who cluster at the edge of the markets. And yet we are not poor, far from it. We are never in want. We have everything we need. We just have a different way of measuring wealth. Among us wealth is having enough—not more than enough.

In Ishlair, larger houses are usually occupied by more people. If extra room is needed little chambers are often added to existing buildings. Sometimes, when they are no longer in use, they fall into disrepair. Then they are torn down again and the pieces reused. Our houses are not so fixed and permanent as those in Eezore. They are more like living, growing organisms, always changing with the needs of the occupants. Among the Hadra the energy of house-pride goes into the details: intricate story-telling carvings on the lintels, brightly colored tiles around the archways, windows of different fanciful shapes, weavings, plants, colors. If we seek to impress it is with our flowers and our decorative handwork. That is the charm of a Hadra settlement.

Wanting to feel myself part of the life of Ishlair again and to make myself useful, I helped Souvir and Chanith and their crew of workers mud the walls of their new room. This space was to become a larger pottery since those two now planned to make wares—bowls and plates and cups and platters—to send off with the Wanderers for sale in other places as well as for use at home.

When the outside had been coated with white clay I painted scenes from my journey on it, losing myself for a while in the work and the wonderful swirl of bright colors. Along with entertaining the eyes this helped to seal the clay against bad weather. Mostly I worked alone, but sometimes I had an attentive audience, watching and commenting with interest and approval, teasing a little as if trying to draw me back into the web of life there.

There was to be a healing for me in hopes of mending my broken powers. Mordica had insisted on it and some of the others had agreed to try. She was very hopeful about the outcome. I was not so sure. In fact I was more anxious than I admitted to anyone, even my mothers. I went about haunted by some strange sense of foreboding, but did not speak of it, afraid of bringing about the very thing I feared. I even tried to shield my thoughts though of course among the Hadra, when feelings are so strong, it is almost impossible to shield them altogether.

The night before the healing I went down and sat by the river with only my candle for company. I needed to prepare myself, to clear my mind and open my heart for what was to come. Trying to find some calm, I watched the slow changes in the night sky and listened to the murmuring rush of the water. I could not come to this healing full of longing and resistance, yet much as I tried to shut her out, Suinyari's name would suddenly leap into my mind. Just when I thought I had some peace in the matter, her face would float into my inner vision or I would hear the sound of her voice in the night breeze. At those moments I would beg the Goddess to help clear my mind. For a little while afterward there would be silence in my head. Then it would all begin again.

At last, in desperation, I shouted aloud, "Stop it, Suinyari! Let me go! Let loose your hold on me! All that is over now. I have already made my decision and it cannot be changed. Besides I have no choice." Then I ended with a sob, "Oh, Suinyari, I am so sorry. I miss you so."

This love had been so easy to slip into. Why was it so hard to get free of? Why did it have to hurt so much? Finally, weary with it all, I lay back on the sand and shut my eyes for just a moment. I thought I was going to struggle with this the whole night and get no sleep. Instead I woke in the dawn light to the sound of women's voices. They were coming for me. All I had to do was surrender to them. This struggle would soon be over.

Groggy from too little sleep and too much inner turmoil, I stumbled to my feet, brushed off the damp sand and stepped forward to greet them. There were five of them altogether. Nazzem, our healer, had organized everything and chosen the others. Akella, my bondmother, was there as well as Mordica, our Councilor, my friend Shaleen and Tenathi, the new healer from Zelindar, the one who was thinking of settling in Ishlair. I bowed to each of them and each of them in turn dipped her hand in the river and pressed her dripping fingers to my forehead in a blessing, saying, "May the Mother heal you and return your powers." Then, on the sand, Nazzem carefully laid down a bright blanket-sized sacred weaving that I recognized as coming from the Zildorn. Meanwhile the others made a large circle of candles around it. Next Nazzem set three bowls of dried sweetherb at three spots in the circle, lit them and drew lines in the air between them so that inside the circle there was a triangle of power. Then they all walked around the circle three times chanting something in the old language, words I did not understand.

As I watched all this, a quiver of apprehension went through me. Would I be the same person after this was over? Then the smell of burning sweetherb flooded my senses, making me dizzy. The flames of the candles quivered before my eyes. I felt myself sinking into a deeper place and my knees began to give way. Before I could fall to the ground, Nazzem took my hand and led me to the circle. At the entrance she stopped and said, "Mother, we bring this daughter before You for Your help. She has lost her way in the world out there and her powers are failing. Please keep her safe and help return to her that which is her birthright." With those words she led me to the center and had me lie down on the bright cloth. The others came in and knelt down, one at each foot and one at each hand while Nazzem knelt just behind my head.

"Close your eyes and empty your mind," she said softly in my ear. "Let yourself drift on the scent of sweetherb." With that they all began chanting again. I could feel their touch on my hands and feet, as well as Nazzem's fingers moving about on my head. Soon I could sense the touch of their Kersh in my mind, like fingers moving about inside my head that sent shivers up and down my spine. I tensed for a moment. Then Nazzem whispered to me, "Let us in, open yourself to our minds, do not be afraid, nothing here will hurt you. Relax, breathe deeply and surrender to the Mother. Let Her do Her healing work and allow us to help."

With that the tension eased. I felt myself floating out on her words, on the sound of the chanting, on the scent of the herb. I was opening up, surrendering, turning myself over to whatever came. I was safe among the Hadra again. I had come home to stay. Then Nazzem knelt down by me, put her hand on my heart and said softly in my ear, "You must let go of that woman and that city and everything that happened to you there."

At that instant my heart was suddenly torn by a pain so sharp that I sat bolt upright with a cry of anguish and my eyes flew open. Nazzem, echoing my cry with her own, collapsed sideways into Akella's arms. I felt her shock ripping through my mind with a sound like tearing fabric. There was a sudden clamor of words from the others. Pushing away all the hands that were on my body, I heard myself saying in a strange voice that I hardly recognized as my own, "No! I cannot do this! I cannot! I cannot! It goes against my heart." I was shaking my head wildly. The words came out as a hoarse, despairing cry. I pressed both hands over my heart to hold against the pain that wanted to tear my body in two.

Nazzem was moaning, lying there limp and gray in Akella's arms, seeming barely conscious. The rest of them were all staring at me in shock and surprise. I saw the look of pain on Mordica's face and felt her hurt stab me in the heart, sharp as a turning knife. She gazed at me intently as if trying to understand, then she leaned forward and said softly, "Donya, we cannot do this healing against your will and you know what will happen without it."

I nodded, not trusting myself to speak.

"Is it because of her?"

I nodded again and for a moment Mordica looked very old and weary. It hurt me to think of the pain I was causing her. Then she straightened suddenly and said in a cool distant voice, "Well, you are not the first Hadra foolish enough to give up her birthright for love and no doubt you will not be the last. You have burned Nazzem with your willfulness. It is her healing we must look to now."

I was dismissed. Her words had a chilling finality as if I had already been written out of the Hadra book of names, as if Donya of Ishlair had ceased to exist. And perhaps, in a way, she had. Desperate to be understood I said, "I tried to turn my will over to the Goddess. I really tried, but I could not. This is what came instead."

"Could not or would not, it matters little in the end. Either way you are at Her mercy. If you cannot be one of us then you are free to go out and meet your fate wherever it calls you." With that she pulled me to my feet. Then, to my surprise, she kissed me on the forehead. "Good luck to you, Daughter. You will need it. That is a hard world out there for a Hadra, especially as your powers begin to wane."

Other women had now found their voices and were beginning to argue with me or with Mordica or with both of us. Shaleen said sharply, "Are you just going to let her go that way?"

Mordica shook her head. "And what do you expect me to do? How can I hold her? What choice do I have? You know you cannot bind a Hadra or bend her will. No matter what you or I may think on the matter we cannot live her life for her. Only Donya can live her own life, make her own choices and accept the consequences. And now we must do a healing for Nazzem since she was wide open and caught the full force of that blast. And you, Donya, you must be far away from her. Quickly!"

Without another word to any of them, I stumbled away alone, going back up the winding path that led to the settlement. Not even Akella came with me. They all stayed there to help with Nazzem.

Once on the streets of Ishlair again I walked fast and kept my head down, looking neither left nor right for fear someone would try to speak to me and the dam would burst. I headed straight up the hill to the Zildorn and was immensely grateful to find it empty. Taking myself to the darkest corner, I sat down on the floor with my back against the wall and my head on a bench cushion. There I burst into tears. I wept as if my heart would break and indeed it hurt as if it had. Full of guilt and pain and confusion I was much in need of healing myself. I felt as if I was the cause of Nazzem's collapse, Mordica's grief, everyone's disapproval and disappointment.

They had come to help me and I had let them all down. At that moment I felt so divided it was as if a knife had cut me in two. I hated the side of myself that I had come to think of as the Shokarn part.

It drove me away from Ishlair and turned my life upside down with restlessness and discontent. It seemed to cause endless trouble for the Hadra I loved. It was making me a stranger among my own people. I thought again of Mauri's bitter words when I had first left for Eezore, and of my bondsister Tiaga's mocking insults, and of Henori's pain and disappointment. And now I would have to face the terrible curse of fear all alone. My powers were failing and there could be no healing for me. I would have to go back out into that world with little or no protection and no idea of how to defend myself. And how did I know Suinyari would even want me back? She had seemed totally indifferent when I left.

Each new thought brought with it another flood of tears. I felt sick and empty, drained of everything. Finally I became aware of Shaleen's presence. She was standing there quietly, watching me cry. When I turned my face away, ashamed of my tears, she came and sat down next to me and took me in her arms. With a groan I laid my head down on her breast and let myself be held like a baby. She even rocked me slightly and crooned softly with no words, stroking my hair, soothing me and bringing me back to myself. I had been wandering in a very dark place, even wondering if I might not be better off dead.

When I was finally able to lift my head and take a deep breath, she said, "You know, Donya, when I have lost direction in my life and am in need of advice, sometimes I come here and ask Tazzi for help."

"What Tazzi? I know of no Tazzi here, save two little girls, much too young to give useful advice."

"The Tazzi of old, our foremother, the one who with Pell brought the first Hadra through all those dangers to find safety on the coast, the Tazzi who founded Zelindar. I come to ask her what she would do in my place. She had to face many hardships and won her way through them. Somehow she always has something to tell me if I let myself listen. Here, you could do worse." With those words she took our copy of Tazzi's first volume from the shelves and laid it on the table in front of me. Then she was gone.

I stared down at our copy of *Daughters of the Great Star.* This was the story of the Khal Hadera Lossien, the first Hadra to appear in the world. With a shrug I opened this book that I had not read since I was a girl. I wondered what Tazzi from that far past could possibly tell me in this troubled present, but in spite of myself I soon got drawn into her epic tale of courage and adversity, of survival against the odds.

Tazzi and Pell had led the new Hadra through endless dangers and hardship to safety on the coast. With vision and tenacity they had created the settlement of Zelindar that was our first sanctuary and the site of our first city. I became so absorbed in the story that I forgot my own troubles for a while and even lost track of time. Suddenly the light was fading. I had been far away in another place and time. Only slowly did I come back to the present.

Thinking of it all, I saw that my own troubles were small compared to what those women had faced. My life was not the tragedy I was making it. In many ways I had been fortunate, but I had made choices that brought me difficulties and now I had to pick up my life and live it boldly no matter what the outcome. "Well, Tazzi," I said aloud to this long-dead woman who seemed to me so real and present in the Zildorn. "You kept us alive and brought us all to safety and that was the adventure of your life. Now I, your daughter's daughter's daughter, have grown restless with safety and need to be on my own adventure. In spite of the danger I need to spread my wings in the world out there and I hope I can have your blessing."

"Are you talking to yourself or is there someone here I cannot see?" Mordica asked as she came in and sat next to me on the bench.

"Both. Looking for guidance, I was just rereading Tazzi's account of the first Hadra and their struggles with each other and with the forces of the Zarns. It was Tazzi I was talking to."

"You could not find a better advisor so perhaps I am interrupting. I was worried and came to see how you were. Shaleen said I could find you here."

"Tazzi has just taken me on her journey and made me realize that mine is not really so hard after all. How is Nazzem? Did I do something terrible to her?" I was almost afraid to ask.

"Nothing that will not mend. Nazzem is resting. She will be fine in a few days. You know, even with your diminished powers you still have far more force than you realize."

"I did not mean to hurt her. I would never do such a thing. You know that, Mordica."

"We all know that." She touched my cheek gently and then laid her hand on my arm. "I had hoped you would come back to take your place here, but it seems that is not to be." I could hear the sadness in her voice. All that lost hope and longing made me want to cry. But she was not angry anymore. I was very glad of that. I could not have stood up under any more anger and accusations. I was too fragile, too weighted down with my own despair and my anger at myself.

"Go do whatever it is you need to do," Mordica said softly. "Perhaps when you have worn out your wanderlust you will come back to us. Perhaps then your powers can be mended."

I knew I needed to leave again, but this time it was not Eezore that drew me. After rereading Tazzi's account, Zelindar was where I wanted to go. Perhaps there would be answers for me in that city or in the great library at the Zildorn there. But first there was something I had to do. I went back down to our house to face my birth mother. I found Henori sitting in the kitchen and sat down opposite her. I could feel her fear and her resistance, but this time I would not be put off. Akella came to stand in the doorway, hands on her hips, watching me warily.

"I cannot have a healing. I am too much of a danger to myself and others, but at least I will have the truth before I leave here. No more evasions, no more pretenses. I need to know who my father was and why it matters so much to you to keep it secret."

"Donya, you cannot force your mother that way," Akella said sharply.

I turned to her. "I will have the truth and this time you will not interfere and protect her. This has gone on too long and cost me too much pain and confusion."

In three strides Akella came to stand between me and Henori. "Donya, you need to leave now. You are causing your mother pain."

"And what about my pain?" I shouted recklessly.

Akella was pointing at the door, about to tell me again to leave when Henori put a hand on her arm. "Maybe it is time. I should have told her long ago."

"Are you sure?" Akella's gaze was full of concern, even pity.

"Yes, I am sure. Leave us for a while. She has a right to know."

And so it was Akella who went out the door instead of me, giving me a warning look as she left.

Spider

We got up by the bell, ate by the bell, came to lessons by the bell, came to work by the bell, went to sleep by the bell. I was surprised we did not have to relieve ourselves by the bell. I suppose I was safe at the House of the Mother, but I certainly was not happy. After all, I had not chosen to be there, there was just nowhere else I could think of being at that moment. I felt exiled from what I now thought of as my true home, Althor House. And I was very angry at Suinyari for disappearing down her black hole of despair and leaving me abandoned just as Imalia had done. I was also angry at Donya for riding back to Ishlair without me when she could so easily have taken me with her to meet the Hadra. Altogether I was too angry to see the advantages of being in that place, all the things I could do and learn there. And of course I did not consider for one moment the kindness of these women in taking in this angry, troublesome child. I am sorry to say that I went right back to my old ways, far more likely to feel resentment than gratitude.

I had been used to having my own room and a good deal of privacy and independence. Now I found myself sharing a room with seven other girls and I was expected to keep my bed and all my things in order. It was especially hard at night. I had to lie there listening to the rest of them whisper and giggle and fart and snore when I wanted to sleep or at least be alone with my own thoughts.

Anyhow I was much too different from those other girls for us ever to be friends. They were all careful, orderly, obedient, eager to learn and totally boring. I found them insufferable and they found me impossible. I knew there was no way I could be "good" enough to fit into their little world and so I reverted to the worst of my street speech and behavior. I would say things to make them blush, to see the look of shock come across their faces. It was so easy and it gave me some sense of power when I was feeling so powerless. For their part they made fun of my speech. They called me a street-rat and a gutter-puppy and worse. They pointed and giggled and whispered among themselves, either stepping out of my way while holding their noses as if to avoid something foul-smelling or purposely blocking my way, bumping me or tripping me. I got into several fights that very first week and took a nasty pleasure in being stronger than any of them. The monster in me needed satisfaction. Hurting one of those haughty girls gave it to me.

Mother Melna tried to talk to us all in her kindly gentle way about loving each other, accepting our differences and caring for one another. Nothing changed. Things might have gotten even worse if not for Mother Olya. She suddenly appeared in our room one morning with Sister Haldrun right behind her, both of them looking very angry. I suppose the noise must have alerted them. I was fighting with Tamlin—she was the worst of the girls—while the others cheered her on. We were rolling around on the floor, each trying to get in a punch or a kick or to find some advantage.

When the rest of them saw Mother Olya an instant hush fell. She was not known for her gentle kindness or her patience either. In fact we were all a little afraid of her. She was not a very tall woman, but solidly built with big, strong, powerful arms. Not bothering to ask who was at fault or who had begun the trouble, she grabbed each of us by the back of our robes, lifted us off the floor and shook us. While we were still dangling there, she said in her rough voice, "Neith, Tamlin, you seem to have too much time on your hands. You will both come with me to the stables to report to Mother Golvini. Shakulu and Reesha will get a vacation this morning. When you have finished mucking out the stables you will report to Sister Ativan in the kitchen. There is still a big pile of pots from last night's meal. When you are done with that you can fold the sheets from the line. You will need to do that together. Do not let the ends fall in the dirt or you will have to wash them again. All that should occupy you for the day. If it does not teach you how to make peace with each other, tomorrow you can do it all over again. And if that is still not sufficient I can easily think of something more for you to do. If any of the rest of you want to continue this nonsense you can join them in the stable."

Sister Haldrun stood watching silently with her hands on her hips. She was glaring at us or rather at me, nodding her agreement to everything Mother Olya was saying, ready, I suppose, to step in if Mother Olya needed any help. Haldrun was no friend of mine. She had already warned me several times not to make so much trouble in the wash house.

I wanted to stamp my foot, to shout, "You cannot make me. I do not have to be here. I can go back to Althor House any time I please," but I held my tongue. No matter how bad it was here it was better than going back to Suinyari's bleak, blank silence. At least there was some life at the House of the Mother. I was afraid if I said anything rude to Olya she might really send me back.

Ordinarily we each had our chores to do, but nothing like this. Sister Ativan made sure we stayed in the kitchen until every pot had been scrubbed shiny and hung back on the rack. All the sheets in the place must have been drying on the line that day and we had to do a nimble dance together so that none of the edges dragged in the dirt. By the end of the day we were both exhausted. We certainly had no fight left in us. We even had a grudging respect for each other. Mother Olya came to look for us in the dining hall. "Well, have you made peace or do you need another day at the stables?"

"We have made peace," we both said in unison.

"Now, if you need to fight you should learn how to do it right and then only use it for self-defense. You are young for this, but perhaps you are ready. Both of you report to Sister Monarko at the practice yard tomorrow. Save your fighting for that place and that place only. I trust I will never need to tell either of you any of this again." We both nodded vigorously.

We never really became friends, but we did become steady sparring partners and we stopped baiting each other. Though I still had a kind of restless, troubled energy that was not satisfied by the ordered and scheduled pace of life there, some of my anger wore itself out in learning the skill of fighting. I found I even had a fair amount of skill at it, enough to occasionally earn Monarko's rough praise or approving nods.

Imalia worried about me and fussed over me in a way I found almost suffocating. She was not at all pleased with my learning to fight. "Oh, Aneithia, I do not think it fitting for a girl to do such things," she told me.

I wanted to laugh when I thought of all the things I had done while living on the streets that were not "fitting" for a girl. "Suinyari would not mind," I answered cruelly. "She would encourage me." With the perversity of youth, now that I had my birth mother's love and affection I no longer craved it, I did not even care much what she thought. It was Suinyari I longed for and missed terribly, Suinyari who was so far gone in grief she had all but forgotten me.

Donya

There was a long silence as Henori gathered her thoughts. I was about to lose patience when she finally began. "You have guessed of course that your father was a Shokarn. What I have never told you is that I was in love with him. He was not some anonymous stranger who wandered into the Gimling. He was a man I cared for so much I was willing to leave the Hadra, give up my life here and go live among the Shokarn or at least among the Kourmairi since the Shokarn would not have tolerated such a relationship. We would each be leaving the safety of our own world to try to make a life together in some Kourmairi town. I would gradually lose my Hadra powers and he would lose all his Shokarn privilege. We loved each other so much we did not care."

She fell silent, staring off into some far place while I waited. Finally I asked, "How did you meet? It seems a most unlikely happening."

"At a Kourmairi market in the town Barzin. He was traveling, exploring the world with all its differences. Being a gentle man who had no wish to be anyone's master, he was not comfortable with Shokarn ways. He certainly did not want to be forced to join the guard and so he was looking for another place to live and another way to be. I had come to the market with some other young Hadra of my age to shop for trinkets. I stayed behind at a stand when the others went on. When I turned he was there, watching me with a look of wonder on his face, much as one might watch a butterfly or a strange new bird. 'Are you really a Hadra? That is what the market women told me. I have never met a Hadra before.'"

"'And I have never met a Shokarn before,'" I told him with a mischievous grin. "'Maybe we should go sit somewhere and get to know each other.' Little did I know what I was saying, what would come of those thoughtless, careless words. We found a bench and sat and talked about our lives. No one had ever paid so much attention to my every word. When my friends finally found me, they were annoyed that I had left them and that they had been forced to look for me everywhere. They were also none to pleased to find me talking to a Shokarn. I went home with my friends, but not till Tengal and I had agreed to meet again, this time alone.

"The next time we met we strolled out of town together, talking intently about everything in our young lives, thinking we were something new in the world. We ended by making love in a field. That is how you were conceived. Not at night and in the secret darkness with an anonymous face over me, but in daylight with a loved face and a bright blue sky overhead, watched over by a whole flock of bobbing brightly-colored wild flowers and a few curious cows.

"After that we met many more times. Tengal had rented some little rooms in the town so he could be near me. When we knew we could not live apart any longer, we made our plans. We moved together into those rooms and played at house, both of us so very young and with so little knowledge of what the world could do. No doubt the Kourmairi thought us strange, but they were kind enough to us, almost protective. We had our year together; the Goddess granted us that. Our love did not wear out. If anything it grew even stronger. When you were born—a lovely baby who was such a wonderful mix of the two of us—it seemed like a miracle and served to strengthen our love.

"Then it happened. A group of Shokarn guards rode into town. We were in the town square at the market. I saw the fear on people's faces and how they backed away from these men. The guards rode right up to us as if they had been looking for us. The leader of them said to Tengal, 'We heard you were living here with a Hadra slut. Now it is time to be done with her and come home where you belong. First we will take care of her.'

"I was standing between your father and those men with you in my arms. I might still have had enough Hadra power to protect us all, but when the guard started to ride at me with his sword raised Tengal leapt between us. Instantly they cut him down with the blows that were meant for me. In their fury at being thwarted they hacked him to pieces in front of me. If I shut my eyes I can still see it all. I can still hear his screams. I was frozen to the spot, unable to move. When they tried to get at me their blows came back to them and several of them were wounded. Finally their captain shouted at them to stop. They gathered their wounded and rode off leaving me with bloody death in front of me, blood all over my clothes and blood on the baby.

"The horrified Kourmairi who had witnessed this attack helped to bury Tengal. I could do nothing, could not speak, could hardly walk, felt as if I had been struck blind. The Kourmairi sent for the Hadra and they came and took us home, back to Ishlair. I was like an invalid, like the walking dead. My own powers had turned back on me and blasted me with Tengal's terror and pain.

"The Hadra of Ishlair took care of me and they cared for you too because I could not. For a long time I could not even look at you. You had been spattered with your father's blood and that was how I still saw you if I even so much as glanced at you. I spoke to no one of what had happened and would not allow anyone to speak to me about it. As best I could I shielded my thoughts with whatever power I had left. Indeed it was almost a year before I was really speaking again. By then Akella had come into my life and was taking care of you. With her I finally began to regain my voice and was able to tell her a little of what had happened. That is why Akella is so protective of me, but I would talk of it to no one else, though of course the Hadra knew the story from the Kourmairi.

"Well, now I have told you your father's name and something of his life and of his death too. That is why I could not speak of it before; it was too terrible. I closed it up in a box and sealed it away in my heart. That is as much as I can say right now. I feel as if I have pulled the scab off an old wound, but perhaps now it will really heal. Maybe later I can tell you more about your father's life if that is what you want. He was a good man who did not deserve to die that way."

So I had been searching for a dead man all these years, most of my life in fact. "You should have told me long ago," I said with sudden bitterness. "Long ago!" Then I felt a surge of hot rage building up inside. "You should have told me! I had a right to know! He was my father!" I shouted at her, furious now, standing up and slamming my fists down on the table. If I could I would have shaken her.

Henori looked stricken. "I wanted to, so many times, but I could not bring myself to speak of it. He tried to protect us, tried to protect his woman and his baby. If he had let me stay in front of him he would still be alive. I saw him die right before my eyes and could do nothing. I blamed myself. All these years I blamed myself. I always felt as if it was my fault, that I should have been able to save him. And whenever I looked at you it reminded me. I am so sorry for what this cost you and how it has come between us." There were tears in her eyes and she was looking at me beseechingly. I had never seen such an expression on her face.

As suddenly as it had come my anger melted away and I was ashamed of it. How could I be angry in the face of so much pain? I stood up and reached out my arms to her. She stood up and let me hold her. "Mother, I have missed you so much all these years," I said softly against her hair.

"And I have missed you too, Daughter, more than you could possibly know. It was agony for me every time you went back to Eezore and to that woman and still I could not speak the truth, my words were frozen. All I could do was fight with you about it. Then, after you left, I would weep. Akella knows; she could tell you."

I held her away and looked her in the eye. "Good, then let this be an end to it. No more secrets between us and no more bad feelings. Can we agree on that?"

She nodded, then gave me a long questioning look. "What about your time in Eezore? Will you speak of that now? Will you talk to me about it?"

"Yes, anything you want to know. I will tell you as much as I can and if there is more you want to hear you need only ask."

"What about that Shokarn woman you fell in love with? What does she look like?"

"Wait, I will show you." I went to find the drawings of Suinyari among my things. Holding one of them in my hands, I felt a stab of pain as I looked at that loved familiar face. I had gained my mother and lost Suinyari. "This does not begin to do her justice," I said as I passed the picture to Henori. She sat staring at it for a long while. Finally she nodded. "Strength in that face as well as beauty," she said as she handed it back to me.

In those next few days Henori and I talked of many things. After a while it grew easier. As the barriers between us began to melt away, so did some of the hard lines in Henori's face. She told me so much about my father that he began to take shape in my mind as a real person, no longer a haunting ghost. I finally had a name for him and I could see his face in her mind, Tengal as a young man, about the same age as I was myself at that moment.

Now a different puzzle began to pester my thoughts and fill my mind. Who would I have been and what would my life have been like if my father had lived? Probably not a Hadra. How strange life is with all its little twists and turns. Would I have traded one for the other? I probably would not even have known. But maybe I would have grown up longing for my lost Hadra heritage, much as I now longed to break free of it.

Henori told me anything I asked. In return I talked to her about Suinyari and spoke my grief at losing her. I finally felt she understood. Perhaps she had understood all along and not wanted to. I also answered all her questions about Eezore. Akella left us alone most of the time, but when she passed through she smiled at me, smiled at us both, and I felt her blessing. Even my young bondsisters began to treat me with kindness and interest instead of contempt.

In that house I felt loved as I never had before. I even felt at home. But not in Ishlair. The failed healing had left me in a strangely disconnected place, belonging neither in Ishlair nor in Eezore nor anywhere else for that matter, not sure where I was supposed to be or what I was supposed to be doing. I avoided Mordica because I did not want to see the disappointment in her eyes. And I found myself uncomfortable and self-conscious around the women who had tried to heal me, as if I had failed them in some way. I think they felt as if they had failed me too and so we were shy of each other. I was also very troubled by having hurt Nazzem that way though I certainly had not meant to. I knew she did not blame me and yet I felt at fault.

I thought I should leave, go somewhere else, start over, but I had no idea where. For a while I was frozen, suspended between two worlds. I had not been able to pledge, not even for the sake of my healing, that I was done with Suinyari and would never go back. And yet day followed day and I did not return to Eezore. For one thing I was not sure Suinyari wanted me back. She had not even said goodbye or wished me well when I left. I kept thinking I should write to her and yet I did nothing. I could have sent a note with Shaleen when she stopped by to see if I wanted to go back with her. She even asked me if I wanted to send word with her, but I shook my head. "Later," I told her. "I will write later, when the next Wanderer caravan goes east. Right now I am not sure what to say."

Very slowly, as summer ended, I began to come out of my stupor and join the life of the settlement, harvesting the gardens, storing food away, cutting wood for the winter, repairing tumbled walls. Just by being there among the Hadra it felt as if I was gradually healing, regaining my powers, though of course I had no way to test my powers of self-defense. Everything in Eezore seemed very far away, much too far to reach out for, and everything in Ishlair seemed very small and close, almost suffocating. And yet, in spite of my sense of strangeness, I seemed to be settling back into the pattern of life there.

Spider

Everything at the House of the Mother was regimented, planned and organized. All the women there were in different levels signified by different color robes which we had to wear all the time. "It makes things much simpler not to have to worry about clothes," Mother Melna told me. I think it was just their way of keeping us under control. Personally I longed for my own clothes. Girls up to the age of sixteen and women who first came there were Yellowrobes. After that young women were Greenrobes and then went on to becoming Redrobes, earned by becoming proficient in some skill. Older women were Bluerobes. The purple robes were for the Mothers, the top of the heap, the ones who gave orders to the rest of us. All the others were Sisters except for the Yellowrobes, who were just "girls." I despaired of ever graduating to a green robe.

There were rules for everything, more rules than I could possibly remember, enough rules to choke on. I felt as if people were watching my every mistake. Lozell, who had helped Mother Melna get my mother off the streets, seemed to feel as if she had been appointed to be my special guardian, my guide to becoming a better girl and on to being a Greenrobe—and perhaps she had. Maybe she was trying to earn her blue robe by being my guard dog. If so I did not appreciate it. I did not even like her and I told her so. I think she did not like me either, but she still stuck to me like an annoying burr. Anishen, the other Sister who had helped with my mother, also seemed to feel some responsibility for me, but she was gentler and kinder with her advice and "guidance," more like Alliya at Althor House. Still she was another hovering watchful presence trying to make sure I obeyed all the rules.

In spite of their attention I felt very alone in that crowded place of busy productive women—and very lonely. My mother, who had become a Greenrobe and then had quickly gone on to earn her red robe, was always busy with her work in the weaving room and had little time for me. Besides we were too different. She was too sweet and timid for my rough ways. There was little real understanding between us. I think I frightened her. And her anxious, hovering love made me feel suffocated. She was always trying to tame me down, make me more acceptable, suggesting gently that I not talk so loud or move so fast. As for Mother Melna, she was far too busy keeping everything and everybody running smoothly to have much time for one troubled and troublesome girl—except once in a while to try and correct my bad ways in her kindly patient manner. As for the other girls, the rest of the Yellowrobes, I had no use for them or they for me. They were all too "nice" and "good," too eager to please their elders. All but one that is.

Nessa was about three years older than I was, but she was also a Yellowrobe, having just come there. She was another street-rat, another outsider. Her mother had been a rag-seller and had barely made enough money to keep them alive, living on the street. Like me, Nessa had learned the skills of snatching food wherever she could. When her mother knew she was dying she had brought Nessa to the House of the Mother, afraid of what would become of her wild daughter if she stayed on the street. "She did not have to bring me to this prison. I could have taken care of myself out there. I am not a baby," Nessa would say scornfully.

But of course it was not a prison and she was not a prisoner. The gates were open all day. She was free to leave anytime she pleased, but she did not. Instead she stayed and complained. Three meals a day and a dry bed no doubt helped to keep her there, but her grumbling drew my discontent. When I heard her say, "Those cursed bells, they make my head feel like it is splitting," I knew I had found someone I could talk to. "As if we would not have enough sense to get up in the morning and go to bed at night without all that clanging," she would say with scathing contempt.

Soon we began to go about together. Whenever we could find a moment away from our work we would hide away in some little corner with food we had snatched from the kitchen. There we would make fun of the other girls, gossip about the sisters and mothers and tell each other the stories of our lives.

Mother Melna was not at all pleased with this new association of mine and told me so quite plainly. "She is not a good influence for you, Neith. Being around her so much will certainly not benefit your life. I am sorry you chose someone like that to be your friend." I think she had hoped the other girls would eventually tame me. Instead I had picked someone who was worse than me in every way and Mother Melna's little talk had made her even more desirable. Nessa's language was cruder than mine, her voice was louder and her manners even more appalling. She was always getting "gently" reprimanded for her ways, but she was the only person there I felt comfortable with, the only one where I did not have to watch myself all the time and feel the strain of trying to be "better" than I really was.

I needed some release for the restless, angry energy that ate at me, burned in my blood. In that Nessa was a good companion for me—or a bad one depending on one's point of view. We did little acts of mischief together and were always in trouble with one of the mothers or sisters. Then she hit on the idea of our sneaking out together at night.

The gate was always closed at nine except for those who had the privilege of keys, and the candles and lamps in our room had to by blown out by ten—more bells, of course. In our explorations we had found a seldom used storage room that was quite close to the outer wall. The room had a small window that would probably not have accommodated a full-grown woman—especially not some of the mothers with their wide hips and broad backs—but it was no challenge to two skinny girls. There was a thick rope, attached to a strong hook in the wall, probably for hoisting things up through the double wooden doors that were now all boarded up. Perfect! Too much of a temptation, really. All we had to do was make some knots in the rope, then throw one end out the window and over the wall. After that we could just scramble down, using the knots for hand-and-foot holds, no great challenge for two street-rats who were used to making quick disappearances.

That night we waited until everything was dark and quiet. It would not do to go out in our yellow robes so Nessa had found us some dark ragged clothes that must once have belonged to boys. She thrust these into my hands and whispered that I should put them on quickly. There was no chance to ask her how she had managed this amazing feat. Instead, quivering with excitement, I tugged on the pants and pulled the rough shirt over my head. I tapped her arm as soon as I was ready.

There were always sisters who patrolled the halls at night to make sure everything was as it should be, but they were easy enough to evade. We were used to slipping around silently in the semi-dark. Street training has its uses. We met in the storage room with just a candle stub for light. Putting a box under the window, we scrambled up one at a time, wriggled out the window and slid from knot to knot down the rope. Without much effort we suddenly found ourselves out on the street, holding on to each other and having to choke back our nervous excited laughter. It had been almost too easy.

I followed Nessa. She knew the city much better than I did since I had mostly stayed in the Rhanthor Market and one little corner of familiar streets near it. Giddy with freedom, we went along peering into people's windows and looking in at inns and taverns, spying on lovers in the alleys, evading the guards and slipping away quickly if someone reached for us or tried to speak to us. Mostly we managed to stay out of sight and unobserved, but sometimes we had to run very fast and disappear quickly. This was a game I knew well, but I had never had a companion to share it with. After each of those chases we would end up breathless and exhilarated, clinging to each other with nervous laughter—victorious again.

The fourth night we went out on one of those ventures we ended up on a street full of women—women walking about boldly and provocatively, women in doorways, women sitting on windowsills, women calling out suggestively to the men who passed. I had never seen so many women on the street before. Except for the markets, men seemed to own the streets, especially at night. All these women appeared to be dressed in elegant but shabby clothes, many with fancy bows and sparkling jewels for decoration. Every once in a while one of them would vanish into the shadows with some passing man, slipping down an alley or into a building. Nessa held me back and made sure we kept ourselves well out of sight.

"What are they?" I whispered to her. "What is this? I have never seen so many women in the street before."

She laughed at my innocence. I think she had brought me here on purpose for a little lesson. "Easy Ladies, Night Walkers, Gutter Girls. They sell their bodies to men. When I lived on the streets I liked to come here and watch the goings-on."

Of course I knew there were women who traded their favors for money, though I had only a foggy idea of what that really meant. Even my mother had done that for a while. I just had never been on such a street. There was music coming from different places, snatches of sudden talk and laughter, strange cries, the sickly sweet smell of drugs on the air and for us the wonderful heady excitement of glimpsing the forbidden. I was having a grand time, watching this dangerous, secret life from our hiding place, feeling very bold and clever and grown-up. Then I heard horses galloping fast in our direction and men shouting. Nessa gripped my arm. She had the sense to be frightened before I did. Women began to scream. The men on horseback rode right into the middle of the scene, many with whips and some with swords. Shouting horrible things they began to lay about them, whipping women, knocking them down, even trampling them under the horses hooves. Even the men who had been on the street were not safe from this attack.

The noise was dreadful. The riders were yelling, "Stab those women! Crush them! Kill them!" Women were screaming, groaning, pleading for their lives. Men were crying out. I could hear the sound of blows landing and bones breaking like snapping branches as horses were ridden into fallen bodies. Where just moments before there had been a scene of dark forbidden gaiety now there was a scene of utter horror with blood in the streets, mangled bodies and people dying. I was frozen in fear, sure we would soon be discovered and killed the same way, but Nessa could still move. She grabbed my hand and gave me a hard tug. Then we ran all the way home without once turning around, sure that any moment we were going to feel the lash of the whip on our backs or the slash of a sword.

We got back breathless to the wall of the convent. I was not sure I would have the strength to climb, but fear drove me, lending power to my arms and legs. When we got into the room again, we helped each other pull in the rope and latch the window. I was about to collapse on the floor when I turned with a start and gave a little stifled scream. Mother Olya was standing there watching us, barely visible in the gloom.

"Do you two have anything to say for yourselves?" she asked with quiet menace. It was as if the darkness itself were speaking.

I was so terrified by what I had just seen and by Mother Olya's sudden appearance that I was struck silent. For once I had no words. Nessa more than made up for it. She poured out the whole story in one long string of words, hardly stopping for breath. There was just enough light for me to see Mother Olya's face change from a look of anger and disdain to one of fear and concern.

"How many are hurt? How far is it from here? Can you show us the way?" Not even waiting for an answer she said urgently, "You must come right now to tell Mother Melna your story."

Suddenly we were rushing down stairs and halls to Melna's room. We met Sister Monarko and Mother Yazeem on the way and they were swept along with us. Once there we breathlessly told the story again. I say "we" because by this time I had gotten my voice back and was able to join a little in the telling. There was no talk now of punishment for our crimes, only another flurry of questions. Soon bells were ringing and suddenly the halls were crowded with sleepy, puzzled and then alarmed women as the story was passed along from one to the other in a hubbub of voices. In no time they were dressing and preparing for a rescue. Monarko quickly and efficiently took charge of gathering supplies: bandages and salves and ropes and knives and whatever else might be needed. No one questioned the rightness of going to fetch those women and bringing them back for healing. They were only concerned with how best to do it and how to get there the fastest way possible. At that moment I saw these women in a whole different way, not as boring and ordinary, living by the bell, but as brave, strong, clever and resourceful warriors, women shaping their own lives in the face of a hostile world.

They dashed in and out, shouting orders and hitching up every available cart and wagon. Then they heaped in ropes and blankets and rugs and jugs of water and piles of clean rags for bandages. As soon as the wagons were on their way, they saddled and bridled all the extra horses. Everything was done with the utmost speed and efficiency. Dizzy with all this activity, I helped where I could and otherwise tried to stay out of the way.

Even though I had seen the raid happen I did not get to go with the rescue party. Knowing nothing of such things and unable to ride, I was of no use to them. Nessa of course went to show them the way. I stayed back with the other Yellowrobes. They left us in my mother's care. Imalia directed us as we laid out mats, row upon row of them, found bedding, ripped clean rags into strips, kept the fires going, boiled huge pots of water, heated food and did whatever else might be useful. We also put fresh bedding on our own beds, which would be used for the most seriously wounded.

It seemed like no time at all before they began straggling back, carts and wagons loaded with injured women, some scarcely alive. The cries and moans were terrible to hear. The moment a wagon stopped we Yellowrobes all rushed forward to help. We assisted in any way we could, getting the women onto beds or mats, cutting off bloody clothing and cleaning wounds, holding arms or legs still while healers salved and stitched and splinted and bandaged. Mother Yazeem was in charge of the healing. I had always seen her as a bent old woman with a soft voice who moved about slowly and with great deliberation. Now she rushed about shouting orders as loudly as any captain of the Guards and going almost at a run.

Those next few days were all a blur, a constant emergency with little time to eat or sleep because we were too busy feeding others and answering their calls of distress. Altogether we took care of some thirty to forty women with varying degrees of injury, a great strain on the healers as well as on the resources of the house. Some of the women died in spite of our best efforts. And some of them, surprisingly enough, were none too pleased to find themselves at the House of the Mother. I think they expected to be lectured for their ways by "women of virtue." One of them said as much to Mother Olya, and she answered tartly, "Our job is to save your lives and get your bodies back together in one piece. What you do with them after that is your business and certainly none of mine. We have enough to take care of here without telling you what to do with your lives." Others of those women were sweet and kind, more like my mother, very grateful for all our help and painfully bewildered by the violence of the attack. Some had already decided to stay on with us after they had healed.

I worked as hard as I could, doing whatever was needed, sometimes under Haldrun's direction with a whole crew of Yellowrobes, digging a grave or carrying huge pots of water to put on the fire, sometimes alongside Redrobes and Bluerobes as they set bones and stitched wounds. I learned to change dressings and apply herbal compresses. I brought food and carried out waste and fell into bed exhausted at the end of the day. I was so occupied with saving others that for a while I forgot my own problems. Sometimes I even forgot my own existence and was nothing but a useful pair of hands or a set of running legs. My eyes were gritty from lack of sleep and my arms and legs ached all the time, but for the first time I felt useful there, part of the life of the place.

When things calmed a little, Mother Melna called me into her office. I thought she meant to praise me for my hard work. Instead she shocked me by saying, "It is time for you to go back to Althor House now. I think Suinyari needs you at home. Besides you cannot stay here any longer."

How typical, now that I finally felt at home there I was being sent away. "But why?" I asked plaintively. "I have been good, done everything I was asked to and much more besides, worked as hard as I possibly could. I will never sneak out again."

"Probably not, but your restless spirit will find some other mischievous thing to do. It is in your nature. This is not the right place for you."

"But if Nessa and I had not gone out that night many of those women would have died."

"Without a doubt and we are very grateful to you, but Olya and I have had a long talk with some of the other mothers about it and we still cannot let you stay. We would send Nessa away too if there was anywhere else for her to go. Besides, I think Suinyari needs you to help bring her back out of that pit of grief she is still sunk in. Bethron is worried about her. She tells me Suinyari is no better."

So after all my hard work no one had spoken for me, not even Monarko who I thought liked me. I wanted to shout that I was just a child and it was not my job to save adults. Then I remembered that it was Suinyari who had saved my life when I was about to give up hope. Maybe she needed me now. "All right," I said sullenly. "I see I am just going to be moved about at everyone's convenience anyhow so I might as well say yes."

I packed my few things and then went to say goodbye to Nessa. She looked older than she had that evening such a short while ago when we had gone sliding down the rope in search of adventure—older and very tired. I was amazed to see that she was wearing a green robe. She gave me a hug. "Be well and stay out of trouble. I am training to be a healer, working with Mother Yazeem. I think I have found my work and my path. Come back soon to visit us." She looked and sounded like a different person. My companion was gone. Though her words were kind I felt as if a door had closed between us that would never open again. After that I said goodbye to Imalia, the only other person there who really mattered to me. She cried a little and held me tight. Then someone called her name and she had to go. I did not bother saying goodbye to Mother Melna or Mother Olya, I was too angry at being dismissed that way.

Lozell took me back to Althor House on the front of her horse. After my first few attempts at talking were met by curt answers we rode in stony silence. Finally she broke that silence to say, "After all the mothers have done for you, you have proved to be a wretchedly ungrateful child. I will be glad not to have you in my care anymore."

Ah, so that was how the wind blew. "Well, I never asked to be in your care in the first place. No one consulted me about it. As to gratitude, that was not something I learned on the streets. It was not a useful skill for surviving there." I choked back my tears, not wanting Lozell to see me cry. No, I would not give her that pleasure. When we rode into the yard I was off the horse almost before it stopped and did not look back to say goodbye or thank you. Instead I rushed up and pounded on the green door. Suinyari herself answered the door. She gave me a surprised and startled look. Lozell followed me to the door and handed her a note. Before Suinyari could say anything, Lozell was back on her horse and gone.

I was fighting tears and very worried about what Suinyari would say to my disgrace. "I was afraid for you," I said quickly. "I wanted to come home and keep you company, help bring you out of your gloom. Besides I did not like it there, too many rules."

I was talking desperately fast while she was reading the note. "Oh, really," she said as she finished and turned to look at me. "This note tells quite a different story. I think you have some explaining to do."

"I missed you and I just wanted to come home," I said simply, suddenly aware that there was some real truth in those words.

Suinyari continued to stare at me in that stern fierce way until I was shaking inside. Then, suddenly, she threw back her head and laughed. "Well, maybe you are going to cheer me up after all. I have missed you too. I understand that you were too much for them. No surprise. I always used to get in trouble when I was there. This note says you had quite an adventure. Come and tell me all about it." As we went in she shouted, "Gammo, Bethron, bring us some tea. Neith has come home."

Suinyari

I have missed Donya terribly this winter, but I suppose that is no more than I deserve. I drove her away with my coldness and have no idea if she ever means to come back. There has been no word from her though several Wanderers have come through the city from the west. Sometimes I get angry at her silence. Then I think, What can I expect after the way I treated her? And I myself do not write though I think of it every day. My heart aches with longing, but I do not know what to say to her.

Neith came back before I sent for her, well before I was ready. They sent her home with a startling letter, the sum of which was that she was too much for them to manage and they wanted me to deal with her. I still felt like a dead thing. I had so little to give. How could I be anyone's mother? How could I give the child the love she needed? But Neith told me quite clearly that she was done with being at the

House of the Mother. "There are too many rules. I feel as if I always have to be good. Mother Melna is too kind, worse than Alliya. And my mother is too sad and loves me too much. Her love feels like a burden, like carrying a big rock up a hill. I am tired of hearing how sorry she is for leaving me—as if that could change anything. Besides I missed you and I wanted to come home."

"That is not what this note says." I shook the paper at her and she blushed. Mother Melna had written me a long kindly note explaining what had happened and Neith's part in it. What this meant about the city was frightening enough and I shuddered to think of the danger to Neith. Mother Olya had added a short curt note at the end:

> *You wanted this child. Now it is time for you to take responsibility for her life and for your own as well. These times are very dangerous, especially for a woman like you. Wake up, Suinyari! This is not the moment to go about sleepwalking and feeling sorry for yourself. It is not safe. You are not the first person to love a fool and end up feeling betrayed and despairing. And you surely will not be the last. We have all been there. Get over it and get on with it. The child needs you and for many reasons we cannot keep her here any longer. Mother Olya.*

As if I needed to see her name at the end to know who had written me that. She was right, I knew she was right. I tried to do as she said, but the melancholy that had fallen on me would not lift.

I think during that sad winter Gammo became Neith's mother. I would hear them talking and laughing together and wonder what there was to be so happy about. I had so little spirit that Alliya finally took over the girl's lessons. At Torvil's insistence I bought Neith a stout black pony that she named Alabout. Torvil taught her to ride and was very proud of his pupil. All the love she had once felt for Gordivan she now transferred to Torvil, following him about and helping in the stable. She never asked about Gordivan and avoided him in that quick, silent way she had whenever he showed his face in the house.

For myself I asked Torvil to teach me the use of the sword and knife in my own defense. I thought he might object. Instead he said, "It is about time. We should have done this long ago. Your father would have approved." I was glad when Neith announced that she was joining us and hoped that it would help to keep her safe on those dangerous streets. She was too big now to slip away and hide the way Spider had. It was one of my few pleasures that dreary winter, sharpening my lethal skills with Torvil's help, killing Nosharn over and over. The business, of course, suffered with Gordivan staying mindless with drink and my having no heart for it, but I had enough money set by to see us through. Besides, I did not even care.

As to Nosharn's death, I found myself waiting, always waiting for the next act in that strange, troubling drama in which I had so unwittingly and unwillingly played a central role. For a while nothing happened. None of his relatives came to inquire. There seemed to be no trouble boiling up on the horizon, though when I asked Mother Melna what was to come she seemed troubled and would not look me in the eye. "I see some terrible chaos in the future and it involves us all, not just you, Suinyari, yet nothing comes clear enough to give us warning as how best to avoid it. But you know my far-seeings are seldom reliable." She was shaking her head. I could get nothing more from her.

In spite of my anxiety, it was a fairly uneventful winter and rather mild as winters go in this northern city. After a while I began to recover my desire for life and started to come back to myself. I even tried to mend the rift with Neith. It took a while and considerable effort on my part, perhaps her way of punishing me for my absence. The girl kept growing taller and more beautiful. Spider with her feral wariness and her sly ways seemed to have almost disappeared, though I know Neith still kept her little knife tucked in her sleeve, not a bad idea since the streets of Eezore were not really safe for a young woman-child.

When the weather allowed it, she rode off on Alabout, going on errands for the house or visiting with Imalia at the House of the Mother, but she never again spent the night under that roof. When the wind blew with a vengeance and deep snow swirled about the streets she stayed home and studied with me as I began to come back into the world, or we sat before the fire and read to each other. She was growing and changing so fast I felt as if I was losing her already, though in truth I never really had her. She had never been the sweet, loving child I had longed for, but she was the only daughter I was likely to have. Even though I shared her with another mother, I much appreciated her company during that lonely winter and was very glad after all that she had come back to Althor House. Finally I was able to tell her that.

Meanwhile Donya stayed away in Ishlair and I was not sure if she was ever coming back. Though Gordivan seemed to be recovering somewhat from his grief—at least enough to begin taking part in the business again—the old easy camaraderie that had been ours since childhood was gone. It had been replaced by a careful, cool politeness between us that cut my heart. I could never really trust him again nor could I ever forgive him for his betrayal. For his part I think he blamed me for the manner of Nosharn's death and his own loss of love. "You have Donya in your life and I have no one," he would say angrily to me. Never mind that Donya was gone or that Nosharn had intended my death and probably his as well. Gordivan had a bitterness at the core. He had lost his innocence. That is something that can never be given back.

As the winter dragged on, I looked forward to the first signs of spring. Indeed when I saw the first blossoms on the fruit trees I thought enough time had passed that my worries about Nosharn were over. Then, on a lovely spring day when we had just opened all the windows to air out the stale smells of winter, I heard angry male voices at my front door. I knew it was no friend; friends ride into my back courtyard. Dondo started barking fiercely and I rushed down the hall to find Bethron trying to block the door. From the other side of it someone shouted, "Get out of my way woman. I am Nosharn's brother, Ormath, and I insist on seeing that woman Suinyari right now."

"Let him in, Bethron. Nosharn's brother is welcome in my house and so are his friends." As Bethron stepped aside giving me a warning look, I swung the door wide and held Dondo's collar. Growling low, the dog tried to lunge as four large men pushed their way into my hall. The tallest one was clearly Nosharn's brother. He looked like a bigger, older, harder version of Nosharn himself, as if that one had suddenly come back to life. A deep scowl and a sullen angry look marred his otherwise handsome face as he glared down at me from his considerable height. "If you are Suinyari I need an accounting from you for my brother's death. I do not credit the story I was told. I think you may have had some part in his death."

"I very much regret that you feel that way. He was Gordivan's good friend and mine as well. He died defending us in a bandit attack and had a hero's funeral in this city. If you have ridden a long way today you must be weary. Come sit in my parlor where we can talk more comfortably and Alliya will get us all some refreshments. Then I will tell you everything I remember of that tragic day."

"I will sit down, but we need no refreshments. We have just come from talking to the Zarn. The old Zarn is half dead and much more concerned with his failing body than with affairs of state. But the young Zarn-to-be, Gunjorn, was very interested in my story. I know from Nosharn's letters that he was no friend of yours, that in fact you hated each other. He told me that he was trying to help Gordivan get back what was rightfully his and you were trying to drive him out of the house. Then, very conveniently, he died. Our father was too ill at the time; I could not come before this. Now that I am here I intend to get at the truth. I demand to speak to Gordivan."

"My husband is not here at the moment. I am not sure when he will be back." I said, trying to keep my calm and looking him right in the eye. "But I am sure he will be glad to see you as soon as he returns." I hoped Gordivan would not come down in a drunken stupor to endanger us all with careless words. Actually I had no idea where he was, but I trusted that if he was anywhere in the house or nearby Alliya had gone to warn him. Ormath and his men stayed until dusk, sitting on the edge of their chairs or pacing about restlessly, grumbling to each other. Finally, much to my relief, they left, promising to be back the next day. After they were gone, Neith came out of hiding.

Donya

Fall in Ishlair turned to winter and winter brought with it unusually harsh weather—snow, sleet and freezing rain—that necessitated long days inside. I grew restless again. Something was tugging at my spirit. When there was a sudden warm spell—melting snow and clear skies—I left Ishlair and began drifting down the coast. I knew this hurt my mothers, especially Henori after our new closeness, but I could not help it. I had an itch of restless discontent and had to keep moving. Promising to be back in the spring, I wandered until I reached the Hadra city of Zelindar, the place that had been calling to me all along.

From the moment I first saw Zelindar I fell in love with her much as one might fall in love with a woman. She had all the excitement of newness and strangeness with delightful surprises at each turn of the street, all the richness and variety of a city, but none of the harshness and fear that stalked the streets of Eezore, no guards, no slaves, no Zarn to rule over everyone. Zelindar fascinated me with her endless beauty and her rich history. All the stories of the Hadra were in the archives of the Zildorn there and I found myself drawn back to it over and over.

This seemed like a good place to spend the rest of the winter. I drew and painted everything I saw, trading my work for food and lodgings. I never tired of looking at the scene in all different weather: the sea crashing against the shore, sometimes bright blue, sometimes sea-green, sometimes silver-gray under dark storm clouds; the three hills covered with white stone buildings; the blue Escuro River winding its way through the city and into the land beyond. It was a painter's dream. I also drew and painted the Hadra of that city in all their amazing variety. Many a Hadra home soon had a portrait of mine hanging on its walls.

When I first got to the city I promised myself I was not going to pine away there. After a while I began looking at other women with an interested eye, thinking that maybe this one or maybe that one could distract me. I knew I needed to get over my longing for Suinyari and move on with my life. But each time the other woman seemed to reciprocate my interest and it came close to happening, something in me drew back and turned away. I lost my appetite for sexual adventure the moment it appeared to be a possibility. It was not as if I had made Suinyari any pledge of fidelity and yet each time it felt like a betrayal, strange since the Hadra are not nearly so rigid about such matters as the Shokarn. Before we are bonded it is not unusual for a Hadra to maintain several sexual connections without any upset or jealousy occurring.

One time I went home with a Hadra named Mushaki, a lively woman with wildly curling hair and the strong supple body of a dancer. I even ended up in bed with her. She was also an artist. We met when she had stopped to watch me paint in one of the city's many parks. I felt very drawn to her as if there was an understanding between us. I was pleased that it had gone this far, excited even, thinking, *Yes, please, Goddess, this time let it happen, please!* She was stroking my body and I was melting into her touch when something she did reminded me of Suinyari. Instantly my body withdrew and closed in on itself. The heat of ardor turned into a sheen of cold sweat that chilled my body and made me shiver. Tears of frustration burned on my closed eyelids.

With a sob I sat up, shaking my head to clear it. When I reached out a hand to her, I was afraid she would push me away. "I am so sorry, Mushaki. I did not mean to lead you on. I really wanted something to happen between us. I hope you are not angry with me. This has nothing to do with you. It is only that I…"

She shook her head. Instead of pushing me away she interrupted my apologies with a gentle hand over my mouth. "Hush, Donya. Enough. I understand. I am who I am and not the one you long for." Then she drew me into her arms. Hugging me against her, she rocked me gently while I sobbed and wept and gnashed my teeth with frustration. After a while she said softly, "I am not angry, dear one, only disappointed. I know what you are struggling with and I had hoped to give you some comfort and joy."

At those words I pushed her away. "Were you making love to me out of pity? Is that what you were doing? I do not need your pity." I felt a little flush of anger rush up my face.

At that she shook her head and laughed. "Not at all! I am not nearly so generous as all that, believe me. I am very attracted to you; you can look in my head and see the truth of that. I was hoping I could be the one to draw you out of your grief. But I know your story; I understood that I was taking my chances. How can I be angry at you? I put myself right in the path of it."

We spent the rest of the night in each other's arms, sharing the stories of our lives. We did not become lovers, but we did become good friends. In the morning she said, "If you ever change your mind, Donya, you know where to find me." Then she gave me a quick kiss right on the mouth and pushed me out the door. After that I stopped looking for bed companions. I settled for friendship and the pleasures of my work.

I thought perhaps I could settle in Zelindar. After all, I had no past there, nothing to weigh me down with guilt or regret. Indeed I had several invitations to stay, including an invitation from the Councilor herself to be the official artist for the Zildorn and make a visual record of life in that city. It was very tempting and I was seriously contemplating it, but when the first hint of spring came—and it comes early in the southland—I found myself on the road north, headed not for Ishlair as I had intended, but for Eezore. I had not been able to rid my mind and heart of Suinyari. Thoughts of her had haunted me all that winter. I had drawn and painted her face many times from memory. Now I needed to see her again and settle whatever was between us. Otherwise I would never be able to live in peace in Ishlair—or in Zelindar either.

Suinyari

It is happening, just as I feared. Twice in the last week I have been called before a magistrate and questioned at length about Nosharn and the manner of his death, tricky questions with many sudden twists and turns. They know little but suspect much. Honesty would be fatal, but even lies are very dangerous and must be carefully thought out, planned and remembered. Ormath has taken his case to the young Zarn-to-be and enlisted his help. The old Zarn is ill, probably dying, and cannot be bothered with such things. Besides, I think he has always had a soft spot for me. But Gunjorn would be only too glad to have a case against me. From what I hear from my spies in the palace, Ormath is feeding it to him. Between them they seem determined to bring me down, Ormath to avenge his brother and Gunjorn because I am a woman of some power and standing in this city. When his grandfather dies, I think he will have no scruples with evidence. Even now I fear that if they find nothing to charge me with soon, they will invent what they need.

They have even brought Gordivan in for questioning. Luckily he sobered up enough to remember our agreed-upon story. Also I suppose his very real grief for Nosharn impressed the magistrate though I warned him not to make too much of a display of his feelings lest they guess the real reason for the depth of them. Aside from that we are barely talking to one another. Not a kind word has passed between us since we came back to the city. Each of us feels such a deep sense of hurt and betrayal we cannot bear the sight of the other. I think it is only a matter of time before one of us contradicts the other or scrambles the tale and we are both ruined.

With every passing day it becomes more dangerous for my kind in this city. Gunjorn and his band of Purifiers—urged on by the Grayrobes—are growing ever more brazen and violent. Raids like the one Neith witnessed are becoming more and more frequent. Often I think it is time to leave now, but how would I make a living elsewhere? Here I am known, I have a whole network of associates. Where would I go? What would I do? I can think of no place where I would want to start over, make a whole new life for myself.

And yet I worry all the time. I think Neith is in danger from living with me, but where can I send her where she would be safe? Certainly nowhere in this city, not even the House of the Mother, that is closed to her now. To the Hadra perhaps. She would probably like that, but she cannot get there without Donya's help and Donya is not likely to be back. The house would seem strange and empty without her. Yet if they take me there would be no one here able to protect her. I hate to think of her back on the streets again or, worse yet, in the hands of the Grayrobes. My head goes round and round in circles and I see no answers.

I have told Torvil he is free to leave any time and no bad feelings. I even offered him some money to start again elsewhere, but he is a stubborn man and refuses to leave me, saying that my father saved his life. "Oh, but that was then and this is now, a very different time," I tell him. I even remind him that he has already saved my life, canceling any debt between us, but he laughs and says I save his life every day just by being who I am. They have questioned him also and he has kept to our story, but I am very afraid they may soon resort to torture and that would be the end for us all.

Ah, so many question and no answers and no one to ask, certainly not Donya, for she has gone back to her precious Hadra. No, that is my jealousy speaking, I should not grudge her that. She had lost some of her powers from living with me in a Shokarn city, living among the Ganja as the Wanderers call us. Perhaps her sisters can heal her and make her whole again, but then will she ever come back or is she lost to me? Every time I think of going to live there among those women, my awful stubborn Shokarn pride stops me. I often think of my father. He always had a plan and so I try to imagine what he would tell me or what he would do in my place. Meanwhile I fret and worry and pace about and do nothing, so different from my usual self who leaps into action. Perhaps I am waiting here to die since I seem so unable to move in my own behalf.

One afternoon, when Neith and I were alone in the house, I heard a desperate knocking, more a pounding really, at my back door. When I opened the door, Granthia was standing there, breathing hard, her face flushed, her eyes wide with fear. "Hide me quickly, I need a place to hide. They burned the inn and the stable and tried to kill me because sometimes the girls..."

"Get in here quickly," I hissed at her as all in one gesture I grabbed her arm, pulled her inside and kicked the door shut. "Did anyone see where you went? Were you followed?"

"No, not that I know of. There was too much smoke and a lot of noise. I ran as fast as I could, but once I got near your house I kept looking back and there was no one after me."

Though her face was red she was shaking with cold. I drew her over by the fire and pushed her down in a big chair in front of it. Then I tossed her a shawl, poured her a glass of strong spirits and dipped a hot poker in it to heat it. "Drink that to warm you. Then talk to me and tell me everything that happened." Chills of fear were running up my back.

She downed the drink quickly and gave a little gasp. When she had caught her breath she said all in a rush, "They just came bursting in with no warning, a whole horde of them and instantly set to smashing chairs and tables and bottles. They had clubs and whips. They whipped people as they ran out. I ducked into the kitchen to hide. I thought they would come there next, but instead they ran upstairs. I heard the girls screaming. I slipped out the back and ran. When I looked back they had set the place on fire, flames and smoke everywhere. They kept shouting that my inn was a brothel because some of the girls, you know...sometimes...They probably killed them all, but what could I do? They would just have killed me too." She stopped with a gasp, then shook her head, burst into tears and did not say another word.

"Who?" I shouted, grabbing her by the shoulders, "Who did this, Granthia? Who are you talking about?"

I shook her hard, but still it was a long moment before she could speak again. "Purifiers, a whole bunch of them in those new black and gray uniforms they have taken to wearing. There was a Grayrobe too, but he stayed out in the street, shouting encouragement. He kept saying, 'Make sure you get Granthia! This is her place so she is the worst of the lot.' They meant to kill me, I am sure of it."

"Your daughter? Where is your daughter?" I asked urgently, suddenly remembering.

"In the country. I sent her to live with my mother when this madness first began."

"Well, you are safe here for the moment. When Torvil comes back he will take you to the House of the Mother and they will hide you away." I was trying to reassure her, but I myself was far from reassured. This was all much too close to home. Granthia was one of my best contacts, part of my web of secret connections, but she never came to my house. That would have been much too risky. Now they had burned her inn. Who would be next? I saw the look of shock on Neith's face. I tried to put my arm around her for reassurance, but she shook me off and drew away abruptly, wrapping her arms around herself instead. I had promised her safety if she came to live with me instead of chancing the dangers of the streets. She had trusted me. Now she saw I could not keep my word.

Mother Melna

So difficult to get a fix on it. Sometimes it seems like my life is just a series of errors, just so many shortcomings and failures. Other times it feels as if everything I turn my hand and heart to blossoms, flourishes and succeeds. Goddess knows Lurghan left me with a heavy burden of responsibility. At times, no matter how I try, I feel that I fall far short of it. Why have I suddenly taken to trying to sum up my life that way? I never did that before, much too busy with the next thing that needed doing. And anyhow, nothing comes clear. Each time I only find myself more frightened and confused.

"You fuss too much," Mother Olya tells me. Maybe she is right. But then perhaps it is because I sense that things are ending here and so I have started looking back. But what is next? Where are we going? Nothing comes clear there either except that this is over and it is time for the next thing. Sorry, Lurghan, I held on to your dream for as long as I could. Now it is slipping out of my hands. Forces far beyond my control are moving.

This city is teetering on the brink of chaos. While the old Zarn lies dying, followers of his grandson get more bold and daring with each passing day. Shouting the name of Rha-ais, god of war, to give them courage, they have bloody skirmishes with the guards. Full of righteous wrath, they stage raids on gaming houses and brothels, driving the occupants out with whips and setting fire to the buildings. Sometimes the night is full of screams and shouts. The next day a pall of smoke hangs over the city.

At the same time the more conservative elements of the city, frightened by these wild young men and afraid they themselves might become their target, are trying to bring the Zarn's minister Khazil to power as the next Zarn. They are seeking to gather as many as they can into their camp, even those from other castes. Meanwhile the Grayrobes keep shifting sides. Lurking like strange, dangerous shadows they do whatever is likely to give them the most power and make others fear them. They are more and more visible on the streets now. Whichever side wins it is clear they will be a power to be reckoned with in the future. And under all that there are other elements who would be only too glad to take advantage of civil strife to make some mischief of their own, the rabble among the common people who love violence for its own sake and the Thieves Guild who are always waiting at the edge of things like birds of prey.

We knew it was almost time. Getting ready to leave, we had cleared everything of value from the House of the Mother and hidden it all in caves and passages underneath, though we were not yet agreed on where to go or when. How could we leave all this? Where could we create again what we had made here? I wanted to send some of the young women out of the city, send them west to some Kourmairi settlements, but they kept saying they would not go without us. "Besides, we would be strangers there, outsiders. How do we even know they would take us in?"

And so we went on day by day. It was hard to go when more and more women were coming to us for refuge. It was also hard to leave the place that had been our home for more than forty years. Olya and I had built this place up from ruins and knew intimately every rock and beam and board. We had laid out the gardens that supported our lives. All the flowers and herbs and vegetables had been planted by our hands or under our direction. Every fruit tree was an old friend. The flowering vine that twined up the arch of the gate and bloomed bright pink and red all summer had been planted by my own hands thirty years ago. I welcomed it back with joy each spring when the new little leaves uncurled from the rough gray dead-looking stem and then the flowers burst out, fragrant and plentiful.

Each day I would say, "We need to go. We need to leave at the latest tomorrow by dawn or tonight in the dark. It is not safe here anymore." Then some other distraught-looking woman would be at our gates and Olya would say, "How can we leave when they need us more than ever now? Where would she have gone if we were not here?" And so, the next morning, the argument would start all over again. Then there would be a few days of calm and I would think, *Perhaps it is not so urgent after all, perhaps it will all settle itself out.* After all, there had been upheavals in the city before and we had always weathered them.

Donya

There were rumors in Zelindar of how bad things had gotten in Eezore, but it was not until Suinyari's friend Zathrun came through with a Wanderer caravan that I knew the extent of it. He said his caravan was turning around and going right back, thinking this might be their last time of trading in that city. I think in truth he came looking for me. When he told me about Nosharn's brother making an appearance I feared for Suinyari's safety. At that moment it no longer mattered to me if she wanted to see me again or even if she loved me. Clearly her life was in danger. I decided to return with the Wanderers and make one last attempt to get her to leave the city, very much afraid I might already be too late.

I was traveling again with a whole troupe made up mostly of men. It was quite an experience for me and one I will write more about later on, but they knew all the roads and got me there much faster than I would have managed on my own. They also made it easy for me to enter the city. Once in Eezore I felt a little hesitant. Not knowing how things stood between us I was not sure whether to go up the front walk and knock on the formal red door or ride into the courtyard and knock on the green door. The green door won, but I never got the chance to knock on it. Just as I rode into the courtyard the door was flung wide and Spider came flying out of it with Dondo barking at her heels. She was shouting, "Donya is back! Donya is back!" Suinyari was right behind her. Without a thought, I was off my horse and into her arms. Then both of us were laughing and crying and kissing each other while Spider jumped up and down with excitement and Dondo flung himself against us barking and licking. Then, except for Gordivan, the rest of the household poured out to greet me, seeming very glad to have me back.

I did not ask Suinyari if she had missed me and she did not ask me either. No need. We said it without words by the way we clung to each other, talking, touching, kissing, following one another from room to room. As soon as it was decently dark we fell into bed together, but we did not get much sleep. All the longing and frustration of the past few months fell away in a storm of loving. We made love and then talked and then made love again and talked some more until the darkness began to gray. Then we finally slept for a few hours. I wondered later how I could ever have thought of loving someone else. I felt as if I had finally come home, though I knew in some other part of my mind that I was separating myself from my Hadra home—perhaps forever.

Though she was very glad to have me back, Suinyari seemed no more ready to listen to reason than she had before. I kept telling her she had to make ready to leave and soon, that the city was growing more dangerous every day, but this woman who was usually so clever and powerful and self-willed seemed to dissolve before my eyes, losing her will and her strength, dithering around in confusion and indecision instead of making the needed preparations. Since she seemed unable to make decisions I set the rest of the household to packing up the valuables and getting prepared for departure. They seemed only too glad for someone to take charge and get things moving. Gordivan of course was no help at all. He was drunk most of the time. At least he had the sense not to go out and frequent the gaming houses that had become a target of Purifier wrath.

When I finally grew impatient and tried to shake some sense into Suinyari, she burst into tears, something I had never seen her do, not even when Nosharn had captured her. "But where can I go? What can I do? This city is my life. I have never lived anywhere else. Everything that matters to me is here."

"This city will be your death. These young men who are going to come to power will not let you live and carry on your business. Even if the Khazil faction wins out—not a likely happening—things here will change. The old Zarn's ways will not continue. And this Ormath is a terrible danger. The man is determined to see you dead and nothing is going to stop him."

"But I have friends in high places who will protect me."

"Those friends will abandon you quicker than a fish on dry land will jump back into water. They may even be the first to denounce you in order to insure their own safety. When the change comes you will be a danger to them and they to you. Nothing will be as it has been. Besides, think of Neith, think of the rest of your household. They will not leave without you and you endanger them all by staying here. You and Neith can come to Ishlair with me and we can find a place for the others in a neighboring Kourmairi settlement."

"But we have already been over this a hundred times, Donya. I cannot live with you in a Hadra settlement and be the only person there with no power."

"Suinyari! That is just your pride talking! Staying here will cost you your life. Things will never go back to what they were. No matter what happens at the top, no matter who wins this struggle for power, the old ways are over and you cannot continue here as you have been."

I think I had almost convinced her when two things happened. First Ormath sent a messenger to say that he been called to Pellor on urgent business, but that he would return soon and would settle with her then. The note ended with the threatening words, "Do not think you will escape punishment for what you have done. I will be back to avenge my brother." In spite of that Suinyari burst out laughing as soon as the man had left. "Ormath is gone. We are done with him. The more time goes by the weaker his case grows and he knows it. He will not be back to plague us, I am sure of it." With that she ripped the note into little pieces and tossed them in the air with a triumphant shout. Nothing I said could convince her otherwise.

The next thing was a rumor going through the city that the old Zarn had rallied and had been seen walking about the palace and even in the gardens. The city took on a strange sort of gaiety as if that terrible old man was something to celebrate.

"You see," Suinyari said with a little of her old spirit shining through. "No need to panic, we only need to wait it out. The wind may soon blow in the other direction, especially if the old Zarn gives his blessing to Khazil as his successor. Then these young hoodlums who call themselves Purifiers may all find themselves being tried for treason and those Grayrobes along with them. That is a trial I would actually enjoy sitting through if only they would allow women to attend. This is not the first time there had been a commotion in Eezore and it will not be the last. I have always landed on my feet before. I am not about to abandon my house or my place in this city."

"Suinyari, Suinyari, how can you be so willfully blind? This is not the same thing."

But I was talking to air. She was not listening to me. Full of energy, she was sweeping down the hall, calling out to Bethron and Alliya about organizing a big party to celebrate the Zarn's recovery. "This time I am not just going to talk about it. This time I am really going to do it, invite all the people who used to come to our parties. Get Gordivan sobered up and on his feet to be the charming host. It is time to move forward, time to end all this gloom and bring some joy back to this city and this house."

Part III

Spider

That day, just before it all happened, I was strolling down Atherton Street on my way to the House of the Mother. My pony was lame. Torvil had told me not to ride him for a few days so I was going on foot. I wanted to see my birth mother again. She was loving in a way that Suinyari could never be, no matter how she tried. Sometimes, now that I had mostly forgiven Imalia, I found myself in need of that kind of love. Truth be told, I also wanted to flirt a little with Nessa. I was afraid she still thought of me as just a child, but I had quite unchildlike feelings for her and enjoyed being in her presence. Since our adventures together I had been back to visit several times, though I always tried to avoid Mother Olya and even Mother Melna.

Suinyari had warned me not to go out. She told me the streets of Eezore were no longer safe for a girl-child alone, that I should only go out with Bethron or Torvil, but that morning things seemed very quiet. In fact the last few days had been quiet. There had been none of those marauding bands about that caused so much trouble. Besides they were usually more active in the late afternoon or early evening. Suinyari had not expressly forbidden me from going out, but she had instructed Bethron to keep watch over me.

Arrogant little fool that I was then, I told myself there was really no harm in going *just one more time*. Besides I had my knife safely tucked up my sleeve in case of trouble. I even imagined myself very clever in evading Bethron's watchful eye. How I hated to be forbidden anything. With blissful ignorance I thought, *I can take care of myself.* After all, I had lived on the streets for years with only my own wits to keep me safe. Of course that was as Spider, who was much more watchful than Neith. She was also faster, cleverer, smaller and thinner, all good qualities for staying safe in a dangerous world. And Spider would have been wearing old gray rags, hardly noticeable, not the new blue and green tunic I had put on to impress Nessa. Also, as Neith, I had allowed myself to be loved and that had made me less wary. Altogether I was very pleased with myself that morning—and very stupid.

I still remember every detail of the day. It was a lovely spring morning. All the trees in the city were in bloom. There were masses of colorful blossoms in the courtyards and overflowing flower stands brightened many of the street crossings. I was looking around me with pleasure, full of energy and delight, feeling strong and healthy, also knowing from the mirror that I was not bad-looking. In fact, Neith had become quite the young lady in the last year or so. I knew I was freer than most young women in the city, far freer than I would have been as the daughter of an Uppercaste Shokarn family. Pinned to my tunic I was wearing the insignia of Suinyari's house which up till now had protected me. It proclaimed me a servant to that house, though in truth I was more like the beloved daughter. Actually I liked to indulge in a little fantasy of myself as the orphan niece, the child of impoverished parents, a child who had been fortunate enough to be claimed and brought home by a mysterious, wealthy and loving aunt. I remember being consciously aware at that moment of how very lucky I was and how happy—probably happier than I had ever been in my life.

Being in no hurry I had stopped for a few minutes to watch the water from a fountain sparkling in the sunlight. When I turned back I was surprised to see that the street had suddenly cleared. People had drawn back into doorways or disappeared inside. As Spider I would have been instantly alert to danger. She would likely have disappeared, quicker than a cat or a bird. As Neith I merely had that one moment to be puzzled before one of those monks in a long gray robe stepped out in my path. He had been hiding in an archway and now raised his arms to block my way. "That one," he shouted, pointing at me.

At Suinyari's table we had often laughed at those monks who were more and more appearing in public places, calling them gray turds for the lumpy gray robes they wore, but there was also an air of menace about them. At that moment it was all menace. I had no inclination to laugh. I was terrified.

Finally aware of the danger I was in, I spun around to escape his reach only to find myself trapped by two guards. Before I could get away they had dropped a net over me, pinning my arms at my sides. I shouted and struggled, but I was too late to save myself. When I tried to kick out at them they merely tightened the net around my ankles and wound a rope around the whole package. Then one guard held me easily while the other went for their horses. Meanwhile the Grayrobe looked me up and down with contempt. With malice and a touch of amusement he said softly, almost as if talking to himself, "A little street-rat putting on airs, a gutter-child all dressed up in fancy clothes. We will strip all those pretensions away soon enough, but first we want to make you sing. There is a lot we need to know about Suinyari and Gordivan and Althor House and all the rest of them. We have bigger prey to trap and you will make very good bait. I think Lord Tarkin will be quite pleased."

I had gone cold with fear, sure my life was about to end soon and in some very ugly way. Too late to heed Suinyari's warnings that now rang through my head like a bell. The other guard came back with a wagon and some horses. My helpless, trussed-up body was dumped into the wagon and the Grayrobe climbed onto the seat. One guardsman sat beside him while the other followed, riding one horse and leading the other. A few daring folk were bold enough to shout insults and bad names at the Grayrobe from the safety of doorways or rooftops, but for all the noise they made, no one had the courage to try and rescue me. I only hoped that someone would run and tell Suinyari; at the same time I was afraid this was just what the monk wanted. Either way I was helpless to change the course of things as I was carried through the city by streets I did not know. Just once I tried shouting for help. The Grayrobe slapped my face and told me they would gag me if I did that again. After that I was quiet.

Finally the wagon stopped. I was rolled out of it and slung over a guard's shoulder. I had just one moment to see the place where they were taking me before I was rushed inside. It was a long, narrow building of dark, ivy-covered stones, so low it could easily disappear among its neighbors. Not a building that wanted to be noticed and remembered, it had none of the usual Shokarn ornamentation. Two guards were standing in front of it. The monk spoke tersely to them, saying, "Let no one pass this door unescorted. If someone tries to claim the girl or to slip past you unnoticed, bring them to me immediately. Otherwise keep watch and stay at this door no matter what screams and shouts you may hear. We need some information from this street-rat and must be free to extract it by whatever means necessary." Then the heavy door shut with a loud clang and the walls closed in around me.

I was not sure if these last words were for the guards or really for me. No need to frighten me more. I was already in a state of frozen terror. Though the day was warm I found myself shivering almost uncontrollably. I was carried over the guard's shoulder down a long dark hall with many doorways. It was lit only by a few sputtering torches. I could not imagine what sort of place this was. The monk opened a door at the end of the hall with a large bolt on the outside and I fully expected to meet with a dank, dark little cell. Instead, as I was set on my feet, I was surprised to find myself in a big sumptuously furnished room. It looked like someone's fancy parlor except that there were bars on the only window. Red velvet floor-length drapes hung on either side of the window. A richly patterned rug covered the floor. I saw couches, chairs and an enormous desk behind which sat a rather obese, extremely white-skinned man with hard, clever, dark eyes. Two other men were in the room. When I was brought in, a gaunt, dark-haired man who had been seated by the desk stood up suddenly. He had an eager, hungry look on his face. I recognized him from some gatherings at Suinyari's house. Arnzil!

The other one was a tall, broad-shouldered man with a dark hood over his face. He was standing by the window in front of a brazier of burning coals such as one might use for shoeing horses. Next to him was a metal table with all manner of tools laid out on its surface. Heating in the brazier was a branding iron. I had no question as to the purpose of this gathering—or who its intended victim was.

As soon as I was set down, the Grayrobe waved both the guards out of the room. "Stay by the door, let no one in and ignore whatever sounds you may hear." The moment they left he shot the bolt on the inside and I was trapped in a room with torturers. Cold sweat was pouring down my face and my stomach was clenched in knots of fear. The monk made a bow to the man at the desk. This Grayrobe, who had himself lorded it over the guards, now turned into an underling. "I found what you sent me for, Lord Tarkin."

So this was Lord Tarkin, right hand man to Gunjorn, the man who held the whole city in a thrall of fear. I tried to sneak a glance at him out of the corner of my eye. He looked slow and ponderous. If I had been free of that net, and it had been a contest between us, I would have been out of reach and out of sight before he could get up from his desk. But the door was bolted and the odds at that moment were not in my favor. The smell of burning coals served to remind me of that.

"Take that net off her and bring her here," Tarkin commanded.

"She is very fierce, My Lord, almost like a wild animal."

"Do as I say. It will be a sorry day in this city when four strong grown men cannot handle one girl-child. Help him, Arnzil."

Arnzil, who had been so eager moments before, looked very reluctant now. Between them they untied me and pushed me forward until I stood in front of the big desk. I made no resistance, could not even imagine it. Terror had frozen my brain. Lord Tarkin looked up at me with a cold hard smile. "Well, girl, why do you think you are here in this room?"

I bowed quickly and said in a choked voice, "I have no idea, My Lord."

At that he laughed, a harsh, ugly sound, more like a bark. "Come now, you must have some idea. Mordrak is not cooking my dinner or shoeing horses in this room. You must have guessed the purpose of that branding iron heating in the fire. We need some information from you about your mistress and her associates. I trust you will not make it too difficult. We even have some papers here we would like you to read and sign. I hear you have been taught to read and write in that house." I saw Suinyari's name on the top page as he spread them out before me.

"Please! No!" I tried to back away, but the Grayrobe and Arnzil held me fast. I knew in that awful moment that I would tell them whatever they wanted to know, betray everyone who had ever befriended me, even Donya, even Suinyari, rather than endure a few minutes of their torture.

"Are you thinking to resist? Perhaps you need a little sample. Hold her! Now, Mordrak!"

Before I could pull away the huge man swung the heated branding iron around and pressed it to my leg. The pain was blinding. I screamed and screamed and in that instant Donya came into my mind. It was not that I thought of her. For the moment I had no thoughts. But she had always said that if I ever needed her I had only to call her in my head, and without intention, that was what I did.

Lord Tarkin was nodding, looking well satisfied. "Well, now you see what we can do. We will start at your legs and simply move up with each question you refuse to answer. I leave it to your imagination how this will end if you do not cooperate with us."

The stench of burning flesh filled the room. I bit my lip against the pain. Yes, I saw only too well how it might end, but Tarkin had made a crucial error. I had been paralyzed with terror until that terrible pain had suddenly cleared my head. "And if I answer all your questions, what then?"

"Then you will not die in pain."

So I was to die one way or the other. It was Neith who had been frozen in fear. The pain had awakened Spider. She was in charge now, back from wherever she had been hiding these past few years. Her clever little mind set to work instantly on a plan. It was as Spider I would live or die. I would much rather live, though I saw little possibility of it, but one thing I was sure of, I would not die at the torturer's hands.

Those fools! They had not even thought to search me for weapons. Too arrogant or confident or both. I would never have been so careless. But I suppose they only saw me as their victim, the bait in their trap. They could not imagine that I would be a threat.

"Sick! Going to be sick!" I shouted, bobbing my head about and beginning to retch. My captors released me and backed away a few steps. "Hurts, hurts, going to be sick." I moaned. Now I was retching in earnest and even beginning to spew some vomit about, a trick I had learned as a child for defending myself on the streets. My head was shaking about wildly. Vomit splattered across the desk, some landing on the very papers I was supposed to sign and some on the monk's sleeve. He instantly stripped off his habit and tossed it onto a chair by the door. Lord Tarkin pushed himself back from his desk with an exclamation of disgust. "Get hold of her, you fools," he shouted at the others. Of course he himself made no move to restrain me.

I began bobbing my head more violently and spewing more vomit. Then, with a groan, I put my hands up to my head as if to hold it still. When Arnzil tried to grab me, I was ready for him. I had drawn my knife from my sleeve. As he reached out, I sliced him from the inside of his elbow down to his wrist. He fell back screaming. Blood began spurting everywhere. Next the Grayrobe tried to grab me. I stabbed him in the hand and he also jumped back.

"Mordrak!" Lord Tarkin roared. He was angry now, frightened too. His face was flushed with rage and his eyes were bulging. This was not to his liking, blood and vomit everywhere and a wild creature loose in his room. Mordrak lunged at me. Instead of trying to run I whirled at him and thrust a chair in front of his feet. The big man went down with a loud crash. I leapt over his fallen body, grabbed up the branding iron and stamped him with it twice. He curled up, screaming in pain. For that moment his mind was not on me. I swung the iron in front of me and the others backed away. I knew I had only a short moment of advantage. The iron would soon cool, then their fear of me would be gone. I quickly backed up to the brazier and kicked it over. The hot coals fell along the edge of the drapes and among the cushions there. Almost instantly flames were licking up the drapes and the cushions began to blaze.

With a shout Tarkin pushed himself to his feet and headed for the door, yelling to the guards. He threw the bolt. The door was about to open. This was the moment when everything would be won or lost. I snatched the tongs from the metal table and used them to grab up one of the flaming pillows. This was even more impressive than the branding iron. When Tarkin turned I was close behind him. I brandished the fire in his face. He jumped back, throwing up his arms to protect himself. By now more of the room was ablaze and quickly filling with smoke. As the guards dashed in, swords drawn, I crouched low and thrust the burning pillow up at them. With shouts of surprise and fear they parted, leaving me space to dash between them. As I darted out the door I threw down the flaming pillow and grabbed up the monk's cloak. Then I slammed the door shut, threw my body against it and pushed the outer bolt home with my heart pounding and my breath coming in ragged gasps.

Some of the doors in the long hallway in front of me were open slightly with people peering out, curious and frightened. Quickly I pulled the monk's cloak around me for a disguise and dashed past their startled faces. Seeing that hated gray cloak they drew back hastily. No one made a move to stop me though the shouts from the room at the end of the hall were growing louder. When I reached the guards at the entrance I growled in my deepest voice, "That little street-rat is resisting and Lord Tarkin has sent me for more tools of persuasion." Whether or not they believed me mattered little. They were far too startled to try stopping me. Without a second's pause I burst out into the street and ran faster than I have ever run in my life, all the while picturing that huge man with a mask chasing after me with his branding iron. Moments later I heard a horse in swift pursuit.

Donya

Spider's call came as I was sitting on Cloud's back, concealed in the dark entrance to an alley. I had been watching while Grayrobes and guards bustled about, loading captured street children into wagons. The children were struggling and protesting, but the men were efficiently brutal enough to force compliance. The sight of it made me sick, though the children themselves were probably almost as dangerous as the men who were herding them toward their fate. It surprised me that they were able to gather so many since such children were usually very skilled at slipping away. There was no possible good outcome to this. The children would end up in child brothels or in the mines or dead. Of late there had been more and more such scenes in the city streets. I was trying one more time to decide whether there was anything I could do to spoil the captor's plans and whether it would do any good. Shaleen had warned me over and over not to try altering the way things were done in Eezore. "We are only here to observe, not to try to change this place. If we interfere we only draw attention to ourselves, endangering our mission and our own lives. The nature of Eezore cannot be changed by a few Hadra foolishly trying to do battle with an old entrenched evil."

In spite of her warning ringing clearly in my head, I had just decided I had to do something, no matter how futile or desperate, when Spider's silent scream suddenly rang in my head, a cry of such pain and panic that Cloud seemed to hear it from my mind to hers. With a snort she bolted forward, straight at the guards and Grayrobes. Shouting in surprise, they scattered out of our way. In an instant we had dashed through and past them, racing toward Spider. I hoped that some of the children behind me had broken free at that moment and would be able to find safe hiding, but there was no chance to look back. Cloud was galloping flat out through the city streets and it was all I could do to stay on her back through the twists and sudden turns. The echo of that silent scream was a red thread of terror that drew me on. My head hurt with the shock of it and my jaw clenched painfully. My vision first blurred, then became unnaturally sharp and clear.

Usually I tried to move about Eezore as unobtrusively as possible, wanting to draw no notice to myself. This call had come with such urgency that I was afraid minutes might mean the difference between life and death. It seemed to take forever to cross the city, even at that headlong pace. Finally, as we came within sight of a long low building with smoke and flames pouring out of it, Cloud began to slow a little. I had been clinging to her neck, afraid of falling at sudden turns. As I straightened I saw in front of us a fleeing figure covered by a Grayrobe cloak. From mind contact I knew instantly that it was Spider. At the sound of the horse she redoubled her speed. I was afraid she would slip into an alley and disappear. Shouting her name, I urged a final burst of speed from Cloud. As we came alongside I reached down and scooped the girl up in my arms, cloak and all. She fought my hold while I told her over and over, "Be still, Spider. It is Donya and Cloud. You called me and I am here. You are safe with us."

Finally she stopped struggling and said in a shaky little voice, "Donya, is it really you? I thought it was the guards coming after me. I was running so fast I felt as if my heart would burst. They were going to torture me and I lit their building on fire. When I heard Cloud I was sure they were riding to kill me. It is Suinyari they want and they thought to use me as bait to catch her. We have to ride back quickly and warn her right away. But first let me get rid of this hateful thing." She was struggling to get loose of the cloak that was all twisted around her.

"No, save it. As things are going it may be useful to us. And save your voice, do not try to talk, just show me in your head what happened." She did as I told her and I shuddered at what I saw, frightened not only for Spider, but for all of us, especially Suinyari. It was no longer the time to talk of plans and possibilities and where we might go. We had waited too long. We had to leave now! It was time for all of us to get out of the city if we still could and head west, going away from Eezore as fast and as far as we could.

When we reached Althor House Suinyari was just going out. She looked up in alarm to see me with a Grayrobe mounted in front of me. That instantly changed to amazement when she heard Spider's voice coming from the confines of the cloak. Before I had a chance to speak Spider had slipped off Cloud's back and thrown herself into Suinyari's arms. Words came pouring out of her in sudden bursts of sound. "Tried to torture me...want you...Lord Tarkin and Arnzil and a Grayrobe... big man branded my leg...set a fire and escaped...Donya found me... have to leave right away...not safe here...Oh, Suinyari, they will come for you soon, very soon...put you in the dungeon and kill me."

Just then Torvil appeared. He looked from one to the other of us in surprise. The moment Spider paused for breath, Suinyari said urgently, "Go to the stable this instant, Torvil, and make ready to leave." Then she grabbed Spider's hand and dashed back into the house.

Mother Melna

Finally I had the answer in my hands, the thing we had been waiting for though we had not known it. Akrun of the Wanderers had brought me a letter from Maktesh with the royal seal on it. I could not imagine what it could be. No one had ever written to us from there, certainly not the Zarna. With shaking hands I ripped it open and read:

> *We hear things have become very dangerous in the city of Eezore, especially for women and we know of the good work you have done as a shelter and refuge for them. Aranella, Zarna of Maktesh, has instructed me to write you a letter inviting you to come to Maktesh with as many as wish to come with you and set up a House of the Mother here. We will give you a building and whatever assistance you need in this endeavor. We guarantee you the safety and welcome of our city. Do not delay. It may soon be too late.*
>
> *– Jolaina, Advisor to the Zarna, Writing at Zarna Aranella's behest.*

I gave such a loud yell that Mother Olya came running along with several others. "Look, look, we have a place to go where we will be welcome." I passed the letter around while the news got shouted back and forth. More and more women gathered, all talking at once in their excitement. I felt such a renewal of hope and energy that suddenly anything seemed possible.

"But you must hurry," Akrun said with a frown. "Things will not hang in the balance much longer. Most of the Wanderers are leaving soon. We are not planning to be back until things here are resolved one way or the other. If Gunjorn comes to power and continues on his course there may be no possibility of coming back at all, certainly no possibility of normal trade here. With Wanderer presence gone, I fear the violence will escalate sharply." I looked at this gentle man with his troubled worried eyes and felt a lump of fear rise in my throat.

We had to leave instantly for Maktesh, but I wondered how long even that city would be safe for us. Gunjorn had said many hostile and insulting things about the "Godless" City of Maktesh and the two muirlla who ruled it. Perhaps he was planning an invasion when his grandfather died. For him it would be a good move, a way of consolidating his power and exerting his leadership over the young men who were his followers. It would give them something to do and he would be able to lean even harder on his people with taxes and conscription. Anyone who objected could be branded a traitor. War elsewhere was always a good excuse for tyranny at home.

I had never been to Maktesh, but the Wanderers tell me it is a prosperous, well-run city. It could be a tempting plum for someone like Gunjorn since his grandfather's excesses had almost ruined Eezore. He could promise his people the riches of Maktesh, just there for the plundering and so get them to forget their own miseries here. I could only hope the troubles in Eezore would not follow us to Maktesh but that was far in the future. For now we had a place to go and we needed to make haste in that direction. I gave the orders to make ready and suddenly the House of the Mother looked like an anthill turned upsidedown. Women were rushing in all directions, gathering bedding and clothes and belongings and pots and food and herbs and books.

Suinyari

What an idiot I was to have waited so long! Neith almost died because of me. It was only her own cleverness that saved her. She may have saved the rest of us as well. We should have left days ago, weeks ago. Donya kept telling me that and I would not listen. I was a careless fool. Now everyone I love is at risk because of me. And my own life is certainly at forfeit.

And what on earth had I been waiting for all this time? As if one could turn back the river! Of course there had been no grand party, no putting things back where they were. The old Zarn's recovery had lasted only a short while, nothing to rejoice in. Now he is sicker than ever and with no hope in sight. Whatever was I thinking of to be staying here, feeling sorry for myself when I should have been taking action?

I was amazed to see Neith again, to have her safely back at my house. A messenger from Lord Arnzil had brought me a note saying that Neith had been captured and was in danger: "If you want to see her again you had best come to Delvini Street, the corner that has the fish fountain with the blue tiles. Come by yourself and come right away or she is as good as dead. I am still your friend and will do my best to help you get her back safely."

My friend? Not hardly! Reading those words I went cold all over with fear. When Bethron had answered the door, the man had said he would speak only to the Lady Suinyari. After thrusting the note in my hands he rode off so fast I had no chance to ask even a single question. He had kept his head down. I had not been able to see his face under his low dark hat. Arnzil, that worm! That traitorous weasel of a man who had once called himself my friend! What was his real role in all this? Donya had warned me about him. I certainly did not think he meant me this much harm.

I knew well enough how this would likely end, but I was willing to bargain my life for Neith's. At that moment my life did not seem to matter that much to me anyhow. I certainly was not doing anything with it. But I had to act instantly. Donya was away and I had no idea where. Gordivan of course was too drunk to be of any use and Torvil was out at the market. I went to tell Bethron the content of the message. Instantly she began shouting at me that I was a fool and if I went out I was as good as dead. "This is a trap. They mean to kill you. Anyone can see that. I have been telling you for weeks that we should leave. Where have your brains flown to, Suinyari? When did you become such a fool? You have been moping over Gordivan for months now when you should have been taking care of business and paying attention to the growing danger in this city. You can see the man is a useless fool, not worth your tears. And now look what has happened!"

"Get out of my way!" I shouted back. "I cannot sit here in safety and let them kill her."

"No way am I going to let you go out there!" Bethron shouted even louder. The noise of our argument brought Gammo and Alliya running. They all three tried to block me from leaving, but I had the force of my fear for Neith adding to my strength. I had just pushed my way past them out the back door and was about to run for the stable when I heard a horse galloping in the street. I froze in place, staring at the others in panic until I heard Neith's voice shouting for me. Next Donya rode into the courtyard with a Grayrobe mounted in front of her. I had a moment of such utter confusion that my heart leapt up into my mouth and I gave a little cry of distress. Then Neith was off Cloud's back before the horse even stopped. Shouting my name again and shedding the cloak as she ran, she threw herself into my arms and began breathlessly telling me all that had happened. At the same moment Torvil returned from market. He stared at the scene in utter astonishment. Finally able to move after being frozen for so long, I shouted urgently, "Torvil, make ready to leave this instant!" Then I dashed into the house with Neith.

Donya

With no further instructions from Suinyari, Torvil set to work. It was as if he had just been waiting for those words. Taking charge of the operation, he moved fast and efficiently, telling the rest of us what to do. He sent Gammo, Bethron and Alliya at a run to bring the already packed valuables out to the stable. While that was happening he had me help him put tack and harness on the horses. The beautiful white and gold carriage was left abandoned in its corner as Torvil and I hitched Suinyari's black team to the farm wagon. Until a few days ago, the wagon had been painted bright green with yellow trim, the House of Althor insignia blazing boldly on both sides. I think Torvil took almost as much pride in the wagon as the carriage. Now there was no insignia to be seen. The wagon was a shabby neglected-looking thing, painted a mottled brown with patches of black as if it had weathered and been long neglected.

As soon as we were done, he amazed me by taking buckets of ashes, dumping them on the horses' backs and rubbing the mess in with some sacking. I stared open-mouthed until with an impatient jerk of his head he signaled me to do the same. The sleek blacks turned gray and blotchy. Cloud's lovely silvery coat darkened to mud color. The tack looked half-rotten, not as if it had been carefully oiled and polished every day. As Spider was underfoot asking questions, he told her sharply, "Make yourself useful. Get the bridle on your pony, then tie the reins to the back of the wagon and throw that old blanket over him."

Meanwhile the others were running out with sacks and stashing them in the bottom of the wagon. Next came bags of their own possessions and a box of pots and pans from the kitchen. On top of that went sacking and old cloaks and then sacks of potatoes, onions and cabbages that were already waiting, stacked by the wall of the stable. All this was done rapidly and almost in silence as if it had been well rehearsed already and each knew their role in the drama.

The moment our part was done, Torvil and I, with Spider following, ran back into the house for Suinyari. She had lost her usual calm and was rushing about frantically, moving very fast and making little progress. With frantic hands she pulled us over to a cupboard that had always been kept locked and whose door was now swinging open. "The rest of the gold! Where is it? Is it gone? Stolen?"

"Already in the wagon, Suinyari. Everything is already done," Torvil said with strained patience. "Now it is time for you to come."

"There were jewels in my bottom drawer."

"Bethron has packed them."

"I have to go up and see if…" She was about to run up the stairs, but Torvil blocked her way. In back of me, Spider was jumping up and down with impatience, shouting, "Suinyari, they are going to come for you! They will kill you! They will kill us all!"

I tugged on her arm. "Suinyari! We have to go! Now!"

Torvil went me one better. "No more time!" he growled. Then, with no warning and not another word, he picked her up and slung her over his shoulder, easy enough since he was a big man and very strong. When she started to struggle and protest he yelled, "Quiet!" To me he shouted, "Out of my way!" Then almost at a run he dashed toward the stable. Spider and I were right on his heels. Bethron, Gammo and Alliya were already scrambling into the wagon. Dondo was barking wildly. Bethron snatched him up and tied a scarf around his mouth for silence. Gammo gave a nod of satisfaction when she saw Torvil with his burden. The way she said, "Thank you," I suspected she had sent him on that errand. He set Suinyari gently in the front seat. Then, in one swift motion, he swept off her red cloak and tossed it to Gammo who quickly rolled it up and stuffed it under some sacks of potatoes. "Much too obvious," he said as he snatched from a hook an old gray one that looked as if it might have done duty lately as horse blanket. He wrapped it around Suinyari quickly as Bethron leaned forward to tuck away the telltale flame of her red hair.

"Gordivan! Gordivan! Do not leave him! With me gone they will torture him! They will kill him! Get Gordivan!" It had been so long since he had been an active part of the house that I had actually forgotten him in the confusion of the moment.

"A curse on his worthless sorry hide," Torvil said angrily. "As man of the house he should have been here helping me get everything ready instead of keeping company in bed with his bottle."

"More like the boy of the house," Gammo spat out with contempt.

"We cannot leave him," Bethron hissed. "He has too many tales he could tell, too many secrets."

Suinyari was struggling frantically to get down again. "I have to get Gordivan!"

"Keep her here," Torvil shouted to the rest of us as he dashed back into the house. Gammo came forward and put her arms around Suinyari, pinning Suinyari's arms against her sides in a tight embrace that was also a firm restraint. "Not to worry, love," she said in Suinyari's ear. "Torvil will fetch him for you."

Bethron said hurriedly to me, "Pass me up the child."

"I can ride my pony," Spider protested.

"Do not be a fool!" Bethron snapped. "It is you they will be looking for. You have cost them a lot of trouble, maybe even some lives. You will be quiet and hide between us in the wagon. Out there on the pony, you would endanger us all, not just yourself."

As she reached down her arms, I boosted Spider over the side and into her hands. No sooner had they gotten Spider tucked down and hidden away between them under the blankets than Torvil came staggering out with Gordivan's limp form over his shoulder. He dumped Gordivan on top of the sacks and tossed his sword down next to him. "Cover the fool. Make sure he stays still, keeps his mouth shut and causes no trouble."

Suddenly uncertain he turned to Bethron. "Where are we going?"

With no hesitation she answered, "The House of the Mother. They can hide us at least for a little while until we can make plans for how to get out of the city. I think there is some sort of tunnel that runs underneath. It would not do for us to get stopped and questioned at the city gate."

"But they do not allow men inside."

"Not to worry, they will hide us all," she said decisively.

I noticed that he did not ask Suinyari and she did not contradict Bethron's orders. She hardly even looked up when Torvil stepped up next to her and shook her gently by the shoulder. "Let me do the talking if it comes to it." Then he pressed the reins into Gammo's hands. "Can you drive?" She nodded. "Good. Follow me and do just as

I say." To me he said curtly, "You will ride behind and keep an eye out for pursuit from in back of us. First slip out in the street and see if you can see any danger lurking. Use that second sight I hear you possess."

I did as he said, glad he had taken charge since clearly Suinyari could not. There were few people passing and none who seemed to have any interest in the house. When I stilled myself and scanned the surrounding streets and houses with my Kersh I could sense no one watching the House of Althor from hiding. I only hoped my powers were working well enough to keep us safe. As soon as the street was empty, I dashed back into the stable yard. Signaling to Torvil that all was clear, I swung up on Cloud's back. With the creak and groan of wagon wheels our little procession left the stable and moved out into the street, a simple farm family in an old wagon pilled high with sacks of produce for market. Hopefully no one had witnessed our departure through the gate.

We had just started out and had hardly turned the corner at the next street when I sensed danger. I felt them before I heard them and well before anyone else heard them. Urging Cloud up next to Torvil's horse, I said in his ear, "Guards riding fast this way, at least six, maybe as many as eight or ten. They will be on us very soon."

He turned to Gammo and said tersely, "Guards coming. No time to take a different street to avoid them. Pull the wagon over to the side to let them go by." Then to Suinyari, he added, "Keep your head down, your hood forward over your face and say nothing if you can help it. The rest of you be quiet and keep a tight hold on Dondo. Make sure he does not get loose."

By then we could all hear the clatter of many hooves. I heard Alliya's gasp of fear and Bethron's muttered curses. The moment the wagon stopped, Gammo slipped her long knife out of her belt and concealed it in her lap under the edge of her shawl. Meanwhile I slipped off Cloud's back and drew her to the side to let the riders pass. I kept my head bowed respectfully like a cowed farm boy.

They were on us in a flash, riding hard and staring straight ahead, very intent on their mission. They did not slow as they passed and seemed hardly to notice us. They certainly did not turn to look or speak. As a simple farm family, we were beneath their notice. I held my breath, hoping they could not feel the fear and rage that poured out from me in waves.

They were almost gone when Dondo broke loose. He gave one

loud furious bark before Bethron and Alliya jumped on him and silenced him again. The last guardsman turned back to stare for a moment, but he had no time to say anything to the others for they were rushing on and he had to hurry to catch up to them. Before we were even moving on again, I heard Suinyari's name being shouted and the sound of angry pounding on a door. Then glass was crashing.

"They wasted no time," Suinyari said bitterly. Her face was very white and her eyes were wide with fear. I had never seen Suinyari look afraid before, but at least there was a semblance of life behind her eyes and alertness in her face. "All is lost now, everything will be destroyed."

"Only wood and stone," Gammo answered gruffly. "With what we have hidden in this wagon it can all be built again. Everything that really matters is right here. Just thank the Goddess we were not still there, preparing to leave."

"That was my father's house. He built it up from nothing. They will torch it."

Torvil shook his head. "Let it go, Suinyari. Done is done. Our job now is to stay alive and get away. We will have to go a different way now, longer but more devious. We cannot stay on this street and risk that when the guards search the house and find no one there they will think to question the farm family they passed." He had us moving on again quickly, only now we went at a faster pace and by many winding streets and narrow back alleys. I thought I knew the city well, but I was soon lost in that unfamiliar place.

The people we passed barely took notice of us. They seemed sunk in their own worries. Twice we saw small groups of Purifiers ride by, the first talking in loud, bragging voices about torching this or that place or catching this or that villain and making him pay, the second talking with obvious pleasure of the horrible things they had done to some poor woman. They hardly glanced at us. People drew away from them in fear, silent for the moment, though they had enough ugly and insulting things to say about the Purifiers when they were gone. I felt a strange, heavy mood hanging over the city, expectant and somber as if waiting for disaster to fall, but perhaps that was not my Hadra senses, perhaps that was only our predicament and those were my own feelings I was projecting onto the city. I was very aware of being afraid, that uncomfortable new feeling that rode with me everywhere now, and I glanced behind us many times to be sure we were not being followed.

When we finally came to the House of the Mother the gates were closed and my heart sank. Then Suinyari called out loudly, "We are in danger and need refuge." With that the gates began to open. I was very glad to see Mother Melna's kindly welcoming face as she stepped out between them. Beyond her the courtyard was a scene of utter chaos. Obviously they were getting ready for a hurried departure. Quickly, women in their long hooded robes of different colors began crowding around us and asking questions. Mother Melna had to clear a space so we could bring the wagon through the gates. When we finally came to a halt inside the yard, Gordivan struggled out from under the blanket that had covered him. He began sitting up groggily and looking about, taking his sword in hand as if he might be in danger. "Where are we? What is happening here? What am I doing in this wagon? Who are all these women?"

Mother Olya rushed forward fussing, "Men! What are men doing in this place? It is forbidden!" She looked accusingly at Torvil and then pointed her finger at Gordivan. "And him with a sword even. What were you thinking of, Suinyari? You know this is not allowed."

Suinyari

I had been in a daze of fear, but my heart lifted at the sight of the arched gateway with the cobbled courtyard and the semi-circle of familiar red brick buildings beyond it. We were safe. We had made our way to the House of the Mother without being stopped. I was sure they would take us in and give us refuge. We would be safe here even if it meant living underground for a while. I was especially gladdened by the sight of Mother Melna's smiling face. As soon as the gates were open, before the wagon even stopped, I was out of it and running into her open arms, feeling like a child again, remembering how she had often comforted me then. "They snatched Neith off the streets," I told her breathlessly. "They were going to torture her to get to me."

Not surprisingly Mother Olya was making some loud objection to our being there with men. I had just turned to her and was about to try explaining what had happened when I heard the great bell of Eezore begin to toll. My mouth closed over whatever words I might have said. I felt the bell striking fear into the very center of my heart. Shaking her head, Mother Melna said softly, "The old Zarn is dead."

Listening to the tolling of the deathbell, we all stared at each other in stunned silence, not so much mourning the loss of the past and the death of an old tyrant as afraid for the future and what this new Zarn in power would mean to us all. The silence among us went on and on until Dondo began barking wildly, and Donya suddenly interrupted, shouting, "Shut the gates! Shut the gates!" After that everything happened so fast and was so confusing it is difficult now to retell the events or even to remember them clearly.

Moments after Donya's warning there was the sound of horses. Everyone was rushing about trying to clear the gates enough to shut them again, but the courtyard was too crowded and too full of confusion to be able to act so swiftly. A troop of young men, Purifiers, I thought, from the black and gray uniforms some of them were wearing, came charging down the street straight at the gates. They all had swords in hand except for two who carried flaming torches. Their leader was shouting, "Kill as many as you can and then fire the place!"

The two Yellowrobes who were struggling to shut the gates were cut down by the first riders. Their cries and Dondo's wild barking stopped at the same moment. Then the raiders were among us, slashing about with their swords, wielding them with far more violence than skill. Mother Olya rushed forward as if to block their way with her own body, waving her arms and shouting in her loud, commanding voice, "You cannot come in here! It is forbidden!" She was instantly knocked down by the horses and trampled under foot. I heard Mother Melna's terrible wail echoing in the courtyard over the shouts of the men and screams of the women. Though they were few and we were many, they had the advantage of weapons and surprise.

Torvil reacted instantly, swinging his horse out of the way of the man who charged him, whirling about and getting his opponent in the back with his sword when the man passed. At that moment Gordivan seemed to come to life. He leapt out of the wagon, finished off the man Torvil had brought down and whirled to face another, ducking under his sword and slashing at the man's legs. Another of the raiders was riding straight at the wagon. Alliya was screaming in terror, but Bethron stood up, swung a sack of potatoes and let it fly, catching him in the middle and unhorsing him. Gammo was out of the wagon and on the man in a flash. She had stabbed him twice with her long knife before he could move. After that he lay still in a pool of his own blood.

I had taken out my knife to defend myself, but now I picked up a fallen sword as it had more reach. Fighting was going on all around me while I was frozen in place with no idea what to do. I was used to living by my wits, not by physical action. All this was nothing like Torvil's careful lessons in the stable yard. This was real blood and real death, with shouting, screaming chaos all around me.

Watching helplessly I saw one man ride by with a torch, heading straight at the stable, probably meaning to set it on fire. Granthia suddenly appeared in front of him, blocking his way with a long pole, the kind used for picking fruit and pruning fruit trees. It had a hook on one end and a sharp curved blade on the other. With a shout of fury, she hooked his arm and sent the torch flying to land harmlessly on the cobbles. Then she swung the other end around and caught him across the throat with the blade. Blood spurted. Flailing his arms with a cry of pain and surprise, the man lost his balance and toppled from his horse. Led by Nafrini, three Yellowrobes with knives were on him in a moment. Then they wheeled about together like a flock of deadly birds, in pursuit of another raider.

As I jumped back out of the way my cloak fell off. Suddenly one of the men started shouting, "Suinyari! There is Suinyari! Get her!" Two of them turned and began riding straight at me. I held my sword out in front of me with one trembling hand and my knife with the other as if that could possibly protect me. I was sure I was dead. I saw Donya struggling to get to me, but her way was blocked. Then it looked to me as if she fell. Suddenly Torvil's lessons came to life and I was able to move. As the first of them came at me, it was my arm that remembered the moves rather than my mind, which had gone numb with horror. I sliced and thrust and thrust again with a fury as if the man attacking me was Nosharn come to life and after me again. "Not this time!" I shouted at him. "You will not get me this time!"

I was like a different person, full of some wild demon energy. For that moment I had no fear as I dodged his blow, gave a loud wordless shout, lunged forward and struck home with an ugly crunch. His descending sword just missed me as he toppled forward, falling from his horse in a burst of blood. I think it was the element of surprise that defeated him rather than any great skill on my part. Clearly he had not expected me to defend myself. There was no time to catch my breath or feel victorious. The second man was riding at me. He was being joined by another. They were both yelling my name.

With a shout, Gordivan leapt between me and my attackers. He caught the first man with a slice across his leg and then an upward thrust. The man was not expecting this since he had been aiming his attack at me. When Gordivan turned to finish him off another man got him in the back with his sword. Gordivan staggered forward and fell almost at my feet. I was sure we were both dead. Then out of nowhere Torvil appeared, leapt on the back of the horse and dragged the other man down with him. They both fell to the ground. With a snort the horse reared and wheeled away, almost trampling the combatants. They were struggling right in front of me, rolling over and over. I wanted to help Torvil by stabbing his opponent, but they were moving too fast and I was afraid of hurting him instead. Torvil had lost his sword, which was of little use anyhow in such close combat. Watching frantically for my chance, I was finally able to lean forward and slip him my knife. I did not even stay to watch for the outcome, though I trusted Torvil to win.

With frantic hands I hauled Gordivan out of the way, afraid he was going to be trampled in the melee. We seemed surrounded by bodies, dead or thrashing about in pain, and by frightened rearing horses. I crouched down to protect him with my own body. Struggling to speak, he was able to whisper, "Cover yourself with that cloak, Suinyari, so they do not come after you again." There was blood foaming on his lips. I could scarcely hear his words, but I quickly did as he said, sheltering us both with the cloak. He looked terrible. His face was gray and twisted in pain. Though he did not cry out he was gasping for breath. "Do not die, Gordivan. Please, brother…husband…friend—I need you now. Please do not die."

"No use, Suinyari, just look at me. I am already good as dead."

"No, hold on, we will heal you. There are many healers here. Do not die now! I forbid it!"

At those words he actually laughed, a terrible, sick sound that left more red foam on his lips. "Ah, Suinyari, you think to give me orders even as I am dying, but it is too late, my love. This time I am beyond your power and your will. Let me go, dearest. I was already dead long ago. I died, at least in spirit, with Nosharn's betrayal and death. I am not sorry. Now the body is going to follow the spirit."

"No, Gordivan, please…"

"Hush, you are making it much harder. Just hold me and tell me you forgive me. And no crying. Please. I just want to go in peace."

I pulled his head into my lap and drew the cloak around us both.

From beyond that shelter I could still hear shouts and screams, horses whinnying and the thud of their hooves on the cobbles. If someone wanted to kill us both now, they could easily do so and there was nothing I could do to stop them. Somehow it did not matter, I was no longer afraid. "Peace, little brother, I forgive you for everything and I love you and I always will." I could barely see his face in the shade of our gray shelter. He smiled up at me and shut his eyes. Then the tears came and I could not stop them, but Gordivan lay very still and did not try to argue anymore. I am ashamed to say that at that moment I did not think of rushing to Donya's aid. I hardly even remembered her. Holding Gordivan while he was dying was all I could manage.

Spider

It was all happening too fast. I could not move. All I could do was watch in terror from my hiding place. My escape from the hands of torturers had taken everything I had. There was nothing left in me to do something clever and swift. For that moment Spider was gone. Also I was in terrible pain from the burn on my leg. And so I huddled there in the wagon, frozen in fear. I saw Bethron disable an attacker with a sack of potatoes. Then she and Gammo disappeared over the side of the wagon and into the battle while Alliya hid under the sacks. I crouched there, clinging to a cudgel that Torvil had left behind, but was unable to use it until one of those men rode straight at the wagon, shouting, "Maybe there are more of them hidden under those blankets." He reached out for the blanket. At that instant my limbs suddenly came back to life. With a roar I stood up and swung the cudgel with all my strength. The force of it knocked the wind out of him and almost propelled me over the side of the wagon and under his horse's hoofs. I caught myself at the very last instant.

My mother must have seen me at that moment. She shouted my name. Then, with no heed for her safety, she ran toward me through that deadly melee. Cursing, my assailant turned toward Imalia with his sword raised. She did not even have a knife for protection. In any case, I doubt she could have used one. My mother was going to die right before my eyes. Spider suddenly came to life again. Forgetting the pain in my leg, I vaulted over the rail and swung my cudgel at the man's knee. He gave a howl of pain and turned back at me with his sword drawn. At that moment Rhosharn attacked him from the other side and then Haldrun joined her. With a scream and a gush of blood, he tumbled off his horse and was trampled.

Without pausing, my mother jumped over his prone form and swept me into her arms. I think she wanted to pick me up and hug me to her as she might have done when I was little, but I was almost as tall as she was now, probably heavier and certainly stronger. I could as well have picked her up. So instead, at great risk to our lives, we clung to each other in the middle of that swirling madness. Very foolish I suppose, but by then the worst of it was over. Most of the attackers lay dead or wounded along with several of our own women. As we stood there together the last two raiders tried to escape, riding fast for the gates. At the sound, Granthia whirled around, shouting, "No! You will not!" as she hooked one of them with her long pole and dragged him off his horse. Rhosharn was on him instantly and cut his throat, but the other man escaped through the gates. With a roar of anger he galloped down the street, fleeing for his life.

Mother Melna

It was over almost before it started, a few minutes, nothing more, but that few minutes had destroyed our lives, changed them forever like a violent storm that comes through so fast you can hardly believe it has been there until you look around at the devastation left behind. I rushed to Olya's side and gave a cry of despair at the sight of her face. Except for the terrible purple bruises she was gray-white. With a groan I dropped down beside her, listened for her heart, felt for a pulse of life. Nothing. I pulled up her robe. The bruises went down the length of her body and her chest looked caved in. Grief was choking me, grief and memories. As if the sound were coming from somewhere outside of me, I heard my own voice wailing over and over, "Oh no! Oh no! Oh no!"

We had come here together as young women, girls really. And then been caught up in the wild crazy dream of building a place from the ruins of the old Witch Convent. And we had done it, done everything we had set out to do and more. For over forty years we had been each other's companions, holding to that vision. Now Olya was gone, her life snuffed out in an instant, and I was alone. I wanted to throw myself down on her body and weep. I was wishing I had died with her so I did not have to feel this awful pain, sharp as any sword wound. Then I heard her voice in my head as clearly as if she had spoken aloud. *Get up, Melna. There is no time for grieving now. You are leader here. Think of the living, not the dead. Save who you can. Move! Quickly! There is much to be done to get away before other raiders come.*

Instantly I bit back my tears. I stood up quickly, meaning to take command. The sight that met my eyes almost drove me back to my knees again. Only moments before our yard had suffered nothing more than the disorder of a hurried departure. Now it looked like a slaughterhouse, what a battlefield must look like after the battle with bodies and parts of bodies, blood everywhere and the wounded screaming. Those still alive were staring about in blank-eyed shock, unable to move, standing with their arms hanging down, weapons slipping from their hands, or sinking to the ground or leaning against buildings for support, or voiding their stomachs in the bushes. Suinyari had thrown back her gray cloak. From the way she held Gordivan's head cradled in her lap and the spreading pool of blood around them, I knew he was dead.

Meanwhile the yard was filling with more and more women who had been down in the tunnel or in the other buildings and were just coming on this scene of horror. Their terrified voices were rising in a chorus, "What happened? What happened here?" again and again with no one answering. And over it all was the sound of the deathbell still tolling for the old Zarn. Much like the others who witnessed the bloodshed, I was stunned, unable to move, until I heard Olya's voice in my head again. *Do something Melna! Quickly! No time to stand about! Get the others moving! Get yourselves out of here! Now!*

"Quiet!" I shouted trying to make myself heard over the groans of the wounded and the flood of frantic questions. "Quiet! Listen to me and do just what I say. One man got away and that is enough to raise an alarm. We will surely be blamed for the death of the others. We only have a few minutes to clear everything away, be in the tunnel and gone from here before they come after us. Now, as fast as you can, Lozell and Enlin, clear the bodies away from the gates. Then shut them, chain them and fasten the chain with a lock. Torvil and Rhosharn, move the dead bodies over that way. Golvini and Monarko, take the wounded toward the stable. Mother Yazeem, go with them to see if you can stop the bleeding. Take Tamlin and Reeja with you to help with bandaging. Nessa and Ulwin, put Mother Olya on a garden flat and lay her gently over there with the other dead. The rest of you finish loading the wagons and get them into the passage as quickly as you can."

Suddenly I heard that gravelly familiar voice I never expected to hear again in this world, not loud but clear enough. "Fools, hammer hands, is that a way to handle people who are hurt." Nessa screamed and almost dropped her end of the pallet. I rushed over to see Olya staring up at me. Her face distorted with pain, she muttered, "You had better hurry with this, Mely, or they will come back and kill us all, finish what they started."

"Put her with the wounded," I told Ulwin sharply. There was no time to cry or fuss. When I turned I saw Torvil trying to take Gordivan from Suinyari's arms. "Too soon," she was saying. "Let me have a little time with him."

"There is no time," I said sternly. "Let him go now, Suinyari, we have no time left."

I thought she would argue or struggle, that Torvil and Rhosharn might have to fight her for the body. Instead, with a deep sigh, Suinyari kissed him on the forehead and stood up. "Goodbye, love. Thank you for my life. I will try to live it well." Then she turned, swung her cloak over a wounded sister and helped carry her into the stable. I saw the bloody body of her dog Dondo being carried away in the other direction with the dead.

Somehow in the swirl of confusion, my words actually mattered and the terrible chaos began to sort itself out. Our wounded were carried to the barn, the dead were hauled into the work shed, theirs and ours alike. Their three wounded were pulled off to the side by Torvil and Rhosharn. I had no idea what to do with them. Before I could say anything, those two had solved the matter by slitting the raiders' throats. I must have had a look of shock on my face. Torvil shrugged and said quickly, "What else were we to do? We cannot take them with us and we cannot heal them. If they are left alive they will tell everything they have seen here. If they survive, they will only kill again in the name of Rha-ais."

"But you…" I stuttered in amazement, looking at Rhosharn.

"I am not the Zarn's sweet-girl anymore, not his little playmate. Men just like this would have gladly slit my throat at the Zarn's orders." She wiped her blade on her robe and went to help Torvil with more bodies. When they were all in the shed, Torvil turned to me and asked, "Now what are we to do, Mother?"

"Spread lamp oil all around and light the shed on fire with a torch from the wall. I trust it is far enough from the other buildings so they do not catch. Besides they are made of stone and have tile roofs, they should be safe. As soon as that is done we have to leave."

Quickly, Torvil went to do as I said. I could hardly believe my own words or the horror of all that had just happened. I remembered building that shed with our own hands, Olya and I, when we first came to this place. It had been our first house and home there, our first shelter, the place where we slept and ate while we set about patching the ruined stone walls and getting roofs over them. Now I was ordering it set on fire. Gutted by grief, dazed and numb of feelings, I stared with horrified fascination as the flames leapt up all around the shed that was to be a funeral pyre for our loved ones and our enemies alike.

I could feel Lozell tugging on my arm, hear her frantic voice calling, "Come, Mother Melna! Come away! It is time to leave!" Some part of me knew she was right, but all that was in another place, another country. I could not turn and take my eyes from that was happening before me. Then Torvil threw down his torch, gave a shout, ran toward me and grabbed my other arm. Suddenly, as if released from a spell, I could move again. Staggering and stumbling, I ran for the barn between them, held on either side like a child.

We were the last ones through the great hole in the barn floor and down the ramp. Several hands were there to help us down, then to slide the missing floor piece back into place and replace the support beams. Other wagons had already left. I could hear their wheels rattling on the stone slabs of the passageway and the echoes of subdued voices. There was just one wagon left for all the rest of us, waiting on the far side of the great stone doorway. I was being urged toward it by those few who had remained. "Olya, where is Mother Olya?" I shouted. "I cannot leave without her."

Rhosharn answered, "Safe, gone on ahead. She said, begging your pardon, 'Tell that old fool to hurry along. I need her with me if I am going to survive.'"

"Get in the wagon!" Lozell told me sharply as if she was the mother there and I the apprentice. Meekly, I did as she said while four women pushed on the heavy stone slab that formed the entrance and a fifth pried at it with a bar. They groaned with the strain and the rock barely moved. Then Torvil jumped down from the wagon and added his force. Very slowly and then faster the great rock slab began to move with the terrible grinding screech of rock on rock until it was finally in place. "The locks…" I called out.

"We know," Ulwin answered as she and Monarko scrambled to fit into their notches the rocks that would pin the slab in place and prevent it from ever again being opened from the other side. Then they were on the wagon and moving. We were now in a tunnel that would bring us out well past the South Gate, a tunnel that hopefully would get us safely away, those of us who were left. Later we could count our dead and mourn our losses. At that moment I was too numb even to grieve. One moment I was wide awake, my head full of worries, the next I was deep into exhausted sleep.

Suinyari

I must have fainted. I woke to the sound and motion of the wagon. Instantly, I saw that Donya was lying next to me. From the way she looked I was sure she was dead. The pain of it was so great I was struck dumb. Unable to cry out or even speak, I could only stare at her in silence. Then I saw the slight rise and fall of her chest and was able to breathe again myself. When I laid my head down between her breasts, I could feel the beat of her heart, though it seemed faint and slow, almost hesitant. I was shocked at her appearance. She did not look as if she was sleeping. She looked to be in some strange place beyond sleep. Her skin had a grayish tinge. She was cold and clammy to the touch.

Seeing that I had come back to myself, Mother Yazeem, who was traveling in the same wagon, said, "She has been like that from the beginning. Torvil found her among the bodies. She is amazingly unharmed, yet nothing we do seems to rouse her." I nodded and said nothing, but I thought to myself that her fragile powers must have been blasted by the backlash of so much pain and terror. I pulled Donya over so that she lay with her head in my lap, stroked her hair and called her name, but there was no response. Nothing changed in that beloved face that was Donya and yet not Donya.

Those first few days on the road south I was nothing more than a body being carried in a wagon, not so different from a sack of potatoes or a basket of apples. Numb with shock, I lay there with no thoughts and no feelings. I am ashamed to say I did not even consider anyone else, did not help care for the wounded or concern myself with the food. During that time I must have eaten and relieved myself, someone must have helped me, but I have no recollection of any of it. I woke and slept to the steady endless sound of the wagon wheels.

Part IV

Spider

When my mother was still my mother—before the streets took her away from me and swallowed her up—she used to tell me stories, old folk tales that have been passed on forever from mother to daughter. There is not much I remember from that time, but I know my favorite story was about a little girl named Michi. She was a street-child, much like the one I was soon to become myself—though of course I did not know that at the time. Michi lived by her wits under a bridge. She never had enough to eat. One day, when she had only a crust of bread left, a young man came by and asked her for some food, saying he was very hungry. He was so shabby and looked so thin she took pity on him and shared her crust of bread, apologizing that it was all she had. He thanked her, ate his half and went on his way.

The next day a carriage stopped near her hiding place. The young man, now elegantly dressed, invited her to the palace. It turned out that he was really the Zarn's son. He had gone about in disguise to see what his people were like and had been deeply touched by her kindness. At the palace she got to eat fine food, sit on the throne—at least for a minute or two—and sleep in a soft feather bed.

I felt as if I had become the Michi of that story. I had certainly not shared my last crust with anyone, that was not my way, but I had gone from being a street-child in Eezore to living as the daughter in Suinyari's fine house to being an invited guest in the Zarna's beautiful palace in Maktesh. Who could have imagined such a thing? After everything that happened at the House of the Mother that day I was amazed to have gotten safely out of Eezore and even more amazed to have ended up in a palace in Maktesh.

Wandering about those rooms, I looked at everything with great curiosity, but I was forbidden to touch by the old woman who had been put in charge of me. There were ornamental archways decorated in patterns of colored mosaics, long tapestries that told a whole story in their panels, brightly enameled vases and urns so big I could have hidden inside one, statues of people both clothed and naked, as well as statues of animals, some tame and some wild. There was even one of an Oolanth Cat, so real it frightened me the first time I saw it. Its emerald eyes seemed to follow me when I walked past and it looked ready to pounce. There were also live birds in huge cages and others that strutted or flew about the gardens, singing or squawking. And on every surface there were beautiful delicate ornaments to tempt my itchy fingers.

The woman who had charge of me was named Zurda. She was the oldest person I had ever seen, even older than Mother Melna, with a map of wrinkles creasing her face. She followed everywhere I went and watched everything I did. At first she had a look of disapproval on her face as if some wild animal had suddenly been let loose in the palace, much against her advice. After a few days she grew friendlier. Finally she said with an approving nod that I had curiosity and spirit and that I reminded her of Zarna Aranella when she was my age. I assumed this was a high compliment, at least I took it as such. Once she even took me to see the throne room. I was allowed to touch the throne but not to sit in it. At my insistence I got to visit the stables though Zurda said she could not imagine why I would want to. There I could pet my pony, but I was not allowed yet to ride alone in the streets and there was certainly no one to go with me. Everyone was much too busy, and Torvil had already gone to the new House of the Mother to help with things there.

The trip to Maktesh had been frightening, especially after the terrors of the raid. It had also been incredibly exciting. I had never been out of Eezore before. In my whole life, all I had ever known were city streets. Suddenly we were out of the city and in a place where the land stretched out before us into blue distance. The familiar landmarks were all gone. There were even long stretches of road where there were no buildings at all. The sky seemed endless, a huge blue eye that floated above us and saw everything. Mountains loomed like great dark shadows, especially as evening came on. And then at night the stars came out!

I wanted to ask questions about everything I saw. It was all so new and strange. But there was no one to talk to, no one to answer me. Donya remained unconscious and Suinyari stayed by her, stroking her hair and murmuring softly to her. Gordivan was dead and we would never talk about anything again. Mother Melna was far too busy trying to make sure everyone was safe and being cared for to respond to my curiosity. She was also grieving for the dead. The same was true of the other mothers and sisters. They brushed me off impatiently. After my first few questions went unanswered or got hushed, I learned to hold my tongue, thinking that later I would get my answers, later it would be better.

We traveled for several days, passing only scattered farms and occasional villages. Sometimes there were towns, but we tried to skirt around them. There were many others on the road, also fleeing Eezore and there seemed to be more each day. After a while there were buildings again and as we neared Maktesh they grew thicker until they were almost on top of each other, another city growing up outside the city walls.

Well before we reached the gates of Maktesh, we had an escort of guards. People lined the road to stare in silence at our pitiful procession. When we finally got to the palace itself I thought my eyes would fall out with looking. Nothing I had ever seen in Eezore had been this grand and beautiful. We were so ragged and shabby, I was afraid they would send us away, but the Zarna herself rushed out to greet us, seeming very friendly with Suinyari and Mother Melna. She had a tall, dark woman beside her who gave orders for us all to be fed as quickly as possible and for the wounded to be cared for immediately.

Later, of course, it was as bad or worse than when we were on the road. No one had time for me except Zurda and she only cared because it was her job. I had been assigned to her. "My little charge," she called me. No one asked me if I wanted her for my guardian. And no one seemed to remember that I had done something good for a change, been clever and brave and saved Suinyari's life, in fact saved everyone in my household, except for Gordivan, of course—but then I think he really wanted to die. No one seemed to care one way or the other what happened to me. It was as if I had fallen through a crack in the pavement, disappeared, ceased to exist. Even my mother, Imalia, was too busy hovering over Donya—as if it took six women to watch one woman sleep. Suinyari of course was one of the hoverers. She stayed at Donya's side day and night, as did Alliya.

Meanwhile Bethron and Gammo went off to help with setting up the new House of the Mother. I begged to go with them. Bethron shook her head, saying firmly and without much kindness, "You are too young. You would only be in the way." Then Gammo added more gently, "Come later with Mother Melna when we have things ready, that would be better. Meanwhile you have this whole glorious palace for a playground. Most girls your age would envy you this opportunity." I thought but did not say, *Then they are welcome to it.* Even Imalia joined in. "Do you care nothing for Donya? I would think you would want to stay to see her healed, watch her come alive again."

Of course I cared for Donya. I even loved her in my own way. But there was nothing in the world I could do for her. So I was stuck in this splendid palace that might well be the envy of all the girls my age, feeling useless and dying of boredom. I even went down to the kitchen to see if I could be of help there. They shooed me away saying they had plenty of hands already. I was the outsider, unwanted. My presence in the kitchen might have interrupted their gossip. I wonder if Michi ever felt as lost and misplaced in her beautiful palace as I did in mine.

Donya

With the sensation of having been on a long and perhaps dangerous journey, I opened my eyes to see Suinyari leaning over me. Her lovely face was set in lines of pain and worry and her forehead creased with it. The instant she saw I was awake she smiled down at me, a wonderful smile of welcome that did not quite reach her eyes or change the look of worry in them.

"Welcome back, Donya. And do not leave again—please! I have already lost Gordivan; I cannot bear to lose you too. This time you have to stay with me."

I had no idea what she meant, none at all. My head ached dully. It felt full of pillow stuffing instead of brains and my eyes seemed not quite able to focus. Glancing past her, I saw an unfamiliar, richly appointed room swimming in my vision and could not imagine what I was doing there. "Where am I? What is this place? How did I get here?"

Suddenly, with a violent jolt, I remembered the scene of horror in the courtyard, the bloody raid on the House of the Mother. At that moment it all came crashing in on me. A cruel rush of memory brought with it the searing red pain of all the suffering and death I had experienced through others, pain that wanted to eat my very soul. Instantly I tried to dive back into the blessed darkness that had been my refuge each time I rose to consciousness, a darkness that was very close to death. But Suinyari would not let me go, not this time. She shook me by the arms and shouted my name. When that did not have the desired effect she threw a glass of cold water in my face. That brought me back with a shock, spluttering and coughing, but the pain of memory did not lessen. I was doubled over with it, moaning, retching, sobbing, weakly trying to push her hands away.

"You will not leave again!" she shouted at me, her voice cutting like broken glass. "You will not! Mother Melna says you might die next time. Or end up witless. Stay with me, Donya! Please!" She went on shaking me, willing me back into a world that I was quite willing to leave. I could feel the struggle of wills between us, lines of power being pulled taut, stretching me out to thinness, dragging me back. Then the line suddenly snapped, and I was instantly free of that blinding pain. It was a relief to have it let go its hold on me. But something else happened at that same moment. I no longer had the reading of minds. When I reached out to Suinyari's, I was met with cold gray silence that filled my head and seemed to go out in all directions.

"It is gone," I said quietly. "The pain is gone and so is my Kersh. My inner world has gone silent." I was caught between relief at being free of that searing pain and a sharp grief for what I had just lost. Some part of me had died to let the rest of me return to life.

"Perhaps it will come back later," Suinyari said quickly as she struggled to get me out of my wet nightshirt and into a dry one. She spoke as if I had just misplaced something, a comb or a shoe, and would likely find it again. I knew it was not so simple. I could not even imagine what that loss would mean in my life, but I was too exhausted by the struggle to argue and so kept my silence.

No sooner was I in dry clothes again and sitting up in bed than Mother Melna rushed in, drawn by the sound of shouting. Several others came in soon after her. Among that small crowd was a beautiful woman with a commanding presence and a crown of gold-blond hair. Beside her stood a tall, dark woman, handsome as any man. Suinyari introduced them and that is how I first met Aranella, Zarna of Maktesh, and her advisor, Jolaina. They welcomed me to the palace. Now I finally understood where I was.

Full of kindness and concern, they began to question me. I tried to answer, but could hardly find the strength or wits to form words. Suinyari soon shooed everyone out of the room, even the Zarna, saying I was too tired to talk much. After the others left Suinyari sat in a chair by the door as if to guard my rest. After a while of silence I asked, "How long have I been this way?"

"It took us six days to reach Maktesh and we have been here for four."

I nodded. Ten days of darkness. I leaned back against the bed cushions and sat looking out the window, remembering everything that had happened, but with none of the terrible pain, just sadness for all that was lost. Now it was memory only, not a beast that leapt into the present with bloody claws and fangs. I could see the scene in the courtyard quite clearly, how we had all come there to take refuge and how the women of the house had been preparing to leave and how the raiders had burst in on us.

I recalled that with the very first killings I had doubled over, gasping with pain, hardly able to breathe and not able to move, feeling every wound and every death in my own body, blinding red flashing before my eyes. At some moment, I had found myself forced to look up. Suinyari was about to be attacked. I knew I had to reach her, to get between her and her attacker. Lurching toward her, I tried to move with all the strength I had left. I even managed to stagger a few steps in that direction before I fell flat out and darkness swallowed me. It was a miracle I was not trampled to death in the struggle that surged around me.

The next time I woke there were bright stars over me in a black sky. I could hear the wagon wheels turning and knew we were far from any city. I had a moment of utter peace and tranquility staring up into the night sky before the stabbing red rush of memory caught up with me and I vanished into darkness again. Now I lay very still for a while, gazing out at the palace gardens and letting myself remember in relative calm what I could of that terrible afternoon. When I finally looked back at Suinyari, I saw she was writing in a little notebook. "What are you writing?"

She looked up startled. "I thought you were sleeping."

"No, I was lying here remembering all that happened but without the pain—trying to gather up the pieces of myself. Kersh is a two-edged sword, not always a blessing, but still I shall miss it very much. It is hard to imagine life without it. Come sit by me awhile."

She came and sat next to me on the bed. Her smile this time had less worry in it. "Is it true that Gordivan is dead?" I asked her. When she nodded, I put a hand on her arm. "I am so sorry, Suinyari. I know how much you loved him."

She nodded again. "I miss him dreadfully. He was my life companion, someone I had known since childhood. He held my past in his hands. We knew so much about each other, shared so many things. There is no one else in the world who knows about that part of my life the way he did, no one with whom to share those memories. All gone now. All lost. But I do not miss who he had become in this past year or so. Since Nosharn's death he had not been himself. Grief and guilt and drink were turning him into an ugly stranger. And he was not sorry to go. He told me so himself. He saved my life, Donya, threw himself between me and those men who intended to kill me. It was as if he came alive just before he died.

"I shall miss him for all the years to come. There will never be anyone like that in my life again. Even now I think of things I want to ask him that only he would know the answer to. Then I remember all over again that he is gone. That voice, those memories—all silenced. He was not very brave or strong and he could sometimes be quite foolish, but he was loving and charming and witty and always very kind. He was more than a husband to me, more than a cousin, he was my other self, my spirit twin. Sometimes others in my household did not understand my love for him. They only saw his failings, I knew his heart."

"I am so sorry," I said again. Then I had another thought. "Dondo? Where is Dondo? Why is he not here beside you? Is he not allowed in the palace?"

She shook her head and looked about to cry. "Dead also, cut down by the first raiders. When they rode in the gates he ran at them barking, wanting to warn us or defend us. He never had a chance. He had been my companion for years. My father brought him home for me in a basket, a little handful of dark fur." After that we sat in silence for a while, each with our own separate memories. Finally I tapped her little notebook. "What are you writing?"

"How we first met and everything that has happened since. I wanted you to have it when…" She looked away and did not finish. It did not take my lost powers to know she meant when I left for home, which we both knew I had to do sometime soon. I took the notebook from her hands, set it on the table and drew her down beside me. "Let us enjoy what time we have together and for now let the future take care of itself."

For those next few weeks Suinyari and I enjoyed a magical time of closeness such as we had never had before. In Eezore we had been too busy with our own affairs and too wary of each other to allow such closeness. Now, for that moment at least, nothing else seemed to matter. I was not strong enough yet to go about by myself, but the others, when they saw I was recovering, went on with their own business. Mother Melna and her women went off to the new House of the Mother. Even Alliya left when Suinyari told her she could go with them. Meanwhile the folk of the palace were frantically engaged in trying to deal with the sudden influx of desperate people into their city. Suinyari refused any offers of help with me, saying she could care for me well enough herself.

Alone that way we talked to each other about everything, like two schoolgirls who have taken a sudden fancy to each other and have all the time in the world. Under that flow of bright talk I sensed something dark and secret, something unspoken. When I asked Suinyari, she just laughed and said I was imagining things. I knew this was not the whole story, but of course I had no reading of minds at that moment with which to probe for a deeper truth. Suinyari had forbidden me to do that to her. At that moment, if I could, I would certainly have been tempted to try. Instead I had to accept her words. She stayed constantly at my side. "I have lost everything else in my life, I am not going to lose you, too," she told me over and over.

Yet I knew well enough that she was going to lose me sooner or later, probably sooner, and that this was in fact just a loving way of saying goodbye. I needed to go home to Ishlair. I could not continue to live in the palace forever in this suspended state of being. This was not my life. But every time I tried to speak about the future, hers or mine, she would put her arms around me and cover my face with little kisses. Soon we would be rolling around on the bed together, deep in pleasure. I knew she was only trying to distract me from further talk, but each time I let myself be seduced without much resistance. What did it matter? We could talk later.

This was the most intense pleasure of the body I had ever experienced. After one such encounter I thought, *I would sell my soul for such pleasure.* And the voice in my head answered, *Perhaps you already have.* For the first time in my life I was loving another person without the advantage of my powers. One would think that I would miss my Kersh terribly at such a moment. Instead there was a perverse pleasure in this. And all my other senses were intensified. My fingertips had to substitute for my Kersh. My skin became an ocean of feelings. Also it made us more equals. For that time it was as if we had no past and no future, only the present and we were alone in it together, the only two people in the world.

Under all that I could feel the clock ticking, the earth turning beneath us. I needed to be home before the cold came, before winter made it too hard to travel. At least Suinyari would be safe here in Maktesh, not in danger in Eezore, and I would not have to worry about her when I left.

Mother Melna

The first time I saw the house we had been given, the one that was to be the new House of the Mother, I gave a gasp of surprise and pleasure. So big! And all ours! I fell in love with it instantly. It won my heart. Though I could see that it was foolishly ostentatious as well as shabby and neglected I still thought it the most beautiful house in the world. And now that Donya was recovering, I finally felt freed to go live there—my new home.

The house was large enough to accommodate all our needs for some time to come, four floors or perhaps five, depending on whether you counted the towers, with several wings and many outbuildings. There was a long low building off to the side that was also to be ours. It had once been a barracks, then a prison, and finally a warehouse, now long abandoned. We would probably make it into a shelter for all our animals: chickens and goats and pigs and sheep when we acquired more than those few we had been able to bring with us. Right now it was sheltering a number of people who had also fled from Eezore. They had set up their camp in its shelter, and several of them were hard at work, helping with the repairs on the house.

Before I could make a full tour of the house, Rhosharn quickly came, took my arm and steered me out to the grounds. I was the outsider, the newcomer there, and she wanted the pleasure of showing me everything. Face bright with excitement, she guided me along winding stone paths to an orchard that only needed a little care and pruning. And then on to wide gardens overcome with weeds and briars, gardens that could easily be planted again. I even saw a fair amount of herbs still holding their own against the invading weeds. To one side a patch of garden was already being cleared and planted. Several sisters were busy working there. They rushed over to greet me and welcome me "home." The smell of fresh-turned earth filled my nostrils, warmed my heart and made me want to cry—better by far than any perfume. With a moan I dropped down on my old knees and sank my fingers into the soil. Then Rhosharn had to help me up again.

The more I looked about me, the more deeply I fell in love. A huge kitchen filled with the scent of baking bread, a cobbled courtyard, a giant water trough for animals, a stone cistern for the house, long many-windowed chambers for sleeprooms and a big central room where we could all gather. When Aranella offered us this house, she told me it had once belonged to some family that the old Zarn, her father, thought to be his enemies. They had all been arrested and killed or else had died in prison. There had been no heir or at least none that dared come forward, and so the house had languished uncared for.

I knew the former owners had been taken from this place against their will and to their great misfortune. I did not want to benefit from another's pain. Goddess knows, I understood such pain well enough myself, but those folk were long gone and probably all dead. Whatever realm they dwelt in now they might be glad for us to be there, caring for the place they had loved and making it into a refuge for others. The house itself was suffering under a heavy burden of neglect. With its sad history, probably no one from Maktesh would come occupy it so it was up to us, the refuse of Eezore, the outsiders in search of refuge, to bring it back to life.

Those first few weeks were so busy with all the things that needed doing that my grief for our dead and the shock of what had happened began to fade. As soon as I had crossed the threshold I had felt as if I were coming home. Even Olya gave her grudging approval. "Not a bad place considering that it is drafty and ugly and has a wealth of cobwebs, especially in impossible-to-reach places. Even with all that I think there is room enough for everything we need and it is cleaning up quite nicely."

I burst out laughing with relief at hearing Olya sounding more like her old self again. I had tried to leave her at the palace, thinking she might be more comfortable there and better cared for. She had insisted on coming and had been brought in a carriage along with the longchair in which she had been convalescing. Aranella had insisted on giving it to her.

"Put my longchair right over there by the fireplace and be gentle when you place me in it," she had said imperiously when they carried her into the gathering room. And there she stayed, hardly moving, surveying everything from the center of her web. I fear for Olya. She does not seem to be getting any better though I try every cure and healing that I know. Then, on some days, she has a little color in her face and I feel more hopeful. I have lost so much, I can hardly bear to lose Olya too, but right now I fear she is far beyond my skills, gone over into the hands of the Goddess.

One morning, looking about me, I thought, *Here I am, starting all over again at sixty, doing the things I did when I was twenty*. Suddenly I was hit by such a wave of nostalgia it nearly brought me to my knees, a flood of memories so sharp it was like physical pain. Scene after scene from those early days flashed through my head: clearing away rubble to find a sudden unexpected treasure of unbroken pots and dishes beneath it; discovering a rosebush blooming among a tangle of weeds; raising the roof on that little shed that was to be our first home. It was not the terrible hardships and crushing despair I remembered at that moment as much as the glorious sense of adventure, the excitement of making something new out of those old ruins, seeing it rise day by day, a dream materializing itself right before our eyes, under our hands. And working next to Olya, the two of us so young and hopeful and in love. And other young women coming to join us. For that moment I forgot the hopelessness and hunger and exhaustion that had so often weighed us down. Olya and I had done such good work together, created a sanctuary for women in that hostile city. I could see it in my head as it had been, the handsome red-brick buildings, the wide cobbled courtyard, the abundant multicolored gardens pouring out their wealth on us. All taken from us in minutes! Everything we had built, forty years of work gone just like that. I felt the tears sliding down my face, blurring the actual scene before me so that momentarily it turned into the devastation of that final day in Eezore. I had to shake myself to come back to the present, remind myself how lucky we were to have a place to start over—and generous help in doing it. "Come on, you old fool," I whispered to myself. "There is work to be done. Crying will not make it any easier." Still I wished Olya were there at my side to share the work and the memories.

Except for that brief moment of nostalgia, I allowed myself no time for mourning the past or grieving for the dead. There was too much to do. I worked to exhaustion each day, we all did. At night I fell into bed so weary I expected sleep the moment my head hit the pillow. But then, in the silence, all those unwanted thoughts that had been held back by the busyness of the day would come rushing in. Often the thoughts came in the form of voices. *It is all your fault. You were the one who delayed. If you had agreed to leave sooner many would not have died. Olya would not be a chair-bound invalid.* Then another voice would quickly answer, *And where would Suinyari have gone? Suinyari and all those with her would have been killed. Besides we had no place to go until that letter came.*

Round and round in my head the voices would argue, leaving me no peace. Sleep would flee and I would be wide awake again. Haunted and harassed, I would soon find myself out of bed and pacing up and down the halls, gliding along silently in the dark like the ghost of myself with all my own ghosts for company. Lurghan was there with me, whispering in my ear, and I would hold long conversations with her, telling her everything that had happened, asking her advice. And the ghosts of all the women who had died on that terrible day would add their voices. And those who had died at the House of the Mother over the years would join in. The ghosts of this house would also come to me whispering of old griefs and terrors, asking my help. Sometimes I almost felt as if I could see them, especially the children, pleading for mercy.

Even my mother's ghost came to keep me company on those troubled nights. I had never gone back to our village, not once, not until the very end. A Wanderer had brought me word that she was quite ill and might not have long to live. When I went back I could not believe how old and wasted she looked. I still remembered her as a young woman. "Why did you stay away so long?" she would ask plaintively in her ghost voice, clinging to my hand. "Why did you never come to see me?"

"We took the money. We were supposed to marry those men. We were afraid to come back."

"What did the money matter compared to losing my only daughter? You were my favorite of all my children. Those were bad men. It was good you did not marry them. You could have come back in a year or so. We would have forgiven you."

"We made another life, Mother."

"So I hear and I am proud of you. Still you could have come back or sent word."

"I am here now."

I stayed for a month in my old village, stayed until she died and was laid to rest. We had that time together, as close as any mother and daughter could ever be, closer in some ways than lovers because we had that ancient bond. I told her everything about my new life, fed her and cared for her, read to her from a book I had brought with me, held her as she was dying and closed her eyes at the end. Even so, nothing made up for those lost years. I am ashamed to admit that in all that time in Eezore I hardly ever thought of her. She was part of the past. I had shut the door on it and ridden away. The young are so cruel, so heedless. Perhaps it is the only way they can go forward, not be mired in the past. Now my mother walked those halls with me, reproaching me, telling me of her love and my cruelty, and I whispered back, asking for forgiveness and guidance in my confusion and uncertainty.

Donya

Once I felt strong enough to be out, Suinyari and I began to go our separate ways again. I walked the streets of Maktesh with the constant awareness of having lost my Hadra powers. I had no idea if the damage could be reversed by Hadra healing or if the condition was to be permanent. For the first time in my life I could not hear the thoughts of others. I was as mind-deaf as any other person on those streets. As to my powers of self-defense, I probably had none. I only hoped I was not challenged by anyone. I had no more ability to fight than a small child since I had never needed to learn such things. Some of the background hum of thoughts was still there, but nothing came clear out of it. This strange silence made me feel unbalanced, as if I might fall over at any moment or perhaps slip away into some dark hole. My powers had already been waning due to my long time spent among the Draiga, even before my memory of the terrible deaths at the House of the Mother had blown away the last vestiges of my Kersh.

At that time I saw little of Aranella and Jolaina as they—and indeed all those responsible for the running of the city—were hard at work trying to find ways to deal with the sudden huge influx of people flowing into Maktesh and seeking refuge. The question was how to find enough food and shelter for them all and also some work to make them useful and keep them out of trouble. An added problem was that not all of them were innocents. Some were dangerous and desperate men who had taken this opportunity to escape the force of the law.

For the next few weeks people continued pouring into the city, a flow of people fleeing the wrath of the new Zarn and his Purifiers. Reports from there grew worse with each passing day, stories of raids and massacres. They all had their own horrors to tell, how they had seen a friend or lover or relative killed right before their eyes. And it was happening to all castes. Even the Highborn were not immune to being marked for violence. The resources of Maktesh were being pressed to the limit by the problem. Then, suddenly, the flow became a trickle. Soon it stopped altogether. The Wanderers told us that Eezore had shut its gates. No one was being allowed in or out. The city had closed in on itself, a giant prison with everyone inside either a prisoner or a jailer. I only hoped that Shaleen had gotten herself safely out before that happened and that she was on her way to Ishlair or perhaps there already.

One unforeseen consequence of my going about the streets of a new city was that I began to draw again. I had not meant to, had not even given it a thought. I just took my little pad with me to write my observations in words. Soon I found myself setting them down in pictures as well, so many wonderful things to look at that I wanted to remember, perhaps even to paint later when there was time, when the future was finally settled. I was fascinated not only by the people and the streets and buildings, but also by what I saw in the shops, especially a certain fantastical style of vessels, bowls, vases and pots made in the shape of imaginary creatures: horses with wings and fish tails, fish with arms and legs, birds with human bodies or humans with bird bodies. They were monstrous and at the same time wondrous. Several such vessels were in the palace and I longed to hold them in my hands. I had never worked with clay. I wondered what it would be like to squeeze it between my fingers, to shape such a thing with my own hands. I drew several of my favorite ones. Then, after a while, I even began drawing some vessels of my own design.

Every day, if I was feeling well enough, I went out into the streets, going to the market or slipping in and out of shops and taverns to hear talk of what was happening in the city of Eezore. I also went to the shelters where people from that city had gathered, listening to stories and asking questions. This would be my last job as a spy and I took it very seriously. I knew I would need to leave soon and go home to Ishlair. I wanted to have as much information as possible to take back with me, some small payment for my long absence. No matter how comfortable the palace or how kindly my treatment there, I knew I could not live this strange suspended life forever. It was going to be very hard to leave Suinyari again, even more painful now that we were so close. At least I would have the comfort of knowing she was safe in Maktesh, not risking her life in the dangers of Eezore.

One afternoon, after Suinyari and I had both come in from our respective wanderings around the city, we were summoned with some urgency to Aranella's chambers. As we entered, I saw a stranger seated there or rather barely seated. Just balanced on the edge of her chair, the woman seemed ready to spring up in an instant. Ragged and dirty, with bruises on her face and arms, she looked drawn and in pain, but her eyes were blazing with anger.

Jolaina said quickly, "This woman has escaped from Eezore. She came here looking for you, Suinyari. We offered her the hospitality of the palace, told her she was welcome to bathe and eat and rest first, but she said that could wait, that it was urgent she speak with us immediately. She asked in particular for Suinyari before she would begin to..."

"Pharym!" Suinyari cried out, rushing toward her. "What has happened to you? You look terrible!"

"Suinyari!" Pharym shouted at the same time as she leapt up from her chair. "So glad when they told me you were living at the palace. Wanted you to be here so I could tell my story just once. So much has happened, so much..." Before they could embrace she sank back in the chair with a groan.

"Are you...?"

She shrugged. "They beat me, but I will live. I am one of the lucky ones. Nothing is broken that will not mend. That was the first time, just a warning. The second time I got in their way, they threatened to arrest me and I ran. My younger brother is in the guards and he helped me slip out of the city. I hope they do not blame my escape on him or he may lose his life for mine. But it is not me I came to talk about. I am here to tell you what is happening to the women of Eezore."

Suinyari was standing awkwardly, her eyes glued on Pharym. She shifted about uncertainly as if she wanted to hug the woman and yet was afraid to touch her bruised body. I was hesitating in back of

Suinyari when Aranella said with some impatience and a wide sweep of her hand, "Sit down, both of you, so we may hear what Pharym has to say. Then we can attend to her hurts, get her fed and comfortable." Turning to Pharym she said, "Tell us everything, starting with your own story of how this happened to you. Then you can tell us about others." Aranella spoke graciously enough, but there was that tone of command in her voice.

Pharym took a long drink from the glass of water by her chair, gave a deep sigh and then began. "I am a market woman. That is how Suinyari knows me. We have done business together. Many of her goods have flowed through my hands and after a while we fell into a friendship. What happened to me and what is happening to women in Eezore is all tangled together so I will tell both as best I can.

"Even in that repressive city where women have so little power, market women are outspoken and independent. Though men also sell at the markets it is the women who run them and make the rules for how things are to be done there, working through the Women's Market Council. One of the absolute rules is that we look out for and protect each other. The old Zarn knew we were a power to be reckoned with. He let us be. Not so the young Zarn. Even before he came to power, Gunjorn and his followers saw the markets as a challenge to their absolute rule. Purifiers would come there to harass and intimidate the women, not just the stall owners, but their customers as well. And for the first time we were not able to defend each other. If anyone made a move to stop them that person's stall was sure to be destroyed and perhaps the owner beaten as well. Some even disappeared completely. And so we began to stand by helplessly while terrible things happened right before our eyes." At this she glanced around quickly as if even here she was afraid of being overheard. Then she gathered her strength again and went on.

"As soon as Gunjorn came to power he abolished the Women's Market Council. From then on the markets were to be run by men. Women would need a special license to have a booth there. The only women who would be allowed to sell there would be women with a male relative in the market, a man who would vouch for their loyalty to the new Zarn—as if any of us, man or woman, would willingly pledge our allegiance to that bandit and his thugs. Every day women vanished from the markets. We were not sure if they were just unable to get the new license or if they had been taken away for some infraction of the rules which changed every day. How were we to make a living? How were we to survive? Of course many women worked the markets because they liked the independence, but many others were there because they had no male relative to support them. They were being consigned to starvation or prostitution though now, with the new regime in power, prostitution is punishable by death.

"My encounter with the Purifiers was over some little Goddess figures that were always part of my display, small clay figures that women liked to keep in their pockets to touch and rub for good fortune. Or set up in little hearth niches to make a household altar. As soon as Gunjorn took over he declared Rha-ais, the god of war, to be the only deity allowed to be worshipped in Eezore. Then he sent his bully boys out to smash what he called 'idols.' The making, selling, owning or displaying of any representation of the Goddess is now against the law so I had hidden mine away under the counter.

"When a young woman came by who wanted to buy one for protection for the baby she was expecting, I glanced all around to make sure we were not being observed. Then I laid out just a few of them on the counter. We both bent over them and soon became engrossed in discussing their relative merits and whose hand they had come from. For that moment we forgot our caution. Suddenly there was a warning whistle. I looked up to see three Purifiers bearing down on us. One grabbed the young woman and began hitting her in the face and punching her belly. The other grabbed me and pinned my arms while the third set to beating me. Then, while I watched, helpless and furious, they knocked over my stand and proceeded to smash and destroy everything I had there. Most of those wares were not even mine. They belonged to others and I owed them part of the money from the sales. I was seeing my ruin before my eyes and of course no one came to our rescue.

"I think those men only stopped beating me because a loud commotion at the other end of the market took their attention. Otherwise they might have arrested me right then. After they rushed off I could hardly stand. I was vomiting blood and bile, but the young woman was much worse off. She was lying on the ground. Her skirt was hiked up and blood was running from between her legs. She was probably losing her baby right there. Now many rushed to help us. I could see shame in their eyes as well as grief, shame that they had not been able to step forward and protect us. The young woman's husband appeared out of the crowd. With a cry of mingled grief and rage he snatched her up in his arms to carry her home, trailing blood, followed by some of the market women who were also healers.

"Others came to help hold me up. They righted my stand and searched about for those few things that could be salvaged. Then some of them even escorted me back to the house I shared with my mother and two sisters who also worked in the market. My mother rushed in moments later, hearing I had just been attacked. She got me to bed and cleaned my wounds, all the while fussing at me, saying in her quarrelsome way, 'I told you not to take any images of the Goddess to the market with you. How could you be such a fool? They are just looking for an excuse to destroy us all. Why do you have to be so hardheaded?' As if she was not my best example of how to be hardheaded. I had gotten many lessons from her.

"I stayed home a few days, nursing my hurts and surrendering to fear. But what was I to do? Now I owed money for what had been destroyed. I had to go back to the market. I hitched up my little donkey to my other cart and took only things I had already bought through Suinyari or the Wanderers. When I set up my stand, I fastened a statue of Rha-ais to one corner and the emblem of the new Zarn to the other, hoping in that way to stay safe and not draw attention to myself. Most of the other market folk were doing the same, not an expression of true belief but only of fear. For two days I sold my goods, minded my own business and hoped for the best. I thought perhaps I would be able to repay what was lost after all. Then they came back, not for me this time, but for the woman who had the stall next to mine. We had sold next to each other for three years and were good friends. They started dragging her off. Without a thought I jumped in their way shouting, 'Let go of her! Leave her alone!'

"Of course they instantly turned on me. One of them yelled, 'That is the one we had trouble with before! We need to arrest her this time!' He grabbed my arm. Full of fear I tore myself away, leaving part of my sleeve in his hand. I was not about to let myself get beaten again, or worse, to land in the dungeon. I found myself dashing through the market as fast as I could go, abandoning Yavini to her fate. I could only hope she got away while they were chasing me. Again no one helped me openly, but I have a feeling that things were moved out of my way as I ran and then shoved back into the path of my pursuers. There were certainly enough curses behind me. Soon I could not hear the sound of their running feet anymore. I ducked through streets and alleys and eventually found my sister. She got my brother for me and he helped me out of the city, a whole other story that does not need to be spoken of here.

"Things have gotten so bad for women so quickly there you can hardly believe it. And not just in Eezore. The talk on the street is that the new Zarn keeps saying it does not do for two young women to control the wealth of Maktesh. As soon as he has set Eezore in order and repaired the damage done by the laxness of the old Zarn, he plans to come do the same in Maktesh, to teach women here their place before God and man. I had to come warn you. I have also come to beg your help for the women of Eezore."

Jolaina and Aranella glanced at each other, a look full of infinite layers of meaning. Aranella shook her head. "We can shelter those who come here though even that is fraught with dangers, but we cannot do anything overt to challenge Gunjorn's rule or even have the appearance of doing so and in that way give the excuse for such an invasion."

Jolaina added, "We grieve for the women of Eezore, but we certainly cannot take up arms in their behalf. Our own rule here is precarious enough."

Pharym sat back with a groan. The eagerness died in her face and all the fire seemed to go out of her. It was as if she shrank down and got smaller. "I had hoped…" she said softly, almost in a whisper. Shaking her head she went on, "It is all so terrible, you can hardly imagine…" There were tears in her eyes.

Jolaina and Aranella glanced at each other again. I sensed they were about to dismiss Pharym to bath and food, but Suinyari leaned forward and began questioning her intently and in detail, almost as if the rest of us were not even in the room. There was none of the usual mockery in her tone, only a devouring intensity and an amazing attention to detail. Pharym seemed to recover somewhat and answered in that same intent manner.

Suinyari

As I listened to Pharym's story and asked her questions, chills went through me. Thoughts began churning in my head that I knew I could not share with anyone but her. Actually these were not new thoughts. It was just that they had taken a sudden dangerous new turn. I had been mulling over those same things ever since we had first come to Maktesh. I am ashamed to say it, but for that moment at least I was glad Donya did not have use of her Kersh and so could not read my plans. Clearly it was not possible to discuss such things with Jolaina and Aranella. They would try to block my way. Nor was it safe to talk to Donya—perhaps Donya least of all since she had such a hold on my heart. Though Pharym needed care recovering from her injuries, more than anything she needed hope. Perhaps I could supply her with some of that. I stayed with her through her bath and her meal, talking softly in her ear of what I had in mind. Then I put compresses on her sores and saw her to bed. While she slept I roamed about the city, sorting through many things in my mind, none of them safe or easy or pleasant.

For the next few days I stayed with Pharym as much as possible. She was both my excuse and my reason. I said that as her friend I should be the one to care for her in this strange place where she knew no one. In truth she would have been well cared for there, with or without me. Mainly I wanted to avoid Donya. I especially wanted to avoid being alone with her. I was very afraid that even with her diminished powers she might be able to probe into my mind and read my thoughts. I took to coming to bed as late as possible, hoping she would be asleep. And when she tried to talk seriously with me I would tell her that I had no time, that Pharym needed her soup or her bath or I was too tired and we would talk later when my patient was feeling better. If nothing else worked I would seduce her into loving and so silence her questions. I felt sick at heart at what I was doing. I knew Donya was deeply hurt by my distance, especially after we had been so close. But I felt as if I had no choice. Besides, soon it would all be much worse. She might as well get ready now. Later I would not be able to shield her from the hurt.

I think I have never felt so lonely as I did on those nights when I lay next to Donya's warm body, wide awake with plans and worries, so close and yet so impossibly far away. When she would roll over with a sigh, wrap her arms around me and snuggle close in sleep I would lie there very still against her. Drinking in the warmth of her body, hearing the sound of her breath against my ear, feeling her heart beating against my back, I would feel my own heart breaking and cry silent tears. But we belong to the world as well as to ourselves. Some things are far bigger than our own lives—however large they may seem to us—and those things cannot be fixed by kindness.

Spider

I love this old house; it speaks to me. Mother Melna and I have at least that much in common. I think it speaks to her too—though perhaps in different ways. Happy people lived here once. I can still feel their joy in these walls. Then terrible things happened to them and I feel their grief here too. After that the house was alone, abandoned for years—lonely. I think the house is glad for our presence, glad we are caring for it and making it whole again. I can feel it welcoming us in.

Though I am very grateful to Suinyari, all she did for me and all she endured of my mischief, I will probably never live with her again. She has no home here in Maktesh and seems content just to live in the palace. I thought the palace wondrous for a while. I was dazzled by its riches and enjoyed playing at being Michi. It was like a story come to life. But I know it cannot be my real home. They do not need me there. I would always be a guest, an outsider, my movements carefully watched by suspicious servants. I would much rather be here where we are starting everything new and I am just as much part of it as anyone else, even Mother Melna and Mother Olya. Here I have a place in the pattern of things and I am needed.

I have even found my own little spot in this house. The sisters share sleeprooms, ten or more to a room, but I was a wild thing on the streets too long. I cannot bear the thought of lying awake at night, listening to ten others breathing around me and always being under observation. I discovered a little room at the very top of the west tower. It is too small to be used for much of anything, but it is high enough that the windows look out over the city in all directions. I love to sit here observing the activity in the streets below, being able to see the whole of Maktesh and even the countryside beyond the walls. I think there was once a girl who sat here before me and loved this place just as I do now. I can feel her here. Sometimes I talk to her when I am sure no one else is about. This little room is just big enough for my bed, a chair, a desk and a clothes cupboard, but it suits me very well. I like small spaces; they make me feel safe.

At first Mother Melna tried to argue me out of it. She said it was too far away from everyone, that I would be safer and better cared for in a room with the others. But I am stubborn and I held out for what I wanted, though it frightened me to go against her will. What if she told me to obey or leave? Then what would I do? My mother even added her voice to Melna's out of concern for me. Finally, in her gruff, gravelly voice, Mother Olya said impatiently, "Enough, Melna. Leave off. Give us some peace. The child is still a street-rat at heart and she always will be, no matter what kind of clothes you put on her back. A street-rat needs a little nest of her own to feel safe in. Let her be. I am sick of this arguing. It makes my stomach hurt and it spoils my rest."

And so it came about that I got my way since no one would go against Mother Olya. Some of the sisters even helped me clear the room of dirt and debris, wash the windows, clear away the cobwebs and block off the broken panes. Huffing and puffing, they hauled the furniture up those endless stairs piece by piece. They even laughed and joked and seemed to enjoy it, rather like playing house instead of the serious work that mostly occupied them. I thought some of them might seek out their own quarters after that, but they seemed to be well content with the sleeprooms and to feel more comfortable there.

Donya

Since Pharym came I had hardly seen Suinyari. She had suddenly abandoned me. It hurt, especially after a time of such intense closeness. Now she was close to Pharym instead. She confided in her and shut me out. It was not jealousy that troubled me as much as feelings of loss and bewilderment, coupled with a terrible sense of unease. Clearly she was hiding something from me and I sensed great danger. Beyond that I could not probe her mind. I would if I had been able to and with no qualms about the ethics of the matter, but when I tried to I was met by a cold wall of silence, partly of her making, partly from my own maddening loss of powers.

At first I would lie in wait for her, hoping to stop her as she went about her day. Or I would try to stay awake long enough at night to trap her. All to no use. She would brush past me with some excuse, saying, "Later, Donya, soon..." And she could stay up prowling the palace halls later at night than I could stay awake.

After a while, though it hurt, I thought it might be for the best. I was going to have to leave soon anyway. There was nothing really for me to do in Maktesh. Even my little drawings were beginning to bore me. It was time to go home. Perhaps that was what Suinyari was doing, perhaps she was already making that separation. I talked to Jolaina and Aranella about leaving, thanking them many times for their kindness. To Suinyari I said nothing since she chose not to confide in me. Then I woke one morning knowing it was time to leave—that day, no more delays.

When I turned I saw that Suinyari was not in our bed. From the smoothness of the pillow I guessed she had not been there at all that night. I had a momentary impulse to go in search of her. Then I thought it might be just as well to leave her a written message and avoid the pain of parting. Let her have her life here and I would go back to mine.

When I went out into the hall where there was a desk that always contained writing materials, I was annoyed and startled to see someone there before me. A stranger with a club of dark hair fastened at the nape of the neck was writing with furious concentration. I was about to say something when the person must have sensed my presence and turned suddenly. We both jumped back a step and exclaimed "You!" at the same time. I was shocked at the sight of her. Suinyari's red hair was cut shorter, hacked off really. It was colored an ugly dead brown and her eyebrows were darkened and thickened. This familiar stranger stared at me with guilt and confusion on her face and defiance in her eyes. The paper she had been writing on was clutched protectively to her chest.

"What are you writing?" I asked. "What have you done to yourself? Suinyari, what is this all about?"

When she kept shaking her head and not answering, I suddenly understood. It did not take Hadra powers to guess that she was about to leave without saying goodbye. "You are writing me a note. You are planning to go off without a word. Oh, Suinyari, how could you do that to me after all we have been to each other? How could you even think of doing such a thing?" In my hurt I conveniently forgot that I had been planning to do exactly the same thing to her. Without a word she handed me her note. Looking me right in the eye, she said in a husky whisper, "I thought it was better this way, no questions, no arguments. Read this note; then you will see." There were tears in her eyes.

With amazement I read,

My Dearest Donya, I know I have been secretive and distant these past few days. I am sorry for that and sorry also for the hurt it must have caused you, but I felt I had no choice. That was because I needed to think some things through and come to some decisions no one else could help me with. I know now what I have to do. With Pharym's assistance I am going back to Eezore to help free those women who are trapped or imprisoned there.

"You want to do what!?" I shouted, forgetting to whisper. "Go back to Eezore!? What kind of a fool are you? It will mean your life! Surely they will kill you!" I wanted to grab her and shake some sense into her, but she stepped back out of my reach and faced me angrily.

"You see! That is exactly why I did not want to tell you!" she whispered fiercely. "I knew you would argue and make a big fuss and try to stop me. But who better than a smuggler for this work? Who better for smuggling women out than someone who has spent years smuggling goods in? I know every secret entrance to the city, every tunnel, every guard who can be bribed, every loose rock in the walls. I have a network of people in Eezore I can trust: people in the markets, members of the Thieves Guild, servants in the Great Houses."

I stared at her, shaking my head. Why not indeed? I could think of a hundred reasons why not, but they all had to do with my loving Suinyari and being afraid for her and my own selfish desire to keep her safe. In all honesty what she said was true. She was the perfect one for this dangerous work. And I was afraid it would cost her life. "Suinyari, you will never be able to do this. You are already wanted in that city. You are a dead woman the moment they get their hands on you."

"Just so, they will not get their hands on me. Do you think I plan to announce myself? To go into Eezore saying Suinyari is here? I will be in disguise, take a new name just as you did. Donya, I have to do this, I have no choice. I cannot stay living here safe and comfortable while the women of my city—many of them my friends—suffer so terribly. I cannot live here in peace doing nothing and knowing I have the power to change things."

Never had I heard Suinyari speak with such passion and

earnestness. Always before there had been a little self-mockery in her voice. Now she took my hand, looked me in the eye and went on as if trying to convince me by sheer force of words. "Before this I was playing at life, standing apart from it, looking out the window at life going by on the street with a little smile of amusement on my face. Whatever danger I was in, whatever risks I took just tickled my fancy, entertained me out of my boredom, made me feel clever. Now, live or die, I will be part of life and every single thing I do will matter. The dangers I encounter, the dangers I will lead others through, they will be real. I will have to use everything I have ever learned to stay alive and to succeed in this mission. And if I lose my life in this at least it will be to some purpose; I will have been of some use."

She did indeed look more alive. Cheeks flushed and eyes sparkling, she was more beautiful than I had ever seen her. I could feel myself falling in love all over again. Yet I had to wonder if this was not just one more game—bolder and wilder—the most dangerous and deadly she had ever played. "You let Pharym talk you into this." As I said those accusing words, I did indeed feel a little tug of jealousy.

She shook her head. "Pharym tried to talk me out of it. I had to convince her to come with me. At first she was too afraid, but she has a mother and sisters and cousins trapped in the city so I finally persuaded her and that is where we will start. I need to work with someone I can absolutely trust, someone I already have contact with before going in. Pharym is the perfect one."

Suinyari

Just as I had feared and worse. Donya was trying to turn me from my purpose without really hearing anything I said. I tried to hush her, but soon our shouted whispers brought others rushing into the hall. In no time at all Jolaina, Aranella, Pharym and several servants were crowding around us. My plans for a secret early morning departure had been spoiled. Donya passed my unfinished note to Jolaina. She read it quickly and passed it on to Aranella. When Aranella finished, she shook her head and said forcefully, "Suinyari, this is foolishness. You will die for it and endanger the rest of us. The city of Eezore is sealed. There is no chance of getting safely in and out."

"But I know the ways and I can..."

Jolaina quickly interrupted, "We cannot allow this. They will assume Maktesh is behind this plot and be even more eager to invade. After all our hospitality, how could you think to do this to us? Surely Donya has tried to talk some sense to you."

Then Donya added more of her own objections. With the rest of them joining in it was even worse than I had feared. They went round and round without allowing me time to speak. Even the servants had something to say on the matter. Only Pharym was silent, her face very pale and the bruises livid against it, a reminder of why I had to do this.

Finally I had heard all I could stand. "Stop!" I shouted at them. "That is enough! This is my life and only I have the right to make such a decision. If you want to stop me you will have to put me in prison, break all my bones and keep me there for life. Otherwise I am going back to Eezore."

Then I turned to Jolaina. "I know your story. I know how you took terrible risks when you thought it necessary and you could have stayed safe. Are you going to tell me I cannot do the same? And you, Aranella, every day that you rule over this city as a woman you are at risk." I could not believe I was talking this way to the Zarna herself, but despair was making me bold and reckless. "And you, Donya, how do you think to keep me safe and control my life when you are returning to Ishlair where you belong? I know you are leaving, that we are each going our own way. Besides, what is there for me to do here? Not my old work surely. Aranella would not appreciate a smuggler active in her city. Anyhow, I have my own life to live and this is how I choose to live it. And, if it comes to that, my own death to meet in my own way."

They were all staring at me in stunned silence. Finally Donya nodded. "It is true that you have the right to choose your own life. It is only that I am very afraid for you. And it is also true that I am going home soon. I had hoped to leave you safe in this city, far from the dangers of Eezore. Now I see that is not to be. It is even true that with all your connections you would be the best person to pull together a network for the purpose of freeing women from there. If you succeed I have no doubt that many women will owe you their lives. And if not, well…" She shrugged and turned away so that I could not see her face. "I will no longer try to talk you out of it no matter what the risks. But clearly this is the end of the road between us. You are going far beyond me, entering a world where I cannot follow." The tone of sadness and finality in her voice made me want to cry.

When Donya finished, both Jolaina and Aranella abruptly withdrew their objections. Jolaina also nodded, saying with some reluctance, "I suppose if I were you I would be doing the same." Aranella added, "Just make sure you are not followed leaving here or coming back—if in fact you ever get that chance."

After that I told Pharym to make ready to leave. Then I packed my few things in a saddlebag and went to the new House of the Mother to say my goodbyes. To the others there I only said that I was going north on some business I had with the Wanderers; to Mother Melna I told the truth. I saw fear flash across her face. Very gently she took my face between hands and looked into my eyes. "Child, we only just got out of that city with our lives. How can you be thinking of going back? You are a marked woman there. It could easily cost you your life, Suinyari."

"So they all tell me," I said dryly.

"Are you very determined to do this thing?"

"Yes." I answered instantly. I was trying to sound very sure. Inside I felt a sudden shiver of uncertainty. What was I pledging myself to do? Before it had all just been talk. Somehow, telling Mother Melna my plans made it seem much more real.

She nodded and stepped back. "Then may the Goddess bless you and keep you safe, for surely this is holy work, Her work, you will be doing. I wish you all the skill of your hands, the speed of your feet, the cleverness of your words—those very things I did not quite approve of when you were doing that other kind of work. Unfortunately I think you are right. You are the best one I can think of to do this, but I will worry for you the whole time you are gone. Bring them here to us if you can. We can care for them, heal their bodies and minds, give them useful work and a place in the world—if that is what they want."

Afterward I went to see Mother Olya. We had not much love for each other. She was always curt and sarcastic. I felt she disapproved of me. She had frightened me when I was a young thing and, truth be told, she still frightened me a little even as a grown woman. Still I had tried to love her for Mother Melna's sake. Now I found her lying in a longchair in the main room, covered with shawls and blanket. Her face, waxy pale and still discolored with bruises, looked so pained and pinched it made my heart ache. She beckoned me over imperiously and I drew a chair close to hers. There was no one else in the room. "Glad you are here. Melna needs some cheering up. She is grieving those we lost and will be for some time to come. It does her good to see familiar faces."

"I am afraid I am not much comfort. I came to tell her I was going north on some business."

"Business eh?" She gave me a long speculative look with just an edge of amusement. "And what kind of business would that be? Just how many women do you think you can get out of that stinking trash pit? Some of them are already in prison."

I gave a gasp of surprise. "How did you know? I only told Mother Melna, no one else here. And I only spoke of it this morning at the palace. Is there a spy there who ran all the way here with news that was supposed to be kept secret?" I felt a flush of anger at the thought.

Olya started laughing. Her laugh quickly turned into a wracking cough. When she could talk again there was a touch of malice in her voice. "So I guessed right. No spy, no one told me. What other business could you have going north? Certainly not your old one. I guessed because that is what I would be doing if I were young and had your skills and connections, getting as many women out of that cursed city as I could. All of Eezore is a prison now. It will take someone very clever and very skilled to get in and get others out. You are probably the best one for that work. Good luck to you is what I say. You always were a plucky one. The luck of the Goddess go with you, not that I have much belief in the Great Lady Herself, but it can do no harm to say it." With that she began to cough again. I went to hold up her head and give her some sips of water.

"So stupid!" she said with disgust. "I should just have died there with the rest of them and been burned on that funeral pyre. That is where my heart really is, not here in this new place where everything is strange and different, and there is nothing to remember. It is for Melna that I stay alive. She thinks she can cure me with her potions and compresses and tinctures and powders and prayers. You know how she needs to care for things and she loves me far too much, more than is good for her or for me either, for that matter. But I am dying and there is nothing she can do about it, only delay it a little. The injuries run far too deep. I think I will not see you again in this life. Bring some women back here for her to care for and that will give her something to do when I am gone, something to cut the pain."

"But you are getting better. Surely if you can hang on just a little longer you can begin to mend."

"Please, no stupid lies! It does not become you, Suinyari. I know the truth of how the land lies. False words cannot change it. Go! Go do what needs doing. I have always admired your cleverness. Now it will be put to good use."

"Is there anything I can..."

"Go, leave me in peace. I am dying and do not have much time left. I do not need to be spending my precious strength chatting with you." *Rude to the very end*, I thought as I left her to her potions and her thoughts.

Gammo and Alliya took what I told them at face value. They were very busy with things at the House of the Mother, so deep in their own lives they did not really question me. But Bethron said, "I sense you are going into danger. I should come with you."

"No, not this time. Maybe later." I gave her a quick hug. I could see she was hurt at my not confiding in her, but I could not bear having another person I loved arguing or giving me warnings and advice.

When I saw Neith I was struck by how much she seemed to have grown, even in the few weeks we had been apart. It was as if her potential growth had been curled up inside her like the curled leaf of the fern all the while she lived on the street. With food and care she had sprung up like a plant that finally gets enough water and sun. I had thought she would stay small because of early deprivation; now I was not so sure. She was doing well there, finding her place in this new House of the Mother. Though I needed to say goodbye to her in case I did not come back, she seemed unconcerned about my leaving and unaware of the danger I was going into. *Better that way*, I thought.

Neith was eager to show me everything they were doing there. This time she seemed to be totally a part of it. I was pleased for her and yet it made my heart ache just a little to see how easily she had let me go. For a short while I went about with her from place to place, but when she wanted to show me her new skill with swordplay I had to tell her, "Not today. Next time when I have more leisure. Then I will spend the day and you can show me everything."

As I was leaving Imalia came up to me and laid a hand on my arm. "Thank you for saving my daughter's life and caring for her when I could not. Without you she might well have died on the streets."

I made a slight bow. "Thank you for loaning her to me for that time. She was the delight of my life. I am glad she has found you again." I did not mention the chaos Neith had caused in my house when she first came there or her theft of my gold, things best left unsaid. I knew now she had never really been my daughter, only a borrowed child waiting to be returned to her birth mother. I had been the waystation, the bridge, the lifeboat to carry her safely to the other shore, I had never been the real mother. And in truth I could not care for her now anyhow. It was all for the best that she was living safe and useful in the House of the Mother, but I still felt the pull of loss and a slight tug of pain for what could never be. As I rode out of the courtyard I looked back just once, hoping to see Neith, standing in the doorway, waving to me. She had already vanished on some errand of her own.

Spider

It was from a high spot that I saw Suinyari riding toward us. I had gone out on the roof to replace some broken shingles that had been letting rain into my room. She had not been to the House of the Mother in a while and I was eager to show her everything, especially my new room. I called out to her, but she did not hear me or look up. She was moving fast. With her head down she rode right into the courtyard looking neither right nor left and soon disappeared from sight.

I went dashing down the stairs. When I got there I could not find Suinyari anywhere and no one I asked seemed to know. Finally Nessa told me she was with Mother Melna in her accounts room. "She has left word that she is not to be disturbed for anything," she said sternly. I did not think I was just anything and I was sure Suinyari would want to see me. I boldly went to the door, but finding it was closed, which it almost never was, I could not quite gather the nerve to open it and walk in. I could hear the murmur of voices, though not the words. Making sure there was no one about I crept close to the door and laid my ear against it. It was true that I was still a street-rat at heart. I had learned to gather information however I could. Who knew when it might be needed for survival. Suinyari had been able to teach me to eat with a knife and fork, not snatch things off the platter with both hands or lick the plate, but listening to private talk was one habit she had never been able to cure.

I was shocked at what I heard, almost sorry I had listened. So she was going to go back to Eezore, that bloody city, and planning to risk her life there for strangers. Did she care nothing for those of us who loved her, those she left behind? And she did not even intend to tell me, that much was clear from what I heard of her talk with Mother Melna. She planned to treat me like a child. When I had heard enough I walked to the kitchen, stiff with hurt and anger, and set to work helping with dinner preparations. I was trying to distract myself with noise and chatter and good smells. My heart hurt with the pain of what I knew, but I said nothing to the others. When Suinyari came to look for me to say goodbye I pretended to be absorbed in my work. Still I could not keep the eagerness from my voice as I told her about my tower room and the new goat pens and how we had cleared the orchard and planted a patch of the garden. I took her hand. "Come with me and let me show you everything."

She came, but I could feel her reluctance. Her spirit was already elsewhere, riding out the gates and down the street. Though she was full of praise and enthusiasm and interested questions, still it did not ring quite true. Or maybe I just knew too much. When I offered to show her the new moves at swordplay Torvil had taught us all she said quickly, "Next time." Her face was closed against the truth she was not telling me and her eyes were avoiding mine. "I have to leave now, but next time I come I want to see it all and you can be my guide. Next time I will stay here for a few days." Then she gave me a quick hug and was gone. *Liar!* I wanted to shout after her. *Liar! Liar! You are going away and leaving me. There may not be a next time. Next time you may be dead!*

As soon as she was out of the house I ran up the stairs as quickly as I could. From my window I saw her leave. She never even glanced up. It was as if she was already gone. I longed to call out to her, "Wait, Suinyari, do not go! They will kill you!" Instead I bit my lip, kept silent and watched her ride off. To my surprise I found tears were running down my face. I brushed them away with an impatient hand. What good would it do to cry? It could not stop her from going. In the silence of my little room I said aloud, "Luck ride with you, Suinyari, and bring you safely back again."

Donya

Home at last! What a joy! And this time for good! This time it really feels like home. Both of my mothers have welcomed me back and urged me to stay at the house, even to settle myself back in my old room. "It is just waiting here for you," Henori tells me with a big smile. After hearing Shaleen's reports from Eezore they had feared for my life, not sure if they would ever see me again. Now they are delighted to find me alive and well, standing on their doorstep.

Akella and I have always had an easy understanding. Now it is time to explore my new closeness with Henori, a thing I had always longed for and never expected to find. We discover we can talk to each other about everything, even the past, even my dead father—no more secrets and silences between us. I can feel my heart slowly mending and healing. My bondsisters also seem glad to see me and treat me with more kindness and respect, though sometimes I find them too curious for my liking, especially Laiden, who follows me about, asking far more questions than I am willing to answer. I am done with the Shokarn world and have no wish to talk about my time there. As soon as I returned to Ishlair, I went instantly to give my book of notes and pictures to Mordica, hoping that would satisfy Hadra questions.

Without Suinyari those Shokarn cities hold no allure for me, not even the beautiful city of Maktesh, so different from Eezore, and yet at the heart of it not so different—no place for a Hadra. After Henori's revelation about my father's death, my search for the lost Shokarn part of myself is over. I no longer need to look for his face everywhere I go. I might well have uncles or cousins among the Shokarn, but they could just as easily be Grayrobes or Guards or Purifiers. No reason to think they would be kind, gentle men like my father. I am no Shokarn. It took living in a Shokarn city to realize how much of a Hadra I really am, even if my skin is lighter than that of the women around me.

Shaleen came home a week or so before me, after making a daring escape from Eezore just as that city was shutting its gates. I had worried she might be trapped there. She, in turn, had feared me dead when she heard about the raid on the House of the Mother. We had a joyous reunion until I made the mistake of asking what had become of the convent. "All gone. They burned what would burn and leveled the rest. Not a stone left standing. Not a tree or wall or fence to mark the place. They filled the compound with rubble and then rubbish. They want it forgotten so that no woman in the future could find it and think to rebuild on the ruins." I was sorry I had asked. Memories came flooding back. Now that she found me alive and safely home Shaleen wanted to talk to me about Eezore. She kept saying, "You were there.

You are the only one who really understands." And I kept putting her off. For myself, I did not want to talk about any of it, not then, perhaps not ever.

However when Mordica summoned me before the Council I knew I had no choice. I had to go and answer all their questions. In that way I was forced to relive one more time that terrible bloody raid on the House of the Mother and tell again about the loss of my own powers. I also had to talk about Suinyari, something I had no wish to do. To my surprise I did not feel the devastating ache of grief and longing I had expected, only a sort of sweet sadness as if for something lost in the far past.

It is not that I have stopped loving her. Perhaps I even love her more, but in a very different way, without passion, with detachment. She has separated her life from mine, going where I cannot follow. I understand now that I am truly loosed from the bonds of that love, free to live in Ishlair again among the Hadra and be one of them. It is time. I have been away too long. Even without my powers, I am very glad to be home among my own people.

Suinyari and I had said our last farewells on the road instead of the palace. After a final round of endless goodbyes in Maktesh, the two of us, along with Pharym, rode out of the city disguised as men, wearing dark longcoats and wide dark hats that hid our faces. We went northwest until we were sure we were not being followed or observed. Then Suinyari and Pharym continued north for Eezore and whatever fate awaited them in that city, while I turned west, crossed the Redline into Yarmald and made my way home to Ishlair. Just before she rode off, Suinyari reached out her hand to me with something in it. "For you, all of this was written for you." Fighting back the tears I put her little notebook in the upper pocket of my shirt, right against my heart.

When we were leaving the palace, Jolaina and Aranella tried to send us with more food than we could possibly carry. They offered Suinyari money, but she already had coins sewed into the seams of her clothes as well as in her pouch. She also had her little set of lock picks and entry keys, carefully hidden away for future use. The pain of leaving Spider and not even telling her the truth hung over Suinyari like a gray cloud. But she thought it for the best and it certainly did not stop her from going. She knew Spider would be well cared for and she herself was impatient to move on.

As I left them, I realized it was the first time I had traveled this way alone. I was very aware of my loss of powers, my helplessness should I encounter trouble or danger on the way. I might have been afraid. Instead I put all my trust in my horse Cloud and asked her to guide me safely home. I could no longer speak in her head or hear her thoughts, but she seemed to understand me just the same. I talked aloud to her the whole way, told her my troubles, my hopes, my fears—far more honest than I might have been with any human companion. When I was not doing that I sang all the songs I remembered from childhood, hoping to weave a spell of protection around us both. And so, guided by my horse and with the help of the Goddess, I was very thankful to make my way back safely without encountering any Shokarn guards or even hostile Muinyairin along the way.

Among the great joys of being home again: being free to speak the truth and always be my own real self; breathing fresh air instead of the stench of city streets; not having to be watchful of danger at all times; walking freely along the banks of the river or scrambling up to the top of the bluff to look down at the Hadra settlement that is my home. Right now I am outside as much as I can be. I can hardly make myself stay in any building for long, not even our own house. Inside I feel trapped, closed in, shut away from what matters. This time, being back in Ishlair, it is not the smallness of our interior spaces that captures my awareness. Instead it is the enormity and absolute beauty of the endless space around us: the sky, so blue and wide in the daytime, not blocked by tall buildings and narrow winding streets, not grayed by constant smoke from many chimneys; the night sky so vast and star-filled without other lights to dim them; the endless hills going blue and purple into the far distance beyond us. I realize I had almost forgotten the moon in her many phases, her bright face a constant reminder of the Goddess. She had become a stranger to me in Shokarn cities, her face hidden away. It is so good to be reminded again that I am a child of the earth, not a child of men's cities, good to see the work of the Mother all around me and to remember that I live always in the palm of Her hand.

Though I was very glad to be back in Ishlair I had yet to find my purpose there. I could not go on forever living off the kindness of my mothers and my time of being a Hadra spy was clearly over. Finding myself wandering around aimlessly, I decided to pay a call on Souvir and Chanith. I thought to see how their pottery was progressing, share with them some of my sketches and paintings from the Shokarn cities I had been to and perhaps even show them some of my new ideas. They were immediately interested in everything, spreading out my paintings on a workbench and poring over my little book of drawings, turning the pages eagerly, exclaiming to each other with enthusiasm over everything they saw. Most of all they were interested in my new ideas, the sketches I had done after seeing those fantastical mugs, cups and vases in the shops and stalls of Maktesh. I had drawn several in my own design, some with women's torsos, birds' wings and horses' legs, others with the Morl, the legendary sea monsters of the Yarmald Coast, rearing back to make the handles with their bodies while their tails wound around to make the bases.

"But you must really make some of these for us," Souvir said excitedly. "We could send them out with our next shipment. I think the Kourmairi of Mishghall would love them. In truth I would love them, all done in bright colors. I want to hold one of these in my own hands."

"Please, Donya," Chanith added. "There is a chunk of clay on that table, already wedged, just waiting for you to start. We have been working together forever, Souvir and I. We need someone in here to give us some new ideas, a little inspiration."

That is how I started working with clay, clay that feels so cool and responsive under my hands, clay that seems to take shape in wondrous forms with only a little help from me. It feels like holding a piece of the earth itself between my fingers. I can hardly believe the strange and amazing creations that begin to fill the workbench. Souvir and Chanith are thrilled and call everyone in to see what I am making. In this way clay lessens the pain of separation and helps me to find my way home again.

Speaking of finding my way home, Mauri and I are beginning to mend our friendship. It seems that it is quickly turning into more than just friendship, but we are reluctant to tell our mothers or Mordica for fear that in their eagerness they will push us faster than we are ready to go, making all sorts of public pronouncements and urging us to be bonded. It is very hard in a Hadra settlement, where minds are so easily read, to keep secret an affair of the heart, but we are trying, playing at it almost like a game of strategy, taking perverse pleasure in our shared secret.

At first I argued against trying a healing again, very afraid of failing a second time. The first time I had done great harm to Nazzem, frightened the other Hadra who were there and caused myself agonizing pain. I was not eager to repeat the experience. Akella kept after me about it, saying, "Donya, you cannot go on in this way with your powers crippled. It is not right, not natural." Then Henori would add, "Besides, we will all be there to help you, Daughter." I kept shaking my head, close to tears, thinking it would do me far more harm to try again and fail and might harm others even more. Mordica all but ordered me to do it, but I could not, not even for her. The fear was too great.

Finally it was Nazzem herself who convinced me that we should try again. "Last time I was not prepared. This time, believe me, I will be ready. You have a lot of force, Donya, more than you know, but I will link with Tenathi beforehand for greater power. Besides, I think you yourself are in a very different place, not likely to react the same way."

"But this time I have seen and heard and felt things that could destroy me if they break through, especially in a healing, things you cannot even begin to imagine living here in the safety of Yarmald."

"The safety of Yarmald? Is that what you think? Not so! You have no idea what I have seen!" She gave a bitter laugh and shook her head. "I have also lived out there in that world and seen things that for a while destroyed my peace and shattered my sleep at night. I only sleep easier because some of my Hadra sisters did a healing for me, insisted on it, though even now some of that ugliness breaks through when least expected. You must sit and talk to me, tell me everything you saw before we do the healing. Then we can draw out some of the poison before we start."

I pulled back, shaking my head desperately. "Not again! Please not again!" But somewhere deep inside me there was a little glimmer of hope. Nazzem laid her hand on my arm, turning to look into my eyes with her eyes that were so deep and compelling. I found I could not look away. "Now," she said firmly. "Start now and say it all."

Very softly and slowly at first and with many hesitations, I started to talk. Then, suddenly, the words came pouring out on their own, a torrent of grief and pain and fear that seemed to have no end. When it was finally over it left me weak and breathless, but I had to confess that I felt a little better. Nazzem smiled at me, nodded and patted my arm. "You will see; this time it will go better."

Mordica tried to take control of the healing, saying we should use the Zildorn for it and have the advantage of all the power already gathered there over the years. Nazzem and Tenathi together overrode her, saying that I needed to be outside to let all of that poison go into the open air, not have it echoing around a closed building. I sided with them and so did Akella. It was decided to use the ritual circle that was only employed for special personal rituals, not for our seasonal ones.

Akella and Nazzem went about setting up the altar in the middle of the grassy glade in a circle of sacred trees. I stood watching from behind a tree trunk. Since it was for me I knew I was not supposed to watch. I think they knew I was there but chose to say nothing. They worked together in serious silence, probably using thoughts instead of words to smooth the way—thoughts I could no longer hear—as they laid out the altar cloth over the large flat rock that had been used as an altar since our earliest memories of this place. Reverently and carefully they set the Grain Mother—the Goddess in her autumn aspect—at the very center. In front of her they placed little clay images of the frog, the turtle and the snake, all sacred to Her. Then they spread out sheaves of tarmar and added fruits and vegetables, all harvested from our gardens. On the far corners, on either side of the Mother, they placed two tall statues of water birds, standing upright, birds with the faces and breasts of women—the Guardians, the Gates to the Other World. Mixed into this I recognized things that belonged to me carefully placed here and there: a necklace, a scarf, a ring, my little booklet of drawings. My life was on that altar and so were my hopes for recovery. In front of the Goddess they had left a large empty space, covered with a bright cloth.

Watching them at their work brought an ache of nostalgia to my heart. I remembered doing this with my mothers when I was very young, the only child of the house at that time. Often I had gone about gathering the things that were needed and then helped to hold the basket for them as they carefully set the altar. Finally Nazzem looked straight in my direction. "Go away, Donya. When the altar is set for you, you are not supposed to watch. Do you want to spoil the outcome?" I slipped away, not waiting to be told a second time.

This time it was going to work. I was sure of it. It had to. I had finally let go of Suinyari. There was still a place for her deep in my heart, probably there always would be, but not a place for her in my life, never again. Our roads had parted. I wished her well, I wished her safety on her very dangerous journeys, but the cord between us had been cut. It no longer tugged at my heart and pulled me to her. I had no wish to go back to Eezore ever again or even Maktesh. The very thought repelled me. With or without powers I was truly a Hadra. But being flightless in a flock of birds was painful. Yes, I wanted my powers back.

We waited for evening, for darkness when the distractions of the day had eased away. Mordica led the way, holding her torch high. I followed with my mothers, one on either side, holding my hands. I was like a child again, loved and nurtured between them, but not the child I had been, the child I had never been. My sisters and my friends followed, Mauri among them, chanting. Nazzem and Tenathi were already there and I heard them chanting in response. I felt carried along on a river of love, ready to turn myself over to it.

Then, as we reached the circle and I saw Nazzem reaching out her hand, a sudden wild terror took hold of me. I wanted to run, go anywhere to be away from that place. I might have if Akella and Henori had not had a firm hold on me. I struggled in their grip, gasping, "I cannot! I cannot! I cannot do it!" Bile came up in my mouth. I thought I might really die of fright.

Nazzem clamped a hand on my wrist, saying in a voice of power, "You can and you will!" She held out a cup to me in her other hand. "Drink this. It will calm your fears and let the Goddess do Her work." She held it steady for me. I drank eagerly as this was the only form of escape available at that moment and I needed something quickly. Almost immediately I began to feel calmer and a sort of peace settled over me. The chanting had stopped. There was a long moment of silence in which all I heard was the sound of my own breathing and the loud beating of my heart.

When Nazzem finally asked me, "Do you release this woman, Suinyari the Shokarn, out of your life?" I was able to answer, "Yes," without reservation. Actually it was Mauri's face that came into my mind at that moment and I wished she were there beside me. I tried hard to shield that thought, but I saw a little smile of pleasure cross Henori's face. I nodded quickly to Nazzem. Then she and Tenathi between them laid me out on a cloth in front of the altar rock and placed a sheaf of tarmar across my chest, a sign of rebirth and renewal. The chanting started again, low and then louder and louder. At the same time the smell of incense began to fill the air, flooding my senses. After a while I felt myself floating out, away from my body, away from the altar, away from the circle and the chanting women, away from Ishlair, up into the night sky where the moon seemed to be looking down at me. Under my breath I chanted, *Let me come back, Mother. Let me come back. Let me come back. I want to be myself again.* I heard the words echoing in my head over and over, but I could hear nothing else.

There was a long pause while I stayed suspended between two worlds. Then I felt a dizzying whirling sensation as if I were a leaf spinning down out of the sky, faster and faster. When I re-entered my body it was with a jolt. I came back to such blinding pain that I found myself clutching my head with both hands, thrashing about and groaning aloud. Nazzem tried to hold me still. Mordica was kneeling next to me, saying in my ear. "It will pass, Donya, breathe, breathe, take a deep breath, now another one." She was right. After a few breaths the pain began to lose its grip on me. I felt Henori's gentle hand on my forehead, stroking back my sweat-damp hair and at that same instant I heard the thoughts of the women around me. It was the first time since the killings at the House of the Mother that I could hear the thoughts of others. I breathed a deep sigh of relief. The long inner silence was finally over. The healing had worked. Now I was really home, back in my place in the Hadra web of knowing, back in the net of connections that was my birthright. My Kersh had returned but the strain of it all had been almost too much for me. I felt myself slipping away. I was trying to fight it, to stay awake, to get clear, but Tenathi said in my ear, "Sleep now, Donya, you need it. You have worked hard and need to get your strength back." She covered me with a robe and I let myself go into a warm darkness that this time seemed full of comfort.

From Jolaina of Maktesh to Donya of Ishlair

Dearest Donya, I trust this finds you safely home and in good health, also in good spirits. And I hope you have been able to regain your powers and heal from the shock of all the violence you witnessed. I am sending you Neith's account of your time together as you asked me to and also some words from Mother Melna to fill out the picture. I must tell you that Neith is getting taller every day. I think she will soon be taller than I am. She is growing in other ways as well. I hear she is an invaluable help at the House of the Mother, very skilled and clever at everything she touches. I think she is happy there, but she says she misses you and Suinyari both.

As for Suinyari, she is still alive and well in spite of the dangerous work she does. We see her whenever she brings women here. She has helped many to escape that death-pit of a city. Not all of them come to us however. Some go to Kourmairi settlements west of Eezore and some even cross the Redline into Yarmald. A great many women owe her their lives.

This last time was particularly hard as she was almost caught on her way out of the city so she has been resting with us for a while. She misses you and thinks of you often, but she says she is where she needs to be and that you, no doubt, are also where you need to be. She is our eyes and ears in Eezore. That city is full of civil unrest which Suinyari no doubt helps to foment, but we here in Maktesh are much afraid that if Zarn Gunjorn ever really solidifies his reign he may look toward a conquest of Maktesh. He has made several threats or pronouncements of that nature. So far he has too much trouble to reckon with at home. Meanwhile we make ready in whatever way we can and Suinyari keeps us informed.

Well, now, I have written on far more than I meant to. It was an honor to have known you even for that short a time. I am sure the Hadra of Ishlair are glad to have you home again. Aranella sends her love and regards, as do all the others in the palace. Suinyari has just come to stand over my shoulder as I finish this and says she wants to add a few words of her own. Until next we meet.

—Jolaina of Maktesh

My dearest love, I doubt we will ever meet again in the flesh, but you are always here in my heart. The work I am doing is much more dangerous and difficult than I had thought when we first spoke of it. Had I known what it would mean, I doubt I would have had the courage to embark on such a course, but I cannot stop now. These women need me. They call me "The Sun." That is their code name for me as my real name is never spoken here, but it is not because I am bright and cheery. I am not. In fact you would not believe how stern and serious I have become. I am called that because their whole world has become a dark prison and I am a ray of light, the only sun of hope in their lives. It is all much worse in Eezore than we could have imagined and we were very lucky to get out when we did.

For me things are made both more difficult and somewhat easier by the power struggle going on between Gunjorn, Tarkin and Khazil. The confusion caused by this gives me a little more room to move about in, but I know it cannot last long. Sooner or later one will prevail over the others, likely Gunjorn since I think he has the most armed men at his command. Right now I can think only of the next day's work, that is all I can manage. Whatever happens in the future, my love goes with you always and I thank you for all the joy you brought into my life.

— Your Suinyari

From Donya of Ishlair to Jolaina of Maktesh

Dearest Jolaina, I am hoping all is well with you and the Zarna Aranella, also that all is peaceful in your beautiful city of Maktesh. I am sorry it took me so long to respond, but it has been a hard, cold winter with much snow and ice blocking the roads. I am sending this with the first Wanderer caravan of the spring passing through Ishlair on the way east.

First, let me thank you for your wonderful letter. It was so good to read your words; I could almost hear your voice speaking them. Thank you also for Suinyari's letter that brought tears to my eyes. And I most especially thank you for the packet of accounts you sent me. Along with Suinyari's which I already had, I have read and reread them over this long winter, laughed and cried and shared them with other Hadra. I have also written my own which I have bound with the others along with some of my paintings and drawings to make a book, a copy of which I am sending on to you.

I am also sending you some of my handwork as a small token of appreciation for the great kindness you and Aranella bestowed on us at the palace, kindness I will never forget. I have put this long winter to good use learning to be a potter. These mugs and bowls were inspired by some of the things I saw in Maktesh during my time there. If you think such work might find a market in your city let me know and I will send some with the next caravan going to Maktesh. Clay has been healing for me and these strange creations seem to spring from my hands and fill the shelves with little effort on my part. I even dream of them at night and wake in the morning with new ideas. I am also sending you some little portraits I painted of you and Aranella from drawings I had made while I was at the palace.

You asked about my powers. Yes, they have come back; at least as far as I know since, of course, there has been no chance to test my powers of self-defense. We did a healing ritual that finally broke through that wall of defense, raised as a shield of protection when I witnessed all that violence. If not for that shield I might have been instantly killed by the impact of it. I must say, the workings of our powers are as mysterious to us as they are to others.

It is wonderful to feel whole again, but I think my time as a spy is over. I cannot risk being in a Shokarn city again and so have pledged to spend the rest of my life in Yarmald, on this side of the Redline. I am well content where I am, but if I ever think of wandering again perhaps I will go down the coast to visit the Hadra city of Zelindar where I spent part of last winter.

This brings me to my question. I want to extend to you an invitation to visit us here and see how the Hadra really live. I know this is quite presumptuous, but it is also an opportunity. I am sure no ruler of a Shokarn city has ever visited the Hadra in their own homes. I would invite Aranella too, but I am sure it is much easier for you to travel in disguise with a Wanderer caravan than for the Zarna to travel in state. Please consider my offer. I hope you do not think me too bold.

—Yours, Donya of Ishlair

For Suinyari

Dearest, you are right that we will not meet again, not unless you come in this direction. For myself, I know I will not cross the Redline again in this lifetime. I have had to cut the cord that bound us together in order to be a Hadra among the Hadra again, just as you had to cut it in order to do your work, but you will always have a place in my heart and I regret nothing of what passed between us. Thank you for your account of those times. Jolaina has mine and will share it with you. May luck ride with you. I say prayers for you each day and ask the Mother to watch over you always, to guide and guard and keep you safe on your dangerous path. Much love to you, Suinyari.

—Your Donya

Publications from
Bella Books, Inc.
The best in contemporary lesbian fiction

P.O. Box 10543, Tallahassee, FL 32302
Phone: 800-729-4992
www.bellabooks.com

CALM BEFORE THE STORM by Peggy J. Herring. Colonel Marcel Robicheaux doesn't tell and so far no one official has asked, but the amorous pursuit by Jordan McGowen has her worried for both her career and her honor.
978-0-96777-531-9 $12.95

THE WILD ONE by Lyn Denison. Rachel Weston is busy keeping home and head together after the death of her husband. Her kids need her and what she doesn't need is the confusion that Quinn Farrelly creates in her body and heart.
978-1-93151-365-4 $12.95

LESSONS IN MURDER by Claire McNab. There's a corpse in the school with a neat hole in the head and a Black & Decker drill alongside. Which teacher should Inspector Carol Ashton suspect? Unfortunately, the alluring Sybil Quade is at the top of the list. First in this highly lauded series.
978-1-93151-365-4 $12.95

WHEN AN ECHO RETURNS by Linda Kay Silva. The bayou where Echo Branson found her sanity has been swept clean by a hurricane—or at least they thought. Then an evil washed up by the storm comes looking for them all, one by one. Second in series.
978-1-59493-225-0 $14.95

DEADLY INTERSECTIONS by Ann Roberts. Everyone is lying, including her own father and her girlfriend. Leaving matters to the professionals is supposed to be easier! Third in series with *Paid in Full* and *White Offerings*.
978-1-59493-224-3 $14.95

SUBSTITUTE FOR LOVE by Karin Kallmaker. No substitutes, ever again! But then Holly's heart, body and soul are captured by Reyna...Reyna with no last name and a secret life that hides a terrible bargain, one written in family blood.
978-1-93151-362-3 $14.95

MAKING UP FOR LOST TIME by Karin Kallmaker. Take one Next Home Network Star and add one Little White Lie to equal mayhem in little Mendocino and a recipe for sizzling romance. This lighthearted, steamy story is a feast for the senses in a kitchen that is way too hot.
978-1-93151-361-6 $14.95

HUNTING THE WITCH by Ellen Hart. The woman she loves—used to love—offers her help, and Jane Lawless finds it hard to say no. She needs TLC for recent injuries and who better than a doctor? But Julia's jittery demeanor awakens Jane's curiosity. And Jane has never been able to resist a mystery. Number 9 in series and Lammy-winner.
978-1-59493-206-9 $15.95

WILDFIRE by Lynn James. From the moment botanist Devon McKinney meets ranger Elaine Thomas the chemistry is undeniable. Sharing—and protecting—a mountain for the length of their short assignments leads to unexpected passion in this sizzling romance by newcomer Lynn James.
978-1-59493-191-8 $14.95

FAÇADES by Alex Marcoux. Everything Anastasia ever wanted—she has it. Sidney is the woman who helped her get it. But keeping it will require a price—the unnamed passion that simmers between them.
978-1-59493-239-7 $14.95

ELENA UNDONE by Nicole Conn. The risks. The passion. The devastating choices. The ultimate rewards. Nicole Conn rocked the lesbian cinema world with *Claire of the Moon* and has rocked it again with *Elena Undone*. This is the book that tells it all…
978-1-59493-254-0 $16.95

WHISPERS IN THE WIND by Frankie J. Jones. It began as a camping trip, then a simple hike. Dixon Hayes and Elizabeth Colter uncover an intriguing cave on their hike, changing their world, perhaps irrevocably.
978-1-59493-037-9 $12.95

WEDDING BELL BLUES by Julia Watts. She'll do anything to save what's left of her family. Anything. It didn't seem like a bad plan…at first. Hailed by readers as Lammy-winner Julia Watts' funniest novel.
978-1-59493-199-4 $12.95

2ND FIDDLE by Kate Calloway. Cassidy James' first case left her with a broken heart. At least this new case is fighting the good fight, and she can throw all her passion and energy into it.
978-1-59493-200-7 $12.95

LEAVING L.A. by Kate Christie. Eleanor Chapin is on the way to the rest of her life when Tessa Flanagan offers her a lucrative summer job caring for Tessa's daughter Laya. It's only temporary and everyone expects Eleanor to be leaving L.A…
978-1-59493-221-2 $14.95

SOMETHING TO BELIEVE by Robbi McCoy. When Lauren and Cassie meet on a once-in-a-lifetime river journey through China their feelings are innocent…at first. Ten years later, nothing—and everything—has changed. From Golden Crown winner Robbi McCoy.
978-1-59493-214-4 $14.95

DEVIL'S ROCK by Gerri Hill. Deputy Andrea Sullivan and Agent Cameron Ross vow to bring a killer to justice. The killer has other plans. Gerri Hill pens another intriguing blend of mystery and romance in this page-turning thriller.
978-1-59493-218-2 $14.95

SHADOW POINT by Amy Briant. Madison McPeake has just been not-quite fired, told her brother is dead and discovered she has to pick up a five-year-old niece she's never met. After she makes it to Shadow Point it seems like someone—or something—doesn't want her to leave. Romance sizzles in this ghost story from Amy Briant.
978-1-59493-216-8 $14.95

JUKEBOX by Gina Daggett. Debutantes in love. With each other. Two young women chafe at the constraints of parents and society with a friendship that could be more, if they can break free. Gina Daggett is best known as "Lipstick" of the columnist duo Lipstick & Dipstick.
978-1-59493-212-0 $14.95

BLIND BET by Tracey Richardson. The stakes are high when Ellen Turcotte and Courtney Langford meet at the blackjack tables. Lady Luck has been smiling on Courtney but Ellen is a wild card she may not be able to handle.
978-1-59493-211-3 $14.95